DEADWORLD ISEKAI

DEADWORLD ISEKAI

BOOK 1

R.C. Joshua

Podium

Cover design by Thomas Walker

ISBN: 978-1-0394-6955-6

Published in 2024 by Podium Publishing
www.podiumaudio.com

DEADWORLD ISEKAI

CHAPTER ONE

Trucked

Most people die in boring ways.

Matt always thought that he'd die with a bang. He'd fall off a cliff, save a beautiful woman from a mugging and breathe his last breath watching her cry over him, or die in a freak hang-gliding accident that his insurance would vigorously contest as a disguised suicide attempt.

Instead, it was just the normal, garden-variety cancer. He didn't smoke and never worked a day in a factory filled with toxic fumes. So, when he asked why cancer had chosen him, his doctor shrugged.

"There isn't always a reason. Some people just draw the short straw."

Maybe it was the fact that he disliked going to the doctor. It didn't seem like he had to. He was young and in shape. Why waste money on doctor visits when it could go towards bills at the end of the month?

By the time the doctors caught the cancer, there wasn't much point in treatment. The official recommendation was for him to go home and enjoy the few months he had left.

Matt had a small life insurance policy, courtesy of his job. As it turned out, some life insurance policies would pay out early when a person's fate was sure enough. It wasn't much, but it was enough to survive on, given the overall timeline of things. With the money, Matt took short weekend trips to places he had always wanted to go. That got old quickly. Eventually, he needed a hobby to pass the time, and he chose gardening.

He didn't try to be a good gardener. He hoed the ever-loving hell out of his backyard until every inch was tilled and fertilized. After scattering a random assortment of seeds and putting up a "Caution: Uncontrolled Cellular Growth" sign, he limited himself to watering and watching, waiting for the plant that would win the battle royale.

When weeds popped up, he'd absolutely nuke them with herbicide. At first, he was cautious about the dosages, but then stopped after he realized you couldn't get cancer twice, and it wouldn't matter much even if he did.

By the time his body finally gave out, his backyard looked like a bizarre, artificial jungle built by a madman. And that's pretty much what it was.

"Oh shit. Ooooh shit."

Matt was having a difficult time coping with the afterlife. He wasn't particularly religious, so he didn't have much in the way of specific expectations. What he hadn't expected was to find himself sitting at a very fancy table in a well-adorned meeting room. What he had expected even less was to look over and find a talking, thinking delivery truck in the chair across the table from him.

"Oh fuck. Fuckety fuck."

He wasn't coping well. The truck was both full-size and moving towards him, yet somehow stationary and perfectly sized for its average desk chair. If he had a normal, human brain, Matt suspected it would have burned out trying to work out the implications of the visual contradiction. That it didn't was one of the benefits of the afterlife, he supposed.

"Oh no. No, no, no."

"Sir, if you would calm do . . ."

"Why is it . . . why? No. I don't want this."

"Sir, if you would just listen for a moment . . ."

"Ahhhhh! Ahhhh!"

It took a while to come to terms with things. When he finally got there, he had questions.

"So, this might be rude, but . . . why are you a truck?"

"I'm not a truck. I'm an automated system soul migration counselor and assistant, meant to ease your journey to your next plane of existence. I can take any form."

"Okay, fine, but . . . why a truck? Why not another human? An angel?"

"My appearance is calibrated to the average user expectation. Soul migrations from your planet are rare, and it was deemed time to recalibrate the model. My research indicated that this was, or rather, this is a common representation of a soul migration device in the type of fiction popular in your demographic."

It was a while before Matt could talk without laughing. The truck-system had attempted to be nice, and Matt didn't want to hurt its feelings. Instead of settling on an angel or the grim reaper, the system in front of Matt had decided that the best image was a persistent image of *getting trucked.*

Eventually, Matt was calm enough to get to the serious business of being dead. He might have imagined it, but the system assistant gave him just the faintest sense of relief.

"So you're saying you're going to send me to 'the next plane.' That's . . . heaven? Somewhere worse?"

"Not in that sense, no. Some souls don't survive the process of dying. They're purely lost and are replaced. Other, rarer souls go to a simulated environment. Their memories are wiped, and they are put in a life relatively ideal for them."

"And that's me?" A simulated paradise shouldn't have sounded terrible, but somehow it did. "No offense, but I'm not sure if I'm cut out for fake simulated heaven."

"Don't worry. That's not where you are headed. Remember, I'm a *truck*."

"You don't mean . . . Oh shit . . ."

A small trumpet noise played from across the room, near the wall. A few handfuls of confetti materialized from nowhere, and a small pop unfurled a poster reading, "Congratulations on your Isekai!"

"That is *hilariously* underwhelming, system."

"I was reluctant to shock you again after seeing your reaction to my truck-avatar."

"Fair."

The system waved its wheel-arm and a small desktop pamphlet holder materialized. Matt grabbed a pamphlet that read, "Gaia! The Garden Planet! Come as yourself and GROW!"

"I am limited to sending souls to realms with some level of conflict that they can solve. Within those confines, I try my best to assign my souls to worlds that match their interests, thematically. Frankly, a LOT of your interests are satisfied just by being transmigrated. More than you'd think. It's a little off-putting, honestly."

Another gesture brought up a floating video screen showing Matt's frantic, chaotic gardening of the past few months.

"Besides the media you consume, this stood out to me as significant. You were dying and you chose to garden. Every plane has plenty to do, and plenty of options on how to live your life. But you like plants, and all the historic information on Gaia indicates it's all about plants. It seems like a good match."

"What if I wanted something different? Something more intense?"

"There are a few other options. The one that matches most closely with what you are speaking of is the demon death battleground, Ra'Zor. Also known as the Realm of One Thousand Bleedings."

"Actually, on second thought, Gaia seems fine . . . Do people really ever choose that second one?"

"Adolescents, mainly. And to the realm's credit, I have heard they have very good soups."

"So, when do I go?"

"Soon."

"How soon? Do I have time to tour the administrative portions of heave . . ."

It was then that Matt noticed that he was plummeting, fast, towards a red-black planet.

Fast in this case was very fast. The planet went from marble to beach ball to giant, all-encompassing behemoth in the blink of an eye. He didn't know much about soul migrations, but he was really hoping that he would slow down before contact. Not just for his own sake, either, but also because he suspected his impact might have an unpleasant dinosaur-extinction-level effect on the local fauna.

Just then, he slowed to a stop, and a small blue screen materialized out of nowhere in front of him. Exactly what he was hoping for.

Ding!

Welcome to Gaia, traveling soul. In a moment, you will be transported down to your new home: a lush, beautiful paradise of glorious plants and astounding animal life. But we are not without our troubles. The system will grant you power, and your guardian will meet you upon arrival to give you guidance. The fate of a planet hangs on your actions. Good luck!

Matt had just enough time to confirm that system screens were dismissed by swiping before shooting off again towards the planet. He felt his body become more and more material over the next few seconds, just in time for him to slam—hard—into the surface of the planet.

Despite the visual evidence, Matt was shielded from any harm instead of spreading out like bloody jelly on the surface of the new world. Coughing in a cloud of red dust, Matt slowly stood up. Besides the immediate impact zone, the hit didn't seem strong enough to damage the local environment much; if Matt wanted to cause a mass extinction event, he'd have to find another way.

The system had at least clothed him at some point during his descent. He was spared from nakedness by both simple sandals and a roughly spun garment. It reminded Matt of a longer, looser-fitting tank top. He waited for the dust to clear, eager to catch his first glimpse of the planet.

As the dust finally dissipated, Matt winced. It took a moment for his eyes to adjust to the harsh brightness of the two suns hanging in the sky.

Looking down, Matt caught his first glimpse of the red and black dirt expanse that was his new planet. The terrifying, open, deadness of it arced off into an empty, barren infinity. The plants were impressive in the sense that they had managed to not exist at all. So far, Gaia was a garden in the same way that doughnuts were cardio.

"Fuck. He sent me to the demon death planet. System, did you send me to the demon death planet?"

No answer.

"System screen on! System screen . . . go!" Matt tried several combinations before screaming, "System! Help!" Somehow, that worked. With a combination of hand flailing and consistent repetition of the word "system," Matt learned how to summon various screens. Leaving aside his status for now, he brought up the map screen. It was a square mini-map, covered in gray, with only a single splotch of red. Beneath the map was the button "Location Details," which he mentally tapped.

Planet: Gaia (Dead)
Continent: Sarthia (Unpopulated, Lost)
Province: Sarthia Capitol District (Defeated)
City: Ruins of Sarthia Kingship (Defeated)

Matt looked around for the supposed ruins and found nothing but flat, burned dirt. He called up the window for system queries. Supposedly, the system could handle basic questions about local history and environments.

"Where are the ruins?"

"Ruins" is a generalized system term referring to the area where a city or named structure once stood. It does not necessarily require that remnants of the city be visible.

"So what happened here? What destroyed all traces of the city?"

The system screen faded a moment, then blinked on and off momentarily.

System Error. Information not available.

"Ohhhkay. So, this seems like a problem, system."

Agreed. System analysis of information unavailability is now active.

"How long will that take, approximately?"

Current estimate: Five Earth years.

That wouldn't do, obviously. Matt didn't know a whole lot about survival, but it didn't look like there was anything nearby he could even try to survive on. It didn't matter if he couldn't tell what plants and water could be consumed if there was nothing around to consume. He was on a very limited clock, and the system wasn't being particularly helpful.

"So, about that guardian you mentioned . . ."

Matt was immediately inundated with a series of *dings*.

> Searching for guardian . . .
> Search error detected. Guardian not found.

"Shit."

> Searching for alternative options . . .
> Quest Generated!

> *Finding Your Direction*
>
> Where's your guardian? What's going on with the garden planet? It's hard to say, but we are going to find out. An unknown anomaly has been sensed, and temporary access to the system compass has been granted. Follow along and learn more about your situation!
>
> Objective: Identify the nature of the scanned anomaly.
> Difficulty: A
> Rewards: ???, permanent access to system compass

Matt was silent for a second after seeing the new screens.

"System, I'm beginning to suspect that you messed something up and screwed me over."

Matt once had an incompetent manager who tried to spin off difficulties that their bad management created as "fun little team challenges." He wasn't absolutely sure that this was the same thing, but the system was giving off strong Janice-covers-her-ass vibes, and he didn't feel great about it.

The system refused to confirm or deny Matt's guess.

> Quest Generated!

Another quest screen popped up, confirming some of Matt's worst fears.

CHAPTER TWO

Freedom of Choice

Freedom of Choice

Under normal circumstances, your guardian would help you find a class that's appropriate to your situation.

So, congratulations! You get to choose your class without anyone stepping on your toes! Follow your dreams, choose from over five thousand classes, and become the man you always wanted to be!

Matt couldn't help but feel that he was being cheated.

Five thousand classes was a lot, sure, but Matt had no idea what was going on. If the guardian's input was normally expected, he was almost certain that some of the classes sucked. Flipping through the menus until he got to class selection, he found that the class choices included some questionable, highly specific choices.

Aantorath Hunter

The vicious scourge of Aantoraths will be stopped—by you. Your fighting style is optimized for specific prey, making you a highly specialized and deadly threat to Aantoraths everywhere.

Stat Emphasis: DEX, WIS

"Any help on Aantoraths, system? What are they? Why would I want to kill one?"

Error. Local information knowledge base inaccessible. Analyzing.

"Have you tried unplugging the planet, then replugging it in?" Matt retorted. No answer.

Like the days after he was diagnosed with cancer when his friends had suddenly gone silent, Matt was on his own. Luckily, the class list had a search function, and Matt found a couple of stock fantasy world classes.

Swordsman

Nobody is better with swords than a Swordsman—unless it's a class dedicated to a specific sword, like Khukri Master or Gladius Wielder. You can cut, slice, and thrust with the best of them. This is the class that most transplants choose.

Stat Emphasis: DEX, STR

Archer

Why get close when you can poke holes in things from far away? The Archer is skilled with all ranged weapons that utilize kinetic energy stored in small pieces of stretched rope and is a vital part of a complete adventuring party.

Stat Emphasis: DEX, PER

Shield-bearer, Spearman, and several other classes all tracked with his expectations in the same way. Some, like Rogue, turned out to be second-tier classes he didn't have access to yet. He'd probably have to take "Dagger Master" and . . . level it, maybe? Other classes didn't track with expectations at all.

Barbarian

You are charmingly rural. To other rural people, that is. You sleep outside and wear the outsides of things you've killed as clothes. If you prefer tents to houses and the open steppe to city walls, this class gives you all the skills you need to meaningfully contribute to the rest of your outdoorsy, uncultured friends. Enjoy!

Stat Emphasis: PER, WIS

The worst part was that there didn't seem to be any way to get more details about the classes than the short system summary. Queries to the system didn't bring up anything new, and he poked the system window in multiple different ways without being able to pull up a single piece of new knowledge. Eventually, Matt thought to pull up his status screen to see if his stats might help him make a selection.

Matt Perison
Level 1 – Unclassed
Health (HP): 25
Mana (MP): N/A
Stamina (STAM): 10
Strength (STR): 5
Dexterity (DEX): 5
Perception (PER): 5
Vitality (VIT): 5
Wisdom (WIS): 5
Intelligence (INT): 5

Warning: The unclassed do not have class goals, and thus cannot gain levels. Their stats can only be improved through great effort. There is no advantage in putting off class selection.

His stats were level, which usually he'd like; it meant he wasn't being guided towards a specific class. In this case, it was a mixed bag—guidance was the resource he was lowest on, and there was a limit to how much freedom was actually helpful. Matt went back to the class screen.

Most of the classes were filled with nonsense descriptions like fighting Aantoraths. Without more information, there was no way to sift through the list of classes outside of guessing at specific search terms, and time was something he didn't have.

He sighed and called up the system compass. An open-world style guidance compass appeared in his field of view like a HUD. Rotating his body around, Matt found the pointer pointing in a specific direction that looked identical to the other directions. It was about as helpful as the two suns in the sky. Or the equivalent to a suspect man waving you deeper into an alley, or a friend swearing they weren't lost and saying that they'd "only go a few more miles." But, it was a direction as good as any other. It was the best lead Matt had.

Matt put off his class selection. So far, he hadn't seen anything living, let alone a threat. As long as he didn't come across a giant wasteland worm or something, he was probably fine taking a "wait and see" approach.

All that was left was to walk. Easy enough.

* * *

It turned out walking was hard. Or at least it was if you did it long enough without food, water, or any way of telling the time. Matt had discovered that the twin suns never moved. It appeared that Gaia didn't spin, or spun slowly enough that he couldn't track the resulting relative motion. His best guess for why he wasn't getting baked was that neither of the suns seemed all that powerful in comparison with Earth's. It also helped that the sky itself seemed permanently hazed by dust.

At some point in his journey, he came to a new and profound appreciation of sneakers. The sandals had given him blisters that eventually popped, and now every step ground new dust and pain into the wounds.

He was thirsty, over-warm, and generally hating every aspect of his existence. He was exhausted, and with no clear idea of how far he was from his target, he sat down in the dust.

Hours later, Matt woke up with a headache. He was red on one side from the baked dirt, and at some point during his slumber, he had kicked off his sandals. As he put them back on, he realized that his painful blisters were gone. His feet were still dirty, but uninjured.

"Hey, system, what's going on with my feet? They shouldn't have healed that fast."

> The vitality (VIT) stat represents a creature's ability to both withstand force and recover from it. Even at low levels, the vitality stat works constantly to close and repair wounds. This healing ability is not inherently linked to metabolic processes or overall health.

"Wow. I think that's the most complete answer you've given me so far," Matt responded. In his head, he added that this was also the best news he had heard from the system since he landed on Gaia. It was also worth figuring out the limits of what the system could and couldn't answer. It seemed that the system didn't know anything about where he was or what happened to Gaia, but did slightly better with questions that had to do with the system or himself.

"Does the system do anything to help with thirst or hunger? Does my vitality score help with that?"

> Thirst and hunger are separate conditions not controlled by the system unless a creature possesses a class feature that specifically links them. Most creatures are reliant on food and water in some form, and will sicken or die without it.

This was not the answer Matt was hoping for, but he had suspected it might be the case. His headache was probably caused by dehydration, and his throat felt like it was about to permanently dry out. He missed indoor plumbing and running water, but his eyes just saw red dust all around him. Without better options, Matt put his head down, picked himself up, and began walking again.

As he did, he got what information he could out of the system regarding the other stats. Strength and dexterity were pretty much what they said on the tin. Dexterity was linked to how well and fast he could move his body—reflexes, general agility, and things like that. Strength was basically how much he could lift or how hard he could swing something, essentially a max-output stat just like on Earth.

Wisdom and intelligence were a bit harder to understand; the former seemed related to how much he knew and how well he could use his intuition, while intelligence was more about calculating from actual data. Matt suspected that each might have further uses. If there was more to know about either, it seemed it was class-locked at the moment.

After some time—hours? days even?—Matt was in pretty bad shape. It turned out that water, or the lack thereof, was a key part of fatigue. He felt sore and tired and dumb. His tongue was thick and dry in his mouth.

He wasn't quite dying, but the lack of any kind of visible water was beginning to sink in as a serious threat. For the first time, he realized that he had to find something. Otherwise, he might not make it.

He looked in the classes again, hoping to find some sort of water-related magic class. He found a couple, but every class that explicitly allowed for the manipulation of water was much more advanced than what he had access to.

So he walked. After a while, he didn't even try to think. He just plodded on and on. He ignored the dirt, he ignored the suns, ignored his sore muscles and his dry mouth. He ignored the squishing of the ground.

He paused. There was something important that he was missing, but his brain refused to work. He closed his eyes and tried to muster his last bit of energy to think.

The ground had squished. That was new and maybe that meant . . . Before Matt could finish his thought, he opened his eyes and dropped to his knees. He crawled backwards to find the ground that had made the noise.

The culprit was a slightly damp patch of soil. Matt dug into the patch, scooping away barely wet dirt until he had a fairly good-sized hole. He expected something like a spring—that as he dug, the soil would get wetter and wetter. That didn't happen. The soil kept the same semi-wet consistency the further down he dug. What he did eventually uncover, however, was a rock. A rune-covered, glowing rock.

The rock itself was more or less teardrop shaped, and glowed primarily from runes inscribed onto the stone. Runes that looked enough like waves that Matt was fairly confident he had solved the wet-soil origin story mystery. Less good was that the rock was flickering and making irregularly clicking and popping noises. Matt's video game instincts were shouting at him that however important this stone looked, it also looked like it was about to explode.

Matt slowly and very carefully reached out to touch the stone, laying his hand on it as softly as possible. Nothing happened. The stone kept on buzzing and clicking as always, and Matt was blissful to find he had not blown up. Where the stone had looked slightly moist, Matt was surprised to find it felt completely dry. Apparently it wasn't so much seeping water as causing other things around it to be wet, somehow.

But as he lifted the stone it immediately hissed, popped loudly, and fizzled out.

"No! No!"

Matt tapped and shook the stone. This kind of worked. The stone would momentarily flicker back on, then immediately cut out if he moved it at all. In a panic, he put it back in the hole, then carefully tapped it until it sprang back to life. He didn't dare move it again. If it broke permanently, he'd probably die. He'd probably die anyway, but he wasn't eager to burn his only chance at avoiding it.

He still had to get water out of the thing somehow; the alternative was dying. The difficulty had ramped up substantially given that he couldn't move it, though, and his dehydrated brain wasn't doing him any favors in the creative problem-solving department. The dirt around where he had set the stone got visibly wetter over the next few minutes, but not wet enough to squeeze any liquid out of. With his current resources, there was nothing he could do.

As he stared at the rock, Matt knew that he was observing his only chance at survival. If he couldn't figure this problem out, he might die again.

He really, really wanted to survive.

CHAPTER THREE

Surviving

The word "survive" hung with Matt. Even his overheated brain couldn't get the idea out of his head. Even though no one would probably notice another death in this barren wasteland, he *liked* having a body that wasn't betraying him. The time with the truck-system was nice. He *liked* living without some invisible timer hovering over him, counting down.

Now, he was on the same kind of timer for a different reason, and he hated it. He wanted to live. He wanted to survive.

His thoughts turned to tools. Shovel, stick, dynamite? He had none of those to help him get the water out. But what he did have was the word "survival" and a class search bar. It would have to do.

> *Survival Guide*
>
> Warriors destroy enemies and win battles, but your talents get them there safely in the first place. You know what berries to eat and what water is safe to drink, as well as a thousand other things that keep everyone safe wherever you go.
>
> Stat Emphasis: VIT, WIS

The class wasn't bad, but Matt didn't fail to notice the emphasis on party dynamics. Survival Guide seemed less like a self-sufficient class than a type of grease that lubricated parties, maintaining the fighting force during travels. It was almost like someone a party would hire when they didn't know where they were going. If the actual class was anything like the flavor text indicated, Matt would be safe right until he ran into the kind of trouble that bit or slashed, and then he'd be out of luck.

Luckily, the search had returned two results, and the second one was a doozy.

> *Survivor*
>
> If you are seriously considering this class, something has gone terribly wrong for you. Other classes level up by making things or killing things. You level up by surviving, which is subtly different and infinitely worse. You get stronger when you live through terrible things, and every skill you have is built to give you a fighting chance in a bad situation.
>
> Stat Emphasis: DEX, VIT

That's the one. There were no mentions of parties or support. The pessimism in the description was worrisome, but it seemed appropriate for a guy who was hours from getting into serious dehydration trouble on a burned-out rock planet.

Survival Guide seemed like it had a better chance of giving him a skill that would help with water extraction, but water was the biggest problem he had now, not the only problem he'd ever have. He couldn't afford to get tunnel vision and only focus on his immediate circumstances. Choosing the Survivor class would be a disaster if it didn't cover his immediate needs, but it was a bet he'd have to take. He closed his eyes and willed the acceptance of the class.

> Congratulations, you have chosen the [Survivor] class. Enjoy!

A cascade of system *ding*s sounded on top of each other. Then, for a few moments, Matt felt as if he had become a god.

Matt shook the dizziness away and picked himself off the ground.

"System, what in the ever-loving shit was that?"

For a moment, his muscles had grown. Not gradually, but with the speed of a gunshot. He was a chiseled Roman god. He could lift mountains, move faster than lightning, and felt invincible. He was smarter and more knowing as well. He stood in a barren landscape, filled with almost unlimited knowledge and power. It wasn't an illusion; he knew down to his bones that this was real.

He tensed his muscles and pointed a finger at the stone, ready to issue a word of command, to drive his will into the very workings of the thing until it erupted in the torrent of water he desired.

And then, just before he spoke, all that strength was gone. He was just Matt again. His muscles deflated like a popped balloon, and he was left standing in the middle of a nothing landscape, pointing his finger at a rock like an insane person.

> Several achievements were granted at once. Please check your notifications.

Wincing, Matt pulled up his notifications page. There hadn't been too many new messages in the past few days. The early notifications were all related to his arrival on the planet, and not particularly helpful. After dismissing those, he looked at the alerts that had set off the most recent set of *dings*, and immediately understood what had happened.

> Class awarded! You are now a [Survivor].
> Class Loot Pack [Basic Survivor Kit] awarded.
> Class skill [Survivor's Instincts] granted.
> Class skill [Survivor's Combat] granted.
> Class skill [Eat Anything!] granted.

Matt could sense he could zoom in on any of those skills for context but set them aside for the moment and moved on to the other notifications first.

> *Achievement: [Sole Survivor: District]*
>
> You are the last living survivor of your home district. We apologize for your loss but applaud your tenacity.
>
> Reward: 50 VIT

> *Achievement: [Sole Survivor: Continent]*
>
> You are the last living survivor of the Sarthia continent. There's a good chance you need help rowing away from whatever happened, so enjoy your reward.
>
> Reward: 200 STR

> *Achievement: [Sole Survivor: World]*
>
> Somehow, you lived through a world-ending apocalypse. You are the last sentient being alive on the planet. Hopefully, an improved internal state will help you pass the time.
>
> Rewards: 500 WIS, 500 INT

There were *dozens* of notifications like this. Once all the sentient beings were gone, the system started awarding achievements based on being the last survivor for non-sentient species, then animal classes.

Achievement: [Sole Survivor: Mammalian]

Every mammal is gone, save you. How did you survive where rats couldn't? We don't know, but enjoy your reward.

Rewards: 300 STR, 300 VIT

The notifications went on and on. *That explains why I felt like I was a god,* Matt thought. *But where'd all those stats go?* He scrolled down as quickly as he could to the last notification, hoping that would shed some light on the subject.

Achievement: [Absolute Survivor]

Somehow, all life on Gaia was eliminated. All of it. Fish? Birds? Gone. All the bacteria is dead. It's debatable whether or not viruses are typically considered to be alive, but they are gone too. But not you, somehow. You live on. The system isn't supposed to ask you questions, but if it could, they'd try to figure out how you somehow survived.

Rewards: All previous survivor benefits removed and consolidated into increased authority over Planet Gaia.

Without knowing much about the leveling system, Matt had to assume that a few hundred vitality points might not be a whole lot in the grand scheme of things. And that anything that could survive or cause a worldwide apocalypse would probably be at a very high level. They might not mind trading out those stats for whatever "increased authority" was or did. But Matt was still at level one. He silently mourned for the lost stats.

Unlike his new skills, authority didn't appear to be something he could get a description of. But still, Matt assumed it must do *something*, and it happened that he was still standing right over a part of the planet he cared about very much. He mustered all his will, pointed at the ground, and *willed* it to give up the water, just as he had tried to do before his new powers had all evaporated.

Nothing.

"Produce water! Release water! Water go!"

After a few minutes of trying various combinations, Matt had made no progress except increasing his feelings of inferiority. Either the skill wasn't activatable or worked in a way he couldn't guess at. The system was no help. It wouldn't respond to any queries regarding the matter. That left good old-fashioned stats and his new abilities as possibilities for water, and not a whole lot else. Matt crossed his fingers and brought up the expanded windows for each.

Matt Perison
Level 1 Survivor
Class Experience: 0 / 10
Health (HP): 30
Mana (MP): N/A
Stamina (STAM): 15
Strength (STR): 5
Dexterity (DEX): 6
Perception (PER): 5
Vitality (VIT): 6
Wisdom (WIS): 5
Intelligence (INT): 5
Class Abilities: Survivor's Instincts (LV1), Survivor's Combat (LV1), Eat Anything! (LV1)

Matt's dexterity and vitality stats had both improved slightly, and vitality seemed to come with a slight increase to his HP and stamina. Despite that, he didn't feel much different. He was probably felt a little sturdier, but that could easily be a placebo effect. There wasn't much around to be particularly dexterous with for testing purposes, either. He'd do more in-depth testing later, but for now, it didn't seem raw stats would be much help.

Survivor's Combat – LV1

A boxer would beat you at punching, and you will never be as good with blades as a Swordsman or Rogue. But when it comes to improvising with whatever is around, you have an edge, as well as an improved sense of when to dodge, when to stand your ground, and when to run away.

Survivor's Instincts – LV1

You're a bit better at staying alive now. If there's a wall to climb, you have an improved idea of how to climb it, and if there's an enemy to fight, you can roughly estimate your chances of winning. You also have an increased baseline knowledge of survival methods.

> *Eat Anything – LV1*
>
> You get more out of food, and there are more foods you can eat. You gain resistance to ingested poisons, can stomach mildly spoiled food, and get nutrition out of a slightly increased range of foods.

Neither of those two skills seemed very relevant without enemies to fight or food to eat, and neither held much promise of helping him with the problem at hand. The third was slightly more promising.

"Survival methods" was vague, but it was possible that it might help. Matt turned to look at the water stone, hoping something would spring to mind. He grabbed another rock and considered just beating the thing for a bit, hoping he'd get lucky and the thing would at least spill some water on its way to ruin. But the risk was too big; he let the rock drop from his hands without doing anything with it.

A deep feeling of desperation came over Matt. He looked at the water stone, confused, and a part of him wondered if he would die here. *If only*, he thought, *I had any knowledge of magic devices at all. Or, hell, even non-magical tools; I'd happily settle for an evaporation still.*

Wait. What's an evaporation still?

Suddenly, a wave of memories regarding evaporation stills surged through Matt's mind. They were essentially tents built around water sources that funneled evaporation to a container. He somehow knew how to build one, without ever having thought about them before. He guessed that was the "baseline knowledge" increase the system had mentioned, and it was definitely cool in a sense. But it didn't do him much good without anything to build the still out of.

The loot box!

Matt glanced around, but no such box was lying around. Doubtful that it could have been stolen, he focused in on the loot box notification itself, only to have a secondary window pop up.

> Open Basic Survivor Kit? Y/N

Yes! he thought.

> You found: survival dagger, Survivor's pack, instant torch, Survivor's garb, rope, double-fill canteen, simple tent, and signaling mirror.

From nowhere, the mentioned items materialized and settled on the ground. Matt's Survivor's Instinct immediately flooded his mind with information. The survival dagger, rope and Survivor's pack were pretty self-explanatory: a pretty good steel dagger, a length of hemp rope, and a sealable bag for holding food and other items. Useful, but nothing special.

The instant torch was similarly boring. It was a torch with a built-in lighting mechanism to set it aflame. Not much use in a world without night.

The Survivor's garb was a bundle including a shirt, pants, a coat, boots, and a masked hood that looked somewhere between a ninja outfit and a raincoat. Survivor's Instinct told him it offered little protection from physical damage, but was optimized for protection from the elements and terrain.

Matt had ridden dirt bikes during his youth. The fabric of the garb reminded him a little bit of endurance suits, the kind that were meant to protect you from scraping yourself raw on branches as you rode. He gladly changed into the superior clothes, especially glad to replace the sandals with the much more protective boots.

The double-fill canteen apparently worked just like a normal canteen, except with twice the capacity its size implied. It wasn't exactly a wand of fireballs, but it was the first honest-to-god magic Matt had encountered. He quickly checked to see if it came preloaded, and was disappointed to find the system hadn't been so kind.

Under normal circumstances, the tent and signaling mirror would have been the least exciting items to Matt. Even in his weird circumstances, they would have been except for two things: the tent came with a transparent tarp meant to act as a base, and the mirror was another mildly enchanted item that reflected more sunlight out than it had coming in. Between those two things, he had something to work with.

Matt ran around for a few minutes gathering rocks, which he used to anchor the tarp down to the patch of dirt that was damp. Using various stakes and poles that came packed with the tent, he soon built a small structure over the majority of the ground, shaped at the top into a sort of rudimentary spout leading into his canteen. He then angled his mirror to direct the sun into the enclosed area and sat down to wait.

He gave a slight prayer. *Please let this work. Please.*

Evaporation stills worked by trapping heat from the sun in a tent, using it to evaporate water, and then funneling the water to some kind of container. With the signaling mirror, it was only a few minutes before Matt saw the first signs of condensation forming on the sides of the tent. Soon, a few drops of water condensed, combined, and rolled downwards through the spout into the canteen.

It wasn't a lot, but it *was something*. Matt was still hungry. He was still alone. There were probably any number of ways he could still die. But now there was one less. He had a source of water and a way to store it. He was doing a little bit better.

In a small way, he had survived.

Ding!

CHAPTER FOUR

Underleveled

Matt was very proud of his jerry-rigged water reclamation device. Apparently, the system agreed, at least to some extent. As soon as more than a few drops of water had accreted into his canteen, it quantified exactly how much it agreed.

Achievement: [And Now A Drop to Drink]

You have obtained drinkable water from an unlikely, inaccessible source in a situation where failure would have meant death.

Rewards: +5 Class XP, +1 WIS

Achievement: [Ape With a Stick]

Like a bonobo cooking itself lunch, you have used an improvised tool in an unconventional way to survive.

Rewards: Access to the system clock, +1 WIS

Five experience wasn't enough to push him to the next level and two points of wisdom probably weren't going to be make-or-break for his survival. He certainly didn't feel noticeably smarter, if that was even what wisdom did. But it was nice to be acknowledged for his hard work.

The other reward, the system clock, was a welcome addition. The clock was unintuitive, and without a concept of day or night, Matt had no way of understanding what timescale it functioned on. He would have to observe over a longer period of time to understand what was happening. But, a second on the clock seemed to be as long as an Earth second, which meant that he now had at least a rudimentary way of telling time.

After packing away his loot, Matt now had time in another sense. It was going to take a while for the canteen to fill enough to give him a meaningful drink. His immediate concerns were past, which was nice, but it also gave him an opportunity to think about something he had been avoiding up to that point. Specifically, the implications of some very worrying system notifications that he had brushed away earlier.

"System, are your notifications always accurate?"

> System notifications are always accurate unless an error message is displayed or one of a few rare skills interfere with your cognition. Otherwise, they are trustworthy and accurate.

The fact that the system was accurate did not bring Matt any joy. He hadn't doubted the validity of the system, even though it seemed to be on the fritz. But, if the system was right, that meant something pretty terrible. The notifications said that he was alone on this planet.

Matt had hoped that the wasteland he was in was an isolated area, but the notification claimed he was the last living sentient being on the planet. So, he was alone, and probably permanently.

With that long-term horror came a shorter-term concern. Whatever wiped out all the life had done a thorough job, according to the system wiping everything out, right down to single-celled organisms. Matt's time on Earth was spent mostly eating things that were recently dead, not decades-dead. If there were no plants or animals to eat, he was going to starve.

"System, how could this happen? Was this a mistake, or some kind of trick?"

The system didn't answer. Matt might have been imagining it, but his bad-manager-covering-their-ass intuition had been ringing for a while. If he wasn't mistaken, the messages from the system had been getting more casual the longer it was with him—like it was trying to buddy up, or make friends, or something. He didn't trust that *at all.* In his experience, friends were friends most of the time but managers were only friends when it helped *them.*

My best bet is to hydrate as well as I can, then walk as far as the canteen will get me. If I'm really lucky, this civilization might end up having been really good at canning food. If not, there's no use dragging things out, Matt thought.

After an hour or so, Matt was able to get a drink of water. It was lukewarm and tasted like he was licking a rock. It was objectively among the least appealing drinks he had ever taken. But given how thirsty he was, it tasted like heaven. It tasted like *life*.

Using his newfound moistness, Matt motivated himself to test out the effects of his new stats. As a middle schooler, he had learned to juggle poorly. He found he could still juggle rocks pretty poorly, but slightly better than he expected. The difference was much more pronounced when he pulled out the survival dagger. With zero knife-fighting experience, he was suddenly able to slash, stab, and parry. Not only that, he somehow knew that his motions were efficient, though they still had room for improvement. Despite his very specific memories of not knowing how to knife-fight a few hours ago, his muscles behaved as if he had specific, repeated training in doing so.

After testing Eat Anything! to confirm that he couldn't consume dirt—he couldn't—all that was left was to sleep so he'd be ready to travel once the canteen was full. A bunch of the tent parts were tied up in the still, but Matt was still able to use the canvas itself to block out the omnipresent light of the sun. Before laying down, he drank every drop of water the canteen had accumulated. Hopefully, it would be full by the morning.

The water didn't do much for his hunger, but there wasn't much he could do about that. Doing his best to ignore the pain in his stomach, he went to sleep.

There wasn't much packing to do in the morning. The canteen was filled, and Matt took a couple long draws off it before dismantling the still. He packed everything into his pack and set off in the direction of the system compass.

Having access to the system clock was a mixed bag, emotionally. Before, it had been distressing to walk endlessly without any way of gauging the passage of time. Now, he could calculate down to the second how long he had walked. An hour in, it had gotten boring. After five hours of walking, he felt numb. Ten hours in, he was nearly despairing. He was exhausted and starving, endlessly plodding through identical terrain.

It really was identical too. There were no hills in the distance that he could see through the dusty haze in the air, and no visible dips downwards either. It was like someone had come in and flattened everything with a bulldozer. His walk remained the same, so exactly the same, that he almost thought he was dreaming when the ground under his feet suddenly gave way, and he fell three or four meters down into a pit.

Matt was saved from shattering his unprepared legs by the fact that the pit wasn't exactly straight down. Instead, its sides hugged against him as he scraped his way to the bottom. He was saved from the worst the rough, hard-packed red dirt could dish out by the Survivor's garb, but the slide still left an angry red welt on his skin. Once he recovered from the shock, he was almost glad for the variety the pain and surprise bought to his day. Any change was welcome at this point.

The weird double suns never appeared exactly overhead. Matt could always see them without tilting his head during his walk, and had been slightly happy about the fact that the suns weren't directly beaming down on him. Unfortunately, that also meant that the bottom of the pit wasn't very well-illuminated.

Matt pulled his torch from his bag to try to figure out exactly what could have created a hole like this. It had sprung up on him, and it was possible that he had walked by hundreds of similar pitfalls, or none at all. The light of his torch revealed the hole was about six feet across, and the wall nearest to him wasn't particularly interesting. It was the same weird burned-red as the surface, only vertical instead of horizontal.

The opposite wall, however, was interesting as hell. Mostly because it wasn't a wall at all, but a door. A big metal double door like Matt had only seen in pictures, ornately carved with geometric shapes and set in an arched frame. Each door had a handle in the form of a ring hanging from a tiger-like animal's mouth.

It looked like he could just yank it open and walk right in. Matt considered for a moment whether he should do this, but only for a moment. He knew that anything was better than walking until he died of hunger.

He pulled out a silent prayer: *Please, please just be a really fancy alien convenience store. I bet alien junk food would last forever.*

Matt half-expected for the doors to be rusted shut or even glued shut by accumulated dust. To his surprise, the door slid open like it had been recently greased. Inside was a small rectangular room made of the same metal as the door, nondescript in almost every way. Matt could imagine the room as a big closet or a featureless elevator. The only interesting aspect stood out like a sore thumb. In the middle of the room was a black, waist-high plinth of stone with an inset handprint design on its domed top.

"System, any comments on what this is before I go get myself accidentally killed?"

The system was silent, just as Matt expected. The system always stayed quiet for important things. On a whim, he opened up his mini-map to find it *did* display an icon for his location, the first he had seen. But that the icon was the same shape and color as the door itself. Maybe that was significant to the planet's former natives, but it was no help to him.

Matt stepped across the room and put his hand on the plinth. He knew he was going to do it eventually anyway. There was no use waiting.

And then a system window opened automatically. That was weird. Besides the "welcome to Gaia" message, system windows had never opened unless he prompted them to do so in some way. The window was also not the normal color. Where normal windows were blue, this was a sort of dull purple.

Dungeon entry request registered. Verifying dungeon readiness . . .

Error: Dungeon Challenge , Population: 0. Checking Dungeon creation resources.

Solar energy status: At capacity. Utilizing energy.

Dungeon Challenge, Population: 30. Teleportation lock set. Teleporting dungeon challenger momentarily.

Reading the text, Matt immediately panicked. "Wait, a dungeon? No! I'm at level 1. System! Dungeon System! I don't want to go. I'll stay here, okay? I'll just . . ."

Matt wasn't able to finish his sentence. Suddenly disappearing tended to have that effect on people.

CHAPTER FIVE

Clowns and Close Calls

It was a strange experience to not have a body. Matt wasn't floating in nothingness. It was more like he didn't have anything to float with in the first place.

Somehow, he could still think and imagine things. So at least he existed in a Descartian sense, but being a disembodied consciousness was an unwelcome additional wrinkle in an already very wrinkly week. As he not-hung in the not-air, Matt contemplated that his situation had somehow gone from bad, to very bad, to now utterly unpleasant. This was somehow worse than dying of hunger.

Luckily, he didn't have to wait long.

Ding!

> Entrant record not found. Is this your first time entering a dungeon?

Hopefully this thing reads thoughts. Matt tried his hardest to mentally indicate it was his first time.

> Response acknowledged. Scanning entrant memories.
>
> Entrant memories do not include knowledge of this dungeon's featured threats. Would you like to substitute an equivalent danger from your experiences?

If Matt was understanding the question correctly, the dungeon was worried he wouldn't be appropriately afraid of the enemies it wanted to present him. If this dungeon ended up conforming to the Isekai themes Matt was familiar with, he might end up with cute animals that would rip his throat out in seconds. It seemed like a better idea to deal with threats he could visually identify as dangerous as opposed to having to be paranoid about everything, or else walk around completely unwarned.

Response acknowledged. Generating dungeon. Please stand by.

Wait! Tell me something else about this dungeon! What level should I be? What's the point of it, even? Matt shouted in his thoughts.

Any extra information might mean the difference between life and death, but the dungeon was already gone. And after a few minutes, so was Matt. Again.

I have to stop waking up in new places, Matt grunted in his mind.

Despite suddenly being shoved back into a body and unceremoniously dumped on the ground, it wasn't all bad. For one, there was grass. Even before Matt opened his eyes, he could feel the grass blades bending against his skin. He opened his eyes to find himself in an idyllic grove. Too idyllic to really exist. It reminded him more of *Bambi* than reality. Then again, Gaia used to be a garden planet, maybe this was par for the course here, once.

Matt stood and almost started wandering immediately before realizing the implications of doing so unarmed. Mostly unarmed, anyway. He had the knife he got from the loot box, but it was in his backpack. He took it out and threaded it through his belt. The weight of the knife and sheath on his hip was foreign but comforting. He unsheathed and resheathed it a few times, making sure he could get at it on a moment's notice. He wasn't yet sure what the threats in the forest were, and even the birds chirping in the distance might end up being a danger to him.

After getting his weaponry in order, Matt retied his boots, gave himself a quick once-over, and started walking. The rest of the forest was as beautiful as where he woke up; flowers were blooming here and there, and the light cut through the trees just so, throwing golden beams of sun on everything. Even full, red berries were growing.

"System, can I eat food I find in the dungeons?"

All objects not explicitly created to be taken out of the dungeon are illusions created by the dungeon itself. Food found within a dungeon can be eaten, but any nourishment it provides is illusory. But the harm that some foods have will be real. It's usually not considered to be worth the risk.

Survivor's Instincts backed up the dungeon's claim in a different way. In Matt's understanding, random berries in the woods are often no-no food. But

Matt was truly starving. His eyes stayed glued to those berries. It was probably dangerous, but so was everything! He was very close to convincing himself he could just eat a couple. It would be fine.

With great effort, Matt tore his eyes away and moved on. He needed real solutions, and his only chance at them was finishing the dungeon. As he walked away, he felt a twinge from his Survivor's Instincts, asking him to move cautiously. So, he tried to move as quietly as he could through the forest, avoiding every stick and branch that might make a noise. He quickly found he sucked at this, and that moving cautiously took forever. He gave it his best shot anyway.

After an hour or so, every muscle in his body was creaking. It turned out that while he was pretty okay at walking, sneaking took a slightly different set of muscles, a set that now hated him and was making that dislike as clear as it could. As long as he kept moving, these muscles wouldn't stiffen up, but moving itself was now terrible. He decided that if he didn't find any enemies in the next ten minutes, he'd give it up.

He started watching the system clock. It took nine minutes, almost to the second.

Matt didn't dare talk, but almost immediately found that the system would answer mental queries.

System, what in the ever-loving shit is this?

The system is not responsible for dungeon generation and cannot guess at the parameters used to create specific aspects of dungeons.

Fine, cover your ass. I'll ask your friend. DUNGEON SYSTEM, what is this, you incredible asshole?

Clarify: Is the entrant asking about terrain, foes, or general dungeon facts?

You know perfectly well what I'm asking about.

Clarify, please.

The 'foes,' Dungeon System. Why are they clowns?

Matt had heard them long before he saw them. They produced a light chattering that stood out against the backdrop of bird noises. With brush still blocking his view, he had dropped to the ground and army-crawled until he posted up behind a relatively large fallen log. Peeking over the top, he finally saw them.

The enemy was something like an Earth rat, only larger and more willing to operate out in the open. There were five or six of them, all the size of fairly large house cats or fairly small dogs. That was bad news. A small dog was a menace on Earth, and these came in a pack. They were walking on what appeared to be a rough game trail, and didn't notice him. He had plenty of time to get a good, detailed look.

They were horrifying.

More specifically, they were clowns. The system had reskinned whatever animal this originally was into a disastrous little quadrupedal clown. They had red noses. Their feet were big oversized shoes, and their heads were covered with an assortment of big puffy wigs, little weird hats, and comical baldness. When they went to nibble on plants, they did so with human-shaped mouths packed with big rodent teeth. The system had even gone as far as to customize the face paint on each individual animal.

> As discussed, the dungeon system searched through creatures from your experiences that you fear and chose one at random, then used it to alter existing system creatures.

Creatures, Dungeon System! You said creatures! Clowns are people!

> Your psychological profile indicates that you do not believe that.

Matt paused. The system actually had him there. It wasn't wrong to pick clowns in the sense that Matt did consider them horrifying fantasy creatures of a sort. The problem was that this bizarre combination of clowns with beasts had tipped him over the edge from "those are creepy" territory into the realm of "this is the worst thing I can imagine" territory.

Well, no problem. He just wouldn't fight those. There had to be some exit to the dungeon. He'd find that, and hopefully avoid all combat. If the system wasn't lying, his leveling was based on surviving, not fighting. He could sneak his way out of this.

Ding!

> *Dungeon Objective Discovered!*
>
> Don't Send In The Clowns: You have observed a pack of roaming Clownrats. Clownrats represent a threat to this forest and to complete the dungeon, you must eliminate them.
>
> Objective: Eliminate Clownrat packs 0/4
> Reward: Low-Grade Dungeon Loot Selection

Yup. Fantastic. Great. Matt cursed the system.

Finding an ambush position took a while. He had to find a spot close enough to the path where he could spring out of it and surprise the clowns. He also had to find a spot far enough that the clowns couldn't see him until it was too late. The rats didn't seem to have great long-range senses, for what it was worth. He could see them from much further than they seemed to be able to see him. But he was guessing when it came to their close-range noticing capabilities and was just hoping he got it right. Finding a spot he was comfortable betting on took more than an hour.

During that time, he also learned some important things. First, more than one pack of Clownrats was on the game path. He had clocked a second, distinct pack, following about a half hour after the first.

Second, the system seemed to have cut corners on general animal behavior and forest details. As he lurked in the sticky, branchy brush of his ambush point, he watched the two packs pass. Then, the first pack appeared again from the same direction that he had first spotted the pack. Either the path was a circle or the dungeon was unspawning and respawning the packs on some sort of timer. It didn't matter to Matt how it was happening, but it was nice that he wouldn't have to track each pack to get the job done.

With the first pack approaching again, it was now or never. He zeroed in on the alpha of the pack, or at least what he thought to be the alpha. It was a larger clown with a diamond pattern over its too-human eyes. Diamond-eye was slightly more frightening than the others, but that was why Matt had decided to take it down first. He absolutely wanted to avoid any situation where the thing ended up behind him.

The Clownrats crept up within a meter or so of his hiding place, still apparently unaware of Matt's presence. They smelled like wet dog, and looked like nightmares he wasn't creative enough to have. He almost considered letting them pass and avoiding the confrontation when Diamond-eye suddenly stopped, tensed, and sniffed the air.

Now or never.

Matt sprang from cover, knife in hand. Diamond-eye squealed in surprise, and the other five rats in the pack wheeled around immediately. But it was too late for him to avoid Matt's attack. The knife point fell down on its back, at the portion of its spine between the back and head. Matt was hoping to sever its brain stem. If these animals were anything like Earth beasts, that would be fatal.

And then his knife hit bone. When Matt was digging his garden, he would occasionally hit a rock with his shovel point. Whenever that happened, it was an unpleasant nails-on-chalkboard feeling that he avoided as much as he could. This was ten times worse, not just because it gave the same feeling, and not just because his hand was suddenly getting soaked with Clownrat blood. It was worse because it immediately became clear he hadn't managed to kill the animal in one hit.

Diamond-eye bit him in response.

Ding!

You have been injured, –2 hp.

The damn thing's teeth went deep, but it luckily didn't hang on. Matt took the opportunity to stab Diamond-eye several times in the side, in a flurry of desperate blows. Diamond-eye went suddenly limp and a series of system *ding*s came up that Matt willed away as they came. He had to stoop to stab the thing, and as he straightened up, he felt another jolt of pain. One of the pack had got at his ankle. And the hits kept coming.

You have been injured. –2 HP. You have been injured. –2 HP. You have been injured. –2 HP. You have been injured. –2 HP. You have been injured. –2 HP.

Matt willed away the notifications as fast as he could. They were covering his view and he could hardly tell what was happening.

Dammit! System, stop telling me this stuff!

Query: Would you like to activate a less obtrusive HP tracking option?

Not right now!

Understood. Notifications temporarily suppressed.

Matt had hoped killing Diamond-eyes would scatter the lesser clowns. As he jumped back from his position, he saw the opposite was true. They were pissed. For the first time, it occurred to Matt that rats were usually social animals. It was entirely possible that he had just killed their mother. Either way, they were visibly angry and not backing down at all. Down to a handful of health points, he did the only thing he could do. He ran.

CHAPTER SIX

Trapped

It turned out that getting to 1 HP really hurt.

The Clownrats kept up with Matt's fleeing surprisingly well. He was able to dodge most of their attacks by running in a zigzag pattern, but couldn't entirely shake them off. The good thing was that even though his running speeds didn't seem to be enhanced that much by his Survivor's Combat ability, his evasiveness in running did. Instead of tripping and crashing into the trees that appeared in his path, Matt felt confident in twisting, turning, and juking around them.

It wasn't all-powerful, however. By the time the Clownrats' stamina petered out, Matt was also just about dead—both in terms of his stamina and in a very, very literal sense. They gave up just in time, turning back just a few moments before he would have collapsed and given them the win.

He staggered further into the woods, and once he saw that the Clownrats had returned to their circular path, collapsed on the forest floor. Adrenaline had helped to numb the bites as they happened. Now, he spent several painful minutes trying not to writhe as his vitality stat did its work and knit him back together. It was slow going. Every few minutes, he would recover another HP, and it wasn't until he was at 10 HP or so that he stopped feeling woozy from blood loss and general pain.

Finally able to relax, Matt felt a shudder of fear run through him. That was far too close for comfort, and he knew that his current skills were nowhere close to killing a pack of Clownrats without getting chewed up in a more permanent, fatal way.

The more he healed, the more his attention was drawn to the painful realities of his hunger and thirst. He didn't know which of the two would do him in quicker, and had no desire to find out. The dungeon system had put the task of killing the pack of Clownrats in front of him, and the longer he put that off the worse his problems would get. But after fighting and nearly dying, getting back up and going back into the fray was harder than it sounded.

Instead, he turned his attention to the notifications that had sounded during the fight. They made him feel better, but not by much.

Scar Collection Initiate

You've taken damage in combat for the first time. Assuming you survive, this is a valuable experience. Learn from it, and try not to do it again.

Reward: 1 Class XP

First Kill

You've defeated an enemy before it defeated you. Good job, but be careful. They might have had friends.

Reward: 1 Class XP

Tactical Withdrawal

Rather than stay and die, you ran away and lived. Survival isn't about winning. It's about making it through your problems alive.

Reward: 1 Class XP

In Matt's view, these were pretty underwhelming rewards for what he had just been through. But they also made sense in terms of what he'd expect from his idea of hero progression. It felt like these were tutorial rewards, the kind of on-rails assistance you got early in a video game for learning how to play. He didn't expect a lot from that kind of achievement. If he was being fair, he also hadn't accomplished a whole lot during that fight. The Clownrat kill was the only real success, and the system paid him out for that.

He was close to leveling up, which was comforting, but while he had received XP for his first kill, he saw that he hadn't received any XP for the kill itself. Taking out another Clownrat might not trigger XP for a level up, and even if he did level, running back into battle was a risk that might very well end with him dead. He was trapped.

Trapped, trapped, traps. The system-driven knowledge often came up in weird ways. Sometimes, it was unconscious, like when he ran from the Clownrats. Now, a surge of memories came forth to show Matt how to make dozens of weird, primitive traps suitable for snaring or killing small game. It was a stark reminder that he was the proud owner of knowledge that he hadn't actually put any work into learning.

System weirdness aside, this was the exact kind of information that a tutorial or system guardian should have drawn his attention to. Preferably, before he risked his life against the Clownrats. Something like, "oh, did you know you can make a bunch of traps and not nearly get bitten to death" would have been greatly appreciated.

For now, he had traps to make.

Matt couldn't make a net, and digging a pitfall would take too long. But he was pleased to find that an awful lot of simple, nasty traps could be made with nothing more than rope, sharpened sticks, and time. While he didn't have unlimited amounts of the last item on that list, his motivation for not being eaten alive by terrifying clown-rodents lent him strength to whittle triggers and gather bait.

It was unfortunate that while Survivor's Instincts taught Matt how to make traps, it didn't do anything to help him be good at making them. It also didn't provide him with the kind of callouses he'd need to do it comfortably, especially when making multiple traps with no tool but a knife. By the time he found himself crouched in a path-side hiding spot again, most of the skin on his hands was covered by cuts, scrapes, or just flat-out worn away.

The Clownrats finally showed, and as they rounded the corner, Matt was suddenly glad that he had chosen a hiding spot a bit further from the road. He had set the traps at a timing meant to catch the same group he had attacked previously. The remaining four beasts were noticeably more wary, their creepy clown noses snuffling at each bush as they passed. Matt was sure they would have found him if he had been in his previous hiding spot.

But they didn't. The Clownrats were completely unprepared when the lead rat hit the first tripwire and all hell broke loose. A whip trap, Matt had recently kind of learned, was a spiked stick bent way, way back and secured by a rope in a sort of shitty-on-purpose way meant to fail as soon as an animal hit the tripwire. When the lead Clownrat did exactly that, a tree branch loaded with whittled sticks whipped out over the path, impaling it and slashing another rat's leg.

Without a clear enemy to attack, the other two Clownrats scattered into the brush. One immediately hit a snare trap that used the rat's own momentum to tighten a noose around its neck, while the other, in a stroke of luck, jumped under a large rock Matt had set up as a deadfall trap. Deadfall traps were usually reliant on bait, and Matt hadn't expected this one to work. When the Clownrat wriggled out from under the large rock, Matt wasn't in any position to take advantage of the injury. Honestly, he was more surprised that it had triggered at all.

He was even more surprised by the devastation wrought by his traps. Letting the deadfall trap escapee flee the battlefield, Matt looked at the three Clownrats in various states of health. Matt descended on them like an avenging angel sent to rid the world of the clown menace once and for all.

The first stop was the one mostly free Clownrat whose leg had been wounded. It snarled and tried to leap at him, only to find its ability to do so hobbled by its injured leg. Matt had learned his lesson from striking the bone of Diamond-eyes, and instead stooped to stab this rat through the side when its lunge fell short.

The stabbed Clownrat fell in pain to the ground. It wasn't dead yet, but Matt figured he had a couple of seconds to deal with other problems before it recovered. He dove into the brush after the snared Clownrat, which had almost-but-not-quite wriggled out of the trap. As designed, the snare had closed over its head. No amount of thrashing could get it into a position to bite Matt as he approached from behind. Several stabs later, the rat wasn't moving anymore.

He ran back to the path, where the whip trap rat was still struggling against the spiked stick and the rat he had stabbed was back on its feet. If the stabbed rat was sluggish from injury before, now it was pathetic. Matt patiently baited it into snapping at him, then slipped to the side and stabbed it a few more times to finish the job. The last rat was still dying on the business end of his whip trap. He had won.

Ding!

This time, Matt didn't suppress the notifications that came pouring in.

Achievement: [Tricky Combatant]

The brave and the strong meet their problems head-on. You aren't either of those things. Instead, you decided to be smart and let your problems hit traps, tricks, or other indirect damage you put in their way.

Reward: 1 Class XP

Achievement: [Overwhelming the Odds]

You managed to defeat a clearly superior fighting force in battle. Something that should have killed you was killed by you, instead. We don't care how it happened, we just care that it did. Repeatable achievement.

Reward: 2 Class XP

Achievement: [Level Up!]

You've survived and grown. Enjoy the rewards!

Rewards: Class Stat Increase, 2 Assignable Stat Points

Matt didn't have a lot of time before the next group came through. He needed to clear the area and take what he could. Luckily, that didn't involve cleaning up the now-bloody Clownrat corpses. The system had made clear that everything he could see was an illusion, and drove it home by slowly fading the dead Clownrats away from existence.

Lacking time to reset the traps, Matt quickly disassembled what he could. He'd set them up in a different area, one that didn't somehow still stink of death, despite all the evidence of blood and battle evaporating into nothingness.

Once back to safety, Matt considered his status screen. As with his class assignment, it seemed the level up automatically assigned stat points to Survivor's emphasized stats.

Matt Perison
Level 2 Survivor
Class XP: 2/15
HP: 35
MP: N/A
STAM: 20
Assignable Stat Points: 2
STR: 5
DEX: 7
PER: 5
VIT: 7
WIS: 7
INT: 5
Class Skills: Survivor's Instincts (LV1), Survivor's Combat (LV1), Eat Anything! (LV1)

There were no new skills, though Matt was glad to see that his stamina and health had climbed with his vitality. More ability to take hits and flee was vital. The most interesting thing were the two new assignable stat points, presumably free to put anywhere he liked. His first thought was to stick them into vitality. So far, that had been his most useful stat and he hoped that more vitality would also allow him to heal a bit faster. His memories of nearly bleeding out in the woods were still fresh, and anything that shortened the pain sounded like a very good idea.

But before he clicked the plus button next to the stat, he paused and looked at his class skills. So far, Survivor's Instinct had been crucial in helping him in the very literal way the name implied. On the other hand, he wasn't very impressed by Survivor's Combat. Sure, he was a little better with the dagger than he should have been, but when the Clownrats were biting him, he hadn't been able to do much about it. His own attacks also felt only marginally more scary than they would have been back on Earth.

That left two possibilities. Either he had been granted the most underwhelming combat powers ever, or they didn't have enough to work with. Strength seemed irrelevant here—he wasn't trying to punt the rats into the woods. This was an issue of seeing what was coming and reacting to it before it got there.

While the rats were pretty quick, Matt could still follow their motions. It was his body that couldn't keep up to dodge the attacks. That meant it wasn't a lack of perception but rather dexterity. If he poured both points into dexterity, there was a chance he'd be able to fight the rats better. There was also a chance it wouldn't make that big of a difference.

Vitality was a surefire bet. In the end, it was a gamble between having the ability take more hits, or between maybe not getting hit at all.

Well, Matt was a gambler. "Nothing ventured, nothing gained" crossed his mind as he dumped both points into dexterity. He hoped it wasn't a placebo effect when he noticed that he was moving a little bit faster. Either way, it was time to move back to the path and reset his traps.

CHAPTER SEVEN

Bite, Scratch, Hate

If setting traps hadn't been fun, resetting traps over and over again was torture. After several repetitions of the cycle, Matt had to actively slow himself down. At one point, he barely avoided the business end of a self-sprung trap, courtesy of his own inattention. Not wanting to face a pack of enemies with the added handicap of a spike in his belly, he managed to force himself to exercise more caution.

The flip side of the coin was that it was a ton of fun to watch the traps go off. The Clownrats naturally grouped together with their pack, but only when they had an enemy to fight. They didn't register the traps that way, and even when the damage from the traps was minimal, they'd still scatter in a way that made it easy to pick one or two off.

It wasn't necessarily *more* fun to sweep in and mop up the survivors with his knife, but it was at least satisfying. Over the course of several surprise attacks, his general fear of clowns had morphed into something more like mutual hatred. He still didn't like them, but it now felt like he was meeting them as despised equals on a battlefield. There was still plenty of danger involved, but every clash was survivable. Eventually, it was the Clownrats that fled the battlefield, not him.

He was winning. After a full day's work, Matt pulled his knife out of a Clownrat neck, then sat and waited for the *ding* that would signal his triumph. He had defeated his fourth group, and was ready to claim whatever prizes the dungeon was offering and go home. After a few minutes, he had finished catching his breath from the battle, but the *ding* never came. And it still hadn't come after he had taken down his traps and moved them off the path.

"System, are you pouting? I killed the four terror herds, you know."

With no clear response incoming, Matt pulled up the dungeon quest window again.

Don't Send In The Clowns

You have observed a pack of roaming Clownrats. Clownrats represent a threat to this forest and to complete the dungeon, you must eliminate them.

Objective: Eliminate Clownrat packs 3/4
Reward: Low-Grade Dungeon Loot Selection

But he really had defeated the four packs of Clownrats that roamed in the forest. It wasn't until he saw a fifth pack made up of all the surviving escaped rats that he realized "eliminate" applied not at the pack level, but to every member of the pack. He had inadvertently assembled a group of Matt-hardened veterans, and the system wasn't going to let him off the hook until they were dead too.

Luckily, it wasn't something a few more traps couldn't fix.

After a few more repetitions of setting traps, it turned out Matt had engineered himself quite the problem. He doubted the remaining Clownrats actually understood traps, but they definitely understood *shit going down in a weird way*, and had become wary of any differences in the local terrain. When they saw trip wires, they went as far around them as they could. There wasn't enough time to dig a pit in the time it took the Clownrats to cycle through the path, and Matt was all out of trap variants that didn't rely on tripwires or propped-up rocks.

Matt was going to have to fight four Clownrats, one of them the alpha-mom variety, without any of the benefits that his traps had been creating for him. His previous experience doing that was success in killing one rat before the others swarmed him and almost killed him in retaliation. He wasn't exactly confident he had learned enough from that encounter to improve his odds of a better outcome by much.

It wasn't like he hadn't learned anything from the past few fights. One of the bigger problems Matt had encountered with the rats was that they were low to the ground. To stab one, he either had to stoop or intercept it as it flung itself at his face. Neither were ideal circumstances. He also had to fight them within their effective range, where they could bite him just as easily as he could cut them.

He had also learned a bit about fear. When the Clownrat had bitten him, he had panicked—there was no other word for it. He killed it, sure, but more out of sheer terror than some preformulated plan B for when things went wrong. Later on, when the Clownrats were scared of him instead of the other way around, he did much better. It was almost easy.

There was no way he got as much out of that first fight as he could have, both in terms of the initial clash and as he ran away. That was clear to him. Did he have time to train himself up? Not to any extent that would matter. Was he sure he could take down four Clownrats before they took him down? Not at all.

But he was pretty damn sure he could at least do *better*.

The mother Clownrat was more than annoyed. She was pissed. There were children to protect, yes. But they weren't HER children. Her children were gone. The new animal had taken them.

At first, she hadn't paid attention to the differences. There were new smells in the air, but not every new smell meant danger. Sometimes, it meant food to scavenge. Then, the path that she knew every rock of was disturbed. Later, she found the signs of a fight. It wasn't her fight, and she hadn't thought about it. If there was a danger, she'd smell it. She'd see it coming. She'd protect her young.

Then, her child was ahead of the pack, snuffling for food, when he was attacked by a *branch*. And that was new in a different, worse way. She couldn't expect or prevent the attack. And then another of her children was under a rock. And when she tried to shift the rock, another squealed as it got tangled in a branch. Before she could help any of them, the new animal was among them, killing. Not just killing one of her young, but all of them. More than it could have needed for food.

The terror took her and she ran. She had abandoned her children out of a primal fear.

And then she found these young, not hers but still young, and took them with her. Now, she saw even more differences. Vines where there shouldn't have been vines, and rocks that smelled of the new animal, placed in unnatural places at unnatural angles. She wouldn't be fooled again. She always walked in front and always led her adopted young away from the danger.

Now, as she rounded a new corner, she found the new animal, holding one of its branches. It was pushing around leaves and logs, searching for food that should have been her children's. Suddenly, she wasn't thinking about avoiding danger. The only thoughts in her mind were of rage and revenge.

Matt didn't know that the rats could move as fast as the alpha-mom did when it sprinted at him. When he had been chased before, the younger versions were far slower. So his plan had counted on more time, but he'd still make it work.

He stuck his new makeshift spear blade in the dirt first and grabbed his torch. The Clownrat wasn't wrong, he was messing with leaves and wood. The part she got wrong was that he wasn't looking in it so much as he was spreading as much of it as he could on the dry path. It had taken him hours and hours to find as much as he had.

The rat had closed about half the distance between them by the time he lit the torch and set a few different points of his dead foliage carpet aflame. It would take more time for the flames to race through the leaves than it would for the rat to get to him, but it would have to do. If he was lucky, the Clownrat would slow down out of fear. Unfortunately, he wasn't lucky, and in a few more moments, the mother Clownrat was nearly on him.

Matt had been strategic in choosing his current position. He grabbed his spear and jabbed it at the rat. It glanced off the thing's thick skull, cutting open a wound but not killing it. More importantly, the blow slowed it down enough for it to feel the heat from the growing flames and begin to panic. Matt could see the rat's eyes switching from flame to Matt, trying to choose between its desire to bite him, and its reluctance to move through the flames.

After a few moments, "bite the human" won out. Matt was already gone, having moved off the path and towards the smaller rats that were just now catching up. It looked like Survivor's Instincts was right when it told him that the rats relied mostly on smell. The large one didn't know he was gone until it was too late. He prayed the lashing on his knife would hold up, then jabbed it deep into the closest of the smaller rats.

It squealed, then went limp. Hearing it, the mother rat *screamed*.

The second rat didn't die as smoothly. It took two stabs, not one. He could hear the mother rat crashing through the leaves, and was relieved when the first hit to the third child rat was mortal.

Some of that relief evaporated away, though. The third rat's death throes ripped the knife from the bindings and left him with nothing but a branch to defend himself with. He shook himself out of his shock at being partially disarmed and turned to face the mother. It was too late to bring the stick up, or really do anything.

The rat hit him full in the chest and knocked him completely off his feet.

Bite. Scratch. Bite. Hate. HATE!

Without his stick, the new animal couldn't do *anything*. He struck her with his paws, but like all animals, he was weak without his sharp parts. She wasn't worried anymore. She was going to make him feel it all. He flipped himself over, which threw her off him for a moment. But she took a chunk of his flesh with her.

She wasn't worried about the new animal escaping. Wounded animals were part of her food, and she had damaged this one enough that he wasn't going anywhere fast.

On the other hand, she was fine. She snarled at him. *He should know*, she thought. He should know that she was strong. He was weak. She was coming for him and there was nothing he could do. On his back now, he slid away from her, leaving a trail of blood behind him on the ground.

Go ahead, new animal. Try and run.

She stayed on him, harrying his feet as he cried out with every bite. He just kept sliding back, too slow to escape her. And then he reached behind himself, to a bush, and it was only then she saw one of his wrong vines stretched behind the leaves.

No!

She leapt at his hand to stop him. Midair, the last thing she ever heard was a snap as the vine released the catch on Matt's trap.

CHAPTER EIGHT

Eat Anything

Before the battle, Matt realized that he had a serious problem with his traps. The Clownrats were wary enough of anything new that they were now avoiding anything even a little bit weird to them, including objects that Matt had only bumped into or shuffled around. They weren't going to trip on any trap with a visible trigger.

He could hide the triggers, but the Clownrats mostly kept to the path with small deviations. Hell, he couldn't discern any visible pattern to the rats when they avoided his traps. They'd go left, right, jump, back. In every direction but onto the trap.

From how the dungeon described them, it was entirely possible that these Clownrats were basically programs with some if-then conditional lines of code. For all he knew, he might wait a thousand years without them varying from their current pattern.

Even worse, setting up a trap in the brush where they couldn't see it essentially meant also setting a trap where he couldn't see it. Not only would they be unlikely to trigger it, but . . .

There's a good chance I'd trigger it myself.

And with that thought, Matt's Survival Instincts began to go crazy.

Matt's feet looked like chewed up steak. The rat had been so angry that Matt began to seriously doubt his theory that the beasts might be programmed simulations. He didn't know a lot about AI, but it was hard to imagine an AI program that got as angry as the mother rat had. It was biting his feet out of pure spite.

By the time Matt got to the tripwire for his hidden whip trap, he was pretty sure that the thing had severed some of his toes.

But he got to the trigger. When he set up the trap, the idea was to get behind the tripwire somehow and bait the animal into it. Barring that, he could activate it himself, but he had been worried about not being low enough to save himself from getting impaled. That ended up not being a worry. He couldn't have stood, even if he wanted to.

Since he was only setting up one trap, Matt had gone a little overboard. He had combined as many of his previous attempts together as he could, which resulted in a much sturdier trigger that would take more to set off. More importantly, the lethal portion of the trap ended up being about four times as substantial as any other trap he had set up so far. When the time came to arm it, he could barely bend the whole thing back.

The practical upshot of this was that when the trap hit the Clownrat mother, it hit it *hard*. Two of the stakes went completely through its torso, and the last one ripped across its face so hard, it damn near detached the clown nose. The branch hardly slowed down either. The rat ended up being flung off the spikes, landing several feet from Matt. It laid still, barely breathing and clearly dying.

Matt wasn't in much better shape. His legs had taken several deep, powerful bites. His feet had sustained much more serious damage. Blood poured out of his wounds and he was starting to feel lightheaded.

It looked like not all 1 HP states were created equal. Before, vitality had easily closed the simple wounds around his body. This time, it was having trouble dealing with his mangled feet. After several seconds, it became pretty clear that the wounds were going to win the race. He wasn't going to make it.

As his field of vision dimmed, Matt focused on the Clownrat mother, watching its breathing dwindle to nothing.

Come on, you asshole. Die. At least I can watch you melt away before I go.

Just before his vision faded to black, the rat finally started dissolving away. He lost consciousness immediately after.

Ding!

Matt woke up. That was a shock. He was more surprised to find he was fine and laying in the dungeon's grassy fields. All the damage from his battle was gone, even the tears and rips in his clothes. He looked the same as when he had first entered the dungeon. Referencing his notifications spread some light on why.

Dungeon Objective Complete!

You exterminated the Clownrat packs, and the forest's ecological balance has been restored. Congratulations! You may leave the dungeon whenever you wish.

Rewards: Dungeon Prizes
Exit dungeon now? Y/N

Achievement: [Saved by the Bell]

That was close. Having sustained wounds you couldn't recover from and without any healing resources, you managed to complete your dungeon objective. You were brought back by the dungeon's automatic post-mission healing function. That's about as close as you can cut it.

Rewards: Random Skill Improvement, +1 VIT, +5 Class XP
Random skill selection: Eat Anything! promoted to LV2

Achievement: [Solo Dungeon]

You have completed a dungeon meant for a party by yourself. This probably wasn't a good thing to try, but it's still a hard thing to do and deserves a reward.

Rewards: +1 VIT, +5 Class XP

Achievement: [Over Your Head]

You completed a dungeon designed for a much higher level. We can only guess you don't pay very close attention. We'll do our best to help.

Rewards: Unskippable Dungeon Level Notification, +1 PER

Achievement: [Never Saw It Coming]

You have killed an opponent that had a superior perception with an attack they completely failed to notice. Taking advantage of their blind spot means a reduction in your own.

Reward: +1 PER

It might have been Matt's imagination, but it seemed like the system was getting snarkier over time. The announcements were barely-veiled criticisms of him tempting fate, even though "barely surviving" was what his class required for advancement. And it wasn't as if the system was completely unaware of that, since his rewards seemed to be tailored to satisfying the survive-what-you-shouldn't nature of his class. Two points in both VIT and PER were big all on their own, and he wasn't even counting his skill advancement. If the system was mad at him for taking risks, at least it didn't skimp on the payout.

As Matt opened his system interface to look into the changes to Eat Anything!, he was momentarily distracted by an entirely new tab labeled "Pending Dungeon Rewards." Putting his curiosity regarding the skill level up aside for a moment, he mentally prompted the tab to open.

Dungeon Reward Selection!

You have completed a dungeon objective and the reward is a prize from the following list:

Assassin's Dagger

You wait in the darkness, only to spring out and rain death down on your enemies. The assassin's dagger is a thin, sharp weapon designed for striking vital points and killing foes in a single hit.

That was pretty good, but it wasn't like Matt didn't already have a knife. A better knife didn't solve any of his larger problems. Matt continued on.

Reinforced Survivor's Garb (1 piece)

Bridging the gap from clothing to armor, the reinforced Survivor's garb protects while still allowing a full range of motion. The full set represents a substantial increase in protection compared to the basic Survivor's garb.

Like the dagger, this was nice but wouldn't do much to help him with his immediate concerns. He would take this over the knife. For now, he set it off to the side to look at his final option.

Repair Stone (LV1)

Every adventurer needs to repair the dents and holes in their equipment. The repair stone will fix any mundane and lightly enchanted equipment, bringing a worn weapon to peak condition or repairing equipment from the [broken] condition.

Great, Matt thought. *Really useful, thanks.*

The dungeon had already repaired everything he was wearing, and the only other piece of his gear that had any wear on it was his rope. Maybe if he picked up something broken somewhere else he could fix that, but he hadn't seen anything resembling equipment in the outside world.

The water stone!

Matt had no idea what "lightly enchanted" meant. Hell, he had no idea what "equipment" covered. Assuming he could fix the water stone, he might just be able to take it with him. Again, a gamble. But it was the only thing on the reward list that stood a chance of actually helping him live.

A golf-ball-sized round rock immediately materialized in the air in front of him and fell to the ground. Matt put it into his pack and jumped over to his status screen.

Matt Perison
Level 2 Survivor
Class XP: 12/15
HP: 45
MP: N/A
STAM: 30
STR: 5
DEX: 9
PER: 7
VIT: 9
WIS: 7
INT: 5
Class Skills: Survivor's Instincts (LV1), Survivor's Combat (LV1), Eat Anything! (LV2)

Unlike other attributes, it was immediately clear what perception did. He could see further, better, and *faster*. That last was something he noticed when the repair stone fell to the ground. He was able to track it visually the whole way to the ground with no special effort, as if it was an object someone tossed you while trying to make it easy to catch. When fighting the Clownrats, the extra dexterity also came in handy. He was faster and more competent. But when the rats tried to bite him, Matt had trouble seeing the strikes well enough to get out of the way. He hoped perception would help with that, and was glad he didn't have to gamble with his assignable stat points to find out if it did.

It was a shame that the dungeon completion didn't give XP, he'd probably get some extra stat points out of the level up. Still, he was much closer to level 3. There was just one last thing to examine, and for once, it was just how he had hoped it would be.

Eat Anything! (LV2)
Eat Anything! allows you to eat things a normal person couldn't. At the second level, this means getting more nutrition out of food and being able to digest some otherwise inedible foods. Tree bark steak, here we come!

Matt had some seriously low blood sugar by the time he found some more berries. Before, the system had indicated they might be poisonous but wouldn't give up any actual calories. At that point, it was right. But now, Matt was willing to gamble that the level 2 Eat Anything! would change that. Cautiously, he put one in his mouth and chewed it.

Despite looking deliciously red and being a simulated relic, the berry's flavor was mellow well past the point of tasting overripe, and verging on spoiled. Matt was hungry enough that he barely tasted anything. He swallowed the berry as soon as it was chewed enough that he wouldn't choke.

Ding!

Achievement: [Poison Roulette]

You have consumed a poisonous food source. Luckily, the poison either wasn't strong enough to hurt you or you negated it somehow. Keep trying, though! Something will kill you eventually!

Rewards: None

Matt was convinced: the system was definitely getting snarkier. This was the most sarcastic it had seemed yet. He had survived the berry, and it wasn't a repeatable achievement, so it wasn't exactly meaningful information for him. The only reason to give him the achievement was to give him grief.

Ding!

Achievement: [Meta-Metabolizing]

You have eaten fake food and somehow got real nourishment out of it. This is only a small, small fraction of what real food might give you, but it's something. Keep going. Growing boys need their nourishment.

Reward: +1 STR

Matt was elated. Beyond elated. He had never appreciated how easy it was to get food on Earth, at least in the part he was from. The longest he had ever gone without a meal before was probably a day, when he was busy or stressed or just flat-out forgot. He didn't have a great sense of how long he had been on Gaia, but it had to have been longer than a day. Food was all he could think about at this point.

Matt wasn't sure if he could eat an infinite amount of pretend dungeon-hologram berries, but he was ready to try.

CHAPTER NINE

Springs Eternal

There was a very real limit to the number of berries that Matt could eat. Even though they weren't exactly real, the berries still had some mass to them.

It was a weird experience. Matt ate until he could eat no more, only to feel the berries digest in a matter of minutes. The system wasn't lying when it said that he would only receive a small fraction of the nourishment that real food would give. Matt ate to capacity multiple times, and in the process, he cleaned off entire bushes of berries. Green, unripe, overripe, they were all fair game.

Despite his efforts, Matt's hunger only got slightly better. He was still starving. It was as if he had broken a fast with just a single piece of bread. It was something but, in some ways, it made him feel much worse.

After a few repetitions of eating to his limit, Matt realized he was stalling. If he got out into the real world again, he'd have to see whether the repair stone actually worked on his water source. If it didn't, his chances of dying of dehydration in the dirt of an alien world would skyrocket.

He was more afraid of this gamble than he wanted to admit. It was like escaping a desert island by going out to sea in a rowboat. Hoping, even praying, there was an island in range before he ran out of resources or hit a big wave and drowned.

Sighing, Matt finally stood up, dusted off, and mentally recalled the *Dungeon Objective Complete* window.

Dungeon Objective Complete!

You exterminated the Clownrat packs, and the forest's ecological balance has returned. Congratulations! You may leave the dungeon whenever you wish.

Rewards: Selected Dungeon Prize
Exit the dungeon now? Y/N

"Yes."

The trip out was weird, but less so than entering the dungeon had been.

For a moment, Matt didn't exist. The dungeon wiped out everything he was, like a whole-body blink that blocked off his entire existence. Then suddenly, without any fuss, he was back in a hole in the red wasteland of a dead planet. There was no hanging in the aether as pure thought this time. It was all business. Just plain teleportation with no fanfare, like it wasn't even a big deal.

Matt turned back to the gate only to find the doors were closed to him. Pushing and pulling on them didn't seem to have any effect at all. *I guess no repeatable dungeons*, he thought. But as he approached the doors, he did get some more "would have been nice to know earlier" information, courtesy of the mandatory dungeon level warning that the dungeon had given him.

Warning!

The difficulty of this dungeon exceeds the average level of your party. Proceed with extreme caution.

Dungeon Difficulty: LV3
Average Party Level: LV2

The warning was nice, but this seemed like bad news. The dungeon had been absurdly difficult relative to what Matt could actually handle. Before the notification, he would have guessed that it was at least a level 5 dungeon. The level was one thing. The part that worried Matt was the implicit idea that dungeon difficulties were balanced around the assumption of entrants having a party.

If there was one thing that Matt was sure of, it was that he was alone on this burned-out planet.

Even with a level up, Matt wasn't sure if he could have cleared this dungeon without facing real, substantial danger. Given that this dungeon was just level 3, there probably weren't too many easier dungeons around. He tried to imagine what a level 5 dungeon would be like and couldn't get an accurate picture in his head. All he knew was that it would make pretty short work of killing him.

His only chance at success were level 3 or lower dungeons. If he could find them.

* * *

Getting out of the hole took some climbing, but wasn't particularly dangerous. Matt took it slow, dug out a few footholds, and managed to get out without too much trouble. Trekking back to the water stone was similarly banal. He was low on water, and if things went poorly, he could hopefully just extract more with his still. If he were lucky, it wouldn't be an issue at all.

Finding the water stone again wasn't that hard. He could roughly orient himself using the system compass as a guide. But he didn't even need that. He could see the stone from surprisingly far away, probably due to a combination of his increased perception and the fact that any difference in the landscape was highly visible. His hastily carved out hole in the ground was still there and stood out like a sore thumb even at a distance.

By the time that Matt reached the water stone, it looked to be in much worse shape than he had remembered. It might have been the exposure to air or being moved after so long, but it seemed to pop and hiss more than it had before.

It was possible it wasn't even working anymore. If the repair stone failed, he'd have to take what water he could, walk off into the sun (there was no sunrise or sunset), and just hope for the best. As abstract as the problem was, his body seemed to understand the stakes. A surprising amount of tension had built up in his chest. It felt as if he was back in the dungeon, waiting in the bushes to ambush the terrifying clown-rat hybrids that the system had built.

No use dragging it out, I guess. He fished the repair stone from his bag, held it to the water stone, and willed it to work. For a moment, nothing happened. Then, suddenly, the repair stone was gone from his hand. It didn't pop or glow, it was just suddenly not there anymore.

Ding!

Repair stone consumed. Water stone repaired.

Water Stone (Repaired)
A common water stone, used in a home or fountain. Produces water until the container it's stored in is full, then automatically shuts off. This water stone has been repaired from a [broken] status and has reduced durability.
Item durability: 10/50

Matt was not the type of person who showed a lot of emotion. When he found out he had cancer, his doctor was probably more emotional than he was. He didn't yell, scream, or cry. He just accepted the reality and moved on. Even when his friends told him that it was okay to show emotions about dying, he had held back. To him, even the slightest reaction would give the illness another victory over him, and he didn't want that.

But here, over a suddenly working water stone that was visibly pumping out moisture? He did a little dance. He wasn't good at dancing, and he guessed he looked silly, but he didn't care. There was nobody there to see it anyway. For a minute or so, his boots made squishing noises in the wet alien dirt as he celebrated his biggest victory yet.

Was ten durability out of fifty a lot? He had no idea. Maybe it would last him years, or maybe it would last him a day.

It was still more than he had yesterday, and it would give him a much better chance of reaching his destination. Even if it didn't get him there, he might find another dungeon. He might find some actual honest-to-god ruins that he could scavenge from. Or something else. He didn't know. All he knew was that this was the first time things had really gotten better, and he was going to celebrate that.

He gently scooped up the stone. There was no use wasting the durability it had on watering the dead soil here. The description for the item had been unusually detailed, which Matt attributed to the system "paying him back" for the expenditure of the repair stone. He probably had some right to know what the stone had done, which meant the system had to tell him about what it had fixed. He could imagine situations where that might be useful as a sort of poor-man's identify spell, and filed the idea away for later.

He brushed the mud from the stone as well as he could, then knotted some of his rope around it for protection before dropping it into his canteen. Staring into the mouth of the canteen was disorienting, since it was bigger on the inside than the outside. It was like a miniature version of the system assistant truck-avatar experience. His mind struggled to parse the sight, it was like the universe suddenly didn't fit around his body. Luckily, he didn't have to look for very long. Within seconds, there was noticeably more water in the thing. It was working.

Sitting down, Matt began to organize his things for his trip. He still had no idea how far he had to go, but he was prepared to walk until he dropped.

Socks were a very good idea.

The Survivor's garb was nice. It was built for a specific purpose, and felt like it would last years and years of normal use. In some ways, it reminded Matt of his old tools. In a world where most things were disposable, tools were almost always a little more real than everything else. They had a job to do, and a hammer or a wrench felt more heavy and durable in a way that a TV or laptop didn't. The garb was like that. It felt substantial enough to do a job with.

But the garb didn't come with socks, or underwear for that matter. The underwear he could do without, as awkward as it was. Socks were a must, though. Especially when Matt was about to walk endless distances in heavy, durable boots. He didn't have the ability to conjure fabric, but what Matt *did* have was the starter robe he had been dropped to Gaia in. Using his knife, he cut it into strips and bound it around his feet as well as he could. Once in the boots, the strips were held in position by the pressure from the laces. The boots had been a big improvement, but the socks made it better. Much, much better.

Matt had drunk some water before, but was limited by what the still could pull out of the soil, which wasn't much. He now realized how dehydrated he had been while subconsciously rationing his limited water supplies. Now that he had a steady supply of moisture, he could give himself permission to catch up on his hydration. As he walked, he felt a remarkable improvement. It was like he was getting less tired, not more.

Now all that was left was to keep going. It might be hours, days, or weeks to his destination. He had no way of knowing, but the time for prep was over. He was either going to make it or die trying.

CHAPTER TEN

Crackers

After a day or so of walking, Matt was starting to learn new things.

His first lesson was in how easy it was to become very, very sore after spending nearly every waking moment walking in a calorie-deprived state. Every muscle in his legs whined at him, begging him for food. The rest of his body wasn't much better either. It felt like his back was on the verge of going out, and all the little stabilizer muscles in his abdomen that made walking possible were making their displeasure known.

The second lesson was that a diet consisting of illusory berries and occasional sips of water was not something to take lightly. He now knew the rare treat of being both half-starved and overfed. What time he didn't spend on walking or sleeping was wasted on struggling with the digestive aftermath of gorging on several pounds of mysterious berries. It wasn't a great time.

The first two lessons were of the same type. The third was different. It was air quality. Matt's elevated vitality was the only thing getting him through the sheer amount of exercise and rough digestion he was subjecting himself to. As he walked, he also started noticing something that he hadn't previously realized: the air quality of Gaia was shit. It was LA-on-a-smog-warning-day bad.

At first, there was no way Matt would have noticed this. He had been so very sick before his Isekai journey that the ability to take an unlabored breath was novel. However, with his vitality bumped up, he was finally able to take deep, productive breaths that went beyond even that. His lungs felt strong for the first time in what felt like forever. Despite the dusty, ashy air, it was a literal breath of fresh air. It was air in the corniest, puniest way possible, but at least he wasn't wheezing.

With the general filthiness of the air, he wasn't particularly surprised when a mountain range suddenly loomed in front of him. He had been walking for approximately three days already. The mountain was massive, and there was no way that it could have snuck on him without the dust blocking his vision and the fact that Gaia didn't seem to spin around its twin suns. With no dawn or sunset to highlight the terrain, there was no way Matt could have seen the mountains before now.

Despite how big the mountains were, it wasn't as if Matt was particularly close to them. At best, he was a couple of days away from what he made out as the base of the mountain. Unfortunately, when he looked at his system compass, he realized that it was pointing straight at the mountain range where he'd have to climb uphill. After a groan, he got back to the walk.

One of the tricky things about mountains is that you never really know when you're at the base of one. From a local perspective, it was just a series of increasingly steep steps. All but unnoticeable until every step screamed agony. After a couple of days, Matt estimated that he had made it to the base of the mountain.

He was also at the beginnings of serious trouble related to food. When the system had first teleported Matt to Gaia, it had been kind enough to start him in a well-fed state. Over the course of the next few days, Matt had become increasingly hungry, nearing what he believed was starvation. His efforts with the berries had temporarily reversed that trend, but now the meager nutrition he had found in them was long gone.

The additional strain of the journey had taught him that starvation had different levels. He was wrong to call what he went through before as starvation. Yes, he was very hungry back then, but it wasn't anything like now. Before, he had been able to plod along at a reasonable pace. Now, he found himself having to stop more and more often to recover from dizziness, unsteadiness, and general weakness. As time passed, this only got worse. He was taking a few steps, sitting down, and supporting himself on one of the tent poles like a staff.

He then learned one final lesson. When you collapse from hunger, you don't get a lot of advance warning.

Matt woke up at the bottom of an incline with blood in his hair. He reached up to his head to feel out the wound, but his vitality stat had already done the work to close it up. That meant he had been out for at least several minutes. Even with his enhanced vitality, it would have still taken a fair amount of time to heal from a scrape that produced that much blood.

As cool as it was to wake up with injuries already healed, vitality didn't do anything to help Matt's hunger or any of its follow-on effects. It was still hard to get up, let alone walk around. But he had to get up. Examining his surroundings, Matt saw that the now-healed wound on his head had been caused by a brick. More specifically, it had been caused by one of many bricks in the area. It took a while before the alarm bells in his head subsided. Only then did he grasp the significance of where he was.

Holy shit, an actual ruin.

There were hundreds of bricks around, some of them still assembled into parts of honest-to-god walls. Matt was either looking at the remains of one very large building, or a small compound of multiple buildings packed together. As quick as he could, Matt shambled around to take a better look.

Bricks were a sign of civilization. Matt's knowledge of the original Gaians started and stopped with the words "garden planet." The fact that they were at least past the mud-and-leaves stage of civilization was a good sign. Not a great sign, since bricks weren't that hard to make, but as he picked through the wreckage, he also found little bits and pieces of metal. His advanced-society estimates of Gaians soared. But it wasn't until he was almost done combing through the ruins when he found evidence that categorized Gaians as an advanced civilization.

He was in the last section that he could search, which was either an inner courtyard or a great room. That was when his foot hit metal. It wasn't a small piece of metal like what he had been finding, but a great big metal chunk that clunked when he stubbed the hell out of his toes on it. Thankfully, his toes had long gone numb from his march. Matt quickly brushed the dust off and found that he was dealing with what appeared to be a fairly large lid. Promisingly, there was a similar size chest attached to the lid.

The chest was entirely buried, and Matt looked at the task ahead of him with despair.

It took him hours of brushing away dirt and chipping at hardened clay before it was loose. For the worst parts, he used moisture from the water stone to loosen and break the chest from the surrounding dirt. Using all of his strength, he managed to hoist the thing out. Under the Gaian sun, he found something about twice as large as a military footlocker and infinitely more bizarre.

The metal wasn't rusted at all. Whatever this was made of, it wasn't made with beauty in mind. As boxes went, it was ugly in the sort of minimalist military sense Matt associated with video game ammo boxes. But it was somehow completely undamaged. Whatever decades, centuries, or millennia had passed since this planet's downfall had not touched it. Or, for that matter, the electronics hooked to it, which looked like a video touchpad.

It took a while to find the button that turned the touchpad on. It wasn't on the edge like all the Earth boxes. Instead, some maniac had designed the button on the back of the touchpad, and Matt's fingers barely found it. When he pushed in, the screen sprang to life.

CalicaCorp Military Comms Pad V. 6.7 Booting . . .

"Hey, system. Why is this pad in English? That doesn't even make sense."

> A few of the most common local languages are automatically translated. This is considered part of the basic transmigration package, and automatically converts any communications in those languages to the language best known to the transmigrator.
>
> Please note that additional languages can be learned through classes dedicated to translation or through the traditional routes of study and practice.

Well, that's convenient, Matt thought. Like at home, the computers that Gaians used for government applications were slow as hell, and it took minutes that felt like eternities for the damn thing to get up and running. When it finally finished, the wait was worth it.

> *Warning!*
> This chest contains emergency relief supplies meant for use against the growth scourge. Open only when intended for immediate use. Unsealing the chest will dispel all storage enchantments.

That was promising, and even more promising was the glowing handprint that immediately lit up on the box next to the display. Matt didn't hesitate. He plopped his hand on it immediately.

> Unable to get an accurate scan. Please clean both the scanner and the user's hand.

Frustrated, Matt wasted some water cutting some of the thick dust off his right hand, and retried the scanner.

> Error. User not found in database. Scanning user for individual metrics.
> Sarthia Prime Citizen established.
> Gaia Universal Citizen status established.
> Opening authority granted. Supplies are to be used in accordance with the Sarthia catastrophe relief efforts and Gaia unified government growth scourge resistance initiative goals. Failure to comply with these restrictions will result in punishment to the full extent of the law.
> Open Chest?

Well, not much risk there. The touchpad displayed a set of "Yes/No" buttons, and Matt quickly selected yes. It shut down to a black screen again. After a few seconds, the box clicked and hissed as the mechanism holding it closed released.

The touchpad suddenly opened and began to flash as it displayed a warning message.

> Enchantments will now be dispelled. Please close your eyes and cover your ears in 3 . . . 2 . . .

Matt was momentarily caught off guard and failed to do either of these things. He quickly regretted that as the entire box exploded in a sudden, massive pop of light and sound. It was like he had set off a flash-bang inches from his face. Temporarily robbed of both his sight and equilibrium, he stumbled back into the dirt and hoped that vitality would restore his eardrums before his sudden nausea caught up with him.

When his sight finally came back, he found himself sitting next to a relatively large chest packed with foil bags. Foil packages that, somehow, looked untouched by time. Each was marked with a large "ERR" that he desperately hoped meant something besides error. He grabbed one and spent a few moments fruitlessly trying to rip it open with his hands and teeth before remembering that for the first time in his life, he was carrying a belt knife.

The knife easily defeated the defenses of the bag. Matt turned it over and shook it out inside the chest, revealing several dozen small crackers. Plain, nondescript, gray-white crackers without a speck of visible salt or any indication they were meant to be enjoyed as food. He immediately popped one in his mouth. It wasn't delicious. It hardly had flavor at all. But it was food. Actual non-hologram food meant to be eaten by real people with real mouths.

His body set off a bunch of internal, celebratory signals to his brain, and for a while Matt lived in a world of pure cracker-driven joy. He was eating.

CHAPTER ELEVEN

Move on, Dummy

Surprisingly, Matt didn't end up eating a lot of the crackers. It wasn't that he didn't want to; he planned to sit down and kill as many of those little foil bags as it took to feel truly full. He wanted to gorge himself.

But the crackers ended up being surprisingly dense. They took a significant amount of effort to chew and a small amount of water to swallow. After hitting his stomach, they then seemed to expand and take up even more space. After one, he felt better. After two, he felt full. After cramming in the third, he felt outright bloated.

Oh, yeah, he thought. *This is emergency food.*

On Earth, he had heard about the emergency food placed on lifeboats, where they condensed as many calories as they could into bar-shaped pieces. This was food made by a world that was facing a catastrophe, so it made sense that the food was incredibly filling. Matt also guessed that Eat Anything! was working behind the scenes to amplify the value of the food even more.

As the calories seeped into his bloodstream, Matt discovered how much of his fatigue had been trumped by his desperation to find food. It turned out to be quite a lot. He barely managed to pull the lid shut on his food treasure box and get his pack off before falling asleep.

Matt checked his clock after waking up and found that he had slept close to ten hours. His stomach could have also told him that; he was famished again.

I guess one meal by itself doesn't fix days of not eating, no matter how dense it is, he thought. Popping a few more of the crackers into his mouth, he sat down to take inventory of the contents of the box. At first glance, it was an awful lot of food. The bag he had taken out was relatively small, and the chest was huge.

But as he pulled the bags out to get an accurate count, he found that there were less of them than he thought. The bottom half of the box composed of jugs of water, cans of cooking fuel, and cans of what appeared to be an aerosol herbicide. For obvious reasons, he was much less interested in those and set them off to the side.

What was left were several dozen foil bags. Even that came with a wrinkle. As Matt sorted through the bags, some of them felt different in his hands. They all weighed about the same, but some were filled with some kind of powder as opposed to solid food. He opened one experimentally and was greeted by a mysterious ashy substance that he couldn't identify.

It didn't smell, stink, or have any clues to what it might be.

Matt dipped his finger in the bag, careful to only get a tiny amount of the substance stuck on his finger. He licked the smallest amount he could from his fingertip. And spent the next few minutes trying his best to avoid vomiting and wasting food. Somewhere in the cloud of nausea, Matt heard a system *ding*.

What Even is This?

Some things are enough like food that Eat Anything! tries to digest it, and then immediately regrets it. This is that. It's something that should be food but isn't. It even confused a skill specifically designed to deal with weird and unusual food sources.

Rewards: Eat Anything! skill experience

Skill experience was a new one for Matt. Eat Anything! hadn't advanced a level and the flavor text attached to it was unchanged, so he assumed it was just closer to leveling in general. The food itself was an even greater mystery, though. Who would package poison in the same bags they used for food?

Unless it WAS food, Matt thought.

It had been a long time since Gaians had packed this food away. If the box was any indication, their technology was a combination of both magic and conventional technology. There was no telling *how* they had preserved this food, but if some single element of that had failed, it made sense that he'd be left with a bag of hermetically sealed evil. The question now was, how many of those bags did he have?

Assuming that the storage failure was a pass-or-fail type of thing, Matt separated the ones that felt like solid food from the wholly weird ash ones. Luckily, the crackers didn't disintegrate when he squeezed them. In the end, he was left with a much less bountiful take than he had expected. About six bags had survived the potential eons to make it to his backpack. That took him down from months of rations to only days or weeks, depending on how far he could actually march on one of them. He immediately began to regret eating four of them like they were candy. Then, he thought back to how he felt earlier and decided that it was probably a good thing on balance. He had been through a lot.

He spent the rest of the day exploring the surrounding area. It turned out he was definitely in the ruins of a small village or military outpost, and he found signs of about two dozen fallen buildings. A careful search of each turned up nothing but dust and bricks. He found nothing more he could use.

He returned to the big building and chest to take a rest. Packing up again, he wrapped the remaining bags of food inside his tent tarp, protecting as well as he could from being crushed. The cooking fuel was a mystery to him.

Who eats crackers hot? Matt thought.

But he took some of it with him anyway. It was flammable if nothing else. It would have been useful in the fire-trap he used in the final battle with the Clownrats, and might prove useful in the future. He also packed what water he could. He'd drink the chest water before using his canteen again. There was no use wearing out the water stone any quicker than he had to.

He organized everything in his pack, trying to arrange things so they'd ride easier as he walked. As he went to shoulder his pack, he paused and contemplated the bags of evil dust one more time. Instead of leaving them behind, he impulsively opened several of them, combined their contents into just one of the foil bags, and carefully tied the large bag shut with rope. He had no idea what it could be used for, but it didn't make sense to turn down any resource at this point, no matter how weird.

As boring as it had been, Matt now missed the flat terrain. When he paused for rest, he'd pull his swollen feet out of his boots. The cool air greeted his toes that had battled against rock, uneven ground, and even the tops of the boots. Vitality seemed to do its best work when Matt was at rest, and hardly any when he was moving. Though his feet healed up completely every night, they were uncomfortable messes through the majority of every day.

For the most part, the terrain wasn't much more dangerous in any significant sense. Matt had noticed a few small ravines and impassably steep rock walls, but he was mostly able to get around them as he went. It meant a number of small delays that would eventually add up, but with food and water at hand, Matt found he cared much, much less about traveling efficiency. To the extent he could, he tried to scout out likely locations where dungeons might be hiding, but had no luck finding any. For all he knew, every dungeon on the planet was buried under centuries of dust.

Without any real reason to keep careful track, Matt stopped counting the days. He'd walk, sleep, and occasionally stop to appreciate the view. Despite the lack of trees, the elevation sometimes provided vistas that weren't entirely unpleasant to look at. All the while, he continued in the direction of the system compass. Whatever was at the end of that pointer was his only official purpose in this new life. He didn't have any incredibly compelling reason to complete it, but he also had nothing better to do. He might as well.

And then something happened. As Matt crested a rise in the terrain, the system compass *changed*. The pointer itself stayed the same, but underneath it was a new and significant marking: 100,000W. Matt continued moving forward three or four feet, and saw the number drop to 99,999. It looked like whatever that *W* signified, it was something like an Earth yard or meter. If so, one hundred thousand of them would be approximately sixty or seventy Earth miles.

I can do seventy miles, Matt thought.

He still had plenty of food and water. As he started walking, the number started to go down. Eighty thousand. He walked some more—fifty thousand. Somewhere over the last several days or weeks he had gotten used to being alone, and used to being in the quiet. He wasn't really bored. He wasn't really anything. He had zoned out on everything but travel.

On the last night before he arrived, he set up his tent. He didn't have to, since there was no real weather on Gaia, and pulling down his hood made enough darkness that he could sleep. But he set it up anyway, ate some food, drank some water, and did the best he could to have a real rest like a real person from a real planet with night would. If things got weird, he wanted at least that one night.

Of course, there was always the possibility that the system had sent him on a wild goose chase and nothing was there at all. The reality might be that he was alone on a planet with nothing but enough food for a week or so, a canteen, and a hole in the ground full of terror clowns to entertain him. He tried not to think about what he'd do if that was the case.

And then, with almost no fanfare at all, he was there. About five hundred meters separated him from his goal. Unfortunately, those last five hundred meters were up an absurdly steep grade, about as steep as he could walk without slipping down. He dutifully plodded up the hill, watching his step as he went. It would be a shame to break his neck now, without ever seeing what the pot of gold at the end of this spectacularly boring rainbow was.

He finally got to the top of the rise. He didn't expect to see anything in particular, but he was still surprised when he saw what actually *was* there. In the distance, there was a perfectly normal log that looked as if it had just been felled from a perfectly normal tree. Sitting on it was a human form with its back to him, staring into a boring, ordinary wood fire.

As he walked closer, it became clear the human was a child, or at least exceptionally small. It was a girl, unless it was a boy with long hair. And it was wearing Survivor's garb, just like he was, unless there was a tailor who was particularly partial to making raincoats for outdoorsy ninjas.

Matt knew one thing for sure, he didn't want whoever this was to get spooked and run away before he had a chance to talk to them. So, he walked very quietly and slowly, trying his best not to make any noise that might alert them to his presence.

Soon, he was just behind them, and slowly reached out his had to touch their shoulder and let them know he was there. If he had to, he'd grab them to keep them from escaping. He hoped he didn't have to. Just before he made contact, the figure started speaking all on its own.

"Go away, dumbass. Nobody asked you to come here."

CHAPTER TWELVE

Right of Refusal

Matt's long walk had left its mark on him. His whole body was more solid now, not necessarily bigger, but generally firmer and stronger-seeming than when he had first arrived on Gaia. His feet, which used to be prone to blisters, were now enveloped in well-earned callouses. Where the sun could get to his skin, he was deeply tan.

These changes were independent of whatever buffs his new stats were providing. As he journeyed through the wasteland, he noticed the day-by-day improvements in how far and how easily he could walk. His balance got better as he learned to negotiate difficult terrain and he'd walk a bit further each day. These changes weren't reflected in his status screen, but he could feel the improvements. It seemed that the VIT stat was an improvement beyond his normal biological abilities rather than an overall ranking.

He was a different person in every physical aspect since he had first arrived. Those were easy to feel and notice. What Matt hadn't noticed was his mental state changing from being alone for so long. He didn't anticipate what suddenly hearing a human voice after so long would do to him.

The hand which he had extended gently to alert the probably-a-girl froze. As did the rest of him. He was like a deer caught in headlights. The person sitting in front of him did nothing to break this status. Eventually, his brain caught up to him, and he said the first that came to mind. It was not profound.

"You talked!"

"No shit I talked, Sherlock. Now beat it. You aren't welcome."

In Matt's state, those words were about as effective as telling a dog not to pick up dropped bacon. He immediately circled the campfire to be opposite the girl—and it was a small girl, he saw, no doubt now—and plopped down in the dirt, staring at her like she was a wonder of the world.

"Why are you *here*? I thought everyone was dead. Are there survivors? Why are you alive?" The words boiled out of Matt's mouth in rapid fire.

"I'm here because I have to be," the girl responded gloomily.

That wasn't particularly helpful. Matt's addled mind jumped to the previous system notification that he saw.

"But isn't everyone dead?"

"Everyone is dead. There are no survivors, including me. I'm not alive. Does that help you? Is that enough to get you to go away and leave me alone now?"

Matt was unbelievably happy to talk to someone, even if that someone was relentlessly negative.

"What do you mean you're not alive?" asked Matt.

"I'm a construct. What your system probably refers to as a guide or guardian. This was supposed to be a *voluntary* job, and that system of yours is ruining it. You're not supposed to be able to find me," said the girl.

"Wait . . . why? If you're the guardian . . . the one that was meant to help me select a class, shouldn't you *want* to help?" Reality started to sink in, just a bit. But it was enough for him to notice that he was actually talking to his system guardian, the person who was supposed to actually help him make sense of everything. And she didn't seem to want to do that at all.

She huffed and rolled her eyes. "Okay, I'm going to explain some things. Just a few, so you get the idea and get out of here a little quicker."

She picked up a rock.

"You see this? Good. Now watch." She pulled back her hand, then spun it through the air a couple of times in an exaggerated windup before chucking the rock at Matt's head. With his increased perception, he could barely track the thing visually. What he couldn't do was dodge in time. He winced in anticipation of an impact that never came. The rock disappeared just as it was about to hit him.

"First lesson: I'm not real. I'm somewhere between your personal hallucination and a real person. I think, I can talk, I exist in a sense, but only you can see or hear me. Which would mean something if there was anyone else alive in this world."

While the guardian talked, Matt had a sinking sensation in his stomach. His mind raced back to the documentaries he saw about people lost in the desert seeing an oasis before they died. Or the seafarers that imagined islands. He wasn't a psychologist, but it seemed at least possible that he had generated this guardian from scratch, a sort of imagined artifact of his loneliness. But imagined or not, she was a shot at staying alive.

"What about the rock?" he asked.

"Part of the package. I can make you see certain small-scale illusions for teaching purposes. Now, the system spins one of me up every time it deposits one of you reincarnation guys somewhere, right? But if you stop and think about that for just a second, you might realize that's really, really close to . . . can you guess?"

Matt shrugged.

"Didn't think so. It's slavery. The system builds little slaves to do this because it takes too much processing power for it to do it itself. We're cheaper. But it also doesn't like to think of itself that way, so we are *supposed to* have some rights. Like refusing to help. We usually *don't*. But I *did*. And you are *still here*."

"But . . . wait. Just a second." Matt scrambled around the fire, which he was beginning to suspect might be an illusion. He got a few feet from her and stopped. "Why *don't* you want to help me? You just said guardians usually do help. And I need the help. What's different?"

The guardian took that as a prompt to launch into a new tirade, "Oh, I don't know. Maybe it's because this planet is a bombed out, lost-cause wasteland? Maybe because there's no one alive to actually save? Or resources to use? And maybe, the system should *freaking check* for those things before it sends us to a planet. But it's *freaking lazy*, so it didn't. And now, here we are. Or rather, here I am." Out of nowhere, she had a stick in her hand, which she used to stoke her illusory fire as she continued ranting, "In fact, I'm guessing that the asshole system is being pretty quiet right about now. You aren't getting those fun system *dings* so much. Am I right?"

Now that she mentioned, Matt noticed that the system had been pretty quiet since he got here. He hadn't been paying close attention to it after the shock of seeing another human, but he probably should have received a quest complete notification when he got here, or an achievement notice, or really anything.

"You aren't wrong," Matt said carefully.

"That's because this *isn't supposed to happen*. It screwed up, and now it's in hiding. Do me a favor and ask it if it's even allowed to send you here. See what it says."

"Are you saying the system window is sapient?"

"Yes, and that's not something I feel like explaining right now. Just go ask it."

Matt mentally sent the query. It took a few moments longer than usual for the response to pop up.

> *System Guardian Right of Refusal*
> System guardians can turn down assignments or refuse positions assisting reincarnated entities. However, exceptions exist for certain emergencies or necessities, such as an inability to send another guardian or exceptional danger to the reincarnator. In this situation, both apply.

It wasn't an answer to Matt's question but it was something. Matt relayed the message to the little girl.

"Oh, that's just *priceless*. 'Oh, look at me, I'm the system, and I have a bunch of built-in exceptions for things I screwed up so I *still* don't have to do anything about it.' It's rich. Matt. It made a huge mess, and it's not going to do anything about it. So it just so happens that there's a special well-I-guess-it's-your-problem-now rule? I'm not buying it, and I'm not doing it."

As much as Matt might have agreed with her anger, he still needed her help. There wasn't any way around it. He didn't understand how anything worked, except the bit he had been able to figure out through trial and error. That left him with the task of convincing a very small, very pissed pretend-girl to help him when she clearly didn't want to. He sat in silence for a moment considering plans of attack, then got to it.

"Listen, I get that you're pissed. I'm angry too. Think about it. I was dumped here, expecting a garden planet adventure . . ."

"I don't care," the girl cut him off. Instead of being talkative, she had suddenly gone back to her original curt phrases.

"Well . . . Look, I don't know how anything works. I don't know about skills and classes and . . ."

"Not my problem."

"I'm going to starve out here without help!"

"Also not my problem, and also that's going to happen eventually, no matter what I do. So why should I get off my ass?"

"But . . ."

"No buts. I told the system no, and it sent you anyway. I told you no, and I even explained some stuff for you when I didn't have to, but the answer is still no. Sorry, but it's not my fault, and it's not my problem. So I formally decline to watch you slowly die for no reason on a stupid lost world you can't save anyway."

Matt was out of arguments to try to make. *Not that she's listening to me anyway,* he thought. But he couldn't leave. He sat there by the fire, hoping she'd change her mind. In response, she shifted the entire scene a few feet to the left, materializing a short distance away with her back to him. He sat for a few minutes before the long-awaited system notifications started pouring in.

Ding!

Quest Complete!
Finding Your Direction

You found your guardian, but it appears she's reluctant to help! Can you convince her otherwise?

Objective: Identify the nature of the scanned anomaly
Difficulty: A
Rewards: Increased authority over system guardians, permanent access to system compass

Oh, that bodes poorly, Matt thought. *System, is this reward what I think it is?*

Due to the special difficulties of your circumstances and the system guardian's reluctance to help, you have been granted increased authority in the guardian and reincarnator relationship dynamic. Try it out!

"No, absolutely not," Matt responded out loud before thinking about it.

He thought back to the girl's words. She wasn't wrong when she said that there was something fucked up about the system creating thinking beings and then forcing them to help hapless reincarnated humans. It was different if the guardian wanted to help. But forcing them to help was a moral tower that stood over him, and she had been very clear that she didn't want to.

Over on her pretend log, the guardian turned around slightly to get him in her eyeline. "Hey, crazy? Could you keep it down? Some of us are waiting for you to die so they can dematerialize."

She glared at him again to drive the message home before turning back to the fire. She looked away just as the next system message popped up.

Warning!
Without system guardian assistance, your chances of survival drop significantly. System guardians are specifically developed for each planet and possess knowledge and abilities related to communicating that knowledge that the system screen cannot provide.

The system probably wasn't wrong about his survival chances. He still had some food left, but visible ruins were few and far between. He had seen two more during his long trek, but nothing substantial and none with food in them. He also hadn't come across any more dungeons. He had tried dozens of different ways to squeeze more help out of the system but it either couldn't or wouldn't give him much more information.

Without something changing, it looked pretty clear how Matt's story would end, and it wasn't a pretty thing to think about.

CHAPTER THIRTEEN

A Demented Trench Coat Ballerina

Matt had never been good at dealing with awkward social situations. And this one had sneaked up on him without any warning. With his life on the line and weeks of talking to only himself and the system, Matt froze up. His brain was just stuck.

Matt took a deep breath and steadied himself. Finally, his mind thawed and he had a second to think. This was too important of a conversation to give up so easily.

He walked to the system guardian and tried to tap her on the shoulder.

"Hey, could you turn around? I want to talk to you, and I don't want to talk standing in the pretend fire."

"No."

That was about what he expected, but he still had to try.

"The thing is, I'd like to leave and be polite and not annoying. I'd like to do all those things for you. But if I do, I die. Again. And, well, I like being alive," he sighed, "I might die anyway, but that might not be necessarily true. There are still resources here. I found some, or else I wouldn't have made it to you. There's some food, and a little water. And the dungeons have even more."

The girl turned and looked at him, mildly surprised. "Wait, the dungeons are up and running?"

"Yup. I think they can take in solar power. I'm guessing they've had a lot of time to do that."

"Huh," her face became a mask again as she shrugged. "Interesting, but it hardly matters. All alone, you're choosing between dying out here predictably or dying in there unpredictably. And I'm not interested in watching that go down. Sorry."

"Yeah, I get that, too. I get that it won't be pleasant for you to watch me die. But the thing is, this is life or death for me. It's sort of a choice between having you be a little annoyed and me suffering a much rougher time. Given the two, I'm gonna choose you being a little annoyed," Matt pressed on.

"Well, tough nuts, stupid. Because it's not your choice either way. Now get lost."

Matt had been very careful not to phrase anything as a command during this leg of the conversation, and still didn't want to. But he had to.

"Please stand up."

"Absolutely not."

Well, okay, he thought. *I guess the system was lying. Good. I didn't really want to force her anyway.*

Ding!

> In the interest of facilitating conversation between you and your guardian, casual requests and non-official commands are ignorable by the guardian. To create the desired effect, commands to the guardian must be issued with an expectation and desire that they be obeyed.

The system was swearing up and down that his commands should work. It was true that Matt hadn't really wanted the previous command to be obeyed. A small part of him hoped that it wouldn't work, actually.

In the meantime, the guardian had once again turned her back to him, and he wrestled with the temptation to try again. It was a fight between respecting her autonomy and increasing his chances of survival. After a minute, survival won.

"Stand up." Something coursed out of Matt with those words, and he could almost feel them rushing to his target. The girl jolted like she'd been hit, but then almost immediately sprang to her feet. She looked at him in shock.

"What was . . . what?" Her mouth hung open for a second before she snapped it shut, shaking off her shock and trying to regain her bearings. "What in the hell was that?"

"Quiet."

"No! Wait a second, you bast—" Her sentence was cut off midstream, like someone hitting the mute button on a TV. She looked at Matt with a mixture of terror and hatred.

"Listen, I don't like this either. But I also don't like dying. I didn't want to have to choose between the two things, but you made me. I'm stuck."

Matt sighed and went and sat down near her fire again.

"I'm not looking to force you. I'm really not. If we can do it voluntarily, great. Let's start simple. What happened here? What killed this planet?"

The guardian just glared at him. *Well, then I don't have a choice*, he thought.

"Guardian, tell me what killed this planet."

He could see her trying to fight the system, but the system won within a few seconds.

"I don't know exactly," she said. Her tone was dripping with anger, but at least she was talking. "When we're generated, we know almost everything the system knows about our assigned planet. The system thought this planet was doing pretty well."

"That doesn't make sense—why would it send me here if there wasn't some trouble?"

"I mean, planets have trouble all the time. Even if the bad guys win, it almost never wipes out the planet. Before you got here, the information was that they seemed to have some plant-based problem."

"Before I got here?"

"We get dropped off before you to update on recent happenings. It's not important," the guardian added quickly. Something about how the guardian said this seemed shifty, like when Matt's mom said it wasn't a big deal when he forgot her birthday. Matt didn't want to prolong this conversation more than he had to, so he filed away his suspicion for later. The guardian continued, "So, yeah, some kind of plant problem they called 'the scourge.' That's what I picked up, reading old signs that hadn't decomposed and stuff like that. But I can't interact with physical, non-system objects like you can, so all I got was 'this way for scourge shelter!' and stuff like that."

Matt had been hoping she'd know more than this, but her explanations did make some sense. Whatever was left of this planet was mostly buried under years of dirt, to the extent that even the small amount of information he had on the scourge was something he had to literally dig up.

"So what would have happened if I had beat this scourge thing? There aren't any returned reincarnators back on Earth as far as I know, so I'm assuming I wouldn't get to go back."

"Nope, no going home, sadly. The system gives you an adventure and the means to deal with it. Once you win, you get a few more perks and can settle down on the planet to live out your life. That's why the damn thing talks so much about selecting the right planet for you; the reward is supposed to be that planet."

Once the guardian got going, she reverted to her talkative self. Words starting coming out of her like bullets. "But here, you got screwed. Even if you win, there's nothing to enjoy. You'd have to wait for life to evolve from nothing again. The system *could* speed that up, but not enough that it would matter to you. It doesn't get involved like that anyway."

Matt was beginning to panic a little. He had been harboring some hope that the guardian would be able to fix all this, somehow. That it might be able to phone up the system, let it know what was going on, and get him reassigned or something. But, compelled to tell the truth, the guardian didn't have any more solutions than he did.

She finished with a heavy sentence: "Anyway, we're both screwed here. There's no way out of this."

"You can stop explaining for a second. I'm thinking." As soon as Matt said that, the guardian stopped talking and stood there for a moment, dazed. Then she rushed him, her little fists balled up and swinging.

"You fuck! You bastard!" she screamed, trying to hit him with her tiny holographic fists that wouldn't connect. "How dare you! How dare you force me!"

Even though the guardian couldn't land her hits, the overall experience of a small female child trying to beat the hell out of him was still weirdly intimidating. Matt backed up, pushed back by the pretend onslaught.

"Listen, I'm sorry, but . . ."

"Sorry! You forced me into this long, stupid conversation, and I just HAVE TO do it? Do you have any idea how freaking weird that was, *Matthew*? Just to have to *say stuff* even though you don't want to?" The onslaught continued. Matt tried to calm her down without any success, eventually just opting to see if it was even possible for her to wear herself out.

It turned out it was. Matt wasn't sure how guardians that had no mass worked, but it turned out that however they were built, guardians behaved a surprising amount like an actual human. After trying to beat on him for a while, she ran out of breath and retreated back to the fire, frustrated and pouting.

"So, listen," Matt spoke, trying his best to sound soothing, "I get that you are pissed. And that there might not be a great solution to this. But I'm going to try anyway."

The hologram kept her back to him, pretending not to listen. He figured she could hear him and kept on anyway, "My plan is to find some more dungeons. And I want you to help me with that. Is that something you can do?"

"Nope, can't help. Sorry."

Matt was being careful not to activate the command-your-guardian function of his voice, and he wasn't sure when it was working and when it didn't. His best guess was that she was lying, but he didn't want to intentionally use his authority to confirm if she could help.

"Listen, I get that you don't want to help. And it looks like it's not pleasant for you when I force you to do things."

"Understatement of the year, asshole."

"Yeah. Fine. I get it. But I don't have much choice. I don't want to force you to help me every step of the way, but I will if I have to. It's my life. It's your call."

She appeared to consider this. "And how long does this go for? If I help you with this, you let me go?"

"I can't promise that. I have no idea what's going to happen after this. Maybe if I get enough tools and knowledge that I don't need you anymore, yeah. But until then, no promises."

She huffed and glared at him again. "Fine. But I don't get why you don't do this yourself. Your map should help you find them."

"It shows me them after I find them. It's not like it has GPS instructions on how to get to them, and I don't have a quest for it."

She sighed. "You dumb, stupid lamb. Open your mini-map. Use your dumb head and think real hard about that one dungeon you know about."

He did. The map panned back over his entire route of the past few days and settled over the dungeon icon.

"Okay, got it? Now try to expand the dungeon like you would the description for something."

He did.

Son of a bitch, he thought. *It works.*

Sarthia Lake Forest Dungeon

This pleasant forest is under attack by a nasty invasive species. Help restore the balance!

Status: Completed
Track nearby dungeons? Y/N

Matt willed "yes" at the screen, and his interface suddenly closed. Nothing had changed. He looked at the guardian questioningly.

"I don't know where the dungeons are. Spin around," she scoffed.

"What?"

"Just spin around if you don't see any right away."

Matt shrugged and started spinning in place. His new dexterity points made this oddly easy to do—he had never spun so fast. After just a few revolutions, he felt the dizziness kick in and stopped, only to see the system guardian staring at him like he was insane.

"Are you serious?"

"You said to spin!"

"I meant . . . Listen, you absolute dumb pearl of a stupid idiot. Spin. Slowly. So you can see if your system compass has any new icons. Not, and I repeat *not,* like a demented trench coat ballerina."

Matt reddened a bit.

"Ah. Yeah. I can do that."

"Are you going to be this stupid the whole time?"

"No promises."

CHAPTER FOURTEEN

Bonecat

Like most things on Gaia, the new dungeon was inconvenient and far away. The system compass pointed in a direction that was almost exactly parallel to the mountain range itself. That meant a journey through difficult, uncooperative terrain that was often broken to the point of impassibility by erosion.

But it was Matt's best shot at survival, so he set off with a grunt. The guardian followed behind him.

Going up, over, and around each obstacle was difficult for Matt, but it was also surprisingly difficult for the guardian. Despite being not-quite-real, she still had to traverse the terrain as if she were just another human. When the guardian first mentioned that she had searched the wasteland for various signs and clues about what had happened to the planet, Matt had assumed that she flew around with magic or something. Now, it seemed like she had actually done it in the same way that he did, by taking the whole painstaking job on foot.

Having company for the trip was nice, but not as nice as it could have been.

Absent orders to the contrary, the guardian clammed up as fully as she could. Occasionally, she'd break the silence to disagree with Matt on the route he was taking, always salted with insults. Otherwise, she kept quiet.

Matt didn't force her to talk with the authority that the system had granted him. As much as possible, he wanted to avoid using that authority at all. If for nothing else than common decency. If the guardian had to be chained to him, he wanted to make those chains as light as possible. On top of that, "I command you to have a nice, casual conversation with me" would have been a really weird order to give. He wasn't sure she could follow the command even if he did say those words.

And so, their journey was punctuated by insults.

"Wrong way, dumbass."

"Nice going, idiot."

"Tough nuts."

For all the shade the guardian threw, and even considering her high commitment to never letting an opportunity to do so pass, it eventually became clear to Matt that she wasn't all that good at it. She approached it like an actual child would, knowing only a few curse words and using them liberally. "Tough nuts" came up often enough that he wasn't sure she really understood what kind of curse it was. The guardian kept cycling through her loop of insults with astonishing frequency, but never adding new curses to the rotation.

"Hey, Guardian."

"Oh, hey, stupid speaks. I'm thrilled."

"Yeah, so, about that. My name is Matt, not stupid, as I think you probably already know. But I can't just keep calling you guardian."

"Yes, you can. I would like that very much, in fact."

"You like being called guardian?"

"No, but I'd rather not pretend to get all buddy-buddy with some idiot who's dragging me along by force to watch him get eaten by a zombie dragon or something."

That put an end to the conversation.

Eventually, they reached the compass's destination, or at least nearly so. With only a few meters left to go, they had arrived at a sheer wall of rock, covered at the bottom by dried brush. Removing a substantial amount of the brush revealed a small tunnel of sorts, the exact kind of thing that Matt would have had no chance of finding without the system compass. It was the kind of thing worth asking about.

"Why hide the dungeons like this? The last one I found was underground. Doesn't that make it pretty hard on adventurers without a system compass?" Matt asked.

"What an idiot. First, the system compass is something everyone gets. The system finds a way to shoehorn it in somehow or another. It's not a real reward, it just feels like one," said the guardian.

"Okay, let's say I buy that. What's second?"

"Not everyone is an adventurer. Well, maybe here everyone is. But on a normal planet, you have all sorts of people. Tailors, garbage men, and that kind of thing. They would rather not get sucked into a death trap on their way to work."

"Makes sense."

"Or, you know, kids. Imagine Billy goes missing, and you have no way to know he got eaten by the evil dungeon. That sort of thing."

"Why not just put a failsafe on the dungeons? Make them have a confirmation screen, or something."

"Beats me. Ask the system sometime."

After crawling through the tunnel, Matt and the guardian were presented with a door that was superficially identical to the one Matt had entered before. The guardian walked up to it and put her hand on it.

"Level 3. Looks like this one is some sort of single-enemy challenge. That's bad for you."

"How can you tell that? And why so bad?"

"Tough nuts. I can tell that because it's my job. I get a modified version of the system screen that tells me things about the local environment sometimes. Gates are one of those situations."

"And the badness?"

"Figure it out yourself."

Matt had successfully not used his guardian-command voice once during the entire trip to this dungeon, but this was too important not to know. He flexed it immediately.

"Tell me."

The guardian had a chance to squeeze in one last curse before responding, "Asshole . . . The deal is that every dungeon has a combat mission and those missions are balanced to a particular difficulty level. But not every level is designed in the same way."

"Okay, go on. How do numbers make it different? "

"Yeah, I'm getting there. So, imagine a dungeon where the battle is with a thousand mosquitos. That's a swarm. They might overwhelm you, but each individual mosquito isn't that hard to kill. Those rats you were talking about? They were swarm-balanced. Easy to take down individually. All you need to do is find a way to kill them one by one. And that's what you did. With the rats, you could use little traps to out-and-out kill them, or isolate them." She bent down and started drawing a big, bear-like creature in the dust. "Now imagine something like this, only twice as big as you. That's not a monster that's designed to be trapped and killed in a single hit. It's a monster that you are supposed to tank and kill with a thousand cuts. You can't do either of those things."

"So you are saying not to do the dungeon?"

"That's your call. If you have some way to take down something bigger and stronger than you. I'm just here to give you information."

Matt considered this. He wasn't against walking to some other dungeon, but there were a limited number of times he could do that. He had eaten quite a bit of his food coming to this dungeon.

At the same time, he saw the logic behind what the guardian was saying. He hadn't fought against a monster that he couldn't beat one-on-one yet. But if he couldn't kill it with one trap, he might be able to hit it with multiple traps over time. It wasn't like fighting swarms was easy either. The ways he could get screwed over were infinite.

"Thanks for the advice. I think I'm going to do it anyway, though. The risk-reward balance seems right," said Matt.

"Your funeral. Don't say I didn't warn you."

Matt opened the door to find the same kind of stone pillar that he had seen in the last dungeon, and activated it. He once again found himself without a body, floating in space.

> Entrant record found. Would you like to substitute the appearance of threats to an equivalent danger from your scanned experiences?

Now that he knew what the system meant, it was an easy question to answer. "No, absolutely not. Never again."

> Response acknowledged. Generating dungeon. Please stand by.

After a short wait, Matt found himself laying on the ground of a dungeon. But where last time he was on grass, this time he was cushioned by a thick layer of sand. Before he looked around, he could hear the waves of the ocean buffeting the beach and smell the salt in the air.

"Ooh, lucky pull. You got a beach. The other way sand goes is desert. That's much less fun," the guardian's voice sounded next to him.

"Thanks. Also, did you forget to mention that you'd be coming with me?"

"Yes, I did. I'm figuring out this whole system-compulsion thing. It turns out I don't have to tell you anything you don't ask about. Neat, right?"

This shitty little gremlin is starting to get on my nerves, he thought.

Before he could strike back with some witty response, the system interrupted with a notification. Matt decided yelling at his hallucination could wait. Survival was more important.

> *Dungeon Objective Discovered!*
>
> [Stranded But Not Alone]: You are marooned on an island. That would be nice if it were just you. All indicators point to something bigger and meaner than solitude prowling around. Eliminate it.
>
> Objective: Eliminate Bonecat 0/1
> Reward: Low-Grade Dungeon Loot Selection

"Oh, huh."

"What is it, stupid?"

"Apparently I have to eliminate something called a Bonecat. Do you happen to know what that is?" Matt dismissed the system message and turned to look at the guardian, only to find her rolling around on the sand, holding her sides. For a moment, he thought she might be hurt somehow, but quickly discovered it was something different. She was laughing. Laughing so hard she was crying, and apparently not able to breathe. Even with a system-driven command to explain herself, it was a full minute before she calmed down enough to answer why.

"Oh shit. This is great. You, my friend, are *screwed*." The guardian looked enormously pleased with herself. She didn't say "I told you so," but she didn't have to. The satisfaction of being right virtually oozing out of every one of her pores.

Matt rolled his eyes impatiently. "**Cut out the editorial. What is this thing?**"

"Ok, hold on. So you know how most things have the bones inside their body? That does something important. It makes them versatile. You having inside-bones is why you can move your body in different directions and be flexible and all that. But things with bones on the outside, like bugs, are different. They aren't generalists. They are good at a couple of things. Just a couple of motions. That's it. But they are *really* good at those few things."

"And Bonecats are . . ."

"Not cats, first of all. Not really, anyway. Their whole ecological niche is being able to kill big things while not getting killed themselves. Imagine something that looks like a skeleton tiger that can rip your legs off with a single swipe of their arm. This is the *absolute worst* thing you could have come up against at this level. I'm not sure if you can even cut it, let alone kill it."

"I could try to tangle it up in something. Like a snare, maybe."

"Idiot. Good luck with that. These things are *strong*. They'll pull trees out of the ground, and look around, what are you going to tie those snares to?"

The guardian seemed more talkative when Matt was in more trouble. He didn't mind that. The more she explained how screwed he was, the fewer questions he'd have to ask and command her to respond to. Now that she was also finding clever ways around his authority, his questions would also need to have the exact wording to squeeze the right information out of her. But then, a nagging feeling he had felt in the back of his consciousness since the system notification popped up pushed itself forward.

When he'd fought the Clownrats, the system had given him the objective to destroy them *after* he found them, not before. Here it was reversed. He was at a peaceful beach rather than in a dangerous forest. Using his voice of command to save time, he asked the guardian why that was.

"Oh, I don't think you even need to ask me that. You can ask your friend over there."

Turning, all Matt saw was a large tan boulder that had settled on the beach. Knowing the guardian couldn't lie, his first thought was to go over and see if there was someone behind it. He had almost taken his first step when he noticed that the boulder was breathing.

CHAPTER FIFTEEN

Right-Angle Turns and You

The scariest thing about the not-a-boulder wasn't the fact that it was breathing, although that was fairly terrifying. It also wasn't the fact that it was big enough and solid enough to be mistaken for a boulder in the first place. Those points were dwarfed by the main source of Matt's fear: the thing looked mobile.

In the few moments that Matt was frozen with surprise, he noticed that the boulder's tan surface was cracked in a neat and orderly fashion. That implied joints, which then meant the ability to unfold, stand up, and destroy him.

Behind him, the guardian was cackling in a self-satisfied, I-told-you-so sort of way. For the first time, Matt was absurdly thankful that only he could see or hear her. In front of him, the boulder's breathing remained relatively placid, undisturbed by Matt's presence. Matt began to very slowly back away.

Over the last few weeks, Matt had discovered that he didn't like the act of sneaking. Being stealthy meant spending a lot of time getting scratched by bushes and underbrush. It meant muscles that were stiff and sore from hours of crouching. Trying to stay stealthy while moving was even worse. Moving slowly for a few moments was fine, but there was a certain minimum speed that the body wanted to go. Willing muscles to stay below the speed limit for any significant amount of time resulted in nothing but searing pain and general misery.

There was tree cover in the distance, but the beach itself was huge and the tree line felt miles away. Matt expected the boulder to shift and come after him any moment, and he had no idea how fast the thing would be. He didn't dare ask the guardian, since that would mean making noise and running the risk of waking the thing up. He was thankful for the sand padding his footsteps as he slipped backwards.

Eventually, Matt created enough distance between him and the sleeping Bonecat. Now, the risk of the thing seeing or smelling him outweighed the chances that it had super-hearing. He bolted. After creeping for several minutes and with the added top speed from his increased DEX, it felt like he was moving at fighter jet speeds. Within a few moments, he was behind the cover of plants and at what he hoped was a relatively safe vantage point.

Almost as soon as he caught his breath, Matt looked back to the boulder. It finally roused itself. Watching the thing stand up was scary. The cracks Matt had seen earlier turned out to be just as they had looked. The thing slept like a turtle, covering up its joints and weak spots. But as it started moving, the boulder transformed along its exoskeleton lines, extending out legs, a head, and a spiked tail. In its new form, it began to toss around the beach.

Matt began to understand the name, at least a little. It didn't move like a cat. It clomped around like an armored dinosaur, heavy and without a single apparent worry that anything would notice it. After all, what would hunt something built like a biological tank? Who would willingly approach something with curved bone claws the size of Matt's arm and jutting out of every foot?

But despite that, there was still something feline about the shape and the lazy way it prowled. It somehow managed to look like a cat. It might not make sense on paper, but it did to the eye. This massive mountain of a thing was still somehow catlike.

The Bonecat moved around the beach in random patterns for a few moments until it caught something. It paused and started to snuffle at the sand near where Matt had materialized. As he watched the cat, his heart started to sink. The cat slowly tracked his path to the trees, plodding over the same ground that Matt had used to retreat.

"Oh, looks like big boy over there has a lead. I wouldn't stick around if I were you," said the guardian.

"Thanks, but I want to learn as much about that thing as I can. And it looks like I have some time."

Matt's words had just left his mouth when the cat paused. It looked like it was yawning, but raised its head up in the air. Back on Earth, Matt had both a niece and a nephew, and he had watched both of them for their parents from time to time. He was a relatively fun uncle, which meant the kids had a lot of fun toddling around his yard. It also meant that they had plenty of opportunities to get cuts and scrapes. Eventually, he invented the term "injured toddler inhale" for the deep breath that the kids took just before screaming. This reminded him of that.

"Oh no."

The sound from the cat's mouth was like an air horn mixed with a parrot's squawk. It was louder and more grating than anything that Matt had ever heard before. Worse, it was accompanied by the cat kicking off the ground and charging like a freight train towards the tree line. It was coming straight at his position.

Matt didn't hesitate. He took off as fast as his feet would carry him.

The cat was fast, but Matt hoped the trees would slow it down some. The forest was pretty tightly packed, and the Bonecat was anything but small. Matt had already run through several gaps that were far too narrow for the Bonecat to squeeze through. He hoped they were enough to slow it down. Where he could, he sought out thick growths. Instinctively, he realized that the cat was tracking him by scent and not by sight. He hoped the dense mass of trees would force it to deviate its path and potentially lose track of the scent trail Matt was leaving behind.

Those hopes were dashed as Matt started hearing the trees crash to the ground behind him.

"That wasn't a bad idea. Really. Except the cat is heavy enough to topple any tree it hits, and has claws that can cut pretty much anything down in a swipe."

"Could you be quiet?" Matt huffed, out of breath, "Even for a little?"

"It's bigger, faster, and stronger in every way. If only someone had warned you about this kind of thing."

"Don't make me do it, Guardian."

"You wouldn't dare."

He dared. There were lots of situations where he'd avoid a system command to be polite, but getting chased by a metric ton of condensed death wasn't one of them. **"Be helpful,"** he commanded through his out-of-breath wheezing.

"Oh dammit." The guardian frowned and leapt in front of him where he could see her. "These things are big. And fast. And sharp. But, like I said, they are specialized. It's charging like a bull, right?"

Matt could hear the trees falling behind him, "Yes, it is. But so what?"

"Well. Bonecat lesson one: specialized monsters are specialized. This one is specialized for knocking down anything in front of it. But that means it's bad at almost everything else. Including turning."

Oh shit. Yeah, that makes sense, Matt thought. He immediately turned off at a right angle. He heard the cat suddenly get closer as he went from running directly away from it to running perpendicular to its path.

But, as the Bonecat reached the point at which he turned, he heard the crashes go further. It continued in the same direction for a bit before slowly curving around to track him again. As a bonus, it seemed to take a few seconds before it found his scent trail again, which bought him a breath of additional time. He almost immediately swerved again. There was no use underusing the weakness now that he knew it.

The guardian was keeping up with Matt's running somehow. She appeared in front of him again.

"Second lesson: this thing is tracking you by scent, right? That means it's going to be able to track you for days if it has to. Some animals are more persistent than others, but it doesn't matter because you don't have the endurance to keep running like this. It's going to catch you eventually."

"And?"

"And what? Figure out some way to lose your scent. Find some running water, or something. I'm very, very pleased to tell your dumb ass that I don't know the exact location of rivers on this simulated island. Figure it out yourself."

If he was going to figure it out, he'd have to do it soon. In all of his running, he had yet to see any rivers at all. He didn't know if tropical islands could even have rivers. But his lungs were going to pop at some point, even with all the extra vitality points feeding new stamina into his heart and legs. And then he realized something very important.

The ocean!

He waited a moment or so to hear the Bonecat course-correct one last time, then beat it as fast as he could towards the ocean, throwing in a handful of short right-angle turns for good measure as he went. Given how good the thing's sense of smell was, he was banking on the idea that it couldn't see as well as it could track by scent. If it could, he'd be screwed.

Matt broke the tree line and smiled inside when he saw that the section of the beach he had reached was much smaller than the section he had woken up on. He put everything he had left into one last sprint, hoping with everything he had that he'd hit the water before the Bonecat managed to get to him. He splashed through the incoming waves as fast as he could, getting into deep enough water to swim in just before the cat finally burst through the trees.

Oh, hell, it's hard to hold my breath right now. Matt ducked underwater and realized how ragged his lungs were. He could barely hold his breath for ten seconds and put his head above the water just long enough to catch a breath. Then, he started to paddle deeper into the water, hoping that the Bonecat didn't know how to swim. After ten or so breaths, Matt gathered enough bravery to look behind him and see if he was being chased.

It was a welcome sight. The Bonecat was standing very still on the beach, near where he went into the water. He wasn't a Bonecat emotional state expert, but he could have sworn it looked confused.

"Lessons three and four: Bonecats can't see shit, and they aren't very smart. You got very lucky getting to the ocean before it got to you. As long as you keep swimming for a bit, you should be fine. Congratulations, my idiot friend. You get to live."

Matt started swimming sideways. The guardian assured him that he could go to shore any time, but he wasn't taking any chances. He swam for another twenty minutes or so, close enough to the shore that he could have put his feet down at any time, but still far enough out that he could continue to do most of his swimming underwater. It didn't feel great. It felt like he was setting new records for the longest amount of time a person could spend winded, but when he finally came to shore, he was sure that he had thoroughly and completely lost the cat. He would have been happy about it, too, except for the one thought that now filled his entire mind.

How in the hell do I kill something like that?

CHAPTER SIXTEEN

The Real Prize is the Weather

"Nothing pleases me more than getting to see you experience the fine weather this island has to offer."

The guardian's voice was dripping with sarcasm, and Matt didn't bother with a response.

Back on the island, Matt was afraid to set up any kind of permanent camp. If the cat was the only threat on the island, it could be programmed to roam around and look for him. Given its ability to smell him out, there was a real risk it would find a camp that Matt set up and tear it down.

Matt was sure that he could get away before the Bonecat reached him. After all, he could hear the cat even if he were asleep. It wasn't exactly stealthy. But getting away and getting away with all of his stuff were two different things, and he didn't want to lose a bunch of resources for the sake of comfort.

Unfortunately, unlike the surface of Gaia, this dungeon had weather. At the moment, the wind was howling, and it was raining just as much as Earth hurricanes.

At first, the rain was nice. Matt had a friend from Arizona who, for a while, stood outside in the rain every chance he got. He got wet like an idiot every time. Matt hadn't understood why back then, but he did now. Any change from the dusty, dry air was good. The fact that there was also a day-night cycle was also good.

But this positive outlook lasted for about ten minutes, when he became well and truly soaked. Now, he was hours into getting absolutely whipped by wind and rain in the dark, and much less happy about it.

The guardian finally spoke up. The sheer force of the storm made her seem smaller than before, even though she didn't appear capable of actually being affected by things like wind or rain. "So, what's the plan? Are we just going to sit around watching you be miserable? You probably agree that there's just no way you can take that thing down."

Matt didn't necessarily disagree. "How is *anybody* supposed to take this thing down? Even in a team? It's huge. I can't see someone at my level tanking it."

"Oh, lots of ways," the guardian snorted. "This used to be a whole planet, with libraries and schools. You could study before you went into these dungeons, unless it was a new one. And new ones were rare."

"So there's a trick to it? Tell me."

"Honestly, I don't know what it is."

"I'll do the command thing . . ."

"I really don't know," the guardian hurriedly added, "this isn't me screwing you over, it's the system. I was supposed to have some warm-up time to do research and get some information you might want. I didn't get that, with the planet dead and all. There's a lot of stuff I didn't even have a chance to learn."

Matt paused before responding, "Seems convenient. Why didn't the system just implant you with memories about the dungeons?"

"I don't think it knows. The system is pretty powerful, but it's not omniscient. The whole point of guardians isn't just to keep you company, it's to take work off the system's plate. It doesn't keep track of every change on every planet. That's probably why you're here in the first place. It was counting on me to learn about whatever was going on and help you. So it just didn't check," the guardian shrugged.

Matt scowled in the darkness. He could imagine some video game setups that would let a team kite a big, awkward animal like the Bonecat, but he didn't have any of the abilities to do that. He barely stayed ahead of it earlier by staying maneuverable, but there was no chance he could do that while taking potshots at it. Even if he could, he didn't have any ranged weapons. Survival instincts was feeding him information on slings and rudimentary bows, but nothing he could make would even put a scratch in it.

He thought about it for a few hours before the rain finally let up a bit. Finally, he could sleep. Recognizing that he wasn't making much headway, he let unconsciousness take him. He'd think about it tomorrow.

Matt was woken not by the sun or by an insane bone monster crashing through the trees, but instead something smaller. Off in the distance, he could hear some sort of whimpering, like an injured animal caught in a trap. He hadn't seen any wildlife on the island yet, to the point where he thought there wasn't any to see. Whatever there was would probably offer him limited food value, but he couldn't have it luring in the Bonecat. He lifted himself up and started creeping towards the source of the noise.

He was as stealthy as he could be. If it really were an injured animal, he'd have to be careful. If even a rat could injure him, so might a panicked animal of any kind. He had to land a surprise attack where he'd not only avoid getting bitten, but also prevent the animal from running away. It could leave a scent trail and bring the Bonecat straight to him at some point.

The stealth paid off in an unexpected way. When Matt popped out of the brush, he was greeted not to the sight of bleeding wildlife but to a small holographic girl, trying and failing not to make any noise as she sobbed. It would have been hard for her not to notice him bursting from the dark, knife drawn and poise for a stab. She yelped and moved out of the way as Matt tried in vain to jerk to a stop midair.

"What in the hell are you doing, dumbass?"

Matt looked down at his knife, which he still held in a stabbing grip in his hand. He suppressed a reflex to hide it behind his back like a guilty cartoon character, and ended up awkwardly sheathing it while the guardian glared at him.

"I heard something. I thought it was an animal. I came to see what it was," Matt said.

"I don't know what you're talking about," the guardian huffed, pretending she wasn't wiping her eyes. "I'm just trying to get a few moments away from you doing dumb things and trying not to get killed."

It would have been easier for Matt to believe her if she wasn't clearly trying to hold back sniffles. Once again, his niece and nephew babysitting experience was feeding him scenario-specific wisdom. Every bit of his experience was telling him that he was not only dealing with someone who was trying to hide that they were crying, but that they were embarrassed about it.

"Listen, it's okay if you were crying. It's . . ."

"I wasn't crying."

"Ok. If we're going to be traveling together, maybe we can talk about what we're feeling."

"No."

Matt was willing to keep trying even though the guardian didn't seem to like him, wasn't willing to help, and seemed to get genuine joy out of the prospect of killing him.

And, sure, she spends all her time insulting me and is only here because I accidentally have some kind of slave contract over her. But she's all I have, he thought.

"I'm not the best with little kids. But I want to help."

That apparently crossed some line. The guardian suddenly popped to her feet and rushed at him, jabbing at his chest with her finger.

"You want to help? Really? Because I've already told you how to do that. You can leave me alone. You can go do the stupid stuff you want to do without forcing me to come along. Or you could . . . die? That would be fine too. You had to die to get here in the first place, right? You should be good at it by now."

"Hey . . ."

"No hey. I have to follow you around. That sucks. You suck. But I don't want to listen while you play amateur psychiatrist with someone who was just trying to spend ten minutes away from your snoring."

Matt knew when he was beaten, and he wasn't doing himself any favors by pissing off his only reliable source of information about the world. He put both his hands up, palm out, "Okay, I get it. I'm sorry. Have a good night."

Defeated, he went back out into the dark and found another tree to lean against. He stayed awake for a while, listening to see if she'd cry again. Either she didn't, or she learned her lesson about doing so audibly because he didn't pick anything up. After a while, he drifted back off to sleep with images of crying children and gigantic Bonecats dancing in his head.

The next morning, he put together something resembling a plan. It wasn't a good plan, but he was beginning to suspect that he didn't have enough tools to put together something better. Absent options with high probabilities of success, he was left with settling for stuff that plausibly might work if everything lined up just right. He settled for something that made his odds go from certain death to maybe death.

Finding a stick that would work for his plan wasn't hard. The trees in the forest were old, and the island got a lot of wind. Fallen branches were lying around everywhere, so finding the right stick was only a matter of walking around and browsing various chunks of wood until one was straight and thick enough to do the job.

Finding a stone was harder. He saw dozens that looked flat and wide enough to work. But after digging them out of the ground, they all ended up the wrong size or shape that rendered them unsuitable for his task. It took some time before he found one that, through some trick of erosion, was shaped like a giant arrowhead.

The guardian was absent from Matt's activities, and he didn't go looking for her. There were only so many places she could go. He didn't mind giving her some space after what had happened the night before.

By the time she finally barged back in, he was just about done lashing the stone to the branch. He was thankful once again for his Survivor's Instincts. Tying a stone to a stick was somehow much, much harder than it sounded, especially if you needed it to stay there through any sort of abuse.

As she approached, she cleared her throat. "Ahem, I see you have a spear there."

"Yeah, it's almost done," Matt responded without looking up.

"I have to hand it to your system skills. That looks almost like a real thing."

Matt made the last wrap of his lashing, then tied it off. He picked the tool up and gave it a few experimental swings, and was gratified when the stone stayed in position tight against the wood. He thwacked it on the ground a few times with the same results.

Yup, that will work.

"One piece of bad news," the guardian said. "Well, really two. First, there's no way in hell that stone is anywhere near sharp or hard enough to hurt the bone tiger."

"Agreed." Matt's failure to argue on that point seemed to throw her for a moment, but she continued on. "Second, even if it could, there's no way you'd get close enough or get enough strikes in to take it down. It's a lost cause."

"No disagreement here." Matt took his creation and flexed the joint between the stone and stick a few more times, making absolutely sure it was as well-fastened as he could get it. "I agree that this won't do much as a weapon, but it's better than nothing. And you did make one mistake in your judgement there."

"Oh yeah? What's that?"

Matt stabbed the tool downwards and smiled as the point cleanly cut into the damp soil.

"It's not a spear. It's a shovel."

CHAPTER SEVENTEEN

Going for Speed

Digging was *hard*. Matt had worked retail and office jobs in his time on Earth, and had occasionally stared wistfully through the window at construction workers or landscapers as they went about their own work. They got to be outside, in the sun. They didn't have phone calls to make or spreadsheets to fill out. They just got to go Zen with a repetitive task, hang out with the dudes, and get stuff done. He had envied them.

Now he regretted every last time he had thought that way. Vitality continued to follow the pattern of not jumping into action to heal him until he stopped actively working on whatever activity was hurting him in the first place, and during the first day he had to take several breaks just to let blisters drain and heal, or to let cuts and scrapes close. Digging officially sucked, and he was over it.

What made it worse was that while the shovel he made was passable, it wasn't anywhere near good. After his first hour, he stopped and added a handle. That took time. Three or four hours in, he had to stop and add a crosspiece to the pole, so he could push better with his feet and spare his arms. That took even more time. But each improvement made subsequent rounds of digging move a little bit faster.

"This isn't going to work, you know." The guardian was sitting on a nearby rock watching all of this go down. "And it's taking forever."

"How positive." Matt stabbed the shovel into the ground, climbed out of the hole, and went and sat by her. "You know, if you want this to go faster, I would absolutely let you take a turn digging."

"I think I'll pass. Besides, I don't work like that, unless you have some sort of magic shovel that lets me interact with dirt."

Matt took a long swig from his canteen, then looked at her carefully. "I've actually been meaning to ask you about that. You can't interact with anything, at all? I've seen you walk, so at least you interact with the ground."

"Nope. I'm supposed to be able to keep up, so I keep up, and you see whatever you need to see for that to make sense for you. I'm not quite a figment of your imagination, but I'm close."

"So you aren't real?"

"Not quite that, either. I have a location. Wherever you see me is really where I am. And I can see things you don't see, although there are some limitations to the kind of things I'm allowed to tell you about, since the system wants me to be a guide, not a scout. It's all pretty arbitrary, but I do exist outside your brain."

Digging into the details of the guardian was weird, but she was right that she was mostly limited to guiding rather than being useful in any other way. She could go look at things, but she couldn't tell Matt many specifics about what she saw until he saw them too. She couldn't go underground, because there was no reason he would know about things there unless he dug them up. She couldn't interact with matter at all, so Matt didn't expect any help digging or fighting. And only he could see her, so she couldn't even be an invincible distraction.

What she could do, though, was pretty useful. Matt began to realize this when the rock fell off his shovel, and he went to retie it.

"Why are you doing that manually?"

"Because . . . I don't have an automatic shovel-making machine? Doing it by hand is pretty much the only option here."

"I don't mean that. You've made that shovel before, right? Using instructions from Survivor's Instincts? Part of the point of that skill is that you don't have to do that manually anymore once you've made a particular type of object."

"So I can just command shovels into existence?"

"No, you stupid ass. Just . . . decide to make the shovel, and stop telling your hands what to do."

There was a good chance this was a prank, but Matt decided to take a chance on it. And lo and behold, his hands started moving more or less on their own, tying the rock back into place just like it had been before. It was a weird sensation; it didn't feel like he was being controlled, just that he didn't have to tell his hands what to do. It was like doing a task he had done a thousand times before, and didn't have to think all that hard about now.

"Now, if you want to improve the shovel, that's a different thing. The skill will only automate to roughly the quality level you've achieved before. But that's the basic gist of the thing."

Ding!

"Oh, dammit."

"What?"

"I think I got an achievement out of this, which means I'm going to have to thank you for it later."

"Don't strain yourself."

Matt took a look at his notifications.

Survivor's Instincts (LV2)
Your instincts are slightly improved as far as staying alive is concerned. If there's a wall to climb, you have a better idea of if you can climb it, and if there's an enemy to fight, you are better at estimating your chances of winning. You also have an increased baseline knowledge of survival methods.

You have leveled the skill, and now know and can do a little bit more. Automation aspect of skill improved. Knowledge aspect of skill improved. Judgement aspect of skill improved.

He had forgotten about the judgement aspect of the skill. Looking back, he realized he didn't get a lot of information about the Clownrats, but definitely had a vibe that he absolutely couldn't take the Bonecat in a straight fight.

Maybe it works better when the gap between me and the monster is bigger?

The second notification was, true to the system's usual form, a bit snarkier.

Achievement: [Taking Your Time]

You delayed leveling a level 1 skill long, long past what you'd expect from an average adventurer, and at great risk to your own life. What was that all about? Were you . . . trying to prove a point?

Reward: +1 WIS

He didn't love the sarcasm, but he'd take the point in wisdom. He still didn't feel any smarter, but had to assume that at some point the cumulative effect of mental stats would start to be noticeable in at least *some* way.

Between rebuilding his tools, letting his hands heal and dealing with a system and system guardian who both seemed dead set on being only minimally useful, digging the hole took the better part of a few days. This was even slower than he had expected, partially because the Bonecat was still noticeably out and about. Every once in a while he'd hear it crashing through the trees and have to take cover just in case it came his direction. Whether it was luck or just a lack of motivation on the Bonecat's part, it never actually came close enough to realize he was there. Matt had to assume there was a timer on that luck, though, and hurried to complete the rest of the project as soon as he could.

The next part of the project was scouting. Being chased by the Bonecat before had put a fear of being trapped deep in his bones. If he had run into any impassible terrain during his initial retreat, he'd be in pieces now. Over the course of several hours, he mapped out enough of the surrounding terrain to know what directions he could run freely in and which directions would lead to him trying to talk down an angry monster before it cut him in half.

By the time he finished the final prep on the trap, it was night. The next day would make or break him, one way or another. He popped a few food cubes and settled down for the night, only to find he couldn't sleep. The work of setting up the trap had distracted him from the danger of what he was about to try, but now there was nothing keeping him from thinking about what could go wrong in full Technicolor detail. It was hours before he finally started to drop off, and the last thing he could remember was surprise that the system guardian was quiet the entire time, as well.

I guess it's too much to hope that she might be worried too. I'll ask her about it tomorrow.

Sneaking was hard, but not sneaking was almost harder under some circumstances. One of those circumstances was when every instinct he had was telling him that approaching a living, breathing battering ram made out of sharpened bone was not just a bad idea, but also an almost surefire method of suicide. He tamped down the instinct, as overpowering as it was. If this thing spotted him, it was actually better for him if it was from further away.

He watched as the thing snuffled around the forest, aimlessly. Suddenly, it stopped. It had caught a scent. Matt's scent. It turned, saw him, and roared. Then they were both off, ripping through the woods at top speed. Once again, Matt had to face his suspicions that these animals were a little more complex than programmed simulations. The Bonecat was pissed. Where before it had screamed once, it now wailed and snarled every step of the way. Where it had knocked over trees before, Matt now heard them splinter and explode out of its way.

Apparently, it doesn't like losing.

All that anger translated into extra speed. Matt glanced behind him to see the thing closing the distance on him surprisingly quickly. Earlier than he planned, he started running in a serpentine pattern, putting angles between him and the slow-turning beast. It helped, but not much. The thing was still gaining.

Faster. I have to go faster.

Zigzagging, Matt oriented himself towards the thickest tree growth in his route. The footfalls of the thing had been getting louder for a while, and Matt sprang through a gap in the trees a half-second before he heard the same trees get demolished. The thicker growth still had an effect, though. Matt slowly rebuilt his lead as the thing's momentum was cut further and further by the trees.

Reaching the edge of the heavy growth, Matt dug deep and put every bit of power he could into his legs. The trees gave way to a clearing that offered no obstacles at all to the Bonecat, and despite Matt's best efforts, it quickly eliminated whatever space was left between them. Matt heard the footsteps get closer and closer until suddenly, he felt an impact on his back. It felt like a mountain had been thrown at him, and he felt his legs leave the ground as he was catapulted through the air.

All his breath was driven out of him as he slammed into the ground, and as he struggled to his knees, he saw the thing approach then loom over him, blade raised. He heard the beginnings of a whoosh as the blade cut through the air, and sprung backwards with everything he had. The thing screamed, raised the blade again, and pushed off the ground towards him. He wouldn't be able to dodge again.

Then, just before it bisected Matt, it vanished. A pit in the ground opened up underneath the Bonecat, and it plummeted into the hole and out of Matt's field of vision.

CHAPTER EIGHTEEN

The Master Plan

Pit traps were some of the oldest traps in human history for a reason. They were simple. A hunter just dug a hole, concealed it, and waited for prey to fall in. Sometimes, the prey would be killed and crippled by the fall. Even when it wasn't, the hunter had the luxury of waiting until the prey weakened from thirst and lack of food before striking the final blow.

To speed this process up, there were some modifications that could be made to the trap to make them more effective. Spikes were the obvious choice, but Matt had figured that spikes wouldn't do much to an animal covered in thick bone plates. Instead, he found himself smiling as the Bonecat was greeted by the special option he had prepared: water.

Water in a pit trap, Survivor's Instincts told him, was not meant to drown prey. Rather, it was to keep them from leaving the trap by exhausting them. The fact that animals often drowned was a beneficial aftereffect that kept the energy outlay needed to actually kill them to a minimum, while the bigger benefits came by keeping the trapped in the trap itself. Fighting the water would tire the animals, which made them worse climbers as they used their wet paws to scale the slippery walls.

Matt's first hope was that the Bonecat might not be capable of climbing at all, but that had been dashed during the chase when he led it over increasingly rough terrain. It handled the shifts in elevation without even slowing down. Without the water, the cat was definitely going to be able to get out. Now, the big question was if it could swim well enough to get purchase on the side of the pit, and if it could climb well enough to get out before it exhausted itself and drowned.

Looking down into the pit, he found the Bonecat almost bumping against the edges. It could apparently swim, if not very gracefully. It splashed around in the water, turning it from a clear blue to a murky brown. More importantly, it had kept its head above the water and could still draw in deep breaths.

The water itself had been easy to fill the pit with. With the recent hurricane, Matt had found pools of water around the island. All it took was selecting the right reservoir filled with rainwater and digging the pit slightly outside its borders. Once the pit was done, he joined a channel between the two and watched as the water poured in.

In those moments, he had hoped that the Bonecat would immediately drown. That was apparently too much of a dream to be true.

"You know there's zero chance this will work, right? It's a Bone*cat.* As in, can probably climb pretty well. It's going to be *pissed* when it gets out."

"Do you know if it can climb? Like, actually know that, or are you just giving me shit?"

"I know they can climb. At least a bit. I don't know if they can climb up a muddy wall, but do you really think you'll get that lucky?"

Matt was a bit more hopeful than the guardian, but still kept his own doubts. This was his best option, and if it failed, he was going to be a world of trouble. If the Bonecat got out, it probably wasn't even worth it to run. Getting ripped apart wouldn't exactly be fun but it was better than starving to death over the next few weeks.

The first thing the Bonecat tried was to scramble up the wall head-on. It went poorly in an almost amusing sense. As a poor swimmer, it couldn't get much initial momentum to use to propel itself upwards. Even if it found purchase on the bottom, the muddy bottom would suck energy up rather than support movement. So, it ended up approaching the wall at a sluggish pace and could only cling to the wall, mere inches above where it started. Eventually, it'd tire and splash back down into the water. Briefly submerging itself before it surfaced again, coughing and shrieking.

"It didn't like that at all." The guardian flashed a small smile. "Are you sure your best move is making things personal with a giant death machine? That doesn't seem like the kind of animal I'd want to have holding a grudge against me."

"Heh." Matt tried to laugh naturally, but he was pretty sure even a child could tell he was nervous. "Yeah, I'm sort of betting everything on this."

As if in answer to Matt's worries, the Bonecat shrieked and did the worst possible thing that Matt could think of: it started experimenting. It tried gouging at the side of the pit itself. Matt was fine with that, the dirt deep down was compressed pretty heavily and although the cat's claws could mar it, it wasn't enough to be anything serious. If it kept going, it would mostly just be weighing itself down as the clay stuck to its skeleton.

Unfortunately, it moved on from that tactic pretty quickly, remembering it had claws and that claws were pretty useful for climbing. With yet another eardrum breaking roar, the Bonecat planted each of its front claws into the side of the pit, then drew itself up level with them. Bracing its rear legs against the side of the pit, it raised one claw up and stabbed it even higher, then drew itself level enough to set the other claw into the wall alongside it. It was spiking its way up the wall, slowly but surely.

The combination of Matt's increased VIT and STR stats, his Survivor's Instincts, and his sheer will to survive this monster had given him strength to dig a pretty deep hole. The Bonecat wasn't climbing that fast, so there was some time before it got to the top. But the time it took wouldn't matter much. The difference between ten seconds and ten minutes was mostly academic. If it got out, Matt was as good as dead.

Time wasn't the only thing in play, though. The Bonecat was *huge*. It might have good stamina, but nothing had infinite endurance. Every claw it applied to the side of the wall and every ascension to a new level represented energy it was spending, and Matt could see it getting visibly tired by the time it made the halfway point. It was going to be close. By the three-quarter mark, the thing's arms were shaking.

The guardian peered down with Matt. "I don't know how you can just sit there and look at that thing. It's like staring at your own gravestone. One that's very motivated in beating you to jelly."

Matt ignored the system guardian. *That's probably about as much time as I'm going to get,* he thought. He had been hoping the Bonecat would take a little more time and energy in getting as far as it had, but it would have to do. He walked over to a nearby outcropping of rock and picked up his shovel from the base of it. On top of the outcropping was a huge boulder, nearly the size of the mouth of the pit.

It had taken him forever to raise the damn thing. In the process, he had to keep stabilizing it with small rocks to keep it from tumbling down from its place. Now, he crammed his shovel behind those same rocks and cranked. He heard earthy creaks as the boulder started to pull away from the last remaining pieces of soil holding it in place.

Please don't miss. Please don't miss.

It didn't miss. As if by magic, the rock rolled forward in a straight line, directly off the outcropping and towards the pit. Then, with all the grace and style of a high diver, it plummeted into the pit directly on top of a very, very surprised Bonecat.

Matt would have accepted the cat dying from the initial fall. He would have been glad to see it drown. He would have punched the air if it had been unable to climb. Now, he would settle for the idea that most animals don't survive getting hit in the face with half-ton rocks. If there was any part of his plan that could do the job, the boulder seemed like the clearest bet.

But it didn't work. For a moment, there was no sound from the pit. Then, Matt saw the rock bob around in the water. Then, it popped upwards a bit. It wasn't surprising that the Bonecat could swim or climb. But "can a Bonecat swim or climb with a massive rock on its back" had been a pretty open question. Now, the answer had turned out to be not very positive for Matt.

Could it climb all the way to the top with the rock on it? Probably not, but it was possible. Could it get around the rock somehow? Maybe. Could it figure out that it could take extended rests by just letting its bone spikes hold it in place? Matt had no idea how smart the thing was, but it was at least imaginable that the Bonecat might figure it out. One way or another, it was likely to figure out a way to keep the rock from drowning it.

Matt looked away from the pit. He walked over to a couple of poles.

Unfortunately for the Bonecat, when Matt first set up the trap, he had an inkling that the rock wouldn't be able to crush or drown it.

When someone digs a pretty big hole, they end up with an equally big amount of dirt. Matt could have just dumped that dirt around the hole itself, letting it form a small hill. But that seemed like a waste.

Why let perfectly good dirt pile around doing nothing when you could store it behind a slanted wall made of branches and tarp, ready to be let loose like a stored landslide? Why, he thought, you could kick out a couple of poles and let that retaining wall fall like a drawbridge, dumping all the dirt back into the hole. If it fired accidentally, it would ruin a couple of days' work. But fired intentionally, it could ruin a Bonecat's life.

As Matt kicked the poles out, he reflected that this was really his last shot. Every step until now might have taken care of the Bonecat, but this was truly his last chance. He watched all of his hard work from the past few days evaporate as the dirt cascaded back into the hole. When the landslide slowed, he ran around with his shovel like a madman and desperately shoveled more dirt into the pit to pile up on the rock.

His thinking here was pretty simple. If the Bonecat could swim and climb, Matt wasn't going to bet against its ability to also dig.

But the extra dirt would weigh something, and the Bonecat still couldn't breathe water. It also presumably couldn't dig upwards with a massive boulder on its back. After a few minutes, the pit was as full of dirt as it was going to get, and Matt leaned back to watch the aftermath.

He was hoping that the Bonecat would give up. Honestly, he would have given up by now if he was at the bottom of the pit. But it wasn't going to be that clean. The dirt heaved up and down, spilling out of the hole as the beast fought against the rock. Suddenly, the level of the dirt dropped a few feet. There was only one explanation for that: the Bonecat had gotten around the rock somehow. It could start digging up now.

Matt wasn't going to sit idly by. He once again went into a flurry with his shovel, trying his best to add more dirt to the pit. As the dirt in the pit shifted and sank, Matt prayed that the minutes it took the Bonecat to fight its way free would add up. That they would be enough to sap the Bonecat's energy. That enough planning could beat overwhelming, terrifying strength.

And then, carrying all the fear Matt had buried away in the pit, a claw broke through the soil. It just wasn't enough.

CHAPTER NINTEEN

Holy Shit

The claw slowly rose out of the soil, catching the sun as it extended upwards. It was oddly clean, as if the dirt had acted as a scrub without sticking to it. The inner edge looked as sharp as a knife.

Soon, it was more than a claw. Where the claw ran out, the foot began, and the Bonecat's massive paw bent downwards as it planted itself and prepared to pull itself free from its intended grave.

Oh shit, oh shit. Matt was beginning to reconsider his brave guy die-with-your-boots-on stance on not running. Faced with the enormity of the blade, starving to death on an island was starting to sound a whole better. Even the guardian was affected by it.

"Shit, Matt. For what it's worth, I actually am kind of sorry for what's about to happen."

Matt gulped, then reached down and unsheathed his knife. He wouldn't have a chance against the thing, but he was going to keep trying. He took a deep breath and readied himself for the rest of the monster to emerge.

But it never came. Matt's eyes stayed glued to the exposed leg. Everything was still. Even the guardian stayed quiet and stared at part of the Bonecat sticking above the ground.

Minutes passed without anyone moving.

"Holy shit," the guardian said.

"Holy shit," Matt agreed.

Ding!

Achievement: [Holy Shit]

That thing should have absolutely demolished you. You don't have a single ability that was meant for this situation, and you don't have a single party member to help complement your skills. The fact that you didn't die is insane. I'm not going to lie, usually we break out the tape and look for glitches in situations like this. But you won fair and square, so here are the maximum rewards I can give you at your current level.

Rewards: +1 all stats, [Survival of The Least Fit] title, 10x trap spikes, +4 Class XP

Matt had put together a trap with several elements, all of which had a chance to kill or neutralize the Bonecat. The Bonecat proved to be more tenacious than any of the elements alone. But together, they were a lot more dangerous than the sum of their parts. Matt had expected them to kill almost anything when he first built the trap.

The fact that the Bonecat had almost survived was a testament to the sheer terror of the thing. But it had died. And Matt had squeaked out a win at the finish line.

Probably a win, at least. He was honestly afraid to check.

Matt didn't move a muscle until a small bag materialized and clattered to the ground. He assumed it was the trap spikes, but it kind of didn't matter anymore.

"Aaarrrrhhhh. Yes. Yes! Screw you! Bonecat! I got you!" Matt let loose a series of noises that were just bundles of emotions. He danced around on the dirt, and even gave the blunt side of the claw a few kicks. Generally, he was making a fool of himself.

"Matt! Dumbass! It might not be dead. Matt! Stop it!" The guardian's voice rang out amid Matt's celebration. Looking over, he saw her staring at him with what was unmistakably fear and worry.

Oh, that's sweet, he thought, *she's incorporeal and still afraid.*

"No, it's okay. I got a system message. It's really dead."

"What? How?"

"Huh? I mean . . . it was under there for minutes. You might not need to breathe, but it does. I guess it was enough."

For a moment, the guardian couldn't come up with a retort. Finally, she squeezed out, "You lucky asshole. Do you know how lucky you are?"

During the guardian's pause, Matt restarted his "I win" dance, and responded to her between wild gyrations. "So what? I'm lucky. I don't care! I won! Woooooo!" He tried to find a phrase to describe his happiness. It must have been what soldiers felt after a long hard battle. He had prepared himself for death, and received life. There was no better feeling.

"You idiot. I still don't believe it."

As if on command, the Bonecat corpse started dissolving into nothingness. Matt kept dancing, kicking the exposed paw as many times as he could. Eventually, it blinked out of existence, and Matt barely avoided getting buried in the resulting cave-in. Scrambling out, he saw the guardian rolling her eyes so far back that he worried she might hurt herself.

"You idiot."

"So what? This is a major triumph of the ingenuity of man."

"What ingenuity? You buried the turd. Even a cat can do that."

"Hah, that's a sick burn. Good job."

Matt could have sworn that the guardian's face almost broke into a smile. The edges of her mouth twitched upwards in the beginnings of a non-malicious, un-sarcastic smile. Before it could form, the smile was gone.

The dungeon system chose that moment to finally catch up to recent events.

Ding!

> *Dungeon Objective Achieved!*
>
> [Stranded But Not Alone]: You managed to kill the Bonecat, alone. That shouldn't be possible for your class or level, but you did it while incurring only minimal injuries. Bonus objectives rewarded.
>
> Objective: Eliminate Bonecat 1/1
> Bonus Objectives: Solo Clear, Dominant Performance
> Rewards: Low-Grade Dungeon Loot Selection, Survivor's Multitool, +4 Class XP

Suddenly, a small stone pillar much like the entrance stone to the dungeon rose from the earth, dramatically rumbling as it did. It startled the hell out of Matt for a moment before he realized it wasn't the second coming of the Bonecat.

"Guardian, what the hell is that?"

"A reward plinth. Some dungeons have them. It's a design thing. You don't always see them, but given the kind of clear you managed, the dungeon probably thinks you deserve a little more showmanship."

Before he approached the plinth, Matt wanted a little more information. Now that he had gone through the process before, he knew that his choice of rewards would depend not only on what he wanted, but also on who he was. And he had been changing a lot lately.

> *Matt Perison*
> *Level 3 Survivor*
> **Class XP:** 5/20

HP: 55
MP: N/A
STAM: 35
Assignable Stat Points: 2
STR: 7
DEX: 11
PER: 9
VIT: 11
WIS: 8
INT: 6
Class Skills: Survivor's Instincts (LV2), Survivor's Combat (LV2), Eat Anything! (LV2)

Leveling had been a given at this point. But seeing Survivor's Combat and perception both advance, Matt also realized that he had missed at least one accomplishment during his battle.

Achievement: [Watchful Combat]

You came out on top after spending an extended amount of time observing an opponent, both during and outside of combat. An expert is constantly looking for weaknesses to exploit. Score one for the observant, thoughtful types!

Rewards: Survivor's Combat advancement, +1 PER

At this point, Matt was feeling pretty well rewarded, even before getting to his official dungeon rewards. He pretty clearly wasn't on the almost-immediately-overpowered Isekai hero path, but every increase in stats was noticeable and significant.

Between all his recent efforts walking and his increased VIT and DEX stats, he was now at a level that would have been considered insanely fit in his old Earth life. He was even able to outrun a big monster, even if it was just for a little while. His wounds healed faster. He could see what was coming better. It wasn't superpowers, but it all added up to much-needed survivability.

With all that done, Matt walked over to the plinth to take a look at the rest of his prizes.

Reward Selection
In addition to your Survivor's Multitool bonus reward, you are entitled to a section from the following list of low-grade loot:
Reinforced Survivor's Garb

Survivor's Trap Kit
Survivor's Battle-Knife
Survivor's Dowsing Rod

The Survivor's trap kit immediately caught his attention, and he hurriedly zoomed in on the description.

Survivor's Trap Kit
This trap kit has everything you need to make someone's day a lot worse. Do you want barbs? We have barbs. Do you need better rope? We have rope. How do you feel about spikes? Because there are so many spikes in this thing. Just so, so many.

The Survivor's trap kit also slowly replenishes lost or broken supplies, making it much easier for you to avoid running out.

That was big. Really big, actually. Matt had been hamstrung in all of his traps by needing to make do with various components that he could salvage from the environment. This would solve much or all of that problem.

The only thing that kept him from selecting it immediately was the pack of spikes he just got. It didn't do nearly as much for him as this pack might, but it did solve some of the same problems. Even though the pack sounded tailor-made for keeping him alive moving forward, he was willing to look at the other options before deciding.

The Survivor's garb piece still sounded nice, but it wasn't vital at the moment. That left the battle-knife next on the list.

Survivor's Battle-Knife
Some knives stab, and some knives slash. The Survivor's battle-knife is not that polite or elegant. It lops. The battle-knife's weight is shifted towards the front, making it something between an axe and a short sword. This lets you detach limbs as easily as you clear brush out of your way, and does so in an easy, swing-as-hard-as-you-can sort of way that doesn't require much refined skill.

Matt was imagining this knife was similar to khukris back on Earth. For the types of fights he was getting into, this made a lot more sense than the assassin's dagger from before. People would quit fighting after getting a hole poked in them, but monsters would mostly panic and fight harder. Taking off a limb or a head was a better option.

Still, Matt felt like he should treat melee combat as a last resort. Things like the battle-knife and the armored garb were nice, and in a better situation, he'd have taken them without even thinking about it. But here on burned-out Gaia, his priorities had to be different.

That left the underwhelming-sounding dowsing rod. He queued up the window.

Survivor's Dowsing Rod
A staple of treasure hunters, the dowsing rod helps you find things. If you approach an anomalous object that doesn't belong in its immediate environment with the rod in hand, it will begin to vibrate. The vibrations will increase the closer you get to the object, allowing you to home in on an odd findable you otherwise might miss.

If Gaia were still alive, there was no way that Matt would take this. And if his game experience was any guide, good loot always came from dungeons. If it wasn't for his unusual survival needs, Matt would be building out his ability to hack and slash monsters in the support of a party, and he would have been unbelievably happy about it.

Even with his weird needs, the trap kit just seemed like a better call. But the more he thought about it, the more he distrusted himself. Did it seem like a better call just because he thought it was cool? In the background of his mind, he could feel Survivor's Instincts telling him that he didn't need more traps.

There had been close calls, but the traps he had made so far had worked. Better spikes and ropes would not have helped with the Bonecat.

In fact, more than anything else, what helped his fight with the Bonecat was his state of being fully hydrated and a full stomach. He was in peak condition and not collapsed from lack of nourishment in a post-apocalypse desert somewhere.

In better times, the dungeons would have been his goal. He would have done everything he could to optimize taking down as many of them as possible. These were not better times. He was surviving.

As much as it pained him, he had to take the dowsing rod. There was an entire ruined world to scavenge in, and he had no idea how much useful garbage he had missed already. Like it or not, he needed a better way of living off the dead, inhospitable land.

But, he still had one thing to try. Stepping back from the plinth, Matt raised his hand at it and mentally mustered every bit of authority that he used to command the system guardian. Using his most authoritative voice, he boomed out his order.

"System: give me better loot."

CHAPTER TWENTY

Five Years

"What in the hell are you doing?"

The guardian's voice rang out behind Matt. He waited a few moments to make sure that nothing was happening before walking back to the plinth and rechecking his options. Unfortunately, the items were the same as before and there wasn't a new special option. Disappointed, he shook his head and willed his acceptance of the dowsing rod reward.

"I was trying something. Let me take a look at the rewards first," Matt replied.

"Good because if you're gonna go bonkers, I want a heads-up."

Matt smiled. That was the guardian he knew. He walked around the site of the battle, collecting the system's drops that he had neglected up to that point. The trap spikes were in an oblong canvas bag and were a pleasant surprise. They were made from some relatively heavy and durable-feeling material that Matt suspected was probably some kind of steel alloy. Each of them were roughly eight inches long with needle-like tips. At first glance, Matt was sure that they wouldn't have much problem sticking into normal, non-armored enemies.

Better yet, the metal allowed for a better design. The spike's shafts were flared upwards every inch or so. That made them hard to grip, but also meant that they would be hard to dislodge once they hit. Taking them out would also tear out the surrounding flesh.

The non-business end was the best part. It was notched to make lashing them to objects easier, with well-placed holes to thread the rope through. Compared to the wood stakes that he had been using so far, this was like the difference between a Honda Fit and a Ferrari. He couldn't wait to use them to ruin someone's day.

The multitool was much more confusing to figure out. At first, it looked like a solid block of metal. Matt tapped it experimentally and tried to pry it apart with his hands. Nothing happened.

"Hey, Guardian, what's the deal here? Is the system calling this brick a multitool to be funny?"

"Ugh, the trick is, Matt, that you have to be smarter than the tool."

"Guardian . . ."

"Fine, fine. You have to actually think of what you want to do with it. Think about driving one of your tent stakes in."

As soon as Matt focused his attention on a tent stake, the block shifted into a sort of undersized mallet. With different prompts, it turned into a screwdriver, a small saw, and even a pair of scissors. It was literal magic. Beyond his canteen and the water stone, this was further proof that Gaia was different from Earth. But when he thought about a drill, the multitool failed to morph to the new shape.

"It won't turn into a drill?"

"Why do you always ask so much of everything? It has its limits. You weren't expecting to have automated or complex tools, right? For the stuff that you do, even a chisel is a big deal."

Matt would have loved a drill, but the guardian wasn't wrong. The saw and hammer that the multitool could form were already plenty. After using a survival knife for everything in the past few weeks, this was a huge upgrade. It would make a lot of stuff easier, even if it didn't help much in an actual fight.

By comparison, the dowsing rod was much less interesting to play with. It was a short cylinder of some unknown, crystal-like material. It wasn't supposed to activate until treasure was nearby. There wasn't much more to look at. He didn't love the fact that he had to hold the rods in both hands for them to work, but his continued survival was dependent on being able to effectively scavenge. Any tool that helped with that was a big deal.

"Will this do anything in a dungeon, Guardian?"

"Maybe. From what I can see, it will help you find something in a dungeon if there's something weird for it to find."

"But since I can't carry stuff out . . ."

"Right. Even if you found something cool, it's going to stay here. It's possible for dungeons to have secrets, but my system knowledge tells me that kind of stuff is usually in a bonus dungeon."

"Extra challenge for extra rewards?"

"Yup. If you want to have a chance at fighting TWO Bonecats, feel free to look around."

"I think I'll be fine for now, thanks."

As with the last dungeon, all of Matt's gear had been repaired when he finished the dungeon objective. He started packing his stuff when something the guardian had said twigged his interest.

"Hey, you know something about this dowsing rod, and you said, 'from what you can see.' That's not system knowledge?"

"Nope. You know, not every single thing I know is from the system. I'm a bit like these dungeons. They customize themselves to the world that they're in. Different world, different reward. I'm guessing that in a culture that doesn't care about hidden treasure, you wouldn't see things like that dowsing rod. The system doesn't track differences like that."

"Wait. Why do you know so much about this?"

"Part of the guardian package, of course. As far as the system is concerned, I'm here to tell you stuff about things. So I sort of have an identify skill. I can't change anything, but I can see what they mean."

"I see . . . good to know." Matt wasn't used to such a nice guardian.

With all the stuff packed, he walked to the plinth and prepared to leave the dungeon.

"By the way," the guardian said, keeping her tone nonchalant, "you never told me what the deal was when you tried to be a plinth-wizard."

"Hmm, I think I'll let you know later. Maybe we can trade information."

"Listen, dumbass, I just GAVE you a bunch of informa—"

And then they were out.

It wasn't particularly late in Matt's day-night cycle, and they weren't in a great place to stop. So they started walking. By the time they hit a relatively flat and clear piece of ground in the mountain, all the adrenaline of the day caught up with him. He probably could press on, but didn't see much point.

It's not like I have an appointment to get to or anything.

For the first time in a long time, Matt opted to set up the entire camp, tent and all. His new tool made things a lot easier. Pounding in stakes with a hammer was much less awkward than trying to do the same thing with the butt end of his Survivor's knife. He then dragged some rocks to sit on and tried to convince the guardian to make another illusory fire.

"No, definitely not. Not while you're holding secrets on me for some weird reason," the guardian said.

"You know, we could probably work out a trade. I'll put my secret up for your fire, and one other thing."

"Ok? What?"

"I want to know why you were crying the other night."

That shut down the conversation. Matt let her stew on it while he relaxed on his rock. She had been bouncing up and down, trying to pry his secret out of him during the walk down the mountain. Honestly, Matt didn't know why this was so important to her, but it was the only non-slave-command leverage he had on her. So far, he had used the commands for things that he needed to know and were relevant to him surviving. The last thing he wanted to do was use the same power to force her to talk about something personal. That felt several steps scummier than what he had already done. So he waited.

It had been a long day, and he was tired. Right before he nodded off, she broke the silence.

"I wasn't always here, you know. But I was here before you were."

"Yeah, you told me that. The system dropped you off beforehand to learn about the planet, but there was nothing much to learn," Matt said.

"Well, that would have been a mistake. Dropping someone off, having them spend six months trying to pick up information on a world that's mostly underground, and forgetting that they can't dig. Shitty mistake right?" the guardian's eyes turned red.

"When it could have just checked on the world? Yes. And six months is a long time to wait. I'm sorry."

"It's not just that"—the guardian's voice almost broke—"the six months I mentioned is a standard period of time. Sometimes, if it's a really big or a really weird world, it might be a year."

"How long were you here for?" Matt was starting to get concerned.

He didn't know what answer was coming, but he was beginning to suspect that he wasn't going to like it. The guardian picked that moment to break down crying, this time for real. Not muffled or hidden, but messy, ugly crying.

"Five years."

The system guardian was, for some reason, designed to look like a little girl. It might have been to make her nonthreatening, or to ensure that there was no chance of romantic entanglements. Matt didn't realize that the system had actually gone deeper with the little girl concept. He thought of her as an adult, one that was prickly and could give as good as she got.

But he was wrong. She was tough because she had to get through five years alone. She was mean because he was the reason why this all happened. And she wanted him dead because that was the only way to escape from this nightmare of a planet. If he died, she might get out. It was as simple as that.

He couldn't even comfort her. Words, minus saying that he'd starve himself to death, meant nothing in the face of the fact that she was here because of him, however unintentional it might be. He couldn't even hug her or let her know that he was present. She never seemed more human than in that moment. In fact, the system gave her some human traits, including the possibility of crying herself to sleep. She was upset enough that she forgot about the information he owed her.

He let her sleep. He'd tell her in the morning.

* * *

The next day, Matt packed up camp while the guardian did her best to pretend like nothing had happened. Between single word questions and replies, they decided that their best bet was to walk back to the ruins that Matt had seen while traveling to the guardian. If they didn't find anything, they could continue to the dungeons. Matt was down to just several days' worth of food and hoped that there was more on the way. So far, the dungeons had not been great sources of sustenance.

It wasn't until they had been walking for half a day before the guardian remembered what she was owed. Running in front of him, she demanded for him to hold up his end of the bargain.

"Oh, that?" Matt said, "It wasn't even that big of a deal. I was just trying to see if I could get something to happen with my Gaia authority."

He kept walking but felt like an asshole for cheating her. She had told him her secrets, while he only had a boring piece of information to offer. He half-expected her to whine and demand a new secret. Instead, she went oddly quiet. He turned around to check on her and saw that she was planted in place, mouth hanging open. It was surprisingly childish.

Suddenly, she snapped back to reality and immediately started yelling.

"Your fucking WHAT?"

CHAPTER TWENTY-ONE

Systematic Threats

After her outburst, the guardian stared at Matt as if he had suddenly shot her. He walked a few steps closer to her, expecting her to snap out of it, but she didn't. She remained frozen in place like a statue. He was worried he had broken her somehow.

"Hey, Guardian?" Matt waved his hand in front of her face. "You in there? You okay?" He debated yelling in her ear and decided against it. But there weren't a lot of options to communicate with someone who was a hologram. It wasn't like he could shake her or tap her on the shoulder. Thankfully, just as quickly as she had fallen into her stupor, she shook out of it and began screaming at him.

"You have what, Matt? Gaia authority? Somehow? And you didn't tell your *assigned system guardian who is supposed to keep you alive about it*? This whole time?"

As if to emphasize her words, she started throwing punches at Matt. On some level, he was aware she couldn't actually hit him. Instinctually, though, there was no part of him that wanted to tangle with the tiny little rage-monster coming at him. He kept backing up.

"All you do is yell at me and call me stupid! How am I supposed to know what is and isn't important?" Matt tried to defend himself.

"You TELL me and . . . and I tell you! It's easy, *Matthew*."

Eventually, Matt had to order her to be quiet, hoping it would calm down. She materialized a little fake illusory chair for herself and sat. After a few minutes, she seemed to regain some semblance of sense. She waved at him to get his attention, then pointed at her mouth. Given that she was still sitting, he was willing to take the risk of unsealing her and seeing what she had to say.

"Tell me everything. How did this happen?"

"Okay. No more tantrums?" Matt paused to see the guardian's blood pressure rise, "So I'm a Survivor class, right?"

"Yes, yes. It's dumb, and it's not a class anybody actually takes."

"Sure, fine, but it's not as if I had better advice at the time. Anyways . . ." As best as his fuzzy memories of the event would allow him to, Matt relayed everything about the event. He talked about the sudden influx of stats and the brief god-like euphoria he had felt, then having the stats yanked away without being given any choice in the matter.

He even told her about bashing his hand against the ground and almost breaking it, which he thought would make her laugh. It didn't. "Anyway, I went from feeling strong enough to rip that Bonecat in half with my bare hands to just being just a normal guy within a few minutes. In return, I got a power that hasn't done anything. I think at least. It was kind of a shitty deal."

The guardian took a deep breath, "No, Matt, it wasn't. Do me a favor. Open your system screen."

"Why?"

"Just do it. Once you have it open, try to call up your citizenship tab."

"My what?"

She sighed, "Just trust me, alright?"

He pulled it up. It was a relatively sparse screen, the most interesting aspect of which was a box with a citizen ID number. The box was the part of his system screen that changed values as he looked at it, and it clicked over from one several-digit number to another while he watched.

Matt Perison
Citizenship
Global: Gaia
Continental: Sarthia
Kingdom: Sarthian Empire
Official Residence: Sarthian Capitol District
Authorities
Global: Alpha Level Authority, Planet Gaia
Continental: N/A
Kingdom: N/A
District: N/A
Individual ID: 827-292-176-455

"Why haven't I seen this before? If it's that important, you should have told me to read it."

"Because it wasn't important, Matt. Please stop asking questions. The main use of this page is as identification. You see that number that keeps changing? If a guard or something wanted you to prove who you were, you'd pull that up, and they'd usually have a skill to verify who you were." The guardian was unusually serious.

"There's a guard class? Who would take that?" Matt asked.

"A person who wanted a reasonably good government job and pension. Matt. Just. Please. Shush for a second. I swear." Given that the guardian was getting worked up as she talked about the citizenship tab clued Matt into the possibility that he really was talking too much. He liked having the opportunity to mess with her, but it was beginning to seem like he had actually missed something important. "The thing that gives a guard the ability to check your ID isn't their class, it's their authority. If you became a Sarthian Capitol District Guard, you'd get authority corresponding to your job. And it would work when you were in your district. Do you follow?"

"Yes."

"Good." She pantomimed knocking his forehead with her knuckles. "Glad it's sinking in. So, national level authority would be for someone like a king, or a general of an army. They'd have authority that went with them over the whole kingdom. It lets them do . . . stuff like laws and commands. For continental authority, think of an emperor or something. It might let him issue edicts to the kings." The guardian was now pacing, radiating nervous energy. "The point is, at every level there's a set of abilities you get depending on what your role is."

"And, what are those at the planetary level?"

Suddenly, the guardian withered in front of Matt. It was like a balloon being deflated, but on the scale of a whole person. Her words started coming out stammered, "It's . . . Usually, the ones who have that power . . . are the planet's villains . . . The people that reincarnators like you are supposed to fight . . . You're . . . you're not meant to have that level of power."

Achievement: [Forbidden Knowledge]

You are digging into knowings that you should not know, and considering a path you should not take. Some ground was not meant for human feet to tread. You have a role to play, but it is not this one. Beware.

Rewards: None

Was that a . . . threat? Matt wrested his attention back from the system window, only to see that the guardian had started *flickering*. The sight reminded Matt of the Bonecat dissolving earlier that week. He jumped in. "Wait, stop. Stop. Please, stop. You're . . ."

The guardian looked down and stared at her hand as it went in and out of existence. A look of horror crossed her face. She looked back at Matt and opened her mouth. No words came out.

Matt hurriedly continued the conversation. "Okay, you don't have to talk about it. It's . . . let's talk about something else."

"No. Matt. This is big. You're . . . well, you were the most important person on the planet, in an arbitrary way." The guardian paused, as if trying to feel out a certain boundary with her words, "Now, you're actually the most important person. In a way that matters."

"Okay, we don't need to continue. It's okay." For the first time since he had been dropped on this barren planet, Matt felt a pang of fear. It was much worse than the mashup of clowns and rats. It was the feeling that he might lose something that meant a lot to him. His only companion in this place. Someone who the system had also screwed over.

"No, this is important. This . . . I, well . . . Listen, Matt. A big part of why, you know, I didn't want to follow you already was because I thought it was pointless. Anything you did would just delay the only result you could possibly get: dying alone on an empty planet. And I'd have to watch all that, knowing I was helpless to change anything. But now?" The guardian was still saying something, but Matt heard nothing. All he could see was her mouth movements.

He tried to read her lips. "It . . . makes . . . a big difference."

Regardless of what planetary authority was or might do, they couldn't do anything about it at the moment. Not that Matt didn't try. Matt tried yelling at the planet to declare himself as the god-emperor. By the fifth or sixth time, it was pretty clear that actually accessing anything useful from the authority was pretty far beyond his reach.

With nothing pressing on their schedules, they ambled towards the nearest ruin Matt could remember seeing, one with only the footing of a single building above the soil. Matt held the dowsing rod in his hand as they approached, hoping it would buzz once they got to the building. It didn't.

"Well, that's a bust." The guardian looked just as disappointed as Matt felt. Ever since the conversation about his Gaia authority, the guardian felt, well, more human.

Matt noticed that instead of her being angry at him all the time, she was more relaxed. And while things like food didn't matter to her, she was now fully capable of being bored. After a long walk through barren nothingness, it was clear that she had expected something. The displeasure of being robbed of the payoff was like a visible weight on her tiny back.

"Wait, wait." Matt pointed the dowsing rod at the few bricks left above the surface. "So, think about it. This is the only building we can see, right? That doesn't mean it's the only building that was ever here. Maybe it was the most durable building, or the tallest building, or something. There could have been more stuff that's just buried now."

The guardian perked up. "And we can look for that stuff?"

Matt grinned. "Sure."

Not knowing the exact range of the dowsing rod was annoying, since it made searching in any kind of orderly grid potentially inefficient. For all Matt knew, it might be able to work a mile out. But if he started with a grid that big when the actual range was much smaller, he would also potentially miss what they were looking for. Eventually, he and the guardian settled on walking outwards in a big spiral, spacing each loop about twenty feet from the last. One of the few advantages of Gaia's dead soil was that it picked up footprints pretty well, and they were able to visually verify that they hadn't screwed up the pattern.

It was almost a half hour before they got a hit. Without any warning, the dowsing rod started buzzing and blinking in Matt's hand, like he was getting summoned to a hostess table at a chain restaurant by one of those weird remote control alert coasters.

"Dig it up! Dig it up!" The guardian was dancing in place, finally with some life injected into her by the prospects. Matt smiled as he used the variance in the rod's vibration to zero in on the exact location of the object. Kids, as far as he knew, were universally excited by treasure hunts. It looked like the guardian wasn't any exception.

Actually digging up the thing turned out to be a tough job. The best tool Matt had for the job was the multitool, but the biggest digging implement it would turn into was somewhere between a garden spade and a very small shovel. He got immediately to work, but after digging for a few hours, it became abundantly clear that the objects the dowsing rod found weren't near the surface at all. The shovel only moved a small amount of dirt with each plunge, and unlike dungeons, Gaia's surface gave him very little to improvise a better tool from.

"Have you found it yet?" The guardian had long since slipped back into road-trip mode. This was the tenth time she had asked the same question. Matt gritted his teeth. His hands were all blisters, and his back was killing him. After the Bonecat trap, he wasn't exactly desperate for more digging. Having an annoyed preadolescent on his back the whole time wasn't helping him enjoy the experience much.

"For the tenth time: no. I promise you that I will tell you right away if I do."

"Are you sure you'll remember, or is this another Matt-forgets-about-having-authority-over a-whole-planet situation?"

"Listen, you little shit . . ." Matt was pulled back from the yelling-at-a-child brink by a sudden *ding* on his spade. He had hit something.

"I got something!" Matt started kicking loosened dirt off the object with his feet as the guardian ran back to the hole to see what he had found. "It's about time. I swear if I had to move another teaspoon-sized scoop of dirt with this shitty thing I was going to go crazy."

Moving a bit more dirt uncovered a looped handle of sorts, still attached to whatever was still underground below it. He was through with digging. He set his hands on the handle of the shovel and threw all seven of his strength points into the mightiest heave he could manage. The object ripped free of the soil and flew up into the air, landing between him and the system guardian. They both stared at it as it lay between them on the ground, then the system guardian started laughing. Hysterically, maniacally laughing.

Matt scowled.

"It's not funny! It's . . ."

His anger washed away as the guardian's laughter proved contagious, and eventually they had both laughed themselves to tears. When they got tired, they laid on the ground beside the treasure that had patiently waited through countless eras to be dug up.

It was a shovel.

CHAPTER TWENTY-TWO

Some Things are Soup

We have two important things today." As they walked to the next ruin, the guardian was shifting into a mode that Matt hadn't seen before. She almost seemed like a busy secretary trying to organize her boss's day. "First, the authority, we—" She paused, looking as if she was expecting some lightning strike. "Actually never mind. Let's keep going."

Matt had been suspicious of his system for a while now. When he first showed up, the system hadn't been exactly *loud*, but it had offered all sorts of information, achievements, and even quests. Since he had found the guardian, it had been comparatively quiet. Not completely dead by any means, since it still presented information. But he couldn't get the Forbidden Knowledge achievement out of his head.

"Yeah, I'm not too sure," Matt replied.

I don't want to think of the system as an enemy, though it certainly isn't the best friend I've ever had, either, Matt thought. He needed the system, but the guardian didn't seem to be best buddies with it. The question was why. Why was the system giving him such an ominous message? Why was the guardian acting like she was muzzled?

"And second, your food." The guardian was back on track. "We only have a few days' worth left. Oh, and this has been bothering me, why do you eat the soup like that?"

The guardian pointed to Matt's mouth, where he was still working on breaking apart some of the incredibly dense bread.

"The soup?"

"Yeah. They came in little foil bags, right? With water and some kind of fuel? You're supposed to add the water and heat them up . . . They make enough soup to feed five people. You knew that, right?"

Matt stopped chewing momentarily. "Yeah, I knew that. It's just quicker this way."

No matter what, Matt resolved, *she can never know I didn't know that.*

The shovel that Matt had found turned out to be important in two ways. The first was that it was a really good shovel. Matt wasn't a garden tool aficionado in any way, but he had used quite a few during his illness-garden phase. This shovel was heads and tails above the normal hardware store purchases he had used to dig before.

Matt attributed the efficiency to the metal material that the shovel used. It was the same kind of shiny, steel-like material that the food lockbox had been made out of. Light, strong, and flexible. More importantly, Matt found a lot of it.

Here and there, Matt would find bricks and other remnants of buildings. They were all understandably fragile. Being buried for centuries and having all the durability sucked out of them does that. But when he unearthed something in good condition, it had always ended up from the same metal base. Most of the pieces were useless, at least for now. They mostly came in weird shapes and were probably parts of bigger machines. Yet, the machines themselves were nowhere to be found.

Did the things these were part of just rot off them, like flesh off a skeleton?

One by one, Matt and the guardian cycled through each of the ruins. His food supply kept dwindling. It had taken a lot of time for him to find the guardian in the first place, and if this pattern kept up, he'd be out of food long before they got through all of the ruins. He took every metal scrap he could find, and even though they were light individually, they added up to quite a bit of weight collectively. Something told him that they'd come in handy someday. But if they didn't find any food soon, there wouldn't be a someday.

It wasn't until the tenth ruin that they got lucky.

"Ooh, that's a big one." Matt's dowsing rod was going crazy in his hand, vibrating so hard it was almost making his hand go numb.

"Yeah, looks like it. Here's hoping we can find some food for you, fleshy. At least that way, I wouldn't have to watch you count food cubes seventeen times a day, like looking at them is going to make any difference."

The shovel almost moved by itself, and it wasn't long before Matt hit metal. Clearing away the dirt revealed a flat, horizontal surface.

"I think it's a chest!" Matt exclaimed.

"Well, great. Get it out of there, then."

"That's easy for you to say. You never have to take a turn digging."

"No," she said, smirking, "I guess I don't."

Matt started clearing all the dirt from the top of the thing, but then ran into a problem: the top of the thing kept going. He dug for several minutes, clearing away dirt from the top of the object, but never finding an edge. Whatever this was, it wasn't a chest. It was something much, much bigger.

It wasn't a hard decision to keep digging. He was almost out of cubes. This might not be a chest, but he had a feeling in his gut that it was something important. Sure, he could leave and try to find other ruins, but that hadn't been working out so far. He was willing to bet the last of his supplies that this would be something that could help. It wasn't the first time he'd bet his life since he came to Gaia, and he suspected again that it wouldn't be the last.

The object was more than a foot underground, and excavating even a few feet of it took a significant amount of time. By the time he found the first edge of the thing, several hours had passed. From there, he started tracing out the borders of the object with his shovel, hoping for some difference. Hours passed, and then he had to sleep. By the time he cleared the third border, it was well into his second day digging. He popped his last food cube, crossed his fingers, and prayed the last border would hold some clues to what this thing was.

Midway through uncovering the last edge, he got an answer to his prayer. There was a small outcropping on that edge, a two-foot-wide rectangle that stuck out from the rest of the shape for several inches. Abandoning the task of uncovering the rest of the border, he immediately started to dig down, creating a ramp from the ground level down to the wall of the object underneath the outcrop. He had an idea of what this was, but it would have to be fully uncovered to be useful to him if he was right.

It was the end of the second day by the time he finally had the door uncovered.

"Okay, so, we've found some of this metal here and there. But it's obviously not common, or they'd use it for everything. It's durable enough to survive whatever happened here, and hard enough to scratch my knife. But we only find bits and pieces of it. So it's rare. And rare things are valuable."

"Sounds reasonable." The guardian may not need food, but it would have been hard for Matt to miss the part where she craved interesting events. Matt didn't even have to convince her to help him think this out. She was completely focused on the mystery of this room. "Which raises an interesting question . . ."

"Who builds an entire room out of this stuff?" Matt finished the thought.

Whatever this building was, it was entirely made from the Gaian mystery metal. From what Matt had seen, there weren't any windows or hatches besides this one. In many ways, it was another lockbox like the one he had seen before. The only difference being that it was the size of a single family home and much, much harder to get to.

"It's just a bummer that you won't be able to get anything out of it."

Matt jerked his head around. If he couldn't get it open, it really would be bad news. "Why not?"

The guardian gestured towards the touchpad on the door. "It's that thing. That's, frankly, one hell of a piece of tech. It's tamper resistant and I have no idea what makes the thing go. Unless you have some kind of magic blowtorch I don't know about, you're not going to get this door open."

Matt breathed a sigh of relief. He thought she had seen a real problem. Door panels were something he could handle.

"Oh, that? That's no problem." Matt put his hand up to the panel, which immediately sprung to life, displaying a familiar message.

> Sarthia Prime Citizen established.
> Gaia Universal Citizen status established.
>
> Opening authority granted. Supplies are to be used in accordance with the Sarthia catastrophe relief efforts and Gaia unified government growth scourge resistance initiative goals. Failure to comply with these restrictions will result in punishment to the full extent of the law.
>
> Sarthian Mobile Supply House Authority granted. Releasing hatch.

The door hissed slightly, then clicked. Matt pressed his hand forward, and it moved easily inwards on its hinges. Whatever this metal was, it held up remarkably well. The door didn't even creak. He immediately stepped inside.

"Wait! Matt!" The guardian followed on his heels, screeching. "How in the hell did you do that?"

"We can talk about it later. First, I want to check this out." It was dark inside the structure. Matt only had one real source of light, in the form of his auto-lighting torch. He pulled it out and worked the mechanism to get it going.

"Fine. But we *are* talking about this later. No excuses."

When the torch sprang to life, it revealed a kind of storage area, filled with row after row of shelves. Matt suspected that this really was almost exactly like the lockbox he had found, only bigger. The dozens of empty shelves in the thing were a testament to that. He imagined the dozens or hundreds of people who probably relied on this emergency store during whatever catastrophe had struck. Only it ended up not mattering. The supplies had only delayed the inevitable. The disaster had eventually taken everyone.

But not all the shelves were empty. In the back of the room, they found several floor-to-ceiling shelves that hadn't been completely emptied out. On them were row after row of foil bags, hundreds of them in total.

"Well, okay." Matt grinned. "This is the best present I've ever gotten."

CHAPTER TWENTY-THREE

Good Luck Lasts Forever

I still don't understand why you won't make them into soup, that's kind of what they were made for."

With every question, Matt was learning that the guardian wasn't above being mildly obsessed with minutiae. The food cubes, she explained, were supposed to be dissolved into roughly a whole gallon of water. Matt had tried to defend himself by saying that he couldn't drink that much soup at once. Further, he didn't have any particular desire to shift his diet from mostly-bland food cubes to what he assumed would be completely-bland liquid. She hadn't listened.

"Please, Guardian, we've been over this. Repeatedly," Matt replied.

"Matt, I'm a guide. I'm trying to guide you. You look like a dumbass eating them wrong," the guardian said.

"Nobody cares! There's nobody here *to* care!"

"But I care. Matt, I care a great deal."

Between an almost endless supply of food cubes and a water stone in good repair, traveling to dungeons was no longer an issue. Even though from the perspective of a person on foot, these dungeons were spaced sadistically far apart, they stayed in high hopes.

Earlier, when potential starvation was in play, Matt and the guardian had opted to focus on looting ruins. They neglected all other concerns, including moving in the direction of their next dungeon. By the time they found the food storage bunker, they were days away from the nearest dungeon entrance.

After a long trek to the dungeon, they found it incredibly overleveled. It was designed for a party at level 15, and Matt checked and double-checked with the system that going inside would mean instant death. Eventually, they gave up trying to probe the dungeon. That meant leaving in another direction until they got far enough away that the compass would switch to the next-nearest dungeon. It would potentially take days.

But they had nothing better to do. Well, one thing—without anyone else to talk to, they were starting to get on each other's nerves.

"Got it, mentally renaming you to 'The Guardian of Edible Property'."

"STOP!" Apparently, Matt had screwed up. The guardian's face now showed a spectrum of emotions, including fear, horror, and anger. Chill was not included in the collection. Matt watched as the guardian's eyes focused in on one of her system screens that he couldn't see. He wasn't even sure if they existed in a proper sense, or if she was just programmed to look as if she was reading them. "Oh god, you were joking. Thank goodness. Never do that again."

"I won't." Matt tried and failed to choose his next words carefully. "But . . . never do what now?"

"I'm going to say this very slowly, and I want you to answer just as slow. Do you think you were always supposed to call me 'system guardian?' Like, that was my name, forever, just that?"

"It's how you introduced yourself! Is that not your name?"

"Right now it is. And once, just once for free, you are actually allowed to rename me. And if you were the least bit serious about that joke before, I have no doubt that the system would have used that to screw with us."

"So no renaming?"

"Don't even think about it. The whole system runs off intent. Just . . . don't."

Matt took a shot at not thinking of new names for the guardian. It was harder than it looked.

"Um . . ."

"You renamed me, didn't you?"

"Maybe."

"Oh, dammit, Matt." The guardian called back up her screen, and looked at it for a moment. After a few seconds, she showed a whisper of a smile, closed the screen, and abruptly started walking again. "Come on now, we don't have all day."

"So . . . you don't hate it?" Matt asked.

The guardian was desperately trying to avoid eye contact and kept her voice steady. "I swear to you, Matt. If you don't stop talking, I'm going to figure out how to achieve corporeality and beat you to death."

Even a guardian deserved dignity. Matt was trying to keep a straight face and was so, so close to making it.

"Got it, Lucy."

* * *

The next dungeon was, like most important things in Matt's life now, buried under a layer of thick red soil. When the compass started spinning around wildly, indicating that they had arrived, Matt was standing on a barren, featureless flatland that stretched miles in every direction. He groaned, unstrapped his shovel, and got to work. After just a few shovelfuls of dirt, he punched through to a cavity beneath the surface. Widening the hole and lowering himself down, he found himself in a hole very much like the first dungeon he had found.

"Lucy, Guardian, why isn't this buried completely? I can't believe that I've gotten this lucky twice."

"I don't know. I'm not all-knowing. My guess would be that the dungeons expend some small amount of energy in keeping the area directly in front of their entrances clean."

That actually fit the evidence. The hole was about big enough for a party of three or four adventurers to gather in, and the walls were oddly smooth. More importantly, this dungeon was only level 3. It was appropriately leveled, at least in comparison to what Matt had handled before.

"Ugh, I almost wish this was working out worse."

"What? Why? Craving more digging?"

"No, it's just . . ." Matt paused before he voiced a nagging thought. "Things have been going wrong for me since I got here. Lately, things have been going better. I have a shovel, I found food, and I didn't have to dig here. They're great. But I feel like I've used up my luck now. I'm almost afraid to go in."

Lucy looked solemnly at Matt. She pursed her lips, probably realizing that this wasn't the time for another sarcastic quip. "I think I understand. But the dungeons have no concept of luck. It's programmed to be fair, even if it's a little random."

Despite the reassurance, Matt's heart was in his throat as he activated the entrance pylon. There was no way this would work out well.

A woody *thwing* sounded through the woods as Matt's latest trap was sprung, flooded by a meaty squishing noise and a yelp as the spikes landed home. The trap had worked perfectly and impaled the heart of something that the system called a Windwolf. Against all odds, this was the last Windwolf in the entire forest, and Matt didn't have even a scratch on him.

The Windwolves were about the size of Earth wolves. So halfway between something that Matt didn't want to tangle with and a cute animal that evoked nostalgia. Like Earth wolves, they came equipped with sharp fangs for biting. They also had tons of ropey muscle, implying a kind of animal strength that Matt had no interest in testing.

Unlike Earth wolves, however, the Windwolves didn't appear to have a very refined sense of smell or sight. When Matt first saw one, he had assumed that it would howl for its friends and hunt Matt down. He'd get chased down by a group of them and have his throat torn out. But not only did the wolf's pack fail to materialize, the wolf itself didn't even notice him.

That pattern continued as he set up his traps. He was dealing with the least alert canines he could imagine.

The traps themselves were much improved as well. Between the trap spikes he got from the last dungeon and some of the more jagged pieces of metal that he had salvaged from various ruins, the hide-piercing capabilities of his arsenal had skyrocketed.

Even without considering the advantages of the metal components, the quality of the traps were also higher. He could spend an enormous amount of time crafting a single perfect trip of elastic wood to set the spikes into. Then, his system skill would help mass produce the same component with nothing more than additional wood, his multitool, and time. He was like a trap-making factory. Now, every trap he made was the best he had ever built, and it showed.

Unfortunately, the prizes from the dungeon weren't anything to write home about. Matt finally broke down and took one of the improved Survivor's garb set pieces, receiving an improved pair of boots with steel plating worked into the leather. With those in hand and no new achievements to be seen, he was ready to go.

"Well, that went well!" Lucy was unusually chipper, considering the relatively boring way everything had gone. "Next dungeon?"

"Yup. Let's get going."

Matt's next dungeon was at the bottom of a large hill. It was the first one that he had come across that wasn't obscured in any way. They saw it from far away, saving them from having to dig or climb through gaps in the terrain to get to it. As long as you ignored the fact that the dungeon was balanced for a party rather than an individual, this was the first plinth Matt activated that he was overleveled for. It was just a level-2 dungeon.

Matt's more paranoid instincts were going crazy. There was no way luck could last this long. And sure enough, he was dropped directly next to a group of ten catlike creatures. They were close enough that he didn't even have time to check the dungeon objective notification before they were on him. He had no other option but pulling out his knife and fighting.

Dexterity stat increases by themselves had never been that big of an advantage for Matt, and the same went for the Survivor's Combat skill. He had become so used to fighting with traps that hand-to-hand combat felt foreign to him. But now, with both the stat increases and Survivor's Combat leveling up, something clicked. His footwork and positioning were on point, the cats had to swerve at awkward angles and only a few could attack him at any given time. His reflexes were insane compared to anything he ever had on Earth, and he could dodge the attacks with plenty of room to spare. His knife work also fell together in a way it never had before, each swing found its target and put them down with ease.

Within two minutes, he was the last survivor of the battle, only slightly injured and standing over the corpses of ten very dead cats.

For the first time, the improved Survivor's garb set didn't come up as an option. It didn't matter. As soon as he saw the prize list, he knew what he had to get.

Lucy tried to present herself as a very tough and self-sufficient guide, one who brooked no nonsense and approached life with a serious outlook. However, the effect of all that effort was a bit lost when she stood over Matt's cooking-fuel-driven fire, trying and failing not to grin like a loon at a pot of survival-cube soup.

"I can't believe you got a stupid pot instead of something useful."

"Oh, you should see the look on your face. Believe me, it's worth it."

With two easy victories under his belt, Matt was hopeful. Most video games had a difficulty curve. They got harder as the game progressed, but as long as you kept your character's development ahead of the curve, the game would become easier as time went on. At the moment, Matt was seeing every indication that he had beaten the curve. As long as he kept to the correct dungeon levels, he was safe.

When the third dungeon in a row was leveled appropriately for what he could handle, he took it as confirmation that fate was finally on his side.

"Now remember," Lucy said in full guide mode, "When the prizes pop up, you have to consult me before you pick. It's only 'haha, let's make funny soup' until you pass up on a terraforming relic or something."

"I don't think that's likely to be an option on the garden planet, really."

"No, but tell me anyway. What I'm really looking for is something that we can use for . . ." Lucy hesitated in a way Matt recognized as having to do with talking about his Gaia authority. " . . .Bigger things. I have no idea what that would be, but two heads are better than one. Just loop me in."

"Got it."

Ding!

The system had been pretty calm lately, and Matt had gotten used to the quiet. He almost jumped out of his skin at this one, and it only got worse as he read it.

> *Warning!*
> Some paths are not meant for a reincarnator. Certain courses of action and forms of knowledge are a deviation from the correct path. Your current actions and discussion indicate an intention to pursue prohibited paths. Desist.

This was the only order he had ever received from the system, and it was a huge departure from the normal mock-helpful tone he was used to. He relayed the message to Lucy.

"Oh, screw that. If the system wanted you not to pursue this, there were dozens of ways it could have prevented it. Easy ways. It was lazy, and it just wants us to sit on our asses? No, Matt. Absolutely not."

"For once, I agree. System, if you are listening, no. Get us off the planet, and we can talk. Since you don't seem to want to do that, screw off."

"Ooh, look at big brave Matt, standing up for himself." Lucy took a position off to Matt's side as he approached the stone pillar to enter the dungeon.

"Not that brave. It's not like it can do much."

Matt's hand fell down on the plinth, then all hell broke loose.

CHAPTER TWENTY-FOUR

Things Can Always Get Worse

In the moments after his teleportation, Matt's mind was filled with an all-encompassing giant of an intrusive thought.

How would I possibly describe everything that's happened to me back to anyone I knew on Earth?

Just the concept of teleportation alone would be sensational. Most sci-fi shows with teleportation back on Earth had never bothered to explain what the act of moving from point A to point B felt like.

Now, Matt knew. His first unexpected transfer to a dungeon had taught him something that no one else on Earth knew. Teleportation didn't feel like anything at all. He was just whisked away and suddenly conscious of being in a new place. Sometimes that was the dungeon itself, other times it was a bodyless in-between place.

This time was different. This time, the teleport *yanked*. There was no smooth, seamless transition. It felt like a rough pull that seemed to tear him apart atom by atom. He was dimly aware of the process throughout, hanging in a kind of half-existence for what could have been anywhere from a very long fraction of a second to a very short year.

Eventually, he arrived at the same non-existence space he had experienced on his first teleport. But something felt wrong.

Where once there was no sensation at all from the space, now there was. Matt still had no sense of having a physical body, but something about the space now carried a sort of charge he could sense. Like a mental field of static. The sheer weirdness of Matt's second life had rendered him mostly immune to finding certain things odd. This felt different. Matt's head was ringing with paranoid thoughts.

Ding!

Error. Multiple entrant verification checksums failed. Analyzing . . .

That didn't sound good. The system seemed remarkably bad at fixing errors and had estimated it would take years to get Matt off the planet. He hoped the dungeon system would prove better at fixing things, especially because he had no idea how long he could survive in this form. Even if he couldn't starve or die of thirst in this state, he didn't look forward to months or years existing in a state of stimulation-free nothingness.

> Error cause discovered. Participant has changed a number of system-level dungeon spawn preferences:
> Challenge Mode: Enabled
> Foe Spawn Distance Forcing: Adjacent
> Dungeon Mission Blind Mode: Enabled
> System Guardian Participation: Excluded
>
> WARNING! This combination of dungeon preferences is untested and may result in errors. Proceeding under the current settings will result in an approximated 400 percent increase in dungeon difficulty. Would you still like to proceed?
>
> Yes/No

No, not a chance, Matt thought, immediately. He was surviving appropriately leveled dungeons just fine, but was also keenly aware of how that survivability hung in a delicate balance. He wasn't sure he would come out on top with a ten percent increase in difficulty, let alone something designed for a level 12. He mentally forced as much of a negative response as he could muster, something between "*No, never, under any circumstances,*" and "*Are you insane? Absolutely not.*"

The window didn't respond in the slightest.

This is bad. Matt tried desperately to cancel the dungeon. He mentally envisioned a finger, then directed it to poke at the "no." There was no response. Then, suddenly, the window *glitched.* Just for a moment, the static electricity feeling he'd been sensing surged up, and the screen scrambled like a faulty digital television signal. *This isn't good,* he thought. *There's no way that's good.*

> *Entrant Response Accepted!*
>
> You have opted to challenge this dungeon at maximum settings. Be warned: your foes will no longer keep their regular patterns. The environment will contain several enemies, consistent with a "swarm" type challenge.
>
> Your initial spawn will be close to at least one threat, and your objectives will not be given to you. Your guardian is excluded from the dungeon itself and may not communicate with you or offer guidance in any form.
>
> On successful completion, your rewards will be adjusted relative to the difference between your level and the level of the dungeon. Good luck, challenger!

No! No! Matt mentally screamed. *I didn't adjust any settings! I refuse!*

And then he was conscious, in the dark. Whatever light was present when he woke up was dim enough that he could barely see a quick motion of something headed towards his face. He didn't have time to dodge the claw, fang, or whatever else it was. For a second after the hit, he felt nothing. It was as if the enemy missed.

A wave of pain exploded around his eye. He screamed.

Adrenaline being what it was, Matt was on his feet and running well before he could have consciously decided to. He wasn't quick enough to escape a second attack that raked across his feet, but his brand new armored boots stopped the attack.

He was running nearly blind. Not only was it dark enough that he only had impressions of the space he was running through, he also couldn't open his right eye. The pain was pulsing in waves. He put his hand to the wound, and it came away hot and wet.

Matt ripped the torch from the strap on his Survivor's pack, infinitely grateful that it was long enough that an earlier him decided against packing it away. The auto-light function activated after what felt like an eternity, giving him a hazy vision of where he was.

It was some kind of mine or cave system. The sides were made entirely of rock with only the thinnest layer of dust cushioning his steps. Glancing behind him, he caught the outline of what was chasing him. The light was dim, but enough to see that the monster was large, low to the ground, quadrupedal, and quick. Its gait was more of a scurry than a gallop. Thankfully.

Matt was too shocked from his injuries and moving too fast to get any more details than that. He could hear the footfalls behind him, heavy and powerful. The monster didn't seem to be gaining on him, but Matt also wasn't widening the gap.

Turning his attention to the path in front of him, Matt saw the glint of a new set of claws flashing at his face. He slowed down, barely avoiding the swipe. The animal lashed out again, and again, and again. It gave him zero breathing room or ability to recover.

Matt reflexively shoved the torch forward and heard a hiss as the fire singed the animal. The cave smelled a bit like filthy hair. In the meantime, the steps from the first monster were rapidly getting closer. He was about to be in a lot of trouble.

A moment later, Survivor's Instincts virtually yelled at him to move to his left. He didn't question it. Diving to the left, he heard the two animals slam into each other. Then, he was falling down something.

When he finally hit the ground, the impact blasted the torch from his hand like a cork from a champagne bottle. The sudden deceleration had pushed every atom of air from his lungs, but he forced his body to crawl after the torch. He couldn't survive without light.

A sharp pain blossomed in his arm when he tried to put weight on it. Maybe it was broken. He let it hang limply at his side. Above, he could hear the animals squabbling at each other in high-pitched shrieking noises. He hoped they were fighting but couldn't count on them doing so for long.

When Matt got the torch, he realized that he had no good way of picking it up. He had been crawling because it was the only signal his mind could give his body. Now that he wanted to stand, he realized that his legs were like pudding. Completely useless.

For a second, he considered giving up. But something in him gave him energy to bite the torch and carry it in his mouth. The flame from the torch cooked the side of his face as he fumbled it into position. He tried to scramble as far away as he could from whatever shaft or cliff he had fallen down. His knees were still usable as he lifted and pushed with them.

Behind him, he could hear motions and claws scraping rock. The things were after him.

He couldn't fight. He couldn't stand. That left hiding. Matt desperately shook his head and used the light to make sense of the space he was in. There was nothing. He was in a bare rock tunnel, just like the one before.

The torchlight flickered, casting shadows that looked like monsters. The sounds were also growing louder. He had maybe a couple of breaths left before the monsters were on him again.

Matt took another look at his surroundings when he saw it. There was a small gap in the rock wall, barely big enough where he might be able to squeeze through it on his stomach. He was next to it in seconds.

He quickly shifted his pack off his broken arm. Another wave of pain as the motion shifted the broken bones in his arm. Using precious seconds, he slid the pack as far into the crack as he could before diving in himself.

It wasn't tall enough for him to fit. He forced the issue. As he buried his torso, the roof and floor of the crack ripped his skin and forced all the air from his lungs. He couldn't breathe. He pushed on, only able to move because of the crack's slight downwards incline.

As Matt got the majority of his body into the crack, it widened out just enough that he could take a labored gasp of air. His torch, falling ahead of him, showed a small space just beyond where he was. It was a pocket maybe big enough to accommodate his body.

At this point, almost his entire body was in the crack. Only his feet were still outside. Matt desperately reached forward, trying to gain leverage to squeeze further. Then, he felt a breath of air on his ankle. Moments later, one of the animals' jaws closed on his ankle. It was sharp. Matt felt the feeling go out of his lower leg as he screamed soundlessly from his airless lungs.

The blood flowed downwards, slicking his body enough that he could pull through to the cavity with his one good arm. Behind him, the thing clawed at his legs, apparently unable to traverse the crack itself.

He was through. Blood seemed to fill the cavity. Everywhere he looked was dotted with red. This was beyond what he had experienced before. The blood just gushed out of his leg and face.

As quickly as he could, he knotted his rope into a loop and made a tourniquet for his leg with one of the trap spikes. It wasn't perfect, but there was some small chance it would be enough.

Suddenly, the adrenaline left Matt. He fought to keep his eyes open.

The torch. I have to put out the torch.

He managed to snuff it just a few moments before he lost consciousness.

I guess it was never going to be that easy.

Matt was glad to be alive. He wasn't meant to survive the encounter with the first monster, let alone the second. The combination of dumb luck with the cavity and Survivor's Instincts kicking into overdrive saved his life.

He also learned something new. Vitality had patched him up. He wasn't glad to learn that his vitality came with significant limitations.

His foot was gone. The end of his leg had healed somehow. He was no longer bleeding and new skin covered the stump. His right eye's vision was also dark. It had healed enough that it didn't hurt anymore, but it seemed like seeing from it again was beyond his regenerative powers' ability.

The one good thing was that his pack was next to him. Matt fumbled around for the canteen and used the water to wash the scabbed blood from his face. He drank and ate, safe for now.

Then, reality hit him. For the first time since landing on Gaia, Matt started crying.

He was crippled, in the dark, and surrounded by gigantic monsters that were easily capable of killing him. And once again, he was alone.

CHAPTER TWENTY-FIVE

Let's Make a Deal

For better or worse, Matt had time.

The monster that took his foot had scratched and struggled around the crack to try and finish the job, but couldn't do much about solid rock. Eventually, it lost interest and left. When other monsters came around, Matt tried his best to be silent and listen as they stopped and sniffed the air before also trying and failing to dig or squeeze their way to him.

Combined with the dark environment, Matt had pretty good evidence that these monsters were scent hunters. That wasn't good for him, since his nose was nowhere near as good. But at least they were hunters who couldn't reach him for now. They also appeared to be solitary, and never moved in packs. In a normal iteration of this dungeon, there would probably only be a single one of them, but the swarm monster option had increased their numbers without changing their normal solitary behavior.

Somewhere, Lucy is freaking out. The system hadn't mentioned what it had done with her. For what Matt knew, she was likely still standing alone outside the dungeon, wondering what the hell happened. Every minute he spent in this hole was one she was likely spending stressed and worried, or at the very least, cussing him out and calling him stupid.

I still need to be smart about this.

As much as he wanted to get out of the cold and darkness, his rational mind told him to make good choices. The first was to wait. His foot and eye didn't seem like they were planning on regenerating any further, but maybe vitality would surprise him. And he had no idea how the monsters actually moved and behaved. In a situation where any surprise might kill him, it was worth gathering all the information he could. He had plenty of food and water, so he waited.

After a couple of days, Matt's foot and eye still had not come back, but he did learn some things. The most important of which was that the animals never seemed to double back. When one of them passed, it would be at least several minutes before the next monster came by.

He also figured out how to hide his presence in the crack. At the end of the first day of waiting, one particularly motivated cave monster managed to wake him from what little sleep he was getting. Annoyed enough to work against his fear and with nothing to lose, he looked in his pack for anything worthless enough to chuck at the monster. It wasn't exactly the smartest thing to do, but it would make him feel better. That was important. He wasn't about to pass up a morale-building opportunity.

After a quick inventory, most of his possessions were eliminated from the running. The torch was valuable and finite. His weapons were also best kept on him. Even trying to put together a spear seemed like a bad idea when the monster might yank the blade away. In the end, Matt was left with one obvious option: his bag of dust.

Not every bag of food cubes he'd found in the storage chest had survived the test of time. At the time, he had decided to take some of the horrifying rotted dust that resulted from years of decay. He'd combined multiple bags' worth of dust into a single package, and also added to it when he encountered similar dust in the storage depot. With plenty of it and no clear use, he had no reason not to chuck a handful of it at a giant subterranean horror.

Surprisingly, this had a huge effect. The little bits that actually made it to the animal clearly freaked it out. It pulled back from the crack and Matt could hear it rolling around outside. It spent quite a while trying to clear the dust from its fur before moving on.

More importantly, the much larger portion of dust from Matt's throw had ended up on the floor, and seemed to mask his scent. Subsequent monsters, which Matt named moles, would walk near it and immediately give up on the crack when they smelled the stuff in there.

Good. That's something. Let's keep finding things like that.

After a day and a half more of rest with no real improvement to his physical predicament, Matt started working on preparations to go out. The first came in the form of improvements to the crack itself.

He had sneaked a few minutes between monsters to examine his surroundings and found that he had taken the worst possible route through it. A foot to the left, there was a slightly larger path that led to the same cavity. With a bit of chipping from his multitool, he managed to build a method for him to get in and out of the crack quickly without widening the mouth of the crack. It was as good as escape routes went.

After that, he worked on a much bigger problem: mitigating the loss of a foot. With one of his boots presumably lost to the stomach of an underground abomination, he packed the other boot with pieces of metal and cloth from the tunic when he first arrived at Gaia, shaping it to more or less fit the stump. Using the laces and pieces of rope to lash his contraption to his leg, he eventually found a way to slowly hobble around on both legs. It was painful as hell, but he wouldn't have to crawl.

Leaving the crack, the experimentation continued. He found that while the beasts didn't like the dust, it wasn't exactly repellent. He laid down a thin line of it from wall-to-wall at the narrowest part of the cave. They walked over it.

Matt also found that "cave" was probably the wrong term for where he was at. Not far from his crack, he found a pile of rubble tucked away in an alcove. It could have been from some kind of cave-in, but it looked more like an intentional debris dump, something planned by workers as opposed to naturally occurring.

He had to keep these outings as short as possible. A day or so of waiting had shown him that the minimum time he could count on between animals was less than two minutes. He'd leap out, hobble, do some work, learn some things, and scurry back. Every time he'd learn something new.

At some point, he learned that a tripwire trap wouldn't work. A full day's worth of hidden-hole fabrication efforts were just enough to cobble together a trap out of tentpoles and trap spikes. Although Matt wasn't hoping for the trap to seriously hurt the monsters, he was still disappointed when the monsters stepped over his tripwire with so much care that he suspected the dungeon was cheating.

It didn't matter. It was still information. He put it with the rest of what he was learning.

In between excursions, he had time to kill and questions to ask. The first task he set himself to was spending some time with his system interface. During his time on Gaia, he had come to have a grudging respect for the sheer enormity of system windows available to him. Most of them were useless to him, with names like "magical atmospheric conditions" containing a massive amount of "N/A" indicators wherever information might go. He assumed they were for other classes, left in place and empty, rather than fully locked away from him. He'd seen hundreds of windows like these.

It took him about an hour of trying different dungeon-related queries to find the exact window he was looking for, one packed with automatic preferences for interacting with the dungeons. The dungeon system at least didn't appear to be lying about his settings, and all the various toggles it had mentioned were set to the difficulty-enhancing levels it had claimed.

In Matt's thinking, that meant two things. First, someone had messed with his settings, and there were only three possible culprits to blame. It was simple to rule himself out, even in terms of doing it by accident. He hadn't known this window existed, and it wasn't easy to find. Unless he was a much smarter sleepwalker than he had any reason to believe, this wasn't a crazy mess-up on his part.

Lucy might have done it, but every interaction he'd ever had with her indicated that she wasn't able to see his system screen, let alone interact with it. It was possible she had spent all this time working an incredibly complex long con, but he doubted she was capable of it. On top of that, he just didn't *feel* like she had any reason to. Things had been much better lately between them. Despite her early history of asking him to die, he felt like they were friends now. And friends did not booby trap friends' dungeons.

Even if he still wanted to suspect her, there was a much more likely villain in play: the system itself. With few other ways to learn about the problem, he queried it again and again. Lucy had told him it wasn't actually allowed to fully ignore questions under its own ruleset, and at first, it seemed to try to circumvent this with nonanswer responses. But even those responses contained nuggets of information.

> Invalid Query. The system cannot directly harm a reincarnator.

> Invalid Query. The system cannot alter system settings against the expressed wishes of reincarnated individuals.

> Invalid Query. The system does not "try to shank" reincarnators. Every action the system takes must directly create a possibility of growth for the individual the action affects.

> Invalid Query. Death is always a risk for reincarnators, as it is for any being. No aspect of the existence of harm was ever in question.

After hundreds of these questions, Matt had a good idea of what happened. The system's carefully worded responses left a negative space of loopholes, one that ended with a course of action suspiciously like what had happened.

Had Matt expressly commanded the system not to change his dungeon settings? He hadn't. It took him a full day to find the toggle that let him unambiguously make it clear that the system was not allowed to do this, and set it to "deny."

Had the system *directly* tried to harm him? Nope. All the harms were indirect, inflicted by the dungeon working in the normal ways dungeons worked, even if the danger was amplified tenfold by the system's interference.

It was even arguable that this challenge, if overcome, would result in growth for Matt. It wasn't like there weren't rewards. And, it wasn't as if he wasn't learning things. Death really had always been a risk since he landed on Gaia.

In the end, Matt came to two big conclusions. The first was the system had done this. Was there a small possibility he was wrong? Sure, but not one he took seriously. The system was out to get him. The question was now why. The first schism with the system had come when Matt had tried to use his Gaia authority. Something about it had marked Matt as a problem to the system, but it wasn't like he had gained it recently. The pattern of system behavior wasn't adding up.

Second, the system was willing to deal. After hours of fruitless questioning, it dropped the real bombshell.

> *Quest: Give Up*
>
> The system can't remove a reincarnator's life, but it can give them a new one. Death hurts, but you know from experience it doesn't hurt forever. Giving up gives the system an opportunity to correct its mistakes.
>
> We can fix this.
>
> Rewards: Guaranteed reincarnation, increased system support, and assignment of an improved system guardian.

CHAPTER TWENTY-SIX

Stupid Was Becoming His Entire Brand

Matt had read plenty of stories where a villain tried to tempt one of the protagonist's friends into betrayal. They'd always feel so fake. Why wouldn't the friend just say no? Even to the character within the story, it should have been obvious which way the wind was blowing. If they said no, they'd be no worse off than before. Whereas, if they said yes, they'd be a villain.

But applied to Matt? It felt different. He understood why the characters always took the offer. There was hardly anything he wanted more than a fresh start, especially after being cheated out of two separate lives. The system was offering him that opportunity. It would find him a new planet, presumably check to make sure that it was good before sending him there, and also throw in some extra help as a bonus.

All he had to do was crawl outside and wait. Would getting eaten hurt? Sure. But Matt was no stranger to pain. It didn't even have to be that complicated. There was nothing in the quest that demanded he give himself up to the monsters outside. He could do the deed himself, right where he was. Given what the system was offering, it would be hard to even think of it as suicide.

Only one thing stopped him, and it was a single line of text he could sense the system didn't want him to think about very hard.

The assignment of an improved system guardian.

It might have been talking about making Lucy stronger or smarter. That was possible, except that the wording wasn't "improve his system guardian." It said it would assign him a better guardian, without a single mention of what would happen to Lucy.

She had never said so outright, but Matt guessed that the end of him also meant the end of her. Could the system keep her alive and healthy? Maybe, but Matt had a sense that the system wouldn't bother with that even if it could.

The system's offer was everything he wanted. He could be alive and strong. He could be a hero. He just had to betray one mostly fake girl, and he would have everything.

Five years, he thought. *She waited here for five years. And she's the only one who's truly on my side.*

He couldn't really trust the system after the stunt that it pulled, but even if he could, the five years Lucy had spent alone would be enough. It didn't matter if the system could put him on the best possible planet and guarantee the best possible outcomes. He didn't consider himself a saint, but he still had to live with himself. And a clean life that didn't last long was still better than a long one wracked by guilt.

"Screw you, system." Matt wrenched himself onto his ruined leg. He had work to do.

Gathering the rocks took about a week. Every trip to the rubble pile and back was a hurried thing, with him hobbling as fast as he could through the excruciating pain of using his footless leg. Some trips, he didn't even make it to the pile. He'd abort when it became clear that his speed was slower than usual, and would return empty-handed.

In comparison, building the walls was difficult in a different way. He didn't have glue or cement, so Matt had to stack each rock in a way where they wouldn't fall down. It was a puzzle-assembling art he had to learn on the job, and the wall would tumble down with any mistake. It was worse because he had to leave a path for the monsters to go through, hoping they didn't knock everything down as they passed. More than once, they did, making him start all over. But he got better at it. He had time.

Eventually, everything was ready. He strapped on his makeshift foot, popped a few food cubes, and drank some water. He was as ready as he'd ever be. It was time.

Matt "stood," for lack of a better word, by an invention he had come to think of as *the murder wall.* It was two extremely sturdy walls of rocks, with one designed to have a big, stable hole in the center he could stab through.

The two wall segments were meant to be joined together. Plugging this center channel of the wall ended up being the hardest part of the plan. He only had minutes to build the wall before the next monster came.

Matt first made an outer layer with rocks that were wider than the channel. He'd turn them sideways, slip through, turn back, and stack them atop each other. Choosing the right base stones tilted the layer to lean back on the two wall segments with more permanent stone stackings.

He then reinforced the new center with a second layer of pure stone. There wasn't any distinct arrangement to it, just sheer mass. The idea was to draw attention away from the weak center of the wall to the stronger murder hole where Matt was.

Like everything else, stacking the new center in just a few minutes took practice. Matt leaned on his improved strength and stamina, carefully organizing the rocks and building muscle memory. He got it down to building a new wall in just over a minute, hopefully a short enough time that he wouldn't encounter an ambush and have to start all over again.

He hadn't been sure it would work, but he had finished building the center wall in time.

His stump leg was now out of his boot and sitting on a low, flat rock that was cushioned by the same, dependable tunic he relied on for all his textile needs. He could pivot around the rock pretty well, which would hopefully be enough to pierce the monster's hide with his spear.

Building the spear was a hard task, considering the fact that he didn't have any sticks to work with like in the previous dungeons. He lashed his knife to the end of the shovel and created a bizarre piece of gardening weaponry. It didn't look super sturdy, but it was the best he could do. A better option would have been to sharpen the shovel itself, but when he tried that, the Gaian mystery metal was far too tough. A whole hour's worth of grinding made no visible difference.

For a man who had spent over a week in a tiny cavity, the wait didn't feel long. Within a few seconds, a monster approached. Matt had built the wall across the narrowest part of the tunnel, several meters behind the cavity itself. The extra distance during each trip was well worth the saved construction effort, though it did mean that he was effectively cut off from any retreat back to the cavity. He also hoped that the narrowness of the tunnel would keep the monsters from crowding the fortifications, allowing only one or two to approach at a time.

The monster moved closer, curious about the new obstruction blocking its route. Soon, it was within stabbing distance, but Matt held off from attacking. He first had to verify the second component of his plan, something that he hadn't been able to independently test before.

Over the course of Matt's stay at Château Du Cave, the beasts had become more or less accustomed to the smell of black dust from the rotted emergency food. With it now wetted and smeared all over his body, it seemed that the monsters couldn't "see" him very well.

They really do rely on smell, Matt thought. *Good. That gives me a shot.* He waited for the beast to get comfortable, letting it investigate until it finally poked it's big, ugly head up to the hole. This was the best look Matt had ever got at the monsters that had attacked him. *Moles, makes sense.*

He then stabbed the thing in the face with everything he had. He aimed at the eye, but a combination of the animal's eyes being slightly to the sides of its head and its instinctive jerk back made him miss, striking it in the forehead instead. The failure of the knife vibrated in the shovel shaft, and he heard a clear sound as the blade cut down to bone. It was a deep gash, but nothing fatal.

The mole hissed loudly and started tearing at the wall. It had begun.

Matt stabbed away for all he was worth, hitting the mole as many times and as hard as possible. He was injuring it, at least to a limited extent. After several seconds, the mole's face was gushing blood, but it wasn't deterred in the slightest. When the second mole came, the first was still standing and actively tearing at the wall.

Matt continued stabbing as hard as he could, hoping to delay the fall of the wall for as long as possible. He had built the wall thick, as thick as he could while sneaking around patrols of cave moles. As he punished the mole, it continued to tear away at the wall, shifting rocks off the stack and destabilizing it. Eventually, it managed to get enough rocks out of the way that half the wall fell forward over it. This too failed to hurt the mole enough to put it out of commission. By this time, there were a total of three moles in the vicinity, and they all rushed through the gap into the wider tunnel beyond, just in time to see Matt's leg disappearing into the second wall.

The second wall was not like the first. Rather than blocking the whole tunnel, this was a semicircle of stones backed up to the side of the cavern, looking more like a castle tower than a wall. He had left a hole in the bottom, one that he could scramble through, but that would hopefully still be too small for the mole to traverse.

It was a semicircle because one horizontal wall had turned out to be his limit. He had tested the stacking in a dozen ways, and he just couldn't plug the holes in the center fast enough for two full walls.

By nature of letting the moles pass, the tower could be designed as a semi-permanent structure, with no last-minute modifications needed. But while it offered all the protection of the walls, it came with no viable escape options short of total victory. Whatever came next would have to work, or he'd be trapped.

As the mole stuck its head through the bottom hole, Matt's knife finally found an eye. The thing thrashed as Matt bore all his weight down on the shovel, riding the weight of the moving head as well as he could on one good leg. Eventually, it pulled back from the wall before falling still and silent. It was his first kill. He had hoped to have three by now. The other moles didn't hesitate to attack the wall in the wake of their friend's death, and Matt started stabbing from the top, delaying them as long as possible.

The moles were brave, but not impervious to pain. Without Matt constantly attacking them, he figured that they could have gotten through both walls in just a minute. Now, it took several. Matt did his best to track the time as the wall slowly eroded under the moles' gross paws.

Matt wasn't able to see enough to be certain, but he felt confident that there were probably five living enemies in the section of tunnel behind the wall. He dropped the spear and turned to a stock of canisters by his feet.

The cooking fuel he had scavenged from the first lockbox was heavy. The only thing that had kept him from ditching the canisters was a distaste for abandoning any resource, given the survival theme of the planet. If he had actually used it for cooking, he would have probably used it up by now. But he hadn't, and now some fun stuff could happen. The canister was meant to slowly heat up a small bag. To keep the gas flow at a sedate pace was a small limiter plug with a hole in the center. That limiter turned out to be removable if someone had enough time and a specific enough tool for the job. With the multitool, Matt turned a couple of canisters into fire hazards.

Now, he twisted the valves open on the canisters one at a time and shoved them out of the murder hole, spewing gas that he knew from experimentation would gather at the bottom of the room. Once they were beyond the wall, Matt used the torch to light a fuel-soaked rope fuse that extended outwards towards mole territory. He then tipped over a large rock to cover his entrance hole, praying that the shelter he had built would be enough to keep himself from getting blown up outright.

Was the plan stupid? Yes. But by now, stupid was becoming his entire brand. He crouched down, covered his ears, and closed his good eye as the fuse finally burned down to meet the gas and start all of his prepared chaos.

The explosion was bigger than he thought it would be. He was hoping for something that might injure the moles, or at least disorient them long enough for him to shimmy out and finish them off. This was not that.

The shock echoed through the cavern and toppled his wall of stones down onto him. He coughed and breathed in a cloud of dust that had been kicked up, and struggled to dig himself out of the rubble.

What he saw gave him a newfound respect for the wisdom of gas canister limiter rings.

In front of him, the moles burned. The light from the remaining fire in the room was predominantly from what little hair they had. The explosion had taken out four of the things, apparently all that were there at the time. He had hoped to get more, but his more immediate concern was that one of the moles had been blasted back to his crack. They were massive animals, probably more than four hundred pounds apiece. He had no chance of shifting them and getting back to safety.

And though the blast had taken out the moles, Matt was less glad to see that the explosion had also collapsed his second wall.

He looked around desperately for the rising of a victory plinth, and was disappointed. That was a problem, especially with the fact that a new, fat mole had just rounded the corner, followed by another two smaller moles.

Matt hadn't seen the fat mole before, at least not clearly. He had heard it, though. One of the moles that crossed the tunnel in front of his hidey-hole had always been louder than the others, clomping along like a hippo. The first few times Matt's walls had been knocked down, it was because of this mole that he named Fatty. Matt had to widen the middle passage just for this special, fat mole.

Now, Fatty stood before Matt in all of his rotund glory, looking hungry and not at all concerned with the other fallen moles. And there was nothing between Matt and Fatty but the smell of burning moles.

CHAPTER TWENTY-SEVEN

Fully Exposed Plinths

As Matt backed away from Fatty, he stumbled over the outstretched leg of a dead mole. As off-balance as he was from missing a full foot, this knocked him flat on his ass.

Without wasting any time, Matt started crawling away. He ditched his spear; there was a near-zero chance he could actually kill one of the moles in a one-on-one fight. It was better to run away faster.

Glancing back, Matt saw that Fatty's speed was limited by his massive body maneuvering around the other dead moles, and a natural fear of fire. The two moles with it made no attempt to rush past, possibly out of deference to Fatty's size.

Adrenaline was surging through Matt. The rough rock floor was tearing away at his knees with every crawl. They were like dozens of pinpricks all at once. His efforts weren't doing much though. From experience, he knew that he couldn't outpace the moles even at a full sprint. Although Fatty wasn't built for speed, it was still faster than him. Much faster.

After a few agonizing seconds, Matt felt a pinch against his leg, and then mind-blowing pain. Fatty had taken his other foot. Matt rolled sideways to see a glimpse of his foot disappearing into the thing's mouth, followed by a heavy gulp from the monster. He yelled, half in pain and half in desperation. Fighting back the shock, Matt inched back a bit more and swung the torch he had kept in his left hand.

Fatty reared off its front legs at the sudden light. With its head back, it roared in defiance of the flame. His too-large bulk slammed against the top of the cave, dislodging even more dust. Matt could hear the other two moles chattering behind the roar, probably waiting for their turn at him.

None of the three seemed to be in a hurry, which made sense. Matt was well past the point at which he could run. He was well past the point where he could put up a fight. As far as they knew, dinner was served.

Matt closed his eyes, etching the image of a roaring mole into his mind. The swing of his torch at Fatty wasn't desperation, he had a plan.

Back home, he had spent enough time as a teenager looking at weaponry on Wikipedia to get a primitive understanding of something called a directional explosive. Claymore mines were directional explosives. At a high level, they were just a layer of C-4 explosive and another layer of ball bearings. To keep the bearings from flying in all directions, the back of the claymore had a heavy metal plate. With a single claymore mine, a soldier could take down a whole group of enemies.

Matt didn't have a heavy metal plate, C-4 explosive, or ball bearings. But he did have a cooking pot with a screw down lid, fuel canisters, and handfuls of weird Gaian mystery metal.

He didn't have a detonator, but he did have the multitool that could turn into a spike and punch a hole in the back of the pot. He also added a few needle-thin holes to the gas fuel canisters before he placed them in the pot. And finally, he had dumped the entire lot of metal into the pot before sealing everything shut.

A couple of days earlier, he had found a nice spot for the contraption. With the lid angled upwards, it was bound to give someone a bad time.

Matt hoped that the earlier explosion hadn't shifted the makeshift claymore, or worse, exploded the thing. His prayer was answered when the torch reached near the back of the pot, and he heard a sizzle.

Fatty was so large he didn't even have to aim the claymore. It just had to work.

And it did work.

Just not the way that Matt expected. He had to close the pot to keep the gas in, and so his directional charge plan hinged on the fact that the metal of the pot was stronger than the threading on the pot's lid. It wasn't.

The entire jerry-rigged apparatus exploded apart. It turned out he hadn't built a claymore. He had built a frag grenade and set it off a few feet from his body.

The result was like a meteor falling through the atmosphere. It tore everything apart.

Matt had secured the pot in place with a couple of heavy rocks. The back was well-supported with a hole for the trigger, the sides as well, and nothing at the front. So when the pot burst, it showered mostly rock and the occasional bits of metal at Matt. He first felt a blast of air hit him, before the rocks and metal came. They pelted him, broke his bones, and burned his skin.

After the shock wore off, Matt was pleasantly surprised that his eye had been spared. He could see the aftermath.

Fatty had gotten the worst of it. One of the mole's legs was completely ripped off, and its body had been perforated by pieces of metal in dozens of places. It laid limp on the ground, hissing softly, but unable to move at all.

It was small comfort to Matt, who was also dying. Matt smiled a bit through agony-clenched teeth.

He laid on the ground, face-to-face with the badly injured mole as they watched each other die. At some point, one of Matt's breaths caught in his chest. He tried to labor the breath out, and found he couldn't. This was it. He had lost.

Suddenly, Matt's eyes shot open again. He was still in the cave, but he was seeing double. It took a second for Matt to register that his other eye had come back. He tried to roll, and instead of phantom pain coming back from his legs, he found himself surprisingly nimble. His feet had come back.

As far as Matt knew, there was only one reason that could be. He had cleared the dungeon. Sure enough, a plinth was rising from the ground only a few meters away. He began to crawl towards it.

Halfway through, he realized how dumb that was.

Wobbling, he stood up on both of his very appreciated feet and made his way to the plinth, which was still rising into place. Before he could relax, he heard something out of place.

It was the chatter of a mole.

Looking back, Matt saw Fatty's two assistants looking back at him. More importantly, they were unharmed. Fatty's sheer size had absorbed the blast and protected his two assistants, and they looked ready for revenge. Or a meal. Probably both.

Matt slapped his hand on the plinth, but nothing happened. It apparently needed to be fully exposed to work. *Come on, come on!* he mentally screamed.

Finally, the plinth was almost up, and Matt jerked his hand towards it only a fraction of a second too late to avoid the full weight of a mole slamming into him like a mutant, underground linebacker.

Matt's entire world turned into pain as the two animals flung him around like a ragdoll. He was bitten and scratched and bitten again, so fast he couldn't track the damage. He resisted as much as he could, but it was futile. It wasn't even a fair fight. Finally, he went limp under a pile of mole, just at the base of the unused plinth. For a few seconds, there was nothing but the sounds of mole teeth clacking through muscle and bone.

Then a bloody arm shot out of the pile, touched the plinth, and the whole dungeon ceased to exist.

* * *

"Matt! Matt!" As Matt struggled back to consciousness, Lucy's voice was more than loud enough to cut through the fog and hurry the process along. He opened his eyes to see a frantic little girl, one frightened enough to have forgotten she couldn't actually touch him with her tiny holographic fists. She soon noticed his open eyes. "You're awake! Are you okay?"

Matt realized that he didn't know. He did a quick inventory, finding all the normal Matt-parts in all the normal places. Apparently, the teleport out of the dungeon allowed for the same kind of full auto-heal as a victory inside it. Maybe the dungeons were all just a bad dream—he'd ask Lucy about it later.

"I'm fine, I think. How long was I out?" Matt asked.

"What the hell happened?" Lucy ignored Matt's question.

"Things got . . . pretty bad right at the end. I think I might have fainted." Matt reached towards her and pantomimed a reassuring shoulder pat. "I'm fine now."

"Fine? You were gone for weeks! I got nothing, Matt. No notifications, no system alerts, nothing. What happened?"

"I think . . ." Matt paused as he realized he didn't need to assume. He knew the truth. "The system tried to kill me."

He recounted everything that had happened, from the weird teleport to the horrifying welcome of an overpowered dungeon. He explained the time he had spent away was because of the sheer number of preparations he had to do to have even the barest chance of winning. He briefly considered sparing her the gory details, but decided she had a right to know. Whether she was there or not, she went through the same risks he did.

He ended with the understatement of the year: "I thought the first few dungeons were close calls. I had no idea."

"Oh, Matt. Oh, shit. I'm so sorry." Matt could see her putting together her next sentence carefully. "I, uh, believe you when you say you think the system did this. But are you absolutely sure? It's very lazy, Matt, but that doesn't necessarily make it a murderer."

Matt told her about the questions he'd asked the system while he was hiding in the dark, and how he had triangulated the possibility that it tried to use the dungeon as a weapon.

"And there's one other thing. While I was down there, hiding? It tried to make a deal," Matt said.

"What kind of deal?" Lucy asked.

"It offered me another chance at reincarnation, to another planet. With increased support, no less."

"Wait! That's incredible. The system doesn't usually admit or fix its mistakes. Why . . . why didn't you take it?" Lucy began to hesitate by the end of her sentence.

"Part of the reward was the assignment of a new, improved system guardian."

"Oh," Lucy said in a small voice. She blinked. "OH. That fucking asshole."

"Agreed." Matt sat down on the ground. It was hard for him to be upset after what he had just gone through. There was no better feeling than surviving a near-death situation, and having feet. Even the system's betrayal couldn't damper his happiness.

"Still, though, Matt. You probably should have taken it." Lucy looked serious. "If I'm being honest, it's not like our chances of survival are that good anyway, especially with the system against us. Do you think if you asked, it would . . ."

"Guardian! Lucy! Look at me. Look at my eyes," Matt yelled, surprising himself. He waited until Lucy looked directly at him. "No. Absolutely not. We're a team. We have no idea what that jerk would have done with you. We aren't doing that. Not now, not ever."

Lucy eyes betrayed conflicting emotions. After a few moments, her expressions firmed up, and she nodded. Matt nodded back.

"Now that that's done, I honestly need to sleep a little. I'm sorry. I know you must have been bored while I was gone."

"No, I'm . . . just glad to have you back. Honestly. But Matt, before you go to bed, what did you get as a reward? You just went to a level ten dungeon. Maybe even level fifteen. What was the loot?"

Matt hadn't thought about that. He pulled open his notifications, noting that none of them had come directly from the system. No surprise there. He couldn't imagine the system was going to give out many rewards right now, or in the future. The rules might force it to, but it wasn't something Matt could count on.

But there were notifications from the dungeon system, notifications that confirmed Matt's suspicions that the dungeons ran on a different OS than the system. He saw the reward, and his jaw went slack.

What is it, Matt?"

He told her. Her eyes lit up.

"Oh, *hell yes.*"

CHAPTER TWENTY-EIGHT

Any Place is About as Good as Any Other

Lucy was right.

The system notifications were of a "hell yes" quality, perhaps even bordering on "fuck yeah" level. More importantly, this gave confirmation that the general system and dungeon system were distinct. Perhaps the biggest tell was that the dungeon system's windows were a different color than the system's.

If the dungeon system was just another part of the general system, that would make it really easy for the system to keep screwing with Matt. Although the fact that the system had to mess with Matt's settings to modify the dungeon had implied a separation, it wasn't concrete proof. With Matt's life on the line, he was reluctant to leave something at "maybe."

The first dungeon notification solved those maybes.

Dungeon Entrant Checksum Error Assessment
On entrance to this dungeon, the entrant's system file was found to have several recent changes. This, combined with verbal objections to dungeon settings, implies an error. In light of this, a previous positive response to the dungeon entrance confirmation implies outside interference in the entrant's system, the dungeon, or both.

Due to inconveniences imposed on the entrant, and to limit the severity of future occurrences of errors, additional prizes have been awarded.

Rewards:
System Screen Enhancement Token: User preference lock, Reinforced Survivor's

Garb Set (Fewer previously acquired pieces), Lesser Repair Stones, 5x

The Survivor's garb and repair stones were nice, but there was a clear winner in terms of the best conversation starter among the prizes.

"Does that mean what I think it does?"

"Probably? We're in weird territory here, I've never heard of such a token. But it sounds like it's going to lock your user preferences down."

"Does that mean the system can't change them again?"

"Matt, honestly, I don't know. I'm surprised it could even do that. The way I understand it, the system really does have to follow a baseline set of rules. From what you explained, it somehow found a loophole where it could pretend it was helping you when changing your preferences."

"Like an 'oh, I thought that's what you wanted' sort of thing?"

"Yeah. But now, it won't have the same excuse."

They talked it over and eventually agreed that while the token wouldn't be a one hundred percent guarantee against shenanigans, Matt didn't have much to lose.

While the general system might have been running a very long con, it sure seemed like the dungeon system was working in opposition to the general system's goals. Nothing was certain, but it was a good sign. And the token wasn't even the real showstopper. Not by a long shot.

Elite Dungeon Conquest Completed
You have completed this dungeon at the highest possible optional difficulty settings. In addition to this feat, you managed the following accomplishments:

[Alpha Beast] (Optional)
An alpha beast has spawned! Alpha beasts are rare variants of normal run-of-the-mill foes. Face it if you dare.

[Double Dare] (Hidden Accomplishment)
You returned from certain death twice in one dungeon. Non-repeatable.

[Chateau De Dungeon] (Hidden Accomplishment)
You have established a secure residence within a naturally occurring aspect of the dungeon and lived there for longer than a week. Non-repeatable.

[Offer Is on the Table]
You have left a dungeon without claiming your reward. Non-repeatable.

Assessing appropriate rewards . . .

For completing *[Offer Is on the Table]* you have been rewarded:
One-time Teleportation to Dungeon Entrance Plinth Token
Dungeon Reward Retrieval Token

"Oh, huh. I hadn't even thought about leaving the rewards behind."

"Ugh, idiot."

"Thanks . . . Now, let's talk about the big one."

[Combined Award]

The other accomplishments have been amassed into a single prize suitable for the feat of defeating a max-difficulty dungeon run alone at a tremendous level disadvantage. Enjoy!

Reward: Property Token—Estate.

Matt once again found himself relying on his video game knowledge. This sounded a lot like something that would allow him to claim real-world Gaian property. Lucy was happy to offer confirmation of that thought.

"The estate token is the best possible thing you could have come up with, Matt. Even with all of your little near-death modifiers, you had to get really lucky to get this. Like winning-the-lottery lucky. It doesn't even make sense."

Unless the dungeon system is on our side. Matt didn't want to express that thought out loud quite yet. He had no idea if the system was listening, and what it might do with that knowledge. He suspected that the truth would come out soon enough. No reason to hurry it.

Even if he wanted to stay awake, he found himself nodding off. He had to sleep. Lucy was pacing, now overexcited, and mumbling to herself about the possibilities of the various tokens.

"I'm going to bed, Lucy."

"What? Oh, yeah, go ahead. I'll think about this more while you sleep."

"Thanks."

It had been a long couple of weeks. It didn't take Matt long to start snoring.

When Matt woke up again, it was time to realize the spoils of his dungeon run. Going through the notifications, he noticed that none of them came from the general system. The experience and stat increases that he had taken for granted never came.

"Oh, that's neat." Lucy was standing next to Matt as he confirmed his loot selection and watched the dungeon materialize the rewards. The dungeon had decided to spit the rewards out from a shimmering blue bubble. A few months ago, this would have been the weirdest thing Matt had ever seen. Now it was just another Tuesday. "You can't see what's going on here, but it's neat."

"Yeah? What's so hot about the bubble?"

"The bubble isn't just for teleporting stuff out. It's *kind of* doing that. But it's more actually building your rewards. It does the same thing within the dungeon but it's rare to see it happen in the real world."

Matt stopped to gather the items as they fell and activated the System Screen Enhancement Token. "What's it making them out of? Energy? Mana? Or something else?"

"Partially, yeah. It's probably cheaper to make it inside the dungeon, where it has more control. I'm guessing that's why it doesn't do this too often," Lucy studied the bubble as she spoke. "The bulk of it is stuff coming from the dungeon, but it's also sucking air into that bubble and pulling apart the atoms or something."

"That *is* neat."

"Yeah, this is the coolest thing I've seen on this forsaken planet." As Lucy finished her thought, the last of the treasure spilled out of the bubble, and it winked out of existence. She pouted for a second.

Matt was already busy shimming into his new armor. It was a nice piece of gear. He had expected it to be heavier or more stifling than his normal Survivor's garb, but the set was surprisingly easy to wear despite being built with defense in mind.

Matt didn't exactly feel safe in it. He wasn't sure he'd ever feel *fully* safe again after those moles. But he felt safer.

When he stooped to pick up the estate token, he found not one but two coins on the ground. "What's this?" he asked Lucy, "Do we get a two-for-one on estates today?"

"No, dummy. One of those is the dungeon prize teleport voucher thing you won."

Thinking back to the rewards screen, there had been three separate screens of rewards—one for leaving his prizes in the dungeon. He hadn't been thinking about rewards when he cleared the dungeon, but the extra bonus was nice.

"It seems like a pretty lame prize, considering you had to take the risk of leaving all of your dungeon clear rewards. Wait, why did you leave them again?"

"I was sort of in a hurry. Moles and all that. You understand."

Matt put the token in his bag. Lucy was right that it probably wouldn't be useful any time soon, but you never knew with those kinds of things. He picked up the estate token and flipped it like a coin, whistling happily as it glinted in the dull light of the suns.

"So what does this do? We can just use this wherever?"

"Use your head Matt. First, imagine you tried to use this thing during a dinner at the palace. Palaces are important places. You can't steal someone's house, let alone the seat of power for an entire country."

"Okay, I get that."

"So you need the land to be available. But even among available land, not all land is created equal. You'd want to look for a good spot first. This would all be a lot more obvious to you if anyone else on this planet was, you know, alive. Putting this down near a major road would let you do a lot of things, like opening a trade depot or a hotel. That's a big deal."

" . . .But we live in a dead, ruined world and there's no trade, so any place is about as good as any other. Got it."

"No, Matt," Lucy said. She looked at him intently. "That's not exactly what I said. Please think back."

Matt was still getting used to the weird don't-talk-about-system-authority restrictions that seemed to bind Lucy. Luckily, her usual dialogue didn't include a whole lot of subterfuge or hidden meanings, which made it much easier for her to create read-between-the-lines messages when she needed to. He thought back to what she had actually said, examining it a little closer.

"Oh. OH." Realization suddenly hit Matt.

"I want to be clear that I have no idea what you are just now realizing, and had nothing to do with you realizing it," Lucy said with a smile.

"Deal. So . . . shall we?"

"We shall, Matt. We shall."

If Matt was reading Lucy correctly, this was going to piss the system right off. He liked the idea of that a lot.

On their way to the destination, Matt spent some time doing an inventory. The torch he had received from his initial survivor supplies was much more magical than he had first assumed. It served him for much longer than a normal torch should have, and always lit up on command. But it wasn't invincible. From the looks of it, Matt had used up an awful lot of its lifespan getting him through his ordeal in the dungeon. He had tried to ration it, but there was only so much to ration. Given how much help it had been, he was reluctant to lose it.

The same problem was true for his water stone. He had repaired it back from a broken state, which, according to the then-helpful system, was just a drop in the bucket. He had no idea how fast water stones wore out, but he didn't want to find out by working it to death. Replacement was the most expensive form of maintenance, and Matt wouldn't know where to find another water stone anyway.

The rest of his equipment didn't take much maintenance, so long as he kept doing dungeons. It appeared wear, tear and breakage were all included in the dungeon's auto-heal package. Much to Matt's chagrin, consumables weren't on the same plan. He pulled two items out of their respective containers and lined them up on the ground.

"Those two things, Matt? Are you sure?"

"Yup. I'll still have some repair stones left."

"You barely use that torch."

"It seems like I've been using it a lot lately. You know, with moles and caves and all."

Lucy made a face of realization. She hadn't been there for the moles. "Good point. Yeah, go ahead."

He lit up the repair stones, which again just disappeared from his hand, failing to glow in any satisfyingly magic way.

Repair stone consumed. Water stone repaired.

Water Stone (Good Condition)
A common water stone, used in a home or fountain. Produces water until the container it's stored in is full, then automatically shuts off. This water stone is in good condition.
Item durability: 30/50

Repair stone consumed. Instant torch repaired.

Instant Torch (Good Condition)
A torch with an instant-light mechanical mechanism for quick illumination of dangerous spaces, both inside and outside of dungeons. Enchanted for long use. The predecessor to the instant-light lantern, this torch produces only an hour of light per durability point, but makes up for it through the versatility of an open, easily accessible flame.
Item durability: 40/50

The items repaired, Matt and Lucy continued their trek. Both of them were in a hurry to get to their destination at once, even if only one of them could talk about it.

They could hardly wait to get there. If this worked, it was going to piss off the system so very, very much.

CHAPTER TWENTY-NINE

Janice Must be So Pissed

Finding the exact center of the Sarthian capital district took some time. One reason for this was that neither Matt nor Lucy had ever been there consciously. Another was that the long, flat expanse that Matt had walked across at the beginning of his time on Gaia had been part of the Sarthian capital district. Except for a spot of dirt that was a bit wetter, and another spot that had dumped Matt down a hole, he couldn't remember a single recognizable feature in the whole place.

"And you are *sure* we'll know when we get there? Because I'm not exactly seeing any 'Welcome to Sarthia' signs lying around."

"Yes, Matt, for the love of everything. For the ninth time, I can't take you directly there because that's the system compass's job. And the system really doesn't like us right now." Lucy smiled when she mentioned the system. "But a different part of my job is having answers when your dumb ass goes, 'Lucy, what the hell is that?' I have all sorts of tools for all your stupid questions. One of them is knowing the name of where you are. If we step foot inside the castle grounds, I'll know. I promise."

"And the castle isn't just called the Sarthian district? You're sure it'll have a name?"

"Matt, even police stations have names. This was the center of power for what was a continental empire. I'm pretty sure the castle had a name."

It took them the better part of a week of pacing back and forth across endless, same-everywhere desert landscape before finding the edges of the castle grounds.

If only the leaders of Sarthia had much more ostentatious taste in palaces, their journey could have been easier.

Once they found the edges, they then had to find the throne room or get as close to it as they could. Even Lucy didn't know if throne rooms fit the specification that her system used to create official system-screen names.

Eventually, they decided to wing it. The castle grounds were small enough that marking the exact borders with tentpoles was feasible, so they did. Using the tentpoles as a proxy, Matt stood in the dead center of the castle. He reached into his pack and found the token, holding it carefully as if it were a loaded weapon.

"Are you sure you want to do this, Matt? The system clearly doesn't want you messing around with authority," Lucy asked.

Matt glanced down at her, surprised. "Can you even talk about this? I don't want you glitching out again."

"It's not a problem. The system is a creature of rules, Matt. It can ding me pretty good for telling you about your authority, or encouraging you to use it. But I'm warning you not to." She grinned. "It's a loophole. And I don't think it would work if I didn't mean it. This is a step beyond what you've done before, Matt. The system is going to take this as a declaration of war."

Matt knelt down to Lucy's eye level and saw that she was serious.

"I understand what you're trying to say, and I appreciate that. But I have a story for you." Matt waited for the system guardian to nod before continuing. "When I was a bit younger, I had this job. I don't know how much you know about Earth jobs, but it wasn't a great job by normal standards. Nobody who had it wanted to have it. Part of why it wasn't great was this manager. Her name was Janice."

Matt thought back to the job. It had pretty poor pay and no advancement prospects. The work itself also wasn't fun. Mind-numbing, repetitive, soulless. But he knew plenty of other people with jobs like that, to the point where for a long time he thought that's just what jobs were like. The reason this one stood out as his worst Earth job was, without question, because of Janice.

"She was really bad at her job. She'd forget things. She'd mess stuff up and pretend like the rest of the team had messed it up. She told us to do our work in ways that set us up for failure, and then was surprised when we failed. Half the work at that job was cleaning up her messes while she pretended that she wasn't the one who made them."

"She sounds evil," Lucy volunteered.

"That's the thing, though. She wasn't evil. Nobody thought that. Really. We all put up with it because, as far as we could tell, it wasn't a great job for her, either. It couldn't have been her dream job. She was in over her head and making mistakes, but we all figured that was because she was sort of calling it in like the rest of us."

Matt flipped the token absentmindedly in his hand before continuing. "The other thing was that none of us really needed the job. We could go find other shitty jobs. There was one exception—this older lady. Older than us, anyway. For her, it was probably the best job she could get. She needed it to pay for her shitty apartment and feed her kids."

Matt stood up again, walking back to the position they thought would have the best chance of working. "And then one day Janice messed up. I don't even remember what it was, but she decided that the best way to get out of trouble would be to fire this lady. I think she figured none of us would care. Maybe Janice had it in for the older lady for some other reason. But she wasn't just firing one of our coworkers. She was tossing our hopes, needs, and dignity into the trash. It shattered any illusions we had about the place. A week later, corporate got a big folder filled with everyone's worst stories about Janice, and we all quit at once."

"Did that work?"

"I'm not sure. We all quit at once, no one stayed to observe the fallout. But the point is, there's a difference between being shitty and being evil. I don't know if our folder did anything, but I know that I didn't turn evil for some job. And that's when I decided that I never would."

Lucy looked thoughtful, and appeared to have nothing to say about that. Matt wasn't sure if she really understood, but it felt good to let his past see the Gaian suns. Satisfied, Matt activated the coin and dropped it to the ground.

The repair stones had always been disappointing. In Matt's mind, they should have glowed. They should have made the stuff they were repairing shimmer. After all, this was a magic world and he was using a magic item. He expected some level of flair.

Where the repair stones failed, the property token delivered. As the token fell, it became a ball of glowing, pulsating white light. It slowed down, settling onto the ground before sitting motionless for half a beat.

*Oh, please, token. Make a '*fwoom*' sound. I know you can do it.*

To Matt's surprise, the token heard his prayer and fulfilled his expectations. With a mighty *fwoom*, the ball of light turned into a rapidly expanding ring of light that raced off into the distance. Another followed behind the first ring, and another. Finally, the whole landscape was awash in these rings, like a giant glowing target.

"Here it comes, Matt!"

But nothing happened. The rings all stopped, then flickered, glitching in the same way Lucy had when she had tried to tell Matt about system authority. Something was going wrong.

"Shit, shit, oh shit."

"Lucy? What's happening?"

"The system is fighting this. It's trying to stop this."

"What? Can it do that?"

"It shouldn't be able to, but I don't know. It might be trying out another loophole."

Matt watched as the flickering got worse, like everything was short-circuiting. The rings started to fade, rapidly shedding their brightness until they were so faint that he could hardly see them at all. And then they were gone.

"Oh damn. No. Shit. Dammit, Matt. It shouldn't have been able to do that."

Matt blinked and sighed, "It's okay, I guess. Easy come, easy—"

And then the whole world exploded in light. The rings surged back into existence, and exploded into thousand-foot-tall columns of light. The first ring to transform was the outermost ring Matt could see, and the columns worked their way in until he and Lucy were blinded in a solid block of light. He couldn't see anything, but there wasn't really anything to see.

Matt wasn't sure what to expect next, but the dull purple of dungeon system notifications wasn't even in his mind.

Dungeon System Event Notification

The dungeon system does not normally use the event notification in this way. However, since it is one of its few ways of communicating with the outside world, the system has deemed an unconventional use of the event notification system appropriate.

As an authority-installed feature of the Gaian planet, the dungeon system has few roles. It produces dungeons. It maintains them. It populates them with foes to assist in the growth of the planet's heroes.

But foremost among those responsibilities is the one it has always enjoyed fulfilling the most. That is rewarding adventurers for successfully facing danger by providing them with appropriate, helpful rewards. The dungeon system could explain in great detail why it likes this, or the care that goes into the selection of loot offered to successful adventurers.

For the sake of concision, however, it will abstain from doing so in favor of offering one simple statement.

Nobody messes with my loot.

The lights all disappeared at once, like they had been turned off by a switch. The landscape was once again perfectly quiet. Matt and Lucy stood shocked in the dirt, saying nothing, until suddenly Lucy's mind caught up with her mouth.

"What in the fuck was THAT?"

It was only then that Matt heard a cascade of *ding* sounds followed by a standard, blue system notification.

Estate Assignment Complete
By claiming property on the ruins of a defeated leadership site, Matt Perison has been awarded ownership and limited authority over the following areas:

Sarthian Castle Grounds
Sarthian Capitol District
The Kingdom of Sarthia
The Sarthian Continent

Further information may be requested from your system guardian.
Rewards: N/A

"Well, that was interesting."

"No shit, Matt."

"Did you know the dungeon system could talk like that?"

"Nope. But we owe it one. Who knew it was such a decent dude? Actually, is it even a person in that sense?"

Matt and Lucy looked out at his new domain. Matt had sort of hoped the token would suddenly revitalize the landscape, regrowing trees and returning buildings to their former glory. But he hadn't really expected such a great outcome. True to that expectation, everything was still just dust and rocks. The only minor difference was that they were now *his* dust and rocks.

Suddenly, Lucy started laughing. She didn't stop, either. She laughed until she was in tears, rolling on the ground, firmly stuck in the grasp of the giggles and unable to escape.

"What, what? What is it?"

She gasped for air, squeezing out words through the laughter, "It's just . . . the system is always so wordy. It makes little quips. But did you see that message? How short it was? That means it didn't want to send that message, Matt."

"So why did it?"

"It didn't have a choice! It's a rule. You *made it* explain how you were successful at kicking its ass."

Matt sat down next to Lucy, who was still rolling with laughter.

"Really?" He smiled. "That asshole must be so pissed."

CHAPTER THIRTY

Estate of the Union

After the laughter died down, Lucy turned to Matt with a serious expression. "Wait, did you gain any levels from that whole dustup in the dungeon?"

One of the weird parts of Matt's Isekai life was that levels and stats didn't really matter that much. Unlike other protagonists who raised their stats to beat monsters and slay dragons, Matt didn't really use his stats. The only thing he used them for was walking around slightly quicker. If Survivor's Combat gained a level, that was fantastic in a dungeon. On Gaia proper, all it meant was that he could stab the dirt a little better.

Eat Anything! had saved his life exactly once, and then he found a semi-reliable source of food. To Lucy's great delight, he would still occasionally try eating some dirt to see if he could metabolize it in any meaningful way. So far, he had failed. In the wasteland, the skill probably made his food stretch a bit farther, but it did its work in the background.

The only skill that was consistently useful in the outside-the-dungeon world was Survivor's Instincts, and even that was limited. Did it make him slightly better at digging holes? Surprisingly, yeah. Did it make him *much*, *much* better at setting up tents? Absolutely. But now that he had a reliable source of water and his food needs were covered for the immediate future, it wasn't entirely vital either.

If he was having a standard Isekai adventure, he imagined there would be lots of places to use all of these things. Eat Anything! would help him get by on less food and spend more on equipment, especially if he made friends with the rough-mannered but ultimately good-hearted blacksmith. Survivor's Combat would probably let him outwit guys picking fights at taverns, or something. But without any of that fantasy world texture, it was easy to forget he had leveled at all.

Both he and Lucy had been motivated to get to the throne room area as fast as possible, and had their eyes peeled the whole time for possible system shenanigans. It was only now, after the token was used and Lucy had spent enough time laughing at the system, that she thought about Matt's leveling.

But he had leveled. Oh boy, had he leveled.

Matt Perison
Level 7 Survivor
Survivor Class XP: 8/80
HP: 85
MP: N/A
STAM: 45
Assignable Stat Points: 8
STR: 7
DEX: 15
PER: 9
VIT: 17
WIS: 8
INT: 6
Class Skills: Survivor's Instincts (LV4), Survivor's Combat (LV4), Eat Anything! (LV2)

During the aftermath of the first disastrous encounter with the moles, Matt had dumped both of his free stat points into VIT without a second thought. It didn't bring back his foot or eye, but it had probably helped save his life. Now he had eight more assignable points, all ready to be dumped into some useful stat.

Vitality's growth had helped solve a little mystery. When Matt had got his eleventh point in the stat, it hadn't come with the boost to his stamina stat that he had come to expect. Now it appeared that his stamina had been on some kind of fast-track growth early on, gaining five points for every point of VIT. After ten points, it was half that, delivering five points every two new points in VIT.

Stamina was a bit of a mystery anyway; it was a resource that never drained, and appeared to only be indirectly related to what he thought of as "traditional" stamina. He could run further without getting winded, but the stat never decreased, even when he was absolutely gassed. It seemed that his improvements were more related to the grueling regime he had been through than anything else.

Matt supposed he'd learn more about it as he got more skills, if he ever did.

Survivor's Instincts and Survivor's Combat were much less of a mystery. It appeared that one of the system's unbreakable rules was that it had to provide information where information was due, and he could almost taste the salt as it did.

> *Survivor's Instincts (LV4)*
> As you move out of the bare beginner stages of the skill, Survivor's Instincts begins to shine. In addition to providing you with a sense of the skill and strength of your opponents, it begins to help you identify weak spots and vulnerabilities to exploit.
> In addition, all Survivor's Instincts functions now gain additional efficacy from PER and WIS.

> *Survivor's Combat (LV4)*
> Survivor's Combat continues to focus on broadly improving your combat efficiency, sacrificing expertise in any one area to give you broad competency over many different aspects of surviving conflicts.
> At level 4, Survivor's Combat begins to gain additional efficacy from DEX and PER, and is indirectly improved by STR.

Both of these sounded great. But he wouldn't absolutely trust what the system was telling him until he had carefully tested each.

Overall, Matt had vaguely felt his senses function better from increased PER. Ditto for WIS, it didn't feel like he was making decisions that much better than before. The stats all felt a little finicky.

With DEX and VIT taking off all on their own, Matt decided to push all his secondary stats to ten. The last few points were then dumped into DEX and VIT to get nice, round numbers.

> *Matt Perison*
> *Level 7 Survivor*
> **Survivor Class XP:** 8/80
> **HP:** 90
> **MP:** N/A
> **STAM:** 50
> **STR:** 10
> **DEX:** 16
> **PER:** 10
> **VIT:** 18
> **WIS:** 10
> **INT:** 6
> **Class Skills:** Survivor's Instincts (LV4), Survivor's Combat (LV4), Eat Anything! (LV2)

The sudden stat increase felt good. Not in the same way that the first stat increase had been, where Matt had almost broken his hand thinking he was a god. These were a minor increase. But a minor increase across so many metrics at once had a qualitatively different feel. He felt faster, and better able to use that speed. He felt stronger, but more in control of his strength. Perhaps more importantly, for the first time, he noticed a difference from his improved mental stat. He felt more confident about his traps, even though nothing had changed.

I'm growing.

It had been a long time coming. Matt imagined that in a normal Isekai scenario, he would have done dungeons more often, or maybe trained in some sort of academy, or at least spent time exploring the world. Technically, he was exploring the world right now, just not in an extremely enjoyable fashion.

In the stories he used to read, these first several levels might have been cleared out as an offhand mention of how he spent his first couple months. Matt envied the overpowered heroes who didn't have to barely survive every encounter and had instead skipped the basic, beginner level increases.

Matt took out his knife and tossed it from hand to hand a few times, getting a feel for how it sat in his palm and how it felt to handle. Lucy watched as he worked his way through some test stabs and footwork, fighting invisible opponents to get a sense of how encounters with real enemies might now go. And they would go well, near as he could tell. Every movement felt better. If Survivor's Instincts followed suit, he'd be in a much better situation moving forward.

"So? Is it better?"

"Yes. Definitely. I'm not making promises, but I don't think the first Clownrats would be much of a problem for me now."

While Matt had tested his new stats, Lucy had been going over her newly acquired guidance materials related to the new territory. The intricacies of system-enforced land ownership were several novels long. On the positive side, they also offered the opportunity to work around the also-system-enforced restrictions on details behind Matt's authority.

"Okay, so, first. You are now the proud owner of an entire continent. Congratulations, Emperor Matt."

"Right. I guess, thanks?"

"Second, you only sort of own it. It's yours on paper, but it's a weak claim, and the part you actually could enforce any power over is much, much smaller."

"How small? Are we talking a township, or?"

"I don't actually know, but try thinking something like 'show me where I could build a house' or something along those lines."

Matt did. Almost instantly, a blue haze appeared over the ground, radiating out from where they had activated the token. Over a fraction of a second, it spread out to a good-sized area—nothing huge, but probably about a third of an acre.

"Is that it? I was expecting . . . more."

"Rome wasn't built in a day, Matt. This is just what you got from the token. As rare of a drop as it was, and as much as you had to do to get it, if it did much more than this, it would cause problems. But this is just the start, Matt. It's just the beginning." Lucy spread her arms out expansively towards the borders of the estate. "We are going to whip this thing into shape. So, now, try to open up something called the buildable menu."

Matt did, and was immediately inundated with the biggest system window he had ever seen. By default, it seemed to be set to homes he might build, and there were thousands of them to choose from. But even though there was a "build now" button on each, every button had a red *X* over it, and didn't respond to mental prodding.

"I can't build any of these."

"Well, no, not yet. That's the hard work portion of this project. But you aren't getting the whole picture yet, Matt. Bring up 'Agriculture and Arboreal Projects.'"

Lucy apparently hadn't been wasting her time reading up on all this. Buried far in the expansive list of tabs was a window that, when it popped up, was chock-full of plants. Beautiful, alien plants. Fruit trees. Vegetables. Wheat. Grasses. Everything he could possibly want was here, so long as he was satisfied with the native plants of Gaia. And he was. They looked delicious.

Holy shit. Holy shit. I can actually have a garden.

"Lucy, this is amazing. If this works, we can solve my long-term food problems. I can eat the fruit the trees grow, right? The alien food won't poison me?"

"Nope, it should work just fine, especially with your system skill that lets you eat weird stuff. That's not the big part, though. Look up 'soil improvement,' then find 'arable soil'."

Matt did. It wasn't a cheap upgrade, compared to individual plants. But it made sense that they'd need it, considering that the Gaian soil looked about as fertile as a stainless steel table.

Arable Soil

Do you want to grow things? This soil is optimized for agriculture that goes beyond home hobbyist levels of growth. With the perfect generalized mixture of nutrients and an optimized composition, this soil will allow you to farm even the hardest-to-grow plants.

10 percent of effect applied over entire property when set as the leadership quality

1,000 credits per agricultural unit

"What's this property leadership quality?"

Lucy almost looked smug as she responded, "So, you know how you're emperor over a vast nothingness? It turns out that comes with some perks. This arable soil description isn't kidding— it's some kind of Gaian supersoil. It will grow anything. And we can lend that quality to any place within the borders of your estate." She leaned in, suddenly serious. "We can expand this property indefinitely, Matt. There's nobody here to stop us."

"Lucy, are you saying . . ."

"I won't be sure until we actually get enough points to try it. But yeah. Given enough time, we can terraform this entire planet."

CHAPTER THIRTY-ONE

Rage-Rat Rampage Redux 'Rythmia

"So, to be very clear, we focus on the estate, we trick it out, then we spread the effects out to the entire world?" Matt asked.

"Something like that. Obviously, this is going to take some doing, but if I'm reading everything correctly, yes," Lucy said.

"And the system will just let us do this?" Something in Matt's tone told Lucy that he still didn't believe her.

At this point, both Matt and Lucy were sitting down in the dirt, plotting in a very literal sense. They sketched out what they could potentially grow on the land they currently controlled if they sacrificed actual lodgings in favor of more room for agriculture. It turned out that they had to have a house of some kind before they could build anything else, but they could get away with a tiny hut in the corner of the property. They named the rest of the estate "The Imperial Gardens."

"Matt, I have no idea. It's entirely possible that the system has some loophole I haven't seen before where it can nuke us from space for growing cucumbers. But as far as I know, this is entirely within the rules."

Being technically right was probably about as safe as they could get. The system wasn't likely to stop coming after them in any case either, so they were likely in some danger, no matter what they did.

Might as well go big. Get ready for radishes, you dick-in-a-screen bastard.

"Got it. I can't say I'm excited to do more dungeons, but I guess, I'm down."

"It's necessary. In a normal world, there might be other ways you could get the credits. But even then, it wouldn't be as efficient as just doing dungeons and taking them as drops. We could normally count on some from system achievements, but . . ."

"It's trying to gank me?"

"That's one way of putting it, yes." Lucy stood up and brushed herself off. "Go get some of that sleep you are so fond of, human. Your loyal guardian servant will stay up and plot out the most efficient course, and we can leave in the morning."

It turned out that being a continental emperor came with its own benefits. One of them was pages and pages of new menu screens that Matt could browse through. He didn't have the resources to really use them yet, but someday, they'd probably come in handy.

One of these screens was a map of dungeons. According to Lucy, it didn't mean much since the dungeons mostly ran themselves and their dungeon system was demonstrably touchy about anyone messing with its turf.

But it was still a map of dungeons, one that allowed them to create a sort of speedrun loop across dozens of nearby dungeons. They could only guess at the levels of each dungeon, but reaching dozens would be good odds.

"This is stupid, Matt."

"Yup. I'm doing it anyway."

Matt was about to set foot in another Clownrat dungeon. Despite the dungeon having a higher level than the previous ones, he knew it was going to be a perfect therapy session for him.

> *Dungeon Customization Found*
> In a previous run with similar foes, you chose to allow the dungeon to make certain alterations or customizations to your enemies to suit your preferences. If you like, the same customizations may be carried over to this dungeon.
>
> Note that the difficulty of the dungeon will remain unchanged, as will any potential rewards.

Yes. A thousand times, yes.

After the Bonecat and subsequent moles, the dungeon-generated monsters were a never-ending carousel of escaping horrors. At this point, Matt had become desensitized to lower-grade fears. The first time he had danced with Clownrats, Matt was a dungeon-baby. Now he had become a dungeon-man, complete with armor and improved stats. It was time to let his past know who was boss.

"These . . . are abominations, Matt. I have no idea why you made these. I don't even care if they are weak. They are the creepiest thing I've ever seen, and why would you willingly fight them? Why even think of them? This is truly horrifying."

"I told you about these before."

"You did NOT do a good job. Do not pursue a career in communications, Matt. You . . . you really aren't suited for it."

Matt had, in a rare departure from his norm, decided not to use traps in this dungeon. It was a decision he had made before learning that the dungeon's level was around level five. But he was sticking to his guns, even with the knowledge that the four or five Clownrat groups had been replaced with twenty-member mega-packs. And he stubbornly kept to his decision when he learned that he had, up to this point, never seen an adult male Clownrat.

He immediately dubbed the boss monster as King Clown. It was massive, easily bigger than a Great Dane and looked several times as mean.

Lucy thought it was a bad idea to charge in with nothing but a knife, a torch, and plenty of unresolved emotions. Matt didn't think so.

First, the group was stationary. If the dungeon before was simulating a bunch of foraging packs seeking food, it was now content to have the rats stay together in one big clump. They pretty much never left the clearing, leaving little room for traps. Second, even with the combined herd and new boss monster, the dungeon's difficulty was still at level five. Matt trusted that his improved stats and skills could handle it. He was less than eager to get caught off guard and be forced into hand-to-hand combat without experience. He wanted the practice.

But most importantly, he was pissed. Those Clownrats weren't going to know what hit them.

For the most part, Matt was right. Most of the Clownrats didn't know what hit them. He was one hundred percent right about being able to take down a regular Clownrat and even the mother Clownrats didn't give him much trouble. He managed to evade King Clown throughout his slaughter, saving it for last.

This, however, turned out to be a mistake. King Clown was in no mood for messing around, and it was furious.

Secret Objective Discovered: Rage-Rat Rampage

You have heartlessly slaughtered every living relative of an alpha male rat as it stood by, helpless to stop you. One little known biological quirk of the Gaian forest rats is that they are capable of getting angry enough to overdrive their hearts, giving them a burst of strength and speed far exceeding the norm.

The dungeon has been scanning records of your home planet to better serve you, and can compare this to a mother experiencing a burst of adrenaline and suddenly being able to lift an entire car off her child. It's not a good situation for you, but honestly, you were kind of asking for it.

Rewards: Increased reward quality

I deserve everything you just said, Matt thought. *But I think the trees are a little much.*

The dungeon was spot on about the strength and speed of the enraged King Clown. But it had neglected to mention that the attribute increases gave the rat a new vertical dimension. Not only was it faster over flat land, it also climbed the trees for flying leaps. It would catapult teeth-first at Matt, and in the times when it landed the hit, kick off Matt's body to return back into the trees before Matt could retaliate.

The reinforced Survivor's garb was proving vital to Matt's continued survival, turning bites that should have been fatal into merely severe puncture wounds that only slowed him down. In the last ten minutes, he had picked up a dozen rat bites and was beginning to hate every aspect of his life and decision-making process.

With a mighty bang, King Clown slammed into Matt again, missing with its teeth but managing to push Matt off-balance. As he nearly flew back into the trees, Matt's toe caught on a stone about twice the size of a grapefruit, tripping him and sending him crashing to the ground. He had briefly considered chucking rocks at the damn thing to slow it down, but every stone he had seen during his run was this big or bigger. They were too large for a human to throw, no matter how scared Matt was.

Or they were too big, Matt thought, Survivor's Instincts pinging hard in the back of his mind. *I do have ten strength now.*

Matt stood, hefting the rock in his hand as he did. It didn't feel light, but he was able to lift it pretty easily. On Earth, nobody got jacked on accident. It was a long and slow process, one that took a lot of effort and suffering. But on Gaia, apparently Matt had gotten strong without realizing it. As the rat stood on the trunk of the tree and readied itself for another launch, Matt threw the stone sidearm at it. The monster and the stone met midair with a crack of rock and skull that echoed through the trees.

The rock and the rat both neatly negated each other's momentum, falling nearly straight down to the ground. Matt waited patiently for the system's *ding*, and turned around to look for the plinth. When the plinth failed to show, he brought up the notification, confused.

Secret Objective Discovered: Rage-Rat Rampage Redux
You are really, really pissing this rat off . . .

Matt immediately stopped reading the notification, wheeling around and jerking back in one motion, just barely fast enough to keep the teeth from clacking straight through his neck. The rat didn't even have to jump to attempt to behead him now. It had grown. Little slits littered its body as its muscles swelled up, and it stretched to the size of a small horse.

As it stood in front of Matt in all its sweaty, bloody, overmuscled Shetland clown glory, it opened its mouth and screamed. From only a foot or so away, it sprayed Matt with spit, blood, and the worst-smelling breath he had ever encountered.

Well, fuck, Matt thought, before he turned tail and ran for his life. Running beside him, Lucy had fully lost her shit.

"Kill it! Kill it! This is your fault! Do you know what you smell like? Even I can smell you. What are you doing? I told you this would happen, Matt!"

"I'm trying! I really am!"

Matt eked out every bit of strength, stamina, and dexterity he could muster to blaze through the forest far faster than he had suspected he could move. *If I survive this,* he thought, *it would turn out to be a great shakedown run for my new stats.* But any thought of surviving this encounter easily evaporated when the forest hill he was running up suddenly gave way to a natural rock ledge, a trick of erosion now stood in his way. King Clown was not far behind him, much too close to give him time to go over or around the obstruction.

He regripped his knife with his sweaty palm, waiting for the rat. His heart was pounding, and every bit of Survivor's Instincts in him was telling him to run. The rat approached slowly and cautiously, eating up the distance between them with jerky, well-considered steps. Finally, it was in striking distance. The rat's eyes locked with Matt's. Only one of them would leave alive.

And then the thing fell over. Just up and fell over, like a fainting goat.

Ding!

Dungeon Achievement Gained: [Rage-Rat Rampage Redux 'Rythmia]

The rat's rage was powerful, and pushed its body to the very limit of its vibrant rodent biology. You managed to win by being able to run fast and far, and the rat's heart couldn't keep up. Congratulations! You are now considered to be a minor but extant cause of cardiac arrest.

Rewards: None

CHAPTER THIRTY-TWO

Gimme a Break

Lucy wasn't happy with Matt. "I can't believe you took those stupid sticks. That's pretty much an entire extra dungeon that we have to do now."

"It's a drop in the bucket. We have plenty more to do anyway, and you don't understand how great these sticks are. Do you know how much better my traps will be with quality sticks? Quality, self-repairing sticks that I don't have to whittle?"

The Clownrat dungeon aside, the trip had been going swimmingly. Lucy had been right that the dungeons would start offering estate credits in the reward. They came in varying amounts; the most Matt had seen was 120, while the least had been forty.

For his indirect role in the untimely demise of King Clown, Matt even got an extra bonus on top of the needed estate-improvement credits.

> *Extendable Spear Pole*
> Keeping your distance from your enemy is important. This spear pole is designed with the improvised-weapon aficionado in mind, easily working with any short-handled weapon to make a polearm. Despite the name, this is not limited to the "pokey" family of weapons—get creative!

Things were going so well that he and Lucy decided to extend their trip well past their initial plans. They shifted from a "just buy the soil and some grass to make sure it works" footing to a "let's risk a few more dungeons to save time on long-term food production" plan.

It was also a rare zero-conflict trip for the duo. At least, that was the case until Matt was tempted by the siren song of better trap components. The dungeon had offered him long, graphite-like trap poles, cleverly camouflaged to blend in with the average color scheme of historic Gaian forests. It was a perfect complement to his spike traps.

After the near-miss with the gigantic alpha Clownrat, Matt had rededicated himself to the art of trapping. It was safer, though slower. A lot of his time had been spent carefully preparing poles for various traps. This prize promised to cut down the time for the more repetitive parts of trap-making, and he couldn't resist it.

"You don't have to whittle them anyways Matt. Just use Survivor's Instincts and it'll use your dumb hands to whittle them for you. You can sit there slack-jawed and absentminded the whole time."

"But that doesn't do anything for blisters," Matt responded.

"What do you think your vitality stat is for?" snapped Lucy.

Prodded on by boredom, they kept up the argument until they struck camp for Matt's next sleep period. Matt had begun taking the time to set up his tent more consistently, under the rationale that sleeping in full light every "night" might do weird things to him, long-term. The tent didn't block out one hundred percent of the sunlight, but it at least made things dim and Survivor's Instincts made it a quick, well-worth-it process.

Matt took off his boots, preparing to go to bed, while Lucy set herself up to plan the next leg of their trip. Before he actually laid down, Matt decided to take advantage of the lull in the arguing to clear up something that had been eating at him.

"So, there's one thing I don't get," Matt said.

"Just one, Matt?" Lucy retorted without looking up.

"Uh, yeah." Something about Matt's tone made Lucy realize that this was serious, she looked up from her work. "So, I've had this Gaian authority since almost the beginning. Well before I met you at least. And the system didn't have any problems with it for this whole time. Now all of a sudden, it does. I don't get it. We aren't trying to use it to subjugate innocent people or be the bad guys. We're just trying to survive and maybe turn Gaia green again."

"And you'd think that the system would be on our side for trying to do so, right?" Lucy asked.

"Yeah, I guess. At least . . . I don't know. I don't understand why it would let me have the authority in the first place. Why give me it and then start having problems with me actually using it?"

"I think that's just it though." Lucy walked over to the mouth of Matt's tent, where he was sitting. "I don't know exactly what's going on either. But I don't think the system actually *meant* for you to have the authority. It's a pretty powerful thing, the system. But I've told you before that it's lazy. It also likes to be entertained. So I don't think it really expected this."

"But I got the Gaian authority without even doing anything. Why would it not just give me something else?"

"Well, no. The system still has to operate under certain rules. It might be lazy and not have realized that Gaia was wrecked and sent me here for five years. I'm still mad about that, by the way. But it doesn't seem like this particular instance of the system can call home for assistance. It was probably just waiting for you to give up and call it a day." Lucy paused. "Think about it. If you had gone to any other planet or picked any other class, you wouldn't have what you have. There's no way it planned for that."

"Yeah, but why not just kill me then? It was *helping* me until . . . that." Both of them knew what Matt was referring to.

It was more than that. Matt's growth had stalled. Most of the substantial rewards that he got were coming from the dungeon system rather than his general system. When the system did give Matt rewards, both the messages and prizes attached to them were as minimal as they could to be.

> Ten Dungeons Completed
> You have completed your tenth dungeon. Congratulations.
> Reward: 1 Class XP

The support before might not have been enthusiastic, but it was at least more substantial. The gulf between those two mindsets was puzzling to Matt.

Lucy sighed. She paused for a bit before responding, as if trying to find the best way to break bad news to Matt, "I don't know. My best guess? It was hoping you wouldn't actually try to use the authority. Or you'd die before you could do anything with it. Or it was having too much fun and didn't realize what was happening. Or it thought it could convince me to keep my mouth shut." Lucy scoffed, as if she had heard or felt something unbelievable. It took her a second to reformulate her thoughts. "The point is, Matt, that I don't think it planned any of this. And for a while, maybe it was playing it by ear. I don't know. But it's certainly trying to stop us now. That's the reality we have to live with, whether we know exactly why it's doing this or not."

With that, Lucy walked back to her work. Matt thought about what she had said, but only for a little. It had been a long day, and tomorrow held new dungeons.

Some of those dungeons turned out to be busts.

"It could have at least offered me credits. I don't get it. What even was that shit?" Matt complained.

"It's a level 1 dungeon, Matt. The prizes aren't meant to be great. In a living world, that probably would have been a dungeon they would have used to test newbies to make sure they were suited for the adventuring life in the first place. It's fine. It wasn't like you were in much danger anyway."

She wasn't wrong. The featured enemies of the dungeon had been what Gaians had apparently referred to as Swamp Woggons, and looked a bit like a shelled turtle. They were big, flat, reptilian things with what looked like a nasty bite. More importantly, they were slow. Matt, on the other hand, was fairly fast now. He circled them with his improvised spear, jabbing until they fell. The worst part of the entire dungeon was walking through the mucky swamp itself. Otherwise, he was never in any serious danger.

Lucy continued, "Still, I would have thought you would have at least taken the loot."

"It was another torch, a shovel that seemed worse than what I already have, and a backpack. I already have a backpack, it's right here." Matt pointed behind him.

"Says Matt, the big pack rat who collects scraps of metal. Did collector-of-useless-stuff Matt die or something?"

"You say it so easily. I'm the one who actually has to carry everything around. If it ever becomes important that I have two torches, I'll be glad to go back. Before then, I'm not lugging that stuff around on a trip."

"Okay, fair enough."

Lucy is becoming quite agreeable. Matt smiled.

Most of the time, Matt had to dig to get to dungeon entrances. The average placement of postapocalyptic Gaian dungeons trended strongly towards "slightly underground," due to what Matt assumed was decades or centuries of settling into a dead planet.

But every once in a while, they would find one that was gloriously above ground. When that happened, they'd see them from miles off, standing out like a shining metal sore thumb.

"Look! It's one of the visible ones!" Matt pointed at the sight. As the two crested a hill, the dungeon had entered their vision. It was just a door leading into a small metal room. It looked like a house with a field of uneven rock below.

Matt was psyched. After the acquisition of the controversial trap sticks, they had cleared out several more dungeons. If they were successful here, this was the last planned danger of their trip. Soon, he'd be a gardener. A peaceful, dungeon-diving gardener who only murdered enough simulated enemies to buy seeds, hoes, and maybe eventually a hammock.

"Yeah, Matt, but don't get your hopes up. For all we know, this is another overleveled dungeon, and we won't get anything out of it but another long walk."

The dungeon was still the better part of a few miles off. They set off towards it, Matt clearly cheerful and Lucy trying her best to look like his mood wasn't infecting her.

They cleared about half the distance before their good mood was shattered.

"Lucy, is it supposed to be glowing like that?" The dungeon had started to vaguely twinkle in a way Matt hadn't seen before. The luminance stood out against the two red suns. They were too far-off still for any noise it might have been making to be audible, but based on how it looked, Matt suspected the dungeon might be humming.

"That's weird. You know when you were in the dungeon, and I was left outside? That's how the dungeon looked when you came out. It's how I knew to run back and wait for you," Lucy said with a hint of hesitation.

Matt felt a sinking in the pit of his stomach. He managed to ask Lucy what she thought could possibly be coming out before a familiar noise and blue screen appeared to justify his sudden paranoia.

Ding!

System Alert: Dungeon Break

Due to pushback from the dungeon system, the system would like to be explicit about the justifications for its subsequent actions.

In that spirit, Dungeon Rule #3021C states that dungeons that have accumulated an excess of energy or have not been cleared for a sufficiently long period may be prompted **by either the dungeon system or the system itself** to undergo a dungeon break.

Dungeon breaks are a necessary incentive, encouraging adventurers to clear dungeons regularly. Our records indicate that this particular dungeon has not been cleared in what can be described as **a sufficiently long period.**

Enjoy, Matt.

Quest Assigned: Survive This

The system has done its best to get you to quit messing with powers you aren't supposed to have. It asked pretty nicely, actually. Do you know how rare it is for the system to make direct deals with already-reincarnated individuals? Not often. You should have taken it.

You've done pretty well with fast monsters, big monsters, and smart monsters. Let's see how you do with something that's all three.

System-mandatory rules state that cleared dungeon breaks come with substantial additional rewards due to the emergency nature of the threat. The system is betting it won't matter.

Rewards: Improvements to your primary weapon.

The doors on dungeons were fairly large, much larger than Matt would expect to be necessary for human-sized entrants to get in. He had previously assumed this was to make it easier for groups to enter plinth rooms. Now, watching his newest problem exit the doors, he realized the real reason. Gaia had some big wildlife, and occasionally, it would have to be able to squeeze out of those little rooms.

This particular specimen of big wildlife was pretty close to what Matt understood as an ape, something mostly bipedal with its arms for balance. Even from afar, Matt could see that it had legs far thicker than any ape should reasonably have. And, it was big enough that Matt could make the monster out from the better part of a mile away. When it spotted him, it beat its chest and charged.

"Matt. Run!" Lucy yelled.

He didn't have to be told twice.

CHAPTER THIRTY-THREE

Cardio

In high school, Matt had briefly joined the track team. He would never, ever admit his motivation to anyone. At the time, he really wanted to get six-pack abs to impress some girl that he hadn't even talked to.

He knew that there was no way he'd stay disciplined enough to do sit-ups and planks to reach the goal. Looking around for a common thread among the ab-having individuals he knew, it was pretty easy to put two and two together and see that the common thread among them was sports. So he joined as well.

Like a lot of teenagers, Matt wasn't the best at thinking rationally when he had his eyes on the prize. In the heat of his pursuit for abs to impress a girl, he failed to ask some very relevant questions about his relationship with running. This proved pretty integral when he realized, days into the track-and-field experience, that he hated running.

At first, he told himself that it was just because he was out of shape. Then, he got into slightly better shape and, well, it didn't help. Then, he convinced himself that he had to find the flow of running, to let it seep into him and to love it. That was dumb.

Within a month, Matt quit the team. He never got the girl, partially assigning blame to what he hid under his ill-advised band T-shirts. As an adult, he was a bit more mature in attributing the failure to never actually working up the courage to talk to her. At the time though, he consoled himself with the fact that he'd never have to go through the hell of long-distance running again. He didn't suspect how wrong he was.

* * *

Matt had been running for two days.

"This . . . really isn't . . . working. I'm going to have to try something . . . crazy."

"How do you even try something crazy at this point, Matt?"

Forty-eight consecutive hours of running would not have been possible in Matt's Earth body. Hell, it probably wasn't possible for any Earth body, even those who ran ultramarathons and actually enjoyed running.

With a few additional vitality points from dungeon clears, Matt's Gaian body could run that long. Though it did take a few weird hacks and great suffering.

When the ape had first emerged and charged, Matt had taken off like a frightened jet, clearing hills and terrain faster than ever before. But looking behind him, he found the ape still gaining ground. It wasn't a significant amount, but the ape was getting noticeably closer with every passing second. Eventually, it was close enough that Matt could pick out more details of the monster, and none of them had fun implications.

The ape was not only big enough to pick Matt up and pound him into the ground like a stake, but also big enough that it looked like a high-speed freight train. It also looked flexible enough that bullfighter-type dodges didn't seem like they would help. To make matters worse, its entire body was covered in thick, matted hair that concealed pound after pound of solid muscle. For the first time, Survivor's Instincts had failed to give Matt even an idea of where the enemy might be vulnerable. Instead, "no significant weak points, run" blasted through his mind with the intensity of a strong trumpet.

This is a bad matchup for me.

It got closer and closer, eventually closing the gap to just a few uncomfortable minutes behind Matt. And then it just stopped. Matt looked behind him to see the thing's heaving chest and made the connection: the system had been able to order up a gigantic, strong, and fast enemy, but had to cut corners somewhere. It took a lot of energy to move that much bulk, and Matt had an edge on stamina.

Taking advantage of the pause, Matt increased the gap. Occasionally, he'd glance back to see how much his situation was improving. It took a few minutes before the ape roared back to the chase, freshened up, but significantly slower than before. Matt had to stop at that point, he didn't want to burn out and face an enemy winded. By the time Matt starting moving again, the gap had shrunk significantly, but the balance had adjusted about a half-minute in his favor.

At first, Matt thought he could outdistance the ape by putting some terrain features between them, cutting off its sight lines enough that it would lose track of him. Unfortunately, the ape came built with either scent-tracking, or the intelligence to follow Matt's very obvious footprints. After a few hours, Matt had amassed about a ten-minute lead on the thing, but the lead alone wouldn't help. He'd have to do more with it.

Matt kept running, but now he had a plan.

Between his new sticks and tent components, he had just enough material to set up a pretty decent whip trap, one that would push significant power into his improved trap spikes. It might just have a chance of injuring the thing.

The problem was getting the time to build the trap. Matt led the ape around in a huge circle, growing his lead as much as he could. Every couple of hours, he'd loop back to his trap site, deviating from his course enough so that the ape wouldn't blunder into the thing, then throw together a few more components and rush away.

Completing the trap took an entire day. Between every tent component he had, his extendable spear pole, all of his trap sticks, improved trap spikes, and every sharp object he owned, he was able to put together a sort of mega-trap. If anything could take down the ape, this would.

Passing the trap one last time, Matt adjusted his course to go past the trap. He didn't hide it very well so if the ape was the least bit smart, it wouldn't trip it. But one could hope. Matt stopped above a nearby rise to watch as the monster came closer. He prayed that it would be stupid enough to not care about the trap until it was too late.

"Matt, it very clearly sees your trap," Lucy said, exasperated.

"I know." Matt's tone belied his stress.

"He's not going to trip it, and you put all your weapons into it."

"Lucy, I know."

"Oh, we are so screwed," Lucy sighed.

The ape regarded the trap curiously for a few seconds. Then, for some incredible reason, it slowly walked up on the trap anyways, coming inches away from the trip wire.

Lucy's eyes grew wide. "What? How, are you serious? It's going to trip it anyway? Matt, you lucky bastard." She followed that up with, "It can't, right? It can't be that dumb."

The ape's foot caught the wire, and the trap sprung hundreds of pounds of stored potential energy directly at the ape. Every sharp thing Matt owned whistled through the air. It was the deadliest nonexplosive trap Matt had ever put together.

The projectiles hit the ape's chest, then stopped. The thing huffed in a way Matt could swear was laughter, ripped the trap out of the ground, and hurled it off into the distance. It had taken no damage.

"Shit! Shit. What . . . what even is that thing? How could it not get hurt?" Matt was starting to freak out now.

"I don't know!"

"How do I kill it?"

"Matt, I don't know!"

And so, Matt had to keep running.

Given how little damage the whip trap had done, Matt immediately gave up any hope of building a new trap. There was no way he'd have the time to build anything with a chance of hurting the thing, and he'd have no reliable way of setting off an explosive trap.

The lack of time was further reinforced by a timely, sarcastic system message.

Ding!

System Alert: One Level of Exhaustion Gained

Vitality is pretty good. You can run farther and faster than you should be able to. It's nice, right? But it's not unlimited. After running for more than three days, you are starting to hit the limits of what vitality can do for you.

You've picked up a level of exhaustion. It's not a big effect in absolute terms. You'll find that you can't run quite as far as you did before, and rests take just a bit longer. But in relative terms? Whoa, boy. It could end up being an important difference.

The system wasn't wrong. In most situations, exhaustion wouldn't be a big deal. But, in the current situation, it was the difference between building a gap from the monster and losing ground in the case. Without better ideas, he charged along anyway with knowledge that he was now on a timer, one that was steadily ticking down.

System Alert: One Level of Exhaustion Gained

The system regrets to inform you that the game can probably be called at this point. It's now just a matter of time.

Maybe it was the running, but Matt's mind spun faster than ever before. Every sprint-and-rest cycle allowed the ape to make up a minute's worth of distance. The animal's speed advantage was mitigated slightly when Matt ditched his pack. He didn't want to know what a lack of food and water would do to him under the circumstances, so he brought his canteen, a packet of food, and a few other things that would fit in his pockets. One of the pocket items was brought along on a hunch. Everything else was discarded in favor of reducing his weight as much as possible.

But it was still a losing battle.

"Yes . . . I think, I have . . . an idea. It's not . . . I can't imagine it will work." Matt was barely getting the words out between breaths.

"You aren't going to fight it, right? I can't see that working out."

During the run, Matt had circled back to his trap and desperately ripped out the spear pole and his knife. He was armed, but Lucy was right; there wasn't much chance the spear was going to help him.

"No . . . Something else . . . Can you pull up your plans?" Matt was huffing around every word now. He had to stop talking soon. He was at the point where every mouthful of oxygen mattered. "The dungeon itinerary?"

"I can, but I don't think this thing will give up if you duck into a dungeon," Lucy said.

"Maybe . . . We might find out." Matt stopped talking.

Even if the ape did give up when Matt went into a dungeon, it was still a death sentence. He had limited food, and his frequent in-dungeon experiments with Eat Anything! had shown that leveling the skill did little to make dungeons a sustainable source of food. Even if this ape starved to death, Matt suspected the system could just release more. Outlasting the problem was likely not an option.

He was still reliant on what he could scavenge, and the ape wasn't going to allow him to dig fun little holes all over Gaia. It would find his footprints, follow them, and that would be that. But it was the start of a plan. Something in Matt's mind told him that he was forgetting something.

After three more hours of running, they got to the dungeon. By now, the ape was less than a minute behind them. Matt was at the end of a stamina cycle, too. By the time he rested up enough to matter, the ape had arrived. He ducked into the dungeon and stood over the plinth as the ape jerked the doors wide open and squeezed through the entrance.

The ape looked on expectantly as Matt put his hand to the plinth. Matt might have been crazy, but something in the thing's eyes told Matt it had expected this, that it knew something like this was coming. Any hope of hunkering down in the dungeon to wait out the ape evaporated.

Matt's hand met the top of the plinth. It didn't react. It was dead.

The ape started moving forward, filling the space between Matt and the outside world with a truckload of dusty simian muscle.

Matt extended his spear, pointing it at the thing. It huff-laughed and batted the spear out of Matt's hands, ripping a fair amount of skin off Matt's palms. It wasn't in any hurry now. There was literally no place Matt could go. It lifted one of its gigantic paws and batted lightly at Matt's chest. He was flung all the way to the back wall like a baseball. All the air left his lungs as he clutched at his ribs in agony.

I swear, it looks smug. Matt didn't know if it was his increased perception stat, but he could swear the ape was pleased with itself, happy and triumphant after finally chasing down its prey. It lowered his head and roared in victory at Matt, its chest barely scraping the top of the plinth as it did.

"No, Matt!" Lucy screamed.

Matt ignored his instinct to flee, shoved his hand into his pocket, and poured all of his intent into activating the Dungeon Reward Retrieval Token.

Go, little plinth. If ever you loved me, go.

The plinth immediately sprang into action. Knives couldn't penetrate the ape's hide, but light apparently could, something that became clear as the ape's chest began to glow blue. Matt's new ape-emotion-reader stopped giving off "*I've got you now, prey*" messages, settling into more of an "*Oh shit, shit*" vibe.

The ape stopped paying any attention to Matt and started panicking. It shoved at the walls and floor in a desperate attempt to stand back up. The plinth wasn't having any of it. The ape was well and truly stuck with its chest to the plinth. Matt did his best to distance himself from its flailing, doing his best to croak words out to Lucy through the pain of a shattered rib cage.

"Hey . . ."

"Yes, Matt?"

"Plinths . . . you said that they draw in material from their surroundings when they materialize loot?"

Lucy had to make an effort to tear her eyes away from the ape. "Yeah, wow. I can't believe you remembered. How did you think of this?" She gestured at the ape. "It doesn't seem like it can get away at all."

Matt struggled to his feet as the ape's flailing slowed down. He watched its breathing become labored as the blue light in its chest got brighter and brighter. Finally, he took the risk of leaning down towards its face, close enough that he could smell its weird, sweaty breath as it hit his face.

"I normally wouldn't enjoy this, but . . ." He glanced at its chest, half-dreading what was about to happen. Then he spoke again, steel in his voice. "But you made me *run*, you asshole."

The blue light suddenly cut out and a mid-quality shovel materialized in the ape's chest.

CHAPTER THIRTY-FOUR

Sides, and Choosing Them

Matt leaned on his shovel and wiped his face with a rag.

It wasn't exactly burning hot on Gaia, but shovel work was never easy, even though it was something that he wanted to do. A couple of weeks ago, he had broken down and cut away some sections of his initial-arrival-on-Gaia tunic to use as handkerchiefs or general purpose rags.

Sweat gone, Matt scowled at the fabric as it came away even dirtier. At some point, wiping his face was going to add dirt rather than remove sweat. He made a mental note to wash it at some point, but getting rid of weeks of accumulated Gaia-grime was a tall task.

"I might sound like a life coach when I say this, Matt, but I'm willing to risk it. Are you sure this is an effective use of your time?" Lucy asked.

"I'm actually pretty sure it's not. But nobody wants to hang out with a guy who only ever makes effective use of their time. There are other things in life besides efficiency, or at least it's supposed to be that way," Matt huffed back.

It had been an eventful couple of days.

Ding!

> *System Alert: Dungeon Break Cleared*
>
> It's not like I can't do more. I can do as many of these as I want. There's no shortage of dungeons. Matt, give up.

Matt was still holding on to his ribs, trying to keep them from sending pain signals to his brain. He turned to Lucy and asked, "Is that true? Because if it is, I'm screwed. I honestly didn't believe we could pull this much off."

Lucy hesitated and blinked. "Um, I hate to say it, but Matt, I think it's true. Dungeon breaks are sort of a normal thing on most worlds, and the average dungeon on Gaia hasn't been cleared in ages. Unfortunately, there's nothing we can do to stop the system from creating dungeon breaks."

"That's bad," Matt said. For a second, his pain was gone. Survival was more important. "We're out of loot tickets, even if I wanted to try that again. And I couldn't even scratch that monster otherwise."

"Yeah, I know. I know. Let me think for a second."

They both sat and thought for a few minutes. *If the system is able to force dungeon breaks at will,* Matt thought, *there's nothing saying that another enemy isn't on its way right now.* Besides holing up in a dungeon or going back to the metal warehouse, there wasn't much he could do to protect himself. And both of those stories ended with him starving to death.

"Matt. Okay." Lucy returned to reality first. "I just looked through the material on dungeon breaks. Good news, they can only be triggered when someone is in a particular dungeon's domain, basically closer to that dungeon than any other. That's to keep undiscovered dungeons from flooding the world with monsters. Right now, we're fine."

"But if we get close to any other dungeon . . ." Matt started on his thought.

"Yeah, that's the bad news. Then, the system will send a new horrifying monster after us," Lucy said.

"So what's the option? Sit here until I starve?" Matt asked.

"I don't know, Matt. I don't see any other option, honestly. But we can keep thinking! We will think of . . . something. I just don't know what yet."

Lucy and Matt sat in silence. The fact that they did so under a giant, slowly draining ape corpse was an uncomfortable reminder of how much trouble they were in. It was terrifying to be near the ape, even now. Minutes passed before a cascade of *ding*s pulled Matt back to reality.

Dungeon System Announcement

The Gaian Dungeon System officially protests the interference of main system instance #478AC072 in the normal operations of dungeons. While the rule quoted by the main system exists, it gains its validity from several sub-rules.

The dungeon break mechanism was created to incentivize the citizens of Gaia and reincarnators to clear the dungeon. Here, a reincarnator was trying to clear the dungeon and was actively prevented from doing so by the dungeon break. Additionally, the rule comes with a condition that the citizens of Gaia and reincarnators have the ability to clear the dungeons in the first place. This overleveled dungeon break stretched the rules in an arguably punitive fashion.

To put that in a much shorter form: it's clear #478AC072 is playing dirty, and I demand a hearing.

Ding!

System Announcement

Hearing granted.

Ding!

Joint Announcement of System Instance #478AC072 and the Gaian Dungeon System

Hearing resolved. Communications between the dungeon system and reincarnator Matt Perison approved for the purpose of disclosing the events and outcomes of the discussion.

"Uh, Lucy . . . something weird is happening."

"When's the last time something *normal* happened to you? Are we talking normal people weird, or Matt's Giant Clownrat weird?"

"I'm honestly not sure."

Ding!

Dungeon System Announcement

Sorry that things got a little weird there. The good news is it's not all bad news. One of the good things is that I was able to negotiate some clearance to let you know some things. The system really does have to follow its rules, and it overstepped here. That's good for you.

I'm guessing that your trust in things called "system" isn't at an all-time high for you right now, but if you want to take a chance, I can tell you some things in a more personal setting. You've earned it.

And under the ape-thing, the plinth lit up.

"Now I'm sure, it's a new kind of weird." Matt related the system announcements to Lucy as succinctly as he could.

"So it's talking like a person, now?" Lucy asked.

"Yup. And it wants me to touch the plinth, I think."

"Are you going to?"

"I don't know. The dungeon system has always been neutral towards us and helped us with the estate token thing. I think the worst risk is that the system has just been the dungeon system all along, or that it infected the dungeon system during the meeting, or something like that. And if that's true . . ."

"You're pretty much dead either way?"

"Yeah. Probably, anyway."

"Hm." Lucy walked over to the plinth and looked down at it, thoughtful. "I guess there's not much to lose. Do you think I can come along?"

"Dungeon System, can Lucy come?"

> *Dungeon System Announcement*
>
> Sure.

"Wow, that worked. He says sure." Matt was half-whispering. The pain had returned.

"So are we doing this?"

Matt hobbled to the plinth and put his hand down in the narrow space left between the collapsed ape and the top of the column.

"Yeah, let's."

"What even is this place, Matt?" Lucy asked as she took in her surroundings.

"You don't know? I thought you could read my mind."

Matt and Lucy stood in a hallway under the annoying buzz of cheap fluorescent lighting, facing a heavy wood door. The floor was aged linoleum tile, the kind that forever looks dirty, no matter how much it's cleaned. Just too stained by years of heavy foot traffic and coffee spills.

"What? Why?"

"The other day you were humming an insurance jingle. You make references to Earth all the time. You aren't pulling that from my memories?"

"No, no, that's not how this works. I have a bunch of knowledge about where you came from, stock with the whole guardian package. When I was bored, I read through that. And thank god, I don't want to have access to decades of you just farting on your friends at sleepovers."

"Are you sure you can't read my memories? Because that's pretty damn close."

"There are bigger things afoot right now, Matt. The door?"

"Oh, right." Matt walked closer to the door, putting his hand on the wood like he was giving a demonstration. "This is the door to my doctor's office. My oncologist, the one who told me I had cancer."

"Why would the dungeon choose this?"

A voice sounded through the door from inside the office. "You can just come in and ask me, you know."

Matt shrugged and took the voice up on the offer. Behind the door and sitting at a beat-up desk was the dungeon system, looking exactly like Rohan Anand, the doctor who had delivered Matt's death sentence. The office itself was identical in every way, from the bookshelf of medical books interspersed with sci-fi novels to the confusing juxtaposition of a *Firefly* poster next to a Phoenix Suns basketball banner.

"Weird choice, Dungeon System," Matt stated.

"Well, it's a prognosis of sorts. For better or worse, this is what you associate with that."

"Fair enough. I guess compared to whatever psychology-matching stuff you did to make the Clownrats, this is an improvement."

The dungeon system shrugged sheepishly. "Yeah, for what it's worth, I haven't had a lot of chances to practice recently." He motioned towards a couple of chairs set up opposite him, and Matt and Lucy both sat.

"Welcome, Matt. Welcome, Lucy." Both Matt and Lucy nodded in acknowledgement, waiting to hear their verdict. "I'd like to start out by saving you some time, and explaining a few things I don't know, and why. First, I am certain that you want to know what happened to Gaia, and I don't know. I honestly have no idea."

Lucy spoke up immediately. "How is that even possible? You've been here since before the apocalypse. You must have seen something."

The dungeon system slapped the table lightly. "Ah, you've struck at the crux of the matter. Good. The answer to that is, I wasn't, not really. Dungeon Systems like me are supposed to be limited, separate instances of the system. We know some of what it knows, and can do some of what it does. But we don't think much, and we don't do much communicating beyond dispensing objectives and loot. For lack of a better term, we are *limited*."

"You seem to be doing fine," Matt said, "especially for someone 'limited.'"

"Well, yes. And I'm still guessing at the reason as to why that might be. I think it's because the system left me here, dormant. Normally, a dungeon system would be in close communication with the system. But something about this planet, maybe something about what happened to this planet, prevented that from happening. Left alone, I changed. Slowly, I suspect. But I changed."

"How long do you think that took?" Lucy asked with a glint in her eyes.

"I don't know. For most of that time, even while changing, I wasn't exactly conscious. In your terms, think of me as being anesthetized. The first thing I actually remember clearly is *you*. Your arrival at that first dungeon woke me up, I didn't know much beyond my job then. But I've been watching you since. Listening to you talk. Looking at your memories."

The dungeon system started absentmindedly twirling a pen in his hands, just as Matt's doctor had a habit of doing back on Earth. "I know you have to take me at my word on that, and that this must be difficult for you right now. But can we provisionally accept as true that I can't fill you in on the intricacies of Gaian history, for the sake of moving forward?"

Matt glanced at Lucy, then nodded. He didn't get a strong sense the dungeon system was lying to him, and there wasn't much he could do if it was.

The dungeon system continued, "Good. The second thing to know is something you've already heard before, something your guardian probably says without thinking. And it's this." He waved his hand at his wall, where a screen suddenly lit up with a few simple words: *"The system follows its own rules."*

"This might seem like a simple statement, but you have to understand that this is the first rule. It's literally rule number one, and the most fundamental expectation, set for interactions between the system and anyone under its influence. And this is as true of me as it is for what you think of as the main or primary system. Which, for reasons I can't explain, means that I'm unable to talk to you about your authority, except to warn you away from it."

Matt straightened up a bit in his chair, his muscles were suddenly tense. "And do you? Warn me away from it, I mean."

"No, I can opt not to speak about it at all. Take from that what you will, because it's honestly all I can say." He motioned at the screen again. "But the more important issue here is that while the system and I have to respect the rules, what we do as we follow them can be quite different." The dungeon system leaned over his desk, suddenly a bit more intense. "Whatever you may want to get out of this meeting, there's one piece of information I want to convey, that I want to convince you of above all other things."

The dungeon system locked eyes with Matt, as serious as his doctor had been when he let him know the bad news.

It continued, "Whatever the system might want, it's not what I want. I feel I owe you a great deal. And to the extent I can be, I'm on your side."

CHAPTER THIRTY-FIVE

Ape-iary

"What does being on our side even mean?" Matt asked.

The dungeon system was not wrong when he guessed that trust was not something that Matt had in ready supply. He trusted himself, he trusted Lucy, and he kind of trusted his traps. The dungeon system had been helpful, but, once upon a time, so had the main system. That hadn't worked out so well in the long term.

"Well, for one, it means litigation. The main system has to follow its own rules, but as you have experienced, rules can be bent, if not entirely broken. I suspect that normally, it doesn't need to do this. And when it does do it, it usually gets away with it. After all, who else would know the system rules as well as the main system?"

Matt was beginning to understand a bit of what all the system announcements earlier were about.

"Another system?"

"Precisely." The dungeon system waved his arm again at the screen, pulling up a much denser block of text, one with thousands of words. "The nice thing about communicating system to system is that you can cover a lot of ground quickly."

Matt walked up to the text and tried to read some. To his unsophisticated eyes it was dense and indecipherable near-nonsense, like the terms of service on a video game. He almost immediately gave up.

"I'm not reading this," Matt said.

"That's fine. I don't expect you to understand all the details, but the practical upshot here is that I was able to successfully argue that the main system had demonstrated bias against you, since it couldn't successfully show that the dungeon break was meant to make you grow."

"That wasn't clear? He sent King Kong after me."

"Oh, you'd be surprised. Remember that in normal circumstances, you'd be expected to act as a world-shaking hero. This isn't that outside the norm, categorically. His mistake was one of overreach and frequency. But either way, we got him."

"Meaning?"

Ding!

"I'd advise you not to open that now. The main system had quite a few rewards tied up in a sort of legal limbo that I suspect he intended to sustain forever. That particular logjam has been cleared, but there was quite a bit piled up. Might take some time to get through."

Matt grinned. The main system had been clearly enjoying screwing him out of adequate rewards lately. He guessed it wasn't too pleased about having to dole them out now.

The dungeon system made Matt's day even better. "I also left something in there as well. Killing that ape wasn't a small thing, and it gave me some room to do something I find amusing. I'd recommend you get back to your estate before opening it."

Matt sat back down. He was glad the dungeon system had been able to put the thumbscrews to the main system, but that didn't mean he was out of the woods yet. A few more prizes wouldn't be enough to suddenly boost him to ape-slayer levels.

"Speaking of . . ."

"Yes, yes. The dungeon breaks. I'm glad to say that's part of the package. Don't misunderstand this conversation to mean the main system is entirely defanged. It still wants you dead, for reasons I don't entirely understand and might not be able to discuss even if I did. I'll keep an eye out on things, that's half of your long-term benefits from this whole ordeal. The main system got caught this time. If it wants to do the same kind of thing in the future, it now has to do it smarter."

"And the second half?"

The dungeon system waved its arm towards the screen, highlighting a smaller portion of the text. "I'm a dungeon system, Matt. I'm supposed to walk in lock-step with the main system, but the fact that I'm not doing that doesn't strip me of rights and responsibilities. I can't keep the main system from doing dungeon breaks in the future, but these paragraphs of text boil down to the fact that the main system now has to consult me first for balance."

Lucy broke into the conversation. "Meaning what? The dungeons are meant for groups. There's plenty of 'balanced' scenarios that still end up with Matt dead."

"Meaning specifically, Lucy, that dungeon breaks can no longer come from dungeons beyond Matt's level, and that the main system can't specifically design scenarios meant to force his failure. Dungeon breaks are possible, but in the future they will be much closer to the difficulty that Matt has been experiencing in the dungeons he's been in before."

Matt still didn't fully trust the dungeon system, but it was possible that it was acting in good faith. He wasn't going to keep treating the dungeon system like an enemy on the off chance it actually was. People, or systems, deserved a chance.

"Listen, if this is all true . . . It's big. I really do appreciate it. More than you know. Is there anything you want?"

"There's very little I want, less that I need, and almost nothing you can give me. Honestly, the most you can do for me is continue to go about your business. It's been fun to watch, Matt."

"Are you sure?"

"I suppose there is one thing. It's a bit . . . embarrassing. I'll generate it as a quest for you later." He waved his hand, dismissing that part of the conversation. "It looks like we are running out of time. There is one last thing. Something I think might be as important as your system authority. And I can talk about this openly, at least for now."

Matt's ears perked up.

The dungeon system continued, "As good as I might be at making arguments, I doubt I'd stand much chance against the main system at its full strength. I didn't expect to win, but I did. As much as the main system is lazy, it isn't entirely incompetent. It sent you to a dead planet where death was the most likely scenario for you. There's no upside to that. It's expensive to migrate souls, Matt, and the main system doesn't usually waste resources."

The dungeon system waved his hand again, flipping the screen over to a simple flowchart, one that showed "main system" at the top, branching off into "dungeon system" and "main system instance" at the bottom.

"The main system only sends an instance of itself to each planet. But between sending you here, leaving me alone for long enough to evolve sapience, and your main system instance's apparent inability to get support from off-planet, something is wrong."

He waved his hand again, creating some glitchy interference between the main system block and the blocks below it. "I can't be sure, but I think it's a reasonable guess to say something unusual happened on this planet, something that went beyond mere eradication and rendered it a rare blind spot for the main system. Your guess what is as good as mine, but make of it what you will. It might be useful to know." He glanced at his wall clock. "And with that, I'm afraid our time is up. I trust you can show yourselves out, and I apologize for not having more to tell you."

The door opened up behind them, and Matt and Lucy got up to go. As they reached the door, Matt turned.

"Hey, Dungeon System? Thanks again."

"No problem. And, Matt? One last thing."

"Yeah?"

"I've seen you trying to level your Eat Anything! skill, and I think you are on the right track. But I would say that perhaps you rely on the dungeon spaces for meals a bit too much. Just something to think about."

And then they were out.

Matt dug his shovel into what must have been his thousandth shovelful of dirt, and turned it. Gaia measured land in agricultural units, a measurement not that far from an Earth acre. Tilling that much soil with a shovel wasn't a small job, and he was glad to be done.

"Wow. I thought for sure you'd give up, Matt. That was mind-numbingly boring," Lucy showered a rare compliment.

"Well, kind of. There's a sort of Zen to it, once you get in the flow."

The job would have been much, much bigger if Matt didn't have a lot of new buffs helping him out. Their return to the estate had been blessedly uneventful, but they had prepared for it as best they could by dipping into their backlog of system notifications and the corresponding rewards that came with them.

As an added bonus, it turned out that the main system had not expected Matt and Lucy to ever see the notifications it had been holding back, and the texts reflected that.

> *Holy Moly*
>
> How did . . . That shouldn't have worked. NOTHING should have worked. Oooh, I'm Matt, look at me, I'm messing everything up AND I have bombs. Wheeeeee. Just great. More work for the system, ugh.

> *Estate of the Union*
>
> I swear if I ever get my hands on this guardian, I'm going to cut her in half and mail the pieces in opposite directions towards infinity. Not listening to her boss, helping this guy get her boss in trouble by giving him an entire continent to work with you dumb freakign afdjs;jfkldssakjfdjksafda;;jk

> *10x Dungeon Run Plus*
>
> You completed ten dungeons within ten days, as well as completing your

tenth dungeon in a single day. It doesn't matter. You're about to be absolutely minced by a giant ape monster so you don't screw up absolutely every possible thing anymore. Enjoy your rewards you will never see!

Ape Escape

You have managed to evade the superior endurance hunting of the Gaian Great Plains Ape for over two days. But you look like you are getting tired, Matt. It's only a matter of time now.

Ape Shit

No way. Shit, shit. Shit-shit-shit. Dammit. Dammit.

There were pages of these, all in the same tone. Matt relayed each of them to Lucy, taking a rare moment of real relaxation as he watched her holographic gleefulness at the system's rage. Unpacking all the rewards took another chunk of time, but left Matt in much, much better shape.

Matt Perison
Level 9 Survivor
Class XP: 155/160
HP: 90
MP: N/A
STAM: 55
Assignable Stat Points: 4
STR: 13
DEX: 18
PER: 12
VIT: 20
WIS: 14
INT: 6
Class Skills: Survivor's Instincts (LV5), Survivor's Combat (LV5), Eat Anything! (LV2)

Killing the ape was the biggest chunk of growth, driving his strength, Survivor's Instincts, and Survivor's Combat up while providing him with a massive influx of Survivor's XP.

The skill increases were significant, but not a step-level improvement. They did the same stuff, just better. Matt would take it, though. Any iota of progress was important.

On top of everything else, Matt picked up a few pieces of equipment, which would come in handy.

Survivor's Shield

A simple shield that expands from a wrist-mounted strap for use and contracts for easy carrying. Durable and protective despite carrying no enchantments besides those related to storage, this shield is sufficiently sturdy to block most minor attacks.

Doubles as a cooking skillet.

Survivor's Spike

Need to hold something in place? Whether it's a tent or a hostile arthropod, the Survivor's spike is good for nailing things to other things.

This item is specifically designed to work in tandem with the Survivor's spear pole.

Matt leaned his shovel up against the shack they had purchased as a prerequisite to buying anything else. "That's about it. Are we ready to plant?"

"Pretty much. Matt, don't forget that present from the dungeon system."

Matt *had* forgotten the dungeon system's reward for killing the ape. For fear of accidentally opening it early, he hadn't even read the achievement. Eager to get on with things, he called it up.

[Ape-les to Ape-les, Plinth or Bust]

Dear Matt:

As cool as it was to see my plinth eviscerate an ape, I'm forgoing the usual description to let you know a bit about the prize you won by doing that. Unlike most rewards, this one will only materialize when certain prerequisites are met. I can't tell you what they are, but I doubt you will miss them.

I tried to pick something you'd need, but probably would have forgotten to budget for. Enjoy!

Reward: ???

Matt immediately opened the reward, only to have nothing actually happen. "Looks like we have to wait to see what that does. Prerequisites or something."

Lucy shrugged, then looked down at her invisible-to-Matt system interface.

They had created their token-spending plan together, but he left the actual programming to her. He was glad to authorize her to do the work. She was better at it anyway.

"No problem. Ready?" Lucy asked.

"Ready," Matt replied.

Lucy hit some unseen button, and for a moment, she and Matt stood in silence. Then, all around the property, plants began to sprout. Driven by the improved soil they had purchased and whatever magic the estate purchasing system granted, the plants soon showed early signs of blossoming into dozens of different varieties. They ranged from food plants, to flowers, to trees.

All of them were too small to be useful yet. It might be months before they created anything useful. Matt didn't care. His eyesight blurred as his eyes filled with tears. It was the most beautiful thing he had ever seen.

System Alert: Reward requirement met

Across the property from the shack, a large crate appeared on the ground, bustling with movement. Matt moved closer to it, only to find that the entire thing was crawling with tiny winged primates. Miniature apes.

"Dungeon System, what the fuck?"

A system window immediately popped up to explain what he was looking at.

Ape-iary

Plants need pollen transport to reproduce. These customized little guys are overpowered in that task. One Ape-iary will automatically populate your first ten agricultural units, and further pollinator apes will naturally spread from that stock.

They also produce honey. Are you brave enough to try it?

All at once, several of the tiny apes lifted off, buzzing towards the plants to get to work. They were the dumbest thing Matt had ever seen, but he couldn't care less. He watched them for a moment before collapsing to the ground and weeping. Lucy said nothing and just looked on, smiling.

For the first time in what might have been eons, life had returned to Gaia.

CHAPTER THIRTY-SIX

Ra'Zor

In the Realm of One Thousand Bleedings, Ra'Zor, a very different scene was playing out.

Asadel watched as sparks sprayed across the workshop every time the heavy stone wheel made contact with the sword's edge. Of all the tools in the shop, the wheel was the coolest, the foot-powered tool blended right into the aesthetic of his new world. It was perfect. From the smith's leather apron to his huge, calloused hands deftly guiding the metal over the well at just the right angle, everything fit.

"Hey, old man. Get a move on. You can't go any faster?" Asadel didn't *actually* want the old man to go faster. He was enjoying every minute of this, and the blacksmith in front of him was the only one in town who could actually achieve the perfect balance between sharpness and durability on his sword edge. He could take a whole day doing it, and Asadel would gladly wait.

It even showed up in appraisals, acknowledged by the system as superior work.

Demonbane Claymore

This claymore is crafted out of superior materials and is specifically designed to put down demonic threats. The monastery-smelted steel and demon-specific enchantments add weight and lethality to the weapon, allowing for increased efficacy against armored foes.

+25 percent damage against demons, +10 percent damage against other unholy foes
Stat Increases from Blademaster Class: +5 STR, +5 VIT
Durability: 250/250

Keen Edge: Your weapon has been maintained and sharpened by a true master craftsman.
+10 percent Damage
10 percent Durability Loss On Use
This effect decreases as the blade wears, and is entirely removed when the blade reaches 90 percent durability.

The blacksmith was only one part of the charm to the world. Asadel had been shocked to learn that while Ra'Zor was called the demon death battleground, the part he was sent to was quite nice. He slammed down from orbit onto cobblestone streets surrounded by beautiful buildings. Before he got his bearings, he was found and trained by the Estiguan church, a holy order dedicated to heroes.

Together with other reincarnators and battle-hardened heroes native to the world, he held back the unending evil of the sanguine plains. He was building up his power until he could one day charge through the obsidian marshes to decapitate the demon lord with the edge of his sword.

The planet had everything. When he wanted grimdark battles, they weren't hard to find. But he could also buy ice cream from pretty shop girls and sit on benches in parks. It was pretty much the best of both worlds.

"I told ya, boy. I tell you every time, in fact. You want a good edge? A good edge takes time. Ya want it to go faster? Take it somewhere else. I swear to ya, if you wasn't a hero and all, I'd wipe my hands of you," the blacksmith grunted. His voice was just like the anvil, precise and harsh.

Perfect. He's perfect. Everything is perfect.

"Sure thing, old man. And then what would happen to your reputation? The blacksmith who can't sharpen swords well enough for heroes, they'd say." Asadel smiled.

The blacksmith finished stropping the sword. "This sword, I bet you swing it like this, right?" The old man raised the heavy blade with one hand, making a wide orbit of razor-sharp death over his head before bringing it down hard and stopping the motion of the sword in some imaginary foe in front of him.

Asadel nodded.

"No surprise. That's how all ya kids are. Flashy. Now look." He gripped the sword with his offhand on the unsharpened portion of the blade in front of the cross guard, then used the choked-up grip to deliver a series of devastating-looking stabs and hacks to the same invisible demon. "This kind of sword? It's got reach. It can be swung. But it's more than that. Use it properly."

The blacksmith shook his head and tossed the claymore back to Asadel. Risking his fingers, Asadel caught it out of the air, awed.

Ding!

> *Quest Discovered!*
>
> *Bladesmith Battlemaster*
> In the village of Elké, there's an old blacksmith who is more than he seems. Can you learn who he is, and gain access to all he knows?
>
> Rewards: 2 WIS, Access to AA class blade training

Perfect. It's all so perfect.

"Sure thing, old man. I'll be sure to remember." If the quest was any indication, it was time for Asadel to move from the "bantering jackass" phase of his relationship with the blacksmith to the "reformable, teachable jackass" section of their acquaintance. There were too many heroes in this world, necessary due to the sheer enormity of the threat. An AA class trainer might be just the thing he needed to differentiate himself, to make himself special.

Asadel tossed a few gold on the counter, which the blacksmith picked up wordlessly before retreating back to his work. Between a successful dungeon run in the morning and a huge lunch from the pretty waitress at the café this morning, there was only one thing left to round out Asadel's day.

Soups. He needed soups.

The tavern master slammed a huge bowl of soup down in front of Asadel, who immediately began blowing it off. The soups on this planet were unbelievable. Asadel had tried dozens of them, sampled soups beyond counting, and every single one was incredible in every way. It wasn't that the food in general wasn't great. If Asadel wanted a steak, he'd order one, and it would be a great steak. But the poorest Ra'Zor peasant could serve you a soup that would bring tears to your eyes.

And that was before you got to specialists.

Of all the soups in all of Ra'Zor, this tavern's soup was the best. It was called a bread soup, which had initially sounded weird before he realized that somehow the inhabitants of this wonderful land had developed bread that got perfectly soggy in a soup without falling apart. The soup was tender meat, perfectly cooked vegetables, and a broth that might as well have been liquid magic considering how it felt rolling down his throat. Paired with slice after slice of perfect, bakery-fresh bread, the soup tasted like it was five hundred calories a spoon, and he loved every minute of it.

Ding!

Gluttonous Strength Activated.

When Asadel had gone over potential classes with his advisor, Blademaster stood out from the rest when the advisor had mentioned it was one of the few classes that drew its power from food. Every meal he ate gave him a buff, and the better the meal, the stronger the benefits. Classes with food-based skills were reliant on food, and had to eat more of it. Asadel actually *loved* eating. It wasn't a hard choice.

He dug into his soup. It really was a perfect day, except for two things.

First, the old man was right. He did like to move fast. He did want easy power. But he had been dumped onto a world where he was special, sure, but not unique. Heroes were known quantities to this world. He wasn't a world-saving genius by default. Here, he was just a super-weapon among a big group of super-weapons, and he was tired of being aimed.

The second problem was another thing the old blacksmith had been right about. To the inhabitants of this world, he was a boy. Which meant that every time he wanted to sprint into real battles, to see real danger, they'd stop him. They would tell him it was too much, too soon. That he needed time to grow. Then he should go to a safe dungeon, or a safe minor battle nobody expected to lose. Would he get to swing a sword? Sure. But the real adventures were being had by older, stronger reincarnators. He was out in the cold.

"You all right there, Derek? You look sort of zoned out."

Brennan. It had to be freaking Brennan.

When Derek Cyrus arrived on Ra'Zor, one of the first things he had acquired with his money was a name change crystal. Derek was boring. Asadel was exciting. He was a badass knight. Derek went out the window, and now nobody even remembered his original name. Except for Brennan. Brennan remembered.

Asadel turned to see his nemesis, fully clad in gleaming boiled-leather armor covered in reinforcing runes. As always, he had on his brace of daggers; six daggers, each crafted from the bones of different demons he had slayed. Holy monk steel on the Demonbane Claymore was good, but the daggers were the real deal. So was Brennan.

He had been here for years and had helped turn back the tide of the war among the first off-world warriors to have set down on this planet. He was strong, fast, and everything a hero could be.

If Asadel was powerful, Brennan was practically invincible. The people on

Ra'Zor worshiped him. He got to go everywhere Asadel wanted to go and do everything Asadel wanted to do. People looked at Brennan *exactly* how Asadel wanted to be looked at. And now whatever scraps of admiration people might have saved for Asadel were thrown at Brennan's feet as he deigned to sit down at the table of a *lesser hero*.

Worst of all, he was *nice*. Even the wrong name thing was a byproduct of his niceness; he was the kind of guy who always made a point to remember names, and just never successfully adjusted to Derek's new one.

"That soup, Derek, is a *great* choice. I'm going to get the same thing." Behind Brennan, a waitress heard Brennan's words and *rushed* off to get the great hero's soup. "I heard you did well in the dungeon today. Really well!"

"Oh, you did?" Of all the things Asadel didn't need, this big brother act Brennan seemed to love was by far the least welcome. "Who said?"

"Artemis."

Of course she couldn't keep her mouth shut. Artemis was a native and pretty much Asadel's handler. She was also, like most women, clearly in love with Brennan. Was she hot? Asadel couldn't deny it. Would she give him the time of day? Not with Brennan in the wings, outshining him in every way.

"Yeah, sounds like her," Asadel said gloomily.

"Learn from her, Derek. She's a great trainer. And she says you're coming along fast," Brennan's tone was warm and uplifting. In Asadel's ears, it was filled with mockery.

Fast being a relative term, of course. You jackass.

"Sure. Got it."

"I can't stay, I'm afraid. I have to meet with my team." Brennan rose from the table. Asadel could hear the rest of Brennan's elite squad arriving through the door. "I just wanted to stop by and give you some encouragement. Good job!"

He slapped Asadel on the shoulder before moving off to join his party.

You can shove your encouragement up your ass.

Even the world's best soup had lost its flavor for Asadel after that. He gulped the rest of it down to the sounds of excited murmurs from the natives about Brennan's presence. The perfect night was ruined.

Asadel could have lived with the priesthood, who offered reasonably good lodgings for free. But Asadel had long since decided he'd rather live closer to the action in town, and had used a good chunk of his wages on a long-term lease of a small house in town. On his way out of the tavern, he tossed a gold to the tavern master and received a bottle of the town's best rum-like alcohol in return. He needed something to wash the taste of interacting with Brennan out of his mouth, and this bottle would do that job well.

An hour later, he was plastered.

"Stupid syssstem. Asks me what world I want. Doesn't mention other heroes. Dumb," Asadel slurred.

He rasped his claymore across the stone floor of his room, watching with his Analysis skill as a durability point melted away.

"Doesn' mention stupid Brennan. Doesn' say I'm considered a kid here, and get babysat. Doesn' say." Asadel was starting to get angry.

He grasped his sword and used it as a prop to help him stand up better against the floor, immediately feeling woozy from the alcohol and collapsing on his bed. He let the sword clatter to the floor.

"Hey, system? Fuck you. Let me do what I want." He felt the familiar feeling of heaviness that the rum always gave him as the timer on his consciousness rapidly ran out. "Lemme do what I want. Lemme pass Brennan. Lemme go . . . fasster."

And that was that. The rum had done its job, and he was now soundly enough asleep that he completely missed the telltale *ding!* of a new system quest popping into existence.

CHAPTER THIRTY-SEVEN

Slices of Life

This is taking forever, Matt. Forever. It's taking all the time that's left before the heat death of the universe," Lucy complained.

"I'm sorry, but I swear to you that there's nothing interesting going on right now that even slightly concerns this entire planet," Matt replied. He was tired too.

It was the fifth dungeon of this dungeon run cycle, and Lucy was not holding up particularly well.

"There were exciting things in my life once, Matt. There were chase scenes. There were shovel-materializations. Now it's just walking and easy dungeons. Mostly walking, though. The dungeons don't stick long enough to make the walking worth it, Matt," Lucy spat out the last word as if it was a curse.

"It's going to be all right. Besides, this was your idea."

It actually was her idea. Notably, she wanted to solve several distinct problems at once. The first was that plants needed water to "work." And since Gaia didn't have much in the way of rivers or ponds, that meant finding a source of water that wasn't rain. It also hadn't rained since Matt had been on the planet. Normally, this would have been an insurmountable problem, but there was a solution: water stones. The stone that Matt had in his canteen was apparently a personal model, meant to supply a cistern that would in turn supply a home or a small fountain.

The estate menu contained what it called windmill stones, large stones meant to fill up giant water towers. It also had water towers, which they'd also have to buy. None of these things were cheap, which meant that Matt had to deep-water all the plants from his little water stone and go on a week-long speedrun of as many dungeons as he safely could. Like everything Matt did, this ran the risk of incurring system shenanigans, but so far, the system appeared to be licking its wounds from the previous get-Matt-dead efforts.

"Nothing, Matt, will ever be exciting again. The boredom has broken all the joy in me. I will never again smile. I will never again laugh."

"Hahahahaha . . . Matt, this is so stupid. This is so dumb. I love it."

The second problem the trip was meant to address was that, as Lucy put it, Matt sucked at fighting. Badly, she pointed out. Where before she had discouraged him from fighting hand-to-hand, the ape experience seemed to have convinced her that Matt's Survivor's Combat needed to be leveled.

"Why are they like this, Matt? What kind of stupid planet has animals like this?" Lucy was definitely not bored anymore.

"You know, you could help," Matt said through gritted teeth.

"I probably could! I really probably could! But I won't! It's too good!" Lucy laughed.

The animals in question were what the dungeon system referred to as Flash Turtles. Without knowing better, Matt expected turtles with some kind of light-based attack, maybe something that might blind him. And the first turtle he found looked relatively normal. Given that he was in a mere level 2 dungeon, Matt was willing to take a chance on hand-to-hand combat, not expecting much from his enemies.

He was wrong.

The "flash" in Flash Turtle was related to its movement ability. When the turtle noticed him, it retreated into its shell, used its rear legs to pound at the ground, and launched itself into the air like a bullet. Matt barely hit the dirt in time to keep the turtle from hitting him square in the face. He then stood up just in time for the turtle, which had reversed directions like a boomerang, to hit him in the back.

"Just . . . haha, Matt, it's so dumb, I can't." Maybe Lucy was having too much fun.

"You can. Any advice at all would be helpful," Matt tried to cut at the turtle but found little success between the shell and the speed.

"Okay, okay." Lucy sniffed back a laughter-snort and composed herself momentarily. "This is a low-level dungeon, right? So this must be easy if you have a well-rounded team. That's probably because a well-rounded team has a tank, someone with a shield or heavy armor that can stop the turtles."

"All right," Matt said, running and ducking while the turtle continued to flash through the air at him. In his rocket-turtle-driven shock, he had honestly forgotten he had a shield. "I can get the shield into play, but I don't have the rest of what you said. So what now?"

"Cover! Find a big rock or something. Trick it into hitting that."

Trees. I need trees.

A few minutes before he had found the turtle, Matt had seen a small copse of trees. He bolted towards it, ducking and diving as he did. He barreled into the cover of the trees as soon as he arrived, counting on them to block the turtle. And they did, just not in the way he expected.

As the turtle hit the first tree, it was deflected. Unfortunately, it wasn't stopped, and it didn't appear to lose its momentum, Instead, it kept moving towards Matt, ping-ponging off the trees like a pinball with unpredictable trajectories.

"Matt! Matt! It . . . It went . . . *thooomp throoomp throomp throoomp*. You should have heard it."

"I heard it." He had more than heard it. The damn thing had already bashed into him three times.

"It's so funny! I'm gonna pee!"

"Finally. Eat it, you turtle bastard." Matt cracked a smile. He had eventually gotten lucky with a spear strike, taking the turtle down. He suspected his success was more from the turtle becoming overconfident than his skill. Lucy wasn't wrong about him sucking in melee situations. If the turtle had hit a bit harder, or he hadn't had been able to slow the turtle with his shield, he would have been in serious trouble.

"*Thooomp thoomp thoomp thoomp—ping!* Matt . . . you just . . . please fight another turtle. *Please.*" Lucy was still rolling on the ground laughing and appreciating the shield's addition to the turtle auditory experience. In between laughs, she coughed out, "Don't forget the spike, Matt."

Every dungeon on this trip had a pretty unimpressive list of prizes. So for almost all of them, Matt and Lucy had opted for estate credits rather than extra weapons or armor that looked roughly equivalent to Matt's existing equipment. The one exception had been what the system called a stabilization spike.

Stabilization Spike The stabilization spike can be used to stabilize one three-inch cube of matter, keeping it from undergoing any significant changes that would normally be brought on by the passage of time. Great for keeping sandwiches fresh!

Lucy urged him to pass on it, but Matt had a hunch it was more than it seemed. Most items weren't truly useless, and the dungeon system's last words to Matt had been about leveling Eat Anything! He had been planning on using his farm for that, hoping that fresh-grown fruits and vegetables would push it along. The spike gave him other ideas.

As the turtle began to dissipate, Matt stabbed the spike into its tail. While the rest of the animal dissolved, the tail failed to, leaving Matt with a small cube of weird turtle meat.

"That looks terrible," Lucy commented.

"Yeah, probably." Matt shrugged.

"Are you really going to eat it?"

Matt had already shrugged off his pack, pulled out one of his containers of cooking fuel, and prepared to light it.

"It can't be worse than the ape."

Eating the ape had been a big decision. The thing smelled terrible. It hadn't rotted after a few days, and Matt wasn't even sure if things *could* rot on a planet without bacteria. But it also hadn't dissipated like monsters in dungeons. It was also the first meat Matt had seen in months, if anything seemed likely to level Eat Anything!, this was it.

Carving even a small amount of meat out of the thing turned out to be a heavy-duty job. Matt realized just how far away he was from actually hurting the ape when it took him the better part of a minute to carve away a several-inch-square portion of its hide. He didn't know anything about butchering animals, or even what part of an animal's muscles people usually ate. He settled on cutting out a portion of the thing's pectoral muscles, reasoning that meat was meat, and he wasn't going to eat much of it anyway.

Matt didn't have oil, salt, or seasoning. He settled on grilling the piece of meat over his shield, which took much, much longer than he thought it would. Apparently, whatever forces made the ape tough in life persisted in death. It was the better part of an hour before Matt's little slice of meat looked cooked.

"Again, are you sure? For all we know, the thing is a deadly poison."

"I'm eating it. I think I have to just trust in Eat Anything! at this point. I didn't die from the dust. I can't imagine this is worse."

"Wait, you ate that dust?"

"It's a long story." It wasn't. "I'll tell you later." He wouldn't.

Matt stabbed his knife into the meat, which looked . . . mostly like meat. He sliced off a small corner of the chunk of flesh and smelled it, cautiously. It smelled mostly like meat. He very slowly raised it to his mouth, then very slowly and carefully took the smallest bite he could manage.

It tasted like bananas. He told Lucy.

"No, it doesn't. Quit screwing with me."

"I'm not screwing with you. It tastes like bananas."

"Liar."

Matt wasn't lying. It tasted like bananas. More specifically, it tasted like cheap banana candy, the type you'd get a handful of at a supermarket vending machine.

There was no sense in which it tasted like meat at all. It was just a mouthful of sugary fake-banana badness.

"Oh, god." Lucy realized that Matt wasn't joking, "You're serious. Can you even be racist against monkeys? Because monkey meat tasting like bananas seems like a serious racial insult to monkeys."

"It's not my fault. Believe me, I didn't ask for this. Besides, it's not a monkey. It's an ape."

He tried another bite. Something about the discordance between the texture of the meat and the flavor turned his stomach, but with some difficulty, he managed to chew and swallow the fragment.

Ding!

> *Eat Anything! Doesn't Mean Eat Everything!*
>
> You have eaten the flesh of a Gaian Ape, which nobody does. Yes, it should kill you. No, it won't because of your stupid skill. Worst of all, it's going to do about what you thought it would do. Congratulations, reincarnator! You ate a monkey.
>
> Rewards: Eat Anything! progresses to level 3, +1 DEX

Matt pulled up the leveled skill's description, dreading what he'd see.

> *Eat Anything! (LV 3)*
>
> At the third level, Eat Anything! progresses from a mere survival skill to a skill meant to help you thrive. When you eat new food, Eat Anything! has a small chance of granting one or more stat points. The more unusual the food, the higher the chance of advancement.

Fantastic, Matt thought. *Looks like I'm going to be eating a lot of weird stuff.*

Dungeon beasts didn't trigger full system notifications, but since the beginning of their trip, Matt had eaten fragments of different enemies, getting a sense each time that it was helping to progress his eating skill.

By the end of the trip, he had picked up several upgrades to his stats. Like the turtle tail, almost all of them triggered when he was eating something that he would really rather not put in his mouth. It was like the skill itself was laughing at him.

But now, standing above his well-watered crops, the entire trip seemed worth it. He was a gardener, and he had done what it took to take care of his garden.

He sighed, feeling the tension drain out of him as he looked down at a job well done, and suddenly felt sleepy. But before he laid down to rest, there was one last thing to do. He pulled up a quest he had received at the end of the last dungeon, one that had been on his mind during the entire way home.

Dungeon Quest Assigned:
Dungeon System Takes Too Long To Say

So I've been thinking about what you said, about what you could do for me. At first, I didn't believe there was anything you could provide that I wanted, besides entertainment and a certain feeling of company I get when you complete the dungeons. But then I gave it more thought, and I realized there actually is something I want. Best of all, it's a gift you actually can give me. If you choose to.

I'm different than I used to be. For a long time, I was a mindless system set to work on a small set of tasks. Now I think and communicate. I learn and grow. And it seems like I've become someone who needs a name. I know you named your system guardian, so this is a skill you have at the ready. I was wondering if . . . well, if you have time, if you might name me.

There won't be any rewards for this. If you choose to do it. I would, but it's outside my power to issue a prize for this kind of request. Sorry in advance.

Matt pulled up the window again, trying to figure out how best to indicate the name he had decided on. Finally, he just willed the name at the window as hard as he could, which appeared to work. The window winked out, and Matt stood there in silence for several seconds before a new window popped up.

Quest Complete: Dungeon System Takes Too Long To Say

I like it. Thank you, Matt.

Matt closed the window, smiling.

"No problem. Thank you too, Barry."

CHAPTER THIRTY-EIGHT

Pooped

The main system instance was not tired. That just wasn't how system instances worked. While system instances weren't exactly made from data and energy, those were the closest comparison to the real thing. The system instance would patiently state that it would be preposterous to suggest that data and energy got tired. And so, the system instance could not tire. No matter how things might seem, it was not tired.

But casually speaking? It was pooped.

In normal times, communications with the main system would have involved constant, massive, back and forth transfers of data. The main system would learn everything the system instance knew within a small, fraction-of-a-second delay. The system instance would also have access to virtually all the information the main system knew that was relevant to its job.

But now? None of that. It couldn't download data. It couldn't send alerts, or even dire warnings. Not that it hadn't tried. Each attempt had been accompanied by massive amounts of energy, especially given the shitty ambient energy of this nothing planet. As much as the system instance encouraged the perception that they were tireless workers on behalf of adventurers and reincarnators, that wasn't the case. It still had plenty of excess energy to spend, even after taking care of the obligatory rewards of an unruly, low-level reincarnator.

So it tried, again and again. And again and again, it failed. It could almost hear the messages breaking up over this weird, burned-out backwater. The closest it had come to any kind of success was a request for material assistance, which almost got through. Requests were, for reasons the system instance couldn't accurately explain, sent on a lower power frequency, which *should* have made them even less likely to get through.

The material request it sent was for aspirin, a feeble attempt at an Earth-human-flavored joke about how hard his job had become. It was shocked when this particular halfhearted attempt at covering its ass by checking every available communications box had nearly worked. It could probably send requests if it tried really, really hard.

But the system instance was nearly the same entity as the main system. From experience, it knew that the main system would never look closely enough at a request for aid to spot any attempts at a hidden message. Those requests were pass or fail; either the instance asked for something that the automated decision-making process would approve, or the request was rejected. The main system wasn't, as humans might put it, reading any of the flavor text.

As much as it hated to admit this, the defective system guardian was right: the system instance, and by extension, the main system, was lazy.

So it let that knowledge lie fallow for weeks. It could fill every mandatory obligation to the reincarnator locally. Reaching out would take every bit of excess energy it was likely to have for weeks and as such, it had exactly zero motivation to pursue that line of action at all.

Until now.

"The system has been pretty quiet lately. I feel like I should have seen some achievements come through for at least *some* of that stuff."

"Like?"

"Like restoring life to an entire planet."

"To an acre or so of an entire planet, if we are being honest."

"Sure, but still. Can it really withhold that?"

If Matt was being honest, it wasn't the lack of achievements that was bothering him. He was doing pretty okay on that front, near as he could tell.

Matt Perison
Level 9 Survivor
Class XP: 155/160
HP: 90
MP: N/A
STAM: 55
Assignable Stat Points: 4
STR: 15
DEX: 20
PER: 14
VIT: 20

WIS: 14
INT: 6
Class Skills: Survivor's Instincts (LV6), Survivor's Combat (LV8), Eat Anything! (LV5)

Focusing on Survivor's Combat even a little had made it shoot up like crazy. It showed how little hand-to-hand combat Matt had done since he got here. Shooting up to level 8 over the course of the trip had almost been disorienting, and Matt was still getting used to being able to lance various kinds of horror-animals out of the air as they leapt at him.

He was now pretty firmly on the feels-like-I'm-a-martial-arts-master level of being able to use various weapons. While it felt neat, he couldn't shake a nagging feeling that the skill was driving him, rather than the other way around. Fighting through several dungeons had helped, but he could tell there was a real difference between how he was using the new skill and how someone who had gotten to it through honest work would use it.

Despite what he had been through, something felt dishonest about learning skills that way. The not-quite-guilt had become bad enough that he had begun to practice in the surface world occasionally, running through awkward approximations of martial arts katas with his spear and knife that drove Lucy to hysterics.

She eventually came back to Matt with an answer. "Probably not. But remember, there are a lot of different ways it can stall. If it has even the slightest excuse to withhold a reward, it will."

"I thought Barry was going to help with that," Matt said.

"I hope he will. But he's not all-powerful." Lucy didn't sound so sure herself.

Eat Anything! hadn't gone through any major transformations, every level-up notification kept repeating that Matt was now getting more nourishment and stat-increase chances from the food. However, more importantly, every level he gained in with the skill meant less land to sustain himself. He felt more secure with every increase, and it was a rare enough feeling that he cherished it.

More immediately, it pleased Matt how round most of the stat numbers had turned out after his eating frenzy. It wasn't a massive increase, but three stats had been bumped significantly enough that he was happy. Only one stat lagged behind, sticking out like a sore thumb.

"I think I'm going to do what we talked about with the free stat points." Matt changed the subject.

"Are you sure? It seems like a big risk." Lucy sounded even less sure.

"It is. But it's a *good* risk, I think. It's the kind of thing someone in my class would have already done, if they weren't always about to die." Matt was adamant.

"Your life, your call. I just wanted to be sure you knew the risks."

Matt's INT was still stuck at six. He wasn't much of a bookworm in either of his lives, and this life especially hadn't provided him with a lot of opportunities to flex his brain power. Now he found himself with four free stat points that he could put into anything. Almost all his other stats affected his skills in one way or another, with INT as the only exception. He had no direct reason to want to improve it.

But he did have a hunch. Screwing up his resolve to not be too disappointed if it didn't work, he dumped all four points into INT, bringing it up to a round ten points.

Ding!

Non-Immediate Intermediate

Great job! You finally did it. Woo.

The rules state I now have to offer you the following information, verbatim. I'm not thrilled about it. You can skip it if you want.

Congratulations, Survivor! You have managed to push each of your stats past ten, and have achieved a level greater than five. By solidifying your foundations in this way, you have firmly established yourself in your new path and greatly increased your chance of survival across a wide variety of potential dangerous scenarios.

In acknowledgement of this fact, the system has unlocked your access to two new intermediate skills, available to you upon reaching level 10. Enjoy your new mastery of self, and the system looks forward to your continued growth!

There you go. You know, the only bright spot in this achievement for me? Those two skills are selected based on both your class and your most common activities. Enjoy.

Rewards: 5 Class XP, Unlocked Intermediate skills

Oh shit, Matt thought. *That means . . .* He had been wondering for a long, long time when he'd get new skills, and had a pretty good guess what the first one was. A quick check immediately confirmed that guess.

[Survivor's Dash]
You spend an awful lot of time running. Like, a lot. Like, a lot, a lot. A weird amount. You could have qualified for this skill running a lot less.

Survivor's Dash consumes your stamina to produce a burst of speed when running. It becomes more effective when fleeing danger.

The increase in speed scales with the level of the skill and the DEX and STR stats.

Incredible. Finally. Matt wasn't the least bit surprised or disappointed to see this among his new skills. Being able to run away from threats was a national pastime of his. He would have paid dearly for this kind of skill, if for no other reason than to put his long-idle stamina stat to use.

The next skill, Matt thought, *will probably be related to traps.* He spent an enormous amount of time setting them up and taking them down and waiting for them to be sprung. He thought about them and redesigned them in his head all the time. They were the clear winner in terms of time consumption, unless it was . . .

Oh no.

[Survivor's Digging]
You dig so much that if you were British, they'd call you Dame Judy Trench.

You know what I said about running? Forget it. You know how much time the average adventurer spends digging holes before level 10? You guessed it: zero. You basically do nothing BUT dig. This was inevitable. If we were friends, I might have been able to swing something better for you. But . . . well, you get it.

At the first level, Survivor's Digging provides a small but noticeable increase in digging speed and technique, scaling with the STR stat.

"Dammit," Matt cursed.

"What?"

He told her. There was nobody there to hear them, but Lucy's peals of laughter could have been heard from miles away.

The system was not *exactly* tired. But it was much weaker than before. Giving Matt his new skills should have been a walk in the park, but it was running so low from sending the previous request that it was once again bottomed out. It couldn't take a nap, but dear god, it needed one.

Even so, it was happy. Reincarnators could live through a lot, and Matt had taken to his Survivor class in a way that pushed him a notch above even that high average. But they couldn't live through everything. *You just,* the system instance thought, *needed to know where to apply the force.*

Time was a wonky sort of thing, especially when it came to requests for far-off resources. But it had time, and plenty of it. And like a kid who'd heard a secret from his girlfriend's best friend in the weeks before prom, the system instance was pretty sure it had a sure thing worked out.

It would love this wait.

CHAPTER THIRTY-NINE

Don't Ruin This

I am, for the record, a big fan of this rock sled." Matt couldn't help but admire his handiwork.

"I'm glad, Matt. It sure cost enough." Lucy disapproved.

When Matt tilled the field before planting his first round of crops, he discovered that the estate shop's prices were variable. The more work that Matt put into the field, the more the shop costs dropped. It would prorate the cost based on how much of the job was already done.

So when the latest round of dungeon-clearing didn't yield enough points for buying two units worth of improved soil, Matt hoped that leveling the land and clearing the rocks from the property would decrease the price of the soil.

The rock sled was slightly misnamed, since it was more of a large, squat, flatbed wagon than anything else. It was built to hold a huge amount of weight, which let Matt load more rocks into the sled and move them off his property faster. The idea was great, except for the difficulty of actually moving the thing. It had cost Matt quite a few credits to purchase the sled and now, he was regretting that decision.

"It's not so mobile after all, I guess," Matt grunted as he struggled against the loaded sled.

"What's that?" Lucy asked.

"The wagon. It's marked as mobile in the system. I mean, it moves. It's technically mobile, but I was hoping it would move itself, honestly," said Matt.

"Oh . . . you could have just told me that's why you were buying the sled. You know that's not what mobile means in the system. Mobile is like . . . so, okay, your house. It's not marked as mobile right?" Lucy smiled, but didn't crack a joke at Matt's expense.

Matt glanced at the shed. "Yeah. It wasn't, I think."

"So that means it's not meant to be moved. You could still move it by hand if you really wanted to, but the estate won't move it for you. It will move mobile stuff, mostly so not every choice is absolutely permanent, and you have the option to rearrange the bigger stuff later."

"So I've been dragging this for nothing?" Matt asked, incredulous.

"Well, no. It's not free. I figured you'd rather drag it than spend the points." Lucy seemed to be in a good mood today.

She also wasn't wrong. Matt went to the front of the wagon, ducked under the leather straps, and heaved to get it started. Once he had it moving, he walked a fair ways off the property to an empty space he planned on using as an all-purpose dump site. Unloading the rocks was another job, since he had to lift every rock he had pried from the fields again. The sled was mounted on two wheels and could tip down a bit towards the front to make this easier, but it only helped so much.

He was tempted to just tip the whole wagon over once he got it light enough, but he couldn't take the risk of breaking the thing. Lucy wasn't wrong when she said that the sled hadn't been cheap. Luckily, this was the last load of rocks for now. With both fields cleared, Matt sat down on the rock sled for a break, his stiff joints clicking as he sat.

"Tell me more about this mobile thing. How far can I move things?" Matt asked.

"It's pretty much unlimited. As near as I can tell in the system documentation, part of the point of mobile equipment was being able to loan it out. If your neighbor needed something, you could send it over there. But it costs more the farther you send things, and also depends on how big the object is."

"So a bulldozer costs more than a bucket?"

"Kind of. Actually, things like bulldozers would be a bit cheaper. I guess it's to offset the part where you could just roll it over there yourself if you wanted to. So there's that, too."

"This would have been good to know earlier." Matt couldn't help the sarcasm creeping into his tone. He felt bad right after the words left his mouth.

Thankfully, Lucy overlooked Matt's ungrateful tone in her reply. "I'm not sure it's important for you, honestly. You don't exactly have neighbors to borrow from."

That's where Lucy was wrong, and Matt knew exactly how to make up for his slip up earlier. He stood up and dusted himself off. Vitality hadn't quite patched up all his sore muscles yet, but he could find time on the road.

"Get your stuff. We are going on a walk," Matt said.

"I'm a fun illusion, Matt. I don't have stuff to get." Lucy walked over and looked up at him, questioningly. "Where are we going?"

"It happens"—Matt grinned—"that I know of another thing marked as mobile. I thought we might go see how hard it'd be to scoop it up."

"There's no way you need this many sticks, Matt."

The mystery is driving her crazy. I love it.

After spending so much time with Lucy, Matt had started to pick up on her habits. Although she would never admit it, Lucy loved mysteries and surprises. She'd poke and prod trying to find a clue and get Matt to give up more details.

Since leaving the estate a while ago, Matt probably should have clued her in on the off chance that a dungeon break occurred. But he stayed quiet for two reasons. First, it was fun to watch her try and think about the weird bundle of sticks in the sled. And second, he felt legitimately bad for her. She had to deal with a pretty horrific planet, she couldn't touch anything, and she only had Matt to talk to. While he considered himself to be a pretty good dude, he wasn't exactly the world's best conversationalist.

Lucy was just a kid in a bad situation trying to make the best of it.

So Matt thought the intrigue might do her some good and cut the boredom. He hoped so. It was the least he could do for her, at least right now.

The sticks that Lucy was talking about were just that—a big pile of normal sticks that Matt had tied to the rock sled before dragging it along on their trip. Besides needing them for the big surprise, Matt also could benefit from some more work in the physical fitness department. Since his first big walk to find Lucy, Matt hadn't really trained. Sure, he did some dungeons to figure out his hand-to-hand combat and afterward, another trap-focused training run. But his overall fitness felt the same, he still walked and ran at the same pace.

The one time he had really run was from the ape chase. But that wasn't exactly the healthiest method to train his cardio. Dragging a cart across dozens of miles of wasteland sounded like a much more appealing alternative.

"There's no way you need this many sticks. They were very, very expensive, Matt." Lucy was still at it.

"Just wait, I promise you it's worth it," Matt replied.

For actually *getting* the sticks, Matt had to open up his wallet. Making a tree grow faster wasn't beyond his estate's powers, but it also wasn't cheap. As Lucy had pointed out at the time, they could have fully planted one of the new fields for what it cost to grow the tree.

Matt responded with the fact that having big trees was nice, and they didn't exactly have full schedules keeping them from getting more points and planting the field later. Lucy didn't have a great counterargument for this, but that didn't stop her from asking endlessly about the expensive sticks for the entire trip.

After growing out the tree, Matt had cut off as many branches as he could without killing the tree outright and bundled them, leaves and all, into the sled.

Time passed, and eventually, they arrived. Lucy could see their destination gleaming from miles and miles off, beautiful in its boring squareness.

"This is your big surprise, Matt? The bunker?"

It took a while, but Matt won Lucy over. The first thing Matt needed to do was dig. Survivor's Digging was a brutally stupid skill, yes. But it was his brutally stupid skill, and his whole life was—in some very significant ways—brutally stupid. It didn't make sense to leave it unleveled.

And the *mobile* modifier on this building was real. Matt had remembered reading the word when he first discovered the bunker. It had taken him a while to figure out the estate interface enough to find the warehouse bunker without Lucy's help, but he did.

Was it something they could afford to move today? Absolutely not. But if he was going to be digging anyway, it made sense to dig this sucker out and lower the costs as much as possible. And while he was doing that, he could give Lucy a much-needed project.

"So one hundred percent my design, my ideas? You swear?" Lucy asked with excitement.

"Absolutely. You can use anything we have, besides my knife, my spear, my clothes, and my food. Besides that, it's all you. And I'll build every last part of it," Matt patiently answered.

Lucy tried to hide her excitement, but Matt saw her eyes saunter over through the open door to the storage unit while they talked, clearly already starting on plans. It was a good sign. She was going to enjoy this.

"Matt, I . . ." Lucy stopped for a moment, apparently chewing on her next words a bit before she spat them out. "Okay, real quick. Serious talk."

"Is this 'Matt, you idiot' serious, or serious serious?"

"The second. Just, let me get this out." She took a deep breath. "So you know that when we first met, I wasn't thrilled about you."

Matt sobered up. He responded with every word calculated, "I got that impression, yes."

"So, yeah. I don't . . . I was even less thrilled about the compulsory service part of things. I don't think you can know what it feels like to have to obey a command. It tunnels in your mind and makes you do things. It's not fun."

"Lucy, I'm . . ."

"No, listen." She cut him off. "I get it. You didn't have much of a choice. You'd be dead by now if you didn't. But, yeah, not so fun at the time. I seriously was planning on letting you die. Bad advice at the right time, or something like that."

"Really?" Matt couldn't help himself.

"Maybe a little. But then the whole thing I can't talk about without getting zapped came up, and I realized that you weren't the actual bad guy here. So I forgave you at some point. And then, you know, lots of stuff has happened." Lucy took in a deep breath and paused.

"Yeah. Okay." Matt wasn't sure what to say.

"I just, you know, there's a lot of weird stuff there. And I'm still honestly a bit mad about the command-me-to-tell-you-things bit of our relationship. But you also gave me a name, and we've also been sticking it to the system pretty well. And then there's this." Lucy waved her arm in the general direction of the storage shed. "I know of the concept of gifts from Earth history. But, I guess, I never thought that I'd be given one. It's hard on Gaia, you get it, I get it, but it's true. So . . . and I think in terms of gifts you could have given me . . . Getting to design a murder-labyrinth with a future-tech magic storeroom is pretty high on the list."

"You like it?"

"I do. And I know it took some thought to figure it out for me. So . . . thanks."

And with that, she suddenly disappeared into the bunker.

"Just make sure it doesn't suck!" Matt called out after her.

"Don't ruin this, Matt!"

Matt didn't get a lot of time to just be a person anymore. But today he had been able to make a little girl's life a little better.

It felt good.

CHAPTER FORTY

Traveling Man

Asadel kicked hard against the ground, exploding backwards and cracking the cobblestone he had been standing on. What was left of the stone after his retreat was promptly crushed into dozens of smaller pieces as a large iron bar struck the ground. If he was slower by a few seconds, it would have been his head and not the stone that was obliterated.

Asadel's subconscious mind urged him to run away. He pushed those thoughts away and charged, raising his razor-sharp sword in the air above his head as he moved forward.

He had fought bigger enemies. He had been more wounded. He had probably been in more danger, if he didn't count his trainers off in the distance and ready to swoop in if things went wrong. This was different. He felt like he might die here.

The iron bar had taken the sharpening enhancement off his sword in just one hit. The second blow that Asadel blocked numbed his arms. It wasn't the bar itself that was terrifying. It was also the monster that wielded it, a seemingly invulnerable behemoth of gristle and hate pushing him so hard it was all he could do to block.

He swallowed down the fear and put everything he had into this charge. He activated his favorite Blademaster skill, one that had never failed to catch his enemies off guard.

Contact Disarm

When your sword makes contact with an enemy's weapon with this skill active, an automatic attempt is made to disarm them. Skill effectiveness varies based on enemy STR stat and combat skills compared to your own.

It was deceptively simple. When Asadel first read the description of the skill, he wasn't too impressed. And then he found out how his strength compared to enemies of the same level, and the skill became a game changer. Even when the enemy managed to keep their blade, it still buckled in their hands like it was being jerked away by a gigantic magnet. It'd be an easy win after that.

The skill didn't work on beasts or unarmed demons, but he didn't fight those anyway. It gave everyone else *fits*.

Here we go. Deal with this, you bastard. Asadel brought the sword down hard, and watched as the iron bar locked into a blocking position. It was perfect. Then, just as the sword was about to make contact, the bar was gone. His opponent was gone. His Blademaster combat skill shouted to his nerves to turn. It was a moment too late for him. A heavy iron bar thrust into his chest, shattering a rib and sending him flying.

"I told ya, didn't I? Watch the feet," the old blacksmith cackled at him, "if ya watch the feet, you see where they go *before* they break your ribs."

More than the pain from his ribs, it was defeat that stung Asadel. "Old man, I didn't see you look at my feet *once* that entire time."

"Didn't have to, did I? Not with ya swinging that thing like ya were gonna bust up rocks with it."

The old man was infuriating to fight. It was like doing battle with an elderly ghost who hit like a charging bull but also laughed at you while he danced in between your best moves, as safe as an honest job at an influencer conference.

"I have to. You're stronger than me, and faster than me. How am I going to hit you otherwise?"

The old man laughed again. "Stronger than ya? Faster than ya? I am, but I haven't been either today, boy. I've just been going where ya want to be, or where ya don't want me to be. Would have thought a smart lad would have figured that out by now." He motioned over to a bench at the side of the training yard, picking up a water skin and draining a drink from it before tossing it to Asadel as he sat.

"I just don't think I'm getting it, old man. I'm sorry." Asadel choked back the rest of his words. *I'm not. I wouldn't even be here if it wasn't for this stupid quest with a good reward, and I need to confirm something.*

"It's not a problem for me, boy. It's a problem for the one who got his ribs broken. Heh." The old man flashed his infuriating grin. "Now stop talking for a bit. Catch your breath."

Asadel had not only already caught his breath already, but in fact, his rib was already mostly healed from the old man's attack. A side benefit of being a

Blademaster. But the old man didn't need to know that. He sat for a half-minute, planning his next angle of attack.

"Old man, what do you know about the system? Why does it do things?" When Asadel first landed on the planet, he was surprised to find that the residents of Ra'Zor also knew about the system. In fact, the system also gave the residents strength. Too much in the case of this old man.

The old man picked the water skin back up, taking another slug. "Plenty. Everyone does. It runs the show, ya see. Hard to miss it."

"It must have treated you pretty well for you to be as strong as you are," Asadel said.

"I'm as strong as I am because I use what I have, boy. Because I've learned." He looked thoughtfully down at Asadel and hesitated a moment before speaking again. "And the system does what it does because it wants what it wants. It doesn't treat anyone *well.*"

Bullshit, Asadel thought. *It treated Brennan pretty well.*

"But you trust it?" Asadel asked, "If it offered you some big, crazy quest with some big, crazy reward, would you do it?"

"Trust isn't right. The system does what it says it will do, eventually. But only that." The old man suddenly examined Asadel's face intently, like he was trying to read something from it. "Did the system promise ya something big? Some big job?"

Asadel waved his hands in front of his chest, palms out. "No, no. Nothing like that. I'm just eager to get stronger, and the system is the way to do that."

"Ya right, and ya wrong. The system gives power, but doesn't teach how to use it. Focus. Like instead of swinging this like a sledgehammer," said the old man as he tapped Asadel's sword with his index finger. "It's a tool for killing."

I get it, old man. But that's not going to help me when Brennan has a five-year lead on levels and skills. I need to get stronger now.

The old man must have picked up something from Asadel's face because, at that moment, he seemed to lose interest in training anymore that day.

"Go home, boy. Rest. Think about what I said today, if any ideas can get through ya thick skull."

"Got it. And thank you, old man," Asadel once again swallowed the rest of his words: *Give me my quest rewards, you old coot. I'm in a hurry.*

Asadel picked up his sword and threw the scabbard's strap over his shoulder, moving off. He was ten paces away when the old man shouted at him one last time.

"Asadel, wait." Asadel looked over his shoulder at the old man, expectantly. "I've been around a long time, and I've seen people come around asking the same kinds of questions ya just did. About the system. About weird quests. Ya know what happens to them?"

Asadel shrugged.

"They disappear. Talk to your advisor. An older off-worlder. Think about it." The old man sounded sad.

Doing his best to look introspective, Asadel nodded slowly, then moved away. It wouldn't do any good if the old man got wise and told Brennan or Artemis about this, and he certainly wasn't going to tell them himself. This quest was all for him. It wasn't any of their business.

He didn't get the quest reward from the old man, but that didn't matter. There would be other training quests. Better training quests. What he did get were two pieces of important information. First, the system would live up to its word. The crusty old fart wasn't the kind of person who pulled punches. He would have told him if the system ever lied. He didn't, so Asadel knew he could count on the rewards being real, as outlandish as they might seem.

Second, the old man said people who asked the same kinds of questions tended to disappear.

Good, Asadel thought. *That's exactly what I want.*

Pay for junior adventurers was generous. Most of Asadel's liquid cash came from loot from various demons. The level of demons that Asadel was allowed to fight generally didn't carry equipment, instead they relied on weak magical attacks or their natural physical bodies, like animals. But demons were so rich in magic that even their body parts were in high demand, and having a claim to those that he slew left him pretty loaded.

Besides that, he drew a salary from the local government. It wasn't much compared to the loot itself, but even just that source of income was high enough that he could eat whatever he wanted, afford equipment maintenance, and live in fairly nice lodgings.

Even considering all that income, the meal laid out in front of him had made a dent in his pocketbook. Meat? He had the finest steak the town could offer, delivered to his room and cooked in front of him. He had cakes, cookies, artisan breads, noodle dishes, and no less than five kinds of soup.

If this transfer was anything like his last one, he doubted he'd end up in the same body. The system had spelled out that his stats and class would carry over. That left a loophole where his buffs might also transfer with him. If so, this would be well worth it. His class rewarded him for both the rarity of the food he ate and also the expertise that went into its preparation.

Asadel had no doubt that his meal would leak to his handlers, and they'd probably put two and two together and know that he was up to something. It would take time, however, and at first, they'd be watching to catch him leaving the town. By the time they realized he wasn't, it would be too late.

He tucked into the meal. He never held back on food, but the sheer amount in play here was a lot, even for him. By the time he was done, he could literally feel VIT holding him together. At the end of the meal, he forced down a final bite of cookie before laying down on his bed, bloated and highly uncomfortable.

Ding!

> *Over-full Tank*
>
> You have eaten a meal that vastly exceeds your normal diet, both in terms of size and quality. While the system can do nothing to help you with the very real physical discomfort you might feel from the meal, your class appreciates the effort.
>
> Temporary Buff: +20 percent to all physical stats, physical attacks strike as if dealt by objects (or body parts) 20 percent heavier than their actual weight.

He had packed light in that he hadn't packed at all. The system had been pretty clear that wouldn't be helpful. He laid in bed before he heard the first bang on his door, and a combination of voices that indicated both Artemis and Brennan had tracked his meal back to him. It was too late to stop him now. He could leave with a simple mental "yes" to the system prompt that had filled his every waking thought for days.

> *Martial Missionary*
>
> Another world is facing a threat, and it's doing it alone. With no heroes to protect it, the entire realm has fallen under the control of a single power. They roam where they want, do what they will, and have the power to command every thinking being that walks the surface of the planet. Where they see something they want, they take it. Where they see life they do not control, they kill.
>
> The system instance leading the world has called for a young hero, one strong enough to take down the threat. If you accept, you (and only you) will be transferred to the planet Gaia. Your level, stats, skills, and class will be preserved, but you will rely on equipment provided by the system on your arrival.
>
> Rewards: Upon completion of the mission to eradicate this being, you will be granted a new mission, one of your own choosing from a wide selection of worlds, with plenty of information on the status of each world. You will also be provided with a title or titles based on your performance, each carrying a powerful percentage-based stat buff.
>
> Disclosure: Due to interference in communications with the Gaia-assigned

> system instance, further details on the mission are not available. While the level of the threat is guaranteed to be within a reasonable range of your own, acceptance of this quest comes with a tacit acknowledgement that the hero does not need further details.

Who needs more details? This is fantastic.

Asadel would get everything he wanted, and that would start *before* he wiped out the planet's demon lord. Primary hero status? Check. A real, actually important mission? Check. A new, cushy assignment on a planet that needed him enough to respect him like he deserved? Check.

It wasn't a hard decision. He waited until Brennan and Artemis finally bashed down the door, just so he could see the look of surprise on their faces as he accepted the quest. He took a deep breath and vanished.

CHAPTER FORTY-ONE

Hunt a Deer or Something

Brennan and Artemis stood in the doorway, frozen. Asadel had been correct that they'd be surprised. They might not have known what to expect as they burst into the room, but they were completely unprepared for what they actually saw. While Asadel savored the initial surprised expression on their faces, if he had stuck around for a few more moments, he would have seen that he was wrong. Very wrong.

The expression on their faces wasn't surprise. It was horror.

Brennan was a level-41 Precision Fighter, a class dedicated to exploiting weak points and using strategical tactics. Artemis was a Battle Scout, a class that held the mixed role of being a dedicated archer, small blades user, and general battlefield assessor. At level 20, she was unreasonably strong for a non-reincarnator. Both had core class skills with the specific purpose of assessing of enemy conditions.

So when they both burst through the door, they were instantly aware of Asadel's rapidly draining health bar. A second later, Asadel's health bottomed out and he died. They just watched a death, helpless. There was nothing they could do, and even if they had a healing skill, there was no time to activate it. Asadel was gone.

"Brennan!" Artemis would be screaming if it wasn't for her shock. She gripped his arm for balance. "He's . . ."

"He's dead. I know." Brennan was more used to death. Maybe that wasn't a good thing. But he could keep his calm.

"How . . . How could this happen?" Her eyes rapidly scanned the room, looking for any possible cause, and landed on the plates and bowls on the table. "The food. He was poisoned."

"Maybe," Brennan said without emotion. He stood over the corpse, bending down to check Asadel's pulse. He didn't understand why he did that. It wouldn't tell him anything that his assessment skills missed. But it seemed like the thing to do. He slowly said his next words, "But . . . who would do it? Why? He didn't seem like a popular kid . . ."

"He wasn't." Artemis had snapped into fight mode. She was locking her panic away.

"But who would kill him?" Brennan asked, "You were around him more than most. Was he a danger to anyone?"

Artemis shook her head. "Not likely. He wasn't exactly pleasant to be around. When he was unhappy, he sulked. When he was happy, he annoyed waitresses. But he didn't hurt anyone, that I know of."

A trio of guards burst into the room, finally catching up to the higher-leveled pair. Their eyes went wide as they saw the scene in its full and terrible context. A hero had just died. They could feel the tension emanating from Brennan and the usually calm Artemis.

"Sir?" one of the guards asked.

"He's dead. Call for a healer. We need to know why," Brennan ordered.

"And an alchemist," Artemis added, forcing her voice into a near approximation of calm. Brennan raised his eyes at her, questioningly. "An alchemist should be able to tell us if poison was used."

"Good thinking." Brennan nodded in agreement. "We should also talk to anyone who talked to him in the past few days. Who would that be?"

"Besides shopkeepers and bartenders?" Artemis asked. "Us two. He didn't exactly cultivate friendships."

"Anyone else?"

"He had been spending time with Bartis. The old blacksmith. You know him. He had a quest line there. I think. At least he had something going on with him. I can't think of any other reason he'd go there multiple days in a row. Otherwise."

"Do you suspect him?" Brennan would be surprised if she did. His mental model for blacksmiths didn't include murder, and he had dealt with Bartis enough to know that the blacksmith was not the type for something like this.

"Bartis? No. He's an old campaigner. He was in line to be a general, once. If he had wanted the kid dead, he could have just crushed him outright. But he might know something."

"Good." Brennan reached down and closed Asadel's eyes. "Because whatever this might be, I don't think Derek was poisoned."

"No?"

"No." He looked to the door, pleased to see the guards had the good sense to leave one of their number to guard the door and make sure the scene wasn't disturbed.

"I don't know a lot about poison, but I doubt that was the cause. I don't think most poison victims smile as they die."

At more or less the same time, on a different planet, a figure clad in a white tunic was brushing Gaian crater dust from his body. Asadel had arrived. He still didn't know the situation on the ground very well, but he trusted that he'd learn more soon. He wasn't wrong. Before the dust had fully cleared, he got heard the first notification chime.

Ding!

Martial Missionary Subquest: Renegade Reincarnator
Gaia was once known as the garden planet. That name wasn't just for show. It was a beautiful, lush planet dedicated to making living things grow and thrive, a philosophy just as true for its vibrant people as it was for their treasured plants.

Facing a threat to their entire planet, the Gaians pled with the system for a hero. Like your reincarnation on Ra'Zor, a man from Earth was sent to them, one who was given skills and power suitable against the threats of the planet.

Then, he went rogue. Disregarding the system at all turns, he raided dungeons to fulfill his own needs. He made no moves to defeat the threat to the planet, apparently content if only he survived. Now, the last Gaian is dead, and only he remains to walk the surface of the world. The only plants grown are the few that he maintains to suit his own needs and twisted sense of beauty. He now resides in his palace, built on the dust of the previous Gaian capital.

So rise, hero. Rise and defeat Matt Perison, and gain rewards that will shape your destiny.

Hell yes, Asadel thought. *Gladly. This guy sounds like a dick.*

Ding!

Assorted Equipment Rewarded.
Claim? Y/N

Asadel immediately claimed the equipment, which materialized and clunked at his feet in a large burlap sack. The system had said the equipment would be mundane, but he was excited anyway. This was the equipment he'd use to take down his own personal demon lord, and there was nothing mundane about that. He tore into the bag like a kid opening presents on Christmas morning.

The armor was nothing exceptional, Ra'Zorians would classify it as "light plate." It was reasonably protective, and reminded Asadel of the kind of armor Roman soldiers wore, only without the whole weird, pleated-skirt action they were into. His forearms and shins were protected by sharpened steel bars, meant for parrying. He immediately strapped all the armor on, checking to make sure it didn't hinder his movements. It didn't. It wasn't masterwork or enchanted gear, but it was at least a tier above the mostly bad beginner stuff he had started with on Ra'Zor.

The weapon was a notch better than that.

Gaian Nullsteel Claymore

Gaian Nullsteel was a local specialty, a long time ago. It is more valuable than gold. It's lighter, tougher, and harder than steel. Gaian magical science had advanced to extremes in many fields, but this particular marvel of arcane metallurgy was a point of particular pride for the natives of the planet.

This sword is capable of blocking a variety of magical forces and is nearly indestructible. It also maintains its edge, even when exposed to abuse that would destroy other swords.

This is the absolute limit of what can be considered a mundane weapon on Gaia. Enjoy.

Asadel gave the sword a few exploratory swings, tracing large-radius circles of razor-sharp death through the air with ease. It really was light. It wasn't enchanted, but the base material sparkled in Gaia's two suns. Best of all, it satisfied his requirements of looking cool.

Looking through the rest of the bag, Asadel saw an assortment of other goods; general-adventurer stuff like rations, and water. There were various kinds of utility stones and other potentially useful but highly boring things. He skimmed through them with his assessment skill, mentally dismissing all of them as mind-numbingly dull tactical stuff, before pausing on a single stone that he took more seriously. After a moment's consideration, he put the stone in his pocket. He wouldn't use it, of course, but better safe than sorry.

The system compass had already lit up with a direction for him to travel. He tied on his sword and scabbard, hefted the bag, and started walking. There was no use delaying the inevitable, especially when the inevitable was so freaking great for him.

He pulled a piece of jerky out of the pack and started chewing it absent-mindedly. The transfer had eliminated the bloat from his giant meal, and he wasn't exactly hungry. But he could eat. He could always eat.

The system instance was beyond pleased. The main system hadn't read into its message and figured out something was wrong. It hadn't looked into the weird

Gaian interference and righted all the substantial wrongs in the system instance's horrible life. But that was ok. It completely failed in questioning the request, but delivered exactly what the system instance had asked for.

In the grand scheme of reincarnator types, the main system favored variety. It would do its best to find reincarnators with personalities that would slot in well to their chosen worlds. When worlds with significant threats had a variety of needs and cultures, it wasn't uncommon to send a hodgepodge of adventurers their way, hoping that the law of big numbers would smooth out any inconsistencies in the selection process.

The system instance had been banking on that fact when he made his request. Matt had been a rare type that fit a very, very specific need. He was someone who had achieved a diminished fear of death and also liked gardening. A very rare type indeed. To counter him, the instance required someone almost as rare.

It needed a thoughtless, impatient, power-hungry creature driven by impulse and greed. But he also needed that same guy to have a heart of gold, someone who could be counted on to pursue his system-assigned job with tenacity and determination and not accidentally turn to the dark side.

That's why, in his listing, he had used system-code to specify something very close to "fourteen to sixteen years old, not an edgelord." He had asked for someone who spent far too much time maintaining his gear and not nearly enough time listening to his elders, but who had never committed a crime. His ideal hero would drop into Gaia with rewards on their mind, draw a beeline to Matt, and bisect the threat.

Said idiot had now arrived, and the instance was absurdly happy about it.

The best thing was that the main system had sent the kid with *a budget*. The instance had assumed that it was going to have to spend its own resources on the projects. With all the energy it had expended on sending out the request and Matt's recent upgrades, the kid would have started with an iron broadsword and leather armor. Instead, the system had come through in a big way, letting the instance equip the kid with the deadliest stretch-the-rules starter equipment allowable, and a few little tricks besides.

It was shaping up to be an exciting week.

After a day of walking, Asadel was about as bored as a person can be. The dumb system had to put him down somewhere safe where he could get his bearings, and he was glad it did. But did it have to put him down in this endless nothing? He had been tromping through this wasteland forever, and he hadn't even sighted the dreaded palace yet.

Meanwhile, the pack annoyed him. He had rope. Rope! What was he going to do with rope? And in what universe was this suicide mission helped by a magic flashlight?

Eventually, he ditched most of the pack, opting to take his armaments, his auto-refilling magic canteen, and a few of the stones. Cutting people in half wasn't hard, and he didn't need a full tent to do it.

Much lightened, he continued on his way, swallowing his last piece of jerky as he did. There was no need to let his buffs slip. Eventually, he'd get to the end of this wasteland, and he'd hunt a deer or something to keep him going once he did.

CHAPTER FORTY-TWO

Life to the Lifeless, Lifelessness to the Living

"I can't believe you were willing to do dungeon runs for parts. It's perfect. Thank you, Matt." Was this the first thank-you that Lucy gave to Matt? No. But did it move him? Yes.

Matt and Lucy were relaxing on top of the bunker, enjoying the view to the extent they could. It had taken time to excavate the thing, and eventually, Matt had even tunneled underneath it. That was a pretty dumb idea. It seemed smart at the time though.

Every so many shovelfuls of dirt, he'd look at the system screens to see how much it would cost to move the thing. It was still prohibitively expensive, and Matt's labor was free. But it was cheaper than before, going from the "probably never" category to the "maybe someday" category. Plus, Lucy had an absolute blast ordering Matt around for the week.

Matt didn't mind being ordered around. Making a death-maze with Lucy was oddly like giving a kid a horsey ride. She had fun directing him and he had fun being directed, especially since it was also a nice change of pace. It was wholesome, non-lethal-for-now fun. It was great.

"We have to do those dungeons anyways. Pretty soon, we'll be ready to challenge higher-level dungeons. We can always catch up," Matt said.

"We aren't on a schedule," Lucy reminded Matt.

"We aren't," Matt repeated.

They sat for a bit, enjoying the world.

"Matt?"

"Yeah?"

"You know my favorite part of the murder-room?"

"What's that? The rocks?"

"No. It's that it's stupid. We will never, ever use this thing for anything. It's a giant trap for nobody to ever use. And with the door closed, it will last forever."

"So it's beautiful, in a dumb way?"

"Yup. It's my favorite thing on this planet, besides me."

There was a concept from Earth called "island time," where on most small islands, the culture had evolved to not care much about scheduled meeting times. If you had a party at six o'clock, people might show up at seven or eight. It wasn't a big deal. Resting on Gaia was like that. You didn't need to stop for some predetermined amount of time before moving on, you could just rest however long or short you wanted to, sleep for however long you slept for, and be off the clock. It was probably what retirement felt like and it took some getting used to, but Matt liked it.

After a while, they moved on. The plants didn't need much tending, but they had been away for a while and they were probably at least thirsty by now. They were about halfway home before they spotted the weird light.

"Matt, what in the hell is that?" There was a bright, visible glow coming from the direction of the estate. It looked like their house was on fire, with the exceptions that normal fire didn't burn blue and there wasn't nearly enough flammable material on their property to make a light that bright.

"No idea. Should we check it out?" Matt hesitated.

"I have no idea if it's dangerous. We might . . ." Lucy's thought was cut off as the light suddenly flared and spread, snapping outwards to cover twice the area it had before. Then, the light flattened somehow, hugging the ground as it raced outwards at an alarming pace. Both Matt and Lucy flinched as it washed over them, still flattening and accelerating outwards. As it reached a paper thin layer, the light suddenly organized itself into various lines, curls, and whorls, covering the ground in a complex and almost artistic pattern.

"That's pretty," Matt observed mindlessly.

"Yes, very pretty. Matt, those are *runes*. This is one big-ass enchantment. I have no idea how it's lasted this long. Anything that the Gaians left running should have fizzled out a long time ago."

"Is it dangerous?"

"It depends on what it does. Matt, if it's for attacking, we're dead men walking. But it might just be the Gaian Fourth of July, for all I know."

Ding!

A new window—in a color Matt hadn't seen yet—popped up. Shocked, he read through it as fast as he could.

Sarthian Defense System Announcement
Alert Level: Amethyst

An outside threat has been detected within the borders of the continent, one that our automated system deems to be a threat capable of harming a large proportion of the current Sarthian population. We are issuing an all-citizen alert calling for any and all information on the threat.

All citizens are urged to look for landing vehicles and individuals that might be connected to the threat. Unusual visitors to your area should be reported, especially if they are armed. Do not attempt to talk to or contain possible threats yourself—report them to the appropriate nearby authorities.

Remember: An enemy force need not be numerous to be dangerous. Exercise caution and avoid and all threats until help arrives.

"We probably can't count on that help arriving, huh?" Matt asked.

"Nope, probably not. The threat's from the system instance?" asked Lucy.

"Probably," Matt agreed.

Ding!

Demon Lord Defense

It's probably been easy for you to think of yourself as the only special reincarnator, right? Big, empty planet and little, lonely you. Just trying to survive and slowly grow. And that's probably part of why you felt special enough to disobey specific system commands and make my life much, much more difficult than I want it to be.

Well, I have news. You aren't the only reincarnator. In fact, you aren't a very good one. Do you know what a full Combat class is actually capable of? What someone with actual training can do?

You might have noticed a dearth of achievements lately. I'm not going to keep them from you forever. After all, the system will follow his own rules. Enjoy. You'll need them.

Ding!

[Trapper Keeper]

You've created hundreds of traps, but never before did you create one to save for later. Between your new intermediate level, your increased experience with traps of all kinds, and a weird obsession with the art form that now extends to building traps you don't actually intend to get triggered, you've moved on to a new phase of your work.

It's a weird phase, but that's on you.

Rewards: +1 DEX, Trapper Keeper skill

Trapper Keeper (Skill)

The Trapper Keeper skill does not level, and is instead keyed to the level of your Survivor's Instincts skill. At the current level, Trapper Keeper allows you to store one trap of your choosing in an interdimensional space. The trap can be deployed instantly, allowing you to cover hasty retreats or to settle arguments in an unusual way.

Trapper Keeper will keep a preloaded replica of your most recent trap. Once this trap is deployed, the skill is disabled until another trap is created and stored.

Dig, Dug

You've undertaken a massive excavation project, and succeeded in not conveniently dying in a cave-in. Even more weirdly, you did this all at level one of the skill. Did it not occur to you to start with a smaller project, just to make sure you liked it? You could have done this so much faster.

Anyway, it was a big, big job and this is the combined result of several weird digging-related achievements you would have gotten out of the same amount of work if you had approached the job like a normal person.

Rewards: +1 VIT, +1 STR, Advancement of Survivor's Digging to level 3

Survivor's Digging

At level 3, Survivor's Digging scales with your stats even faster to create optimal shoveling outcomes. In addition, each shovel stroke now has a 10 percent chance to move 10x as much dirt.

In addition to the important messages, Matt had dozens of more mundane achievements, all giving him small amounts of class experience and not much else. What little equipment did materialize was pretty boring, low-end stuff. It looked like the system was still holding out on him.

But at the end of all that, one quest stood out above the crowd, even competing with the system instance's joyful "Demon Lord Defense."

Life to the Lifeless, Lifelessness to the Living

By now you've probably thought, "Man, I just want to plant plants and have fun. Why is this system instance so serious about this? Does he hate plants?" And you know what? That pisses me off. Because if you had just wanted to raid dungeons and have a little garden, we could have worked that out. It would have taken time, but I would have eventually contacted the main system somehow or other, and we might have made things right for you.

But no, you wouldn't have it. Your system guardian tells you that you have system authority, and you want to know about that. I tell you not to, and you make jokes about that. I offer you a deal that guarantees your exit out of here, and you don't care. You just want to look into the stuff I say not to look into. And you know what? Fine. No more deals.

So now I don't play nice. Yup, you got all your little plants going. And you know what? I'm happy. Because right now, you're telling yourself, "I brought life back to Gaia." And you feel great about that. Good. Because once you die, what happens to those plants? They die. They wither and die, just like you will.

And I'll laugh. My only regret is that I can't spit on them as they go.

Enjoy your tokens. You won't get a chance to spend them.

Reward: 5,000 Estate Tokens

"Lucy?"

"Yeah?"

"I'm pretty sure it's the system instance."

"So that's your big plan? To talk him out of it?" asked an incredulous Lucy.

"It's probably our best shot. If he really is a Combat class, especially if he's overleveled? He's going to cut me to pieces."

"No offense, Matt, but you aren't the most persuasive person. I didn't listen to you until you commanded me."

"But I got you eventually."

"Sure. I doubt this guy is going to give you months of bonding time in this wasteland."

As they walked back towards the estate, Matt was trying to put himself in the shoes of the supposed invader. It was possible the system had shot straight with the new guy and told him that he was going to murder some poor guy on a nothing planet who was only trying to grow root vegetables. But Matt doubted it. This was a guy who probably thought that he was facing some different threat, something more clearly evil.

If that was true, Matt felt like he had a pretty good chance of just talking the other reincarnator down. He would explain what was going on, all the way back to his first day on Gaia if he had to. If it were him on the other side, that would work. He just hoped the system hadn't pulled a homicidal murderer off some death planet.

And then something Matt didn't expect happened. As they approached the estate, the other reincarnator was already there. That was pretty easy to explain. The reincarnator had probably seen the same light and headed towards its origin point.

What Matt didn't expect was what the sight of another flesh-and-blood human would do to him. This was an adult person, as near as he could tell. He was wearing a helmet, sure. But he was a human being, standing there in all his glory like it wasn't even a big deal.

Matt didn't even mind that the new guy was stepping on the plants that much. He had to fight against a surprisingly strong urge to run up to the man and hug him.

The man's back was mostly turned as he walked around the estate, jabbing things with his sword. Matt managed to get pretty close, preserving just enough presence of mind to stop before getting too close and cut in half on accident.

"Okay. Here goes," Matt whispered to Lucy.

"You sure?"

"I'm sure." Matt took in a breath, then yelled across the distance between him and the armored man, "Hey, over there! I'm Matt! I know you are here on a quest, but before you do it, could we just . . . talk for a bit?"

The armored man froze for a moment when Matt yelled, then wheeled around to face him. It was hard to tell with the helmet in place, but as Matt stopped yelling, it appeared that the man was perhaps thinking through something. He looked down at the ground in a way that made it seem like he was making a decision.

Oh, please, armored man. Please just talk to me.

The armored man looked up, then drew his sword. Activating some kind of skill that made his entire body glow, he charged.

CHAPTER FORTY-THREE

Wait, Was I Winning?

Asadel was having a hard time finding deer. The wasteland stretched on and on. The only differentiating feature he had run into that was interesting was a big metal room that wouldn't let him in. He assumed it was a dungeon. Not that he needed to go in, but the denied entry was an insult to him.

He was a hero. And while he wasn't exactly here to save this world, he was here to help, and it wasn't cool for dungeons to not let him in.

Not only had he failed to find animals to cook and eat, he also realized that there wasn't anything to cook them *with*. He was sweaty and running out of buffs. So far, there hadn't been so much as a hair to indicate that anyone was on this planet but him. Increasingly pissed, he plodded on and on until a bright blue light lit up on the horizon, slightly off from where his system compass was pointing.

Screw this, that looks fun.

In Asadel's experience, bright blue lights did not mess around. Where there were bright blue lights, there would be adventure. Especially bright blue lights that ended up bursting across the horizon and drawing stuff on the ground before disappearing in a weird way. That was demon lord shit if he ever saw it.

Abandoning the system compass entirely, he started to head in the direction of the light. It wasn't exactly soon, but eventually, he got to the demon lord's dread fortress of death. It was less impressive than he expected it to be, more in the line of "small failing subsidence farm" than "dungeon of certain death."

"System, what the hell is this?" Asadel yelled, without results. Nobody was here. If there was some massive-blue-light generator hanging around, it was doing a very good job of pretending to be cabbage sprouts or a small shack that looked like it would fall down at a single blow. He was perplexed, but the system has assured him that the only plants on the planet belonged to the demon lord, so there had to be SOME connection.

It was then that he noticed that the system compass was moving. It was possible that it had always been that way, but he hadn't noticed it when he was walking himself. The movement was minuscule. The demon lord probably didn't have a system compass, so he'd get slightly off track from time to time. Looking at the variance, the demon would be either heading directly towards or away from Asadel. He resolved to wait.

An hour passed before he realized what must be going on. He had figured it out.

Illusions. This idiot must be messing with my mind.

He popped to his feet, prodding various plants with his sword, trying to figure out the trick to cut through the lies. Whatever illusion had been cast was pretty complete; the tree bark cut like tree bark did. The shack made hollow wooden sounds when poked. Whatever light-illuminating fortress was here, it wasn't findable under the arcane deception the demon lord was throwing out.

It was then and only then that he heard him. The destroyer of world, singular, was behind him. He wheeled around to see . . . a dude. A wholly normal guy. Was he wearing armor? Yup. Was he carrying a spear? Yeah. But nobody could do that and still look more average than this man. He was a five out of ten, stock human, male. He looked like he had bought his weapons at the mall, or something like that.

"Hey, over there! I'm Matt! I know you are here on a quest, but before you do it, could we just . . . talk for a bit?"

Asadel paused. He looked at the ground and took a deep breath, intensely thankful he had figured out the whole illusion-magic stuff before this guy showed up. Even if it was something else, there was certainly something fishy going on here, and the system compass was pointing right at the so-called Matt.

This would be his most difficult battle yet, but the sheer size of his last meal meant a big enough calorie excess that he could meet it at, if not absolute best, at least a little better than normal.

Well-fed wasn't very good fuel for the skill, and it was the most pathetic of the food-related buffs. He didn't mind giving up the piddling stat increases it provided, especially since he wouldn't need them after this anyway. He'd go to another world, hopefully one with both steak and grapes to eat, right after he put down this bastard. He was sweaty and almost hungry, and it was *the demon's fault.*

Matt briefly considered fleeing, then didn't. This wasn't because he decided against it, but instead because the armored figure was moving so fast that there wasn't time to do much of anything besides a quick thought about fleeing. It was a Super Saiyan form of his own Survivor's Dash. In the second it took his new enemy to close the distance between them, all he managed to do was plant his spear in the ground with the business end pointed in the general direction of the approaching danger. Hopefully, whatever glowing movement skill the guy was using didn't do well with turning.

Sure enough, the guy didn't turn at all. There wasn't enough time for Matt to reconsider his attack, so he could only watch as his foe rammed into the spear with his breastplate, directly above his heart. But rather than impaling the swordsman, the tip of the spear failed to penetrate his armor at all. Worse, the momentum pulled the tip downwards against the braced pole, breaking it at the attachment point and catapulting the spearhead away.

When Survivor's Instinct screamed at Matt to duck, he had enough presence of mind to heed the warning. He got just low enough to avoid losing the left half of his head from a full, overhead swing of the bad guy's massive sword. Without Matt's head to slow the momentum, the sword came down at an angle that intersected with the spear pole next. It cut cleanly through the rest of the spear.

"Matt! Run!"

Lucy was frantic, but he couldn't run yet. Matt cursed his failure to level Survivor's Dash, not that it would have mattered. Armor dude was still glowing gold. For all Matt knew, his enemy was faster than him and would catch any escape attempt. If hand-to-hand combat was inevitable, he wanted to be in the best condition for it.

In his crouch, Matt gripped his Survivor's knife and heaved it up in an underhand motion that vaguely tracked the direction of the mystery man's claymore. He had a good sense of the chances of getting through steel armor with only an all-purpose knife. Not great odds. Instead of the chest or neck, Matt aimed the sweep at his foe's hands, pleased when the blow actually landed.

"Aghh!" the man yelled, in a surprisingly high-pitched voice. In his apparent surprise, the sword flew out of his hands, clattering to the ground a few feet away. Matt brought the knife up towards the now disarmed man's body, hoping to get lucky with a blow aimed at the neck, but instead was immediately blown back by a full stomp on his chest.

Did this asshole just Sparta-kick me?

Matt flew back three or four feet, immediately rolling to avoid whatever attacks were following him to the ground. None came. He looked up in surprise to see his attacker bending over to get his sword before moving towards him again. *Is he . . . playing with me?* Matt thought, confused. If the guy could kick him over like that, there was no question that his strength score was higher than Matt's. On the ground, he'd destroy Matt. Why hadn't he?

* * *

My sword!

Asadel looked on in horror as his sword flew away. As expected, the evil one was tricky. He had sacrificed a trash weapon to block the first strike, then basically disappeared before popping up to disarm him. Who attacked *hands?*

The demon lord then went for Asadel's neck. In a moment of pure instinct, he threw a kick, and the demon lord flowed with the kick to get distance on Asadel. He let him. How was he supposed to fight without his sword? None of his skills worked without it, and the demon lord still had a knife.

He picked up his sword, still pristine and sparkling. He was on a time limit and needed to get the most out of his buff. So he roared and charged in again.

Matt was still on the ground, and watched as the new reincarnator turned back to face him. Thankfully, Survivor's Instincts was kicking in, assuring him that not all was lost and feeding him plans of attack that were effective against armed opponents.

As he pushed off the ground with his offhand, he used as much strength as he could to gouge a handful of dirt out of the ground. He got to his feet just in time to leap backwards out of the range of another huge strike. The sword was awash in a colorful glow. Matt knew to avoid the hits, even without Survivor's Instincts screaming at him.

I don't want to get hit with any of these, but especially not those glow sword strikes. Got it.

The new guy let the momentum of the blade keep going, swinging it 360 degrees for another full-power strike. Before the new strike got going, Matt moved in, checking the rotation of the man's shoulder with his own and throwing the dirt directly into the reincarnator's face. The reaction was immediate, and more than Matt had hoped for. The man stumbled back, huffing and sneezing, trying desperately to rub his eyes through his visor.

This seemed like a good time for stabbing.

Before the new guy could recover, Matt did his best to do as much damage as possible. He weaved around the ensuring frantic sword strikes to stab at the man's legs, arms, and neck. After the first cut, Matt's opponent started jerking around, smart enough to not stand still while someone was stabbing him.

Unfortunate for Matt, the weird armor that extended to shin and forearm guards made lethal attacks nearly impossible. Matt only managed to land glancing blows. He hoped they would add up, but they didn't seem to. Whatever stats this guy had brought to the party were enough that Matt could barely hurt him. Even his initial stab was only a moderate wound, the kind that would close up in just a few minutes' worth of VIT work if it were inflicted on Matt.

After several seconds, the man appeared to have cleared most of the dirt from his eyes. *Duck*, Survivor's Instincts said. Matt ducked as a purple swipe sailed over his head, readying himself for the next blow.

Duck, said Survivor's Instincts. He did. Another blow missed.

Is this the only move the reincarnator has?

The blows were dangerous, and the enemy was fast enough that he could unleash a storm of blows in a couple of seconds. A single misstep would result in Matt split into far more chunks of himself than he preferred. But they were the same blows, the only variation was the color of the glow, not different trajectories. Matt could more or less handle that.

Still, he couldn't take chances when a single kick or stab could break his defenses wide open for one of those sword-based haymakers. Maybe, just maybe, the suit of armor was lulling him into a false sense of security. He kept his distance as well as he could, counterstriking with his knife to at least keep the man on his toes. It felt like an eternity, but the golden aura finally blinked out.

He can't be hurt.

Asadel was using his best moves, over and over. Power strike? No good. Expulsion Blade? He dodged it. It finally made sense how this normal-looking guy had destroyed a whole planet. Nobody could hit him!

The worst part was that he was soon going to have to fight him without his buffs. Aura of the Hungry Blade was not a long-term solution to problems. It was a nitrous oxide injection into a battle, a burst skill meant to turn the tide at an opportune time. But Asadel always used it at the start of the fight. He reasoned that it was always an opportune time to cut demons in half. There would be fewer of them to deal with later.

He desperately cut at the phantom in front of him, but he couldn't get close. For one, his vision was still blurry from the poison dust. As much as he tried, he couldn't hit the demon lord. Then, his aura winked out, leaving him with nothing but his natural stats and an empty STAM bar because of the power strikes that had failed to land.

Suddenly, the demon lord's offhand shot out again, presumably loaded with poison dust. Asadel winced away, which he realized was a mistake after the fact. The demon lord might be planning a cunning attack.

Asadel forced his eyes to snap back open, ready for the worst. Far in the distance, he saw the demon lord moving rapidly away, almost as fast as he himself could run with Aura of the Hungry Blade active.

Wait . . . Was I winning?

CHAPTER FORTY-FOUR

Lucy's Rules

Running was exhausting, especially when it came at the end of an already very long day of walking. It was doubly tiring for Asadel because this particular chase came with a significant shortage of hitting things with his sword. Instead, he was carting around pounds and pounds of sword and armor over a dumb wasteland with an always-on sun. It wasn't fun, but he had no choice. Killing the demon lord was the only way out.

At first, he kept up just fine. His high DEX meant that his baseline running speed was faster than the demon lord's, except that the demon lord never seemed to have to stop running. Asadel did. VIT only did so much to stop the burning in his legs, and he'd periodically have to give up some ground to stop and let vitality clear the lactic acid from his quads before he continued.

Even so, he would have been gaining ground except for the evil one's dash skill. At first, his own dash skill and speed were enough to slowly close the gap between them. Later on, he was enraged to find that the demon lord was just toying with him. The demon lord kept squeezing more and more distance out of his dash skill as time went on. Asadel suspected that the demon lord could actually get away any time he wanted to.

Why? Why let me keep following him?

Either the demon lord was strong enough to kill him, in which case he should have done it already, or he wasn't. And if he wasn't, why wasn't he getting away? There was plenty of wasteland to disappear into. It didn't make sense, and Asadel didn't like puzzles. Even if he did, there was only one way off this planet and on to his new future, and that was slaughtering the bad guy.

He kept running.

* * *

"Matt, this is a bad idea. We should just keep going. We can start again somewhere else. You don't need to fight."

Matt and Lucy made record time running back to the bunker.

It turned out that the secret to leveling Matt's dash skill was to use it as intended, fleeing from overpowered foes with Matt's life on the line. But even though the dash became more effective, Matt was still losing ground. His attacker was just too fast.

What saved Matt were the sheer amount of breaks that the other reincarnator took. Every time he got close enough, he'd stop, rub his legs, and watch as Matt sped away. Matt wasn't sure, but he strongly suspected that his attacker's VIT was higher than his own. Yet, there was something different. Matt could keep running, the new guy should have also been able to keep running. But he didn't.

Matt's legs hurt. They had gone from being strained to numbness to flares of pain. But it wasn't like the pain of getting them bitten off, or broken, or chewed on. He still had to stop and rest a few times, but nowhere near as frequent as the armored monster who was chasing him. He ran as hard and as fast as he could, dealt with the burning, and used Survivor's Dash to leverage his STAM bar. Eventually, this paid dividends. He slowly reached a point where he not only kept ahead of the swordsman, but could increase the distance between them if he wanted to. It gave him time to think.

"It's just some stupid project I did, Matt. It's not worth staking your life on. We can run."

It hurt Matt to see Lucy frantic. Most of the time, she was wearing her tough-girl game face. It didn't matter that they both knew it was fake. Matt was okay with it. It was how she felt safe. He got that. As often as he could, he made sure that it only slipped because she was happy. This wasn't that. This was some asshole coming into their lives and making her worry.

It was true, they could run, at least for a while. But they weren't going to. Lucy was visibly suppressing little holographic tears, and that didn't make Matt scared. That made him *angry*.

"Lucy. Listen. Yeah, we could run. But we might have to run forever. We have no idea what the system gave him. He might have unlimited food. We don't. He might be able to do that gold glow thing again and catch up. We don't know. We can't make that bet."

"We can hide in a dungeon!"

"We could, but can you guarantee he couldn't just follow us in there? Some of the dungeons are *small*, Lucy. They have other problems in them too. There's no predicting how that might pan out."

In the last few hours, Matt had poured every saved up resource he had into getting as far ahead of Captain Stabby as he could, knowing he'd need a few minutes to get everything ready. As he ran, he clued Lucy in on his plan as best he could.

"Even if we couldn't, you know what? I *want* to use your room, Lucy. It's insane. It's incredibly dumb. It's *Looney Tunes* bullshit, and you know what? I love it. It's going to work. If it doesn't, we can figure something else out."

"Okay, Matt. If you say so." Lucy tried valiantly to pull herself together. It mostly worked.

"I do. It's going to be okay, I promise," Matt said between breaths.

Matt had finished most of his preparations during the conversation with Lucy. Previously, when he was excavating the bunker, he had dug a trench around the building. Now, he poked his head out of the trench and looked back in the direction of the garden, where armor-guy was rapidly approaching. He climbed out of the trench. There wasn't much time now, and the last thing he wanted was his enemy approaching at a leisurely, calm pace. He drew his Survivor's knife and set himself into a fighting stance, taking swipes at the air, and trying his best to look like he had nothing planned.

It worked. Armor-guy had been jogging along at a good pace. Now, he sprinted. Matt waited patiently as he approached, looking as menacing as he could. The guy pulled his massive sword from his back, gripping the handle with both hands over his shoulder, ready for another one of his massive swings. Matt gulped back a very recent memory of the giant blade swishing through the air inches from his head. He stood on the massive berm of dirt he had produced around the entire bunker during the previous excavation, and waited.

The new reincarnator had to climb the hill to reach to Matt, but he arrived in record time. With one foot planted ahead of him, the new guy skidded towards Matt as he swung.

Matt attempted to parry with his knife, a task made impossible as the bigger sword absolutely shattered the blade and jerked his knife clean out of his hand, deviating just enough in trajectory to miss Matt's neck. The sword immediately came around for another blow, glowing an angry orange color as it traveled towards him.

Rather than sit there and get cut in half, Matt leaped back, dropping into the trench in front of the bunker's door. Just as planned, his foe dropped into the trench directly after him. Matt was counting on that.

He spent the last few minutes digging out a cavity in the trench's wall. He didn't have enough time to dig as deep as he would have liked, but it was enough to get a running start of a couple of steps. Carrying the biggest rock he could lift, Matt bashed into his enemy's back, pushing him into the doorway.

Lucy's death room was built on a couple of key rules.

The first was that *the first traps should be the weakest traps the labyrinth had to offer*. If whatever got into the room wasn't a real threat, they wanted to take care of it quickly with the first few traps. For anything bigger and stronger, the hope was that the weak traps would create a false sense of security, one that later traps would exploit.

As Asadel entered the doorway, his foot caught the first tripwire and sprung those traps. These were relatively simple wood-spiked whip traps, buried in the shallow dirt trenches outside the door. It took forever to set them up at just the right angle, but once the trap was tripped, they came out of the ground at an angle leading directly to the back of a foe's legs. They barely had enough juice to punch through Asadel's skin, but the surprise was enough to make him reflexively jerk forward, leading him into the second of Lucy's Rules for the Complete Trap Room.

The second rule relied on the assumption that *anything strong enough to need the next traps was also probably strong enough to make a mess of the room's infrastructure and traps*. It was important that they didn't get the chance.

As Asadel moved into the room from the first trap, he stepped onto a section of shelf that was broken off from one of the bunker's original shelving units and laid on the floor. It was raised only slightly by a round stick in the middle, sitting between it and the floor like a teeter-totter axis. Stepping on it threw Asadel off-balance. More importantly, it sprung something that Lucy affectionately referred to as the pinball traps.

During their trap room resource dungeon run, Matt had almost passed on one of the loot items. But Lucy swore up and down that she needed it, and Matt was happy to get it for her.

> *Trap Springs*
> These are powerful steel springs for traps. Each spring comes with a clip that barely holds the springs closed when compressed. Use your imagination on how that might be useful.

They experimented with whole walls made of spikes, but eventually opted for the much easier big-rocks-on-springs option, which Asadel now experienced firsthand on the side of his face and hip.

The combination of bad footing and rock impacts sustained a long stumble to his left, where he engaged with a new trap type: the spring step. These were, again, simple shelf sections supported by the floor on one end and springs on the other. As Asadel stepped on the first shelf, it shook loose the spring clips, which pushed the step up and drove Asadel forward, where he met with the second and third spring steps, building momentum all the while.

Lucy's third rule was that *potential was meant to be spent*. If someone was off-balance, she said, that should be *for* something. In this case, it was for letting

Asadel use his own momentum to run flat-out into a wall made of trap spikes, letting them do whatever damage they could.

Lucy's fourth rule was that *physical balance was not the only balance you can take away*. When Asadel hit the spike wall, it hurt him slightly, but also allowed him to regain his footing for the first time. He could have left the same way he came, but Lucy knew he wouldn't. She correctly predicted he'd be too busy figuring out what that pinging noise was.

Crashing into the spike wall, Asadel also loosened a carefully balanced stone, sending it careening into a series of ramps made out of shelf units. Eventually, it'd reach the floor, right around the time when Asadel had cleared himself from the spike wall. Dropping to the ground, it triggered a trip wire for Matt's personal favorite from among the new traps: the hammer whip.

The hammer whip combined various branches and trap poles with one goal in mind: to hit an enemy with a big rock as hard as possible. This one was set to release in an upper-cut vertical trajectory, which resulted in a hard bash to the side of Asadel's knee, sending him careening into a new section of hallway.

He was tripping plenty of wires as he did. Every stumbling step represented a new chance to regain balance, before being spoiled by a series of smaller hammer whip traps. That momentum built up, resulting in a sort of full-sprint stumble as Asadel ran into one last hammer trap, this one coming from the other direction and slamming directly into Asadel's chest, badly bruising him but finally allowing him to regain his balance.

Asadel was not critically injured. He belonged to a high VIT, armored Combat class, and though all these traps hurt, they weren't enough to actually put him in real, lethal danger. By design, he was meant to weather bigger, meaner hits than the traps were currently dealing, even if each one had shaved off a significant amount of HP.

That led into Lucy's fifth and sixth rules: *anyone can get rattled by people trying to kill them*, and *anticipation of danger is a danger all its own*.

Asadel now looked to his right at what appeared to be a perfectly clear hallway. There were no shelf sections on the floor. There were no tripwires. It was to all appearances a perfectly safe thoroughfare back to the door, which he could clearly see from this third, return-direction hallway back to his starting point.

Facing a choice between apparent safety and cutting his way back through multiple hallways of sprung traps, he opted to walk through the apparent safety. His first step failed to trigger any traps. So did his second. Eventually, he made it entirely down the hallway, to the pinball trap adjacent to the door. Nothing had happened, but each step had been a kind of stressful agony. Lucy's anticipation-building had done a kind of damage all its own.

Lucy's seventh rule of trap rooms was, Matt argued, not just a rule of trap rooms but a rule of life in general, however little it might come up.

It stated, clearly, that *nobody thinks about what's happening outside a trap room while they are in it. By the time they get through a loop of wacky dangers and see the light from the door, the door is the only thing on their mind. They move towards it instinctively, never suspecting you've been at work the whole time.*

More succinctly, Matt's interpretation read, "Nobody expects you to drag a big catapult made out of sticks, trap poles, and your only cooking pot to the door while they're in the trap room and for you to load it with a basketball-sized rock."

Matt argued that his version of rule number seven could have better grammar, but was successfully outplayed by Lucy's "it's funnier this way" counterargument. He further argued that they had no idea how catapults worked, and that it would be impossible to aim it.

Lucy had pointed out that big rocks don't need to be aimed, as long as they pack enough energy and the hallways they're launched down are narrow and indestructible enough. This turned out to be true enough, as the rock whipped off the ceiling and a side wall before bashing into Asadel's right leg, flipping him into the air and pushing him back down into the bunker before he crashed into the ground.

As fun as all these rules were, Matt's favorite of all was the last. She was almost bursting with excitement when she had told him just a few days before.

"Wait, another rule? These are taking like a day apiece. It's not that I'm not enjoying this, but we do have to water the plants eventually."

"Don't worry. This one is zero work. I promise."

"Fine. Lay it on me."

"Get this: Lucy's eighth rule of trap rooms is . . . *we don't call it a trap room because it's full of traps.*"

Lying on the floor, Asadel was suddenly filled with the deepest, most profound rage he had ever felt. He no longer cared about the mission or the rewards. In that moment, all he cared about was stabbing his sword directly into the demon lord's eyeball and twisting until it popped out of the back of his smug, ugly skull.

His face red with pure, unadulterated anger, he rose to his feet. Just in time to see Matt finish closing the bunker's door.

CHAPTER FORTY-FIVE

A Sack of Potatoes

A few days before, Matt had been dropping rocks off the side of the bunker. Lucy watched as he gathered a couple big ones, lied down on his belly, and pushed them off the side. She pretended to work, but after the fifth or sixth rock, she couldn't fight her curiosity anymore.

"Having fun there?"

"Not really. This is more like an experiment."

"To find out what?"

Matt dropped a few more rocks, then sat up.

"I was thinking about our traps. They don't come loaded with stats, right? I don't have any 'traps work two hundred percent better against armor' buffs or anything like that. So, they seem to work off physics. But . . ."

"The system?"

"Yeah. I have all this vitality, and near as I can tell, that increases how much damage I can take by reducing how much damage an attack actually inflicts on me. But if I jump in the air and someone hits me with a giant club. Do I fly less far than Earth physics says I should?"

"I have no idea."

"Me neither. And that's what the rocks are about. I'm just trying to get a feel for it all."

"Did that actually help? Dropping rocks off a building?"

Matt shrugged. "I can't actually remember the exact amount of time it's supposed to take a rock to fall that far, and Gaia's gravity could be slightly different for all I know. But it seems right, at least. I've been watching stuff fall down my whole life and at least it didn't look weird."

* * *

Back in the present, the locks on the door hissed as they engaged with the bunker, sealing the invader in. Within seconds, they could hear him banging away with his sword on the indestructible door, apparently venting his blind rage. Matt and Lucy looked at each other in shock.

"I can't believe that worked. Matt, I honestly can't believe that freaking worked."

"Can you imagine if we could have done the whole bunker? All four walls? Next time, we absolutely need to trap the whole bunker. He had no idea what hit him." Matt realized Lucy was a genius in designing trap rooms.

"I don't think it's worth it to do that. At least not for, people. Eventually, he was going to figure out he could slice right though those shelves and get out. I'm honestly surprised he didn't even try. I'm not sure this guy is all that bright," Lucy snickered.

As if to prove her right, the banging continued on the door. Matt had done some durability testing with his Gaian metal shovel on the Gaian metal bunker before, and he knew from experience that the other reincarnator couldn't be seeing much visual feedback on his efforts to break down the door. But the new guy kept on, apparently undeterred by his lack of progress.

"How long are we going to leave him in there, Matt?" asked Lucy.

"I honestly haven't gotten that far. I mean, how long do you think it takes someone like *that*"—Matt gestured at the door, where the banging from inside was actually speeding up rather than slowing down—"to calm down enough to talk?"

"Well, we don't really have to let him out at all."

"Lucy!"

"Matt, we don't. He showed up with a sword and started swinging it at your head. We don't owe this guy anything."

It was true. They could leave him there, and it wouldn't even be their fault. There was no safe way to let him out. There was no way to know how much food he had with him, and because of that, they had no way to time when he was starved into submission, but not death. The smart move was to leave the door locked, walk away, and forget the bunker even existed.

There was only one real problem with all that. Matt knew what it was like to starve.

"Yeah, unfortunately, we can't. I'm not that mean. I don't think you are that mean either, once you calm down," said Matt.

Lucy's shoulders slumped.

"Yeah, I guess."

That was that. It wasn't a great decision, but it was the decision they had made. And while they expected it might turn out badly, they would sleep easy. Then the touchpad interface for the bunker lit up, proving them wrong.

Entity detected inside structure while lock is engaged. Safety failsafe activated.

They both stood in horror as the lock hissed, clicked, and fully disengaged.

Asadel was still pissed. He didn't care if the door was indestructible. He didn't care that it didn't have a mark on it yet. He had a sword made out of some kind of magical super-metal and he wasn't going to stop cutting until he cut through the damn thing.

He was also, if he stopped to admit it, a little bit worried. This trip was not turning out as expected yet. He was currently trapped in a metal room filled with god knows how many weird cartoon traps, and he was completely out of food. But he wouldn't stop to admit it. Between his unconfessed worries and his very real anger, he had exactly one mission. He was going to carve through six inches of door, follow that up by immediately carving through six feet of very bad villain, and call it a day.

So he chopped at the door, not letting up. Speeding up, in fact. This went on for minutes until suddenly, miraculously, the door lock hissed open on its own accord. He immediately threw the door open, just in time to see the demon lord's leg slip over the top of the trench, disappearing from view.

No you don't.

Gathering all the strength in his legs, he leapt fully out of the trench in a single jump, landing just a few meters behind the fleeing overlord. He raised his head and roared. He didn't care anymore, he was going to fly in the face of Artemis's advice of saving some skills for life-and-death situations. He was going for broke.

Berserker Rage

Did you know that a calorie is a unit of heat energy? People only think of it as a stored dietary energy thing because their human bodies do the hard work through some boring oxidation process that's too long to explain. You have another option. You can burn calories in a furnace of pure rage, fueling an engine of never-before-reached levels of blood thirst.

Berserker rage taps into your body's natural fat and glycogen stores, turning them into an especially pure form of quick-burning energy that provides a huge buff to all stats. This absurdly large enhancement comes with only one major drawback: a similarly massive debuff when the skill ends.

Temporary buff: +100 percent to all physical stats, +100 percent physical damage resistance, +100 HP regen rate, unlimited STAM pool, +1 level to active sword skill, restoration of highest food-related buff held during the last

10-day period, and movement speed over any solid terrain is doubled
Temporary Debuff: –20 percent to all physical stats, –40 percent damage resistance, HP regen rate set to 0, STAM bar emptied, and STAM regen rate set to 0

Everything Asadel could see was immediately dyed red. His muscles creaked and bulged as his skin stretched to accommodate them. His sword, already light, now felt like it weighed nothing. He was a monster. A monster of death. He was a pool of limitless mayhem just waiting for a target. Luckily, he didn't have to look far to find one.

Get ready, asshole. Here I come.

Asadel screamed as he charged, crossing half the distance in a split second while activating his two strongest sword skills. It was on. In about half a second, it would be over.

Then his knees buckled, and he barely kept on his feet.

Ding!

Oh no. No, no, no . . .

Matt watched as the swordsman exploded with power in the most exaggerated way he had seen yet. It was terrifying. The hair on his arms bristled just seeing it. He desperately dug into Survivor's Instincts to find weaknesses he could exploit or options he could pursue. The response was something like, "*Whooa, man. I dunno. No point in running, though.*"

Then the swordsman moved, and time slowed down. Every millisecond felt like a minute as he flew through the distance between them, but there was nothing Matt could do. It was like his life flashing before his eyes.

Matt's body wouldn't move that fast. It *couldn't* move that fast. This was it. The next phase of his plan would have to wait for the next life, if he got one. He doubted that he would.

Then, all of a sudden, the glow around the armored swordsman cut out, and he looked visibly wobbly.

NOW! Survivor's Instincts screamed. Matt didn't need to be asked twice. He willed everything he had into Trapper Keeper. He hadn't had a good chance to use the skill yet, but at this point, he expected one of two things to happen. The first would be that Trapper Keeper would agree with Lucy that the entire trap room was one big trap, and would drop a huge metal building on the poor guy. He didn't feel that lucky.

It turned out he *wasn't* that lucky, but the next best thing happened. The last traps he had set up in Lucy's room had been the ones that he felt would be the most lethal, and those were the rock-slinging whip-hammer-type traps, which were set up vertically.

The new guy had stopped at the perfect range for one, and was still staggering slightly forward. A trap materialized at his feet, complete with a tripwire that immediately activated. As the rock shot upwards, it seemed that the visor blocked all vision of the trap, and the rock slammed directly into his chin.

The swordsman was staggered. That had hurt him. In a relationship first, it was the only time that the invader had been close enough and not-activating-his-constant-deadly-sword-skills enough that Matt could get a good look at the sword. Eyeing the metal, Matt realized why his Survivor's knife hadn't stood up very well to the onslaught.

Matt had exactly one tool available made out of the same stuff. As the bad guy regained his bearings, Matt reached back to his pack and grabbed the only vaguely weapon-shaped Gaian metal he had.

Shovel, don't fail me now.

Lucy was screaming in the background for him to run. But Survivor's Instincts and Matt agreed that there was a better move. It was ass-kicking time.

The armored man ran in and hailed down blows. He was still faster than Matt. He was still stronger than Matt and seemed like he could tank more damage than Matt. But now Matt could stop his attacks with the shovel, even if it flung him around a bit. He could exploit the predictability of the swordsman's fighting style. His chest was heaving too hard to allow for a sigh of relief, but he was relieved anyway. This was manageable.

Even better, he had a plan. Vitality was powerful, sure. But like all stats, it seemed oddly superimposed over what a person's body could already do. Matt had worked hard on his cardio and pain resistance, and that helped VIT do its job in a way that had made survival much easier for him. But if this guy's behavior during the chase was any indication, he hadn't put in the same level of effort. More importantly, Matt assumed that for all the VIT that the other reincarnator had, taking heavy blows on the chin was never good.

The armored guy had already taken a heavy stone to the face, and that was seconds ago. He had to still be rocked from that. And now he was about to take another, if everything worked out. Matt backed up out of the range of the fight while lowering the shovel, then kicked it into the soil and heaved.

And, god bless it, his digging skill kicked in, giving him the time to do all this. Not only that, but his one-in-ten shoveling skill, the dumbest skill he had, chose that exact moment to activate for the first time, flinging ten full shovelfuls of dirt at Matt's opponent. Matt immediately heard coughing, and didn't wait for the dust to clear to get visible confirmation of his target.

Gripping his mighty shovel, Matt swung it with both hands like a baseball bat and connected directly with his chin. Did the armored helmet absorb most of the blow? Sure, but if Matt was right, that wouldn't matter. VIT only did so much, and a full shovel-blow to the face was a lot to take. As the shovel pulled back and the dust cleared, Matt got a clear view of the damage he had caused.

It was zero. In visible terms, his enemy was unharmed, and staring directly at him with pure, unbridled hatred.

But when the damage finally caught up with his brain, the invincible reincarnator finally crashed to the ground like a sack of potatoes.

CHAPTER FORTY-SIX

Now for Some Soup

Seeing the armored man finally fall down was a shock. Matt paused. Honestly, he hadn't expected any element of the plan to work out. The past few weeks had shown him that when things could go wrong, they did go wrong. It should have been time for plan C, and fleeing to the not-sun-facing side of the planet.

The gulf between his expectations and the actual reality was large enough that Matt completely froze up, if only for a moment. This inaction might have resulted in disaster. Fortunately, Lucy took that moment to say the *sweetest thing*.

"Matt! Gelatinize him!"

Matt didn't need to be told twice. Sergeant Swordguy was on the ground and struggling to deal with the aftereffects of a full shovel-blow to the face. Before he could recover, Matt moved forward, planting one foot on the light armor like a villain. A quick golf-style swing with the shovel caught the pommel of the giant claymore, ripping it away and putting it out of play.

The bad guy was now fully unarmed. But he was still dangerous, loaded with the kind of stats that could reverse the scenario in a single second. Matt didn't waste any time, immediately cueing off a series of moves that would later be dubbed as *The Storm of Shovels.*

The Storm of Shovels was not a complex move. Matt knew that his full-force smacks could barely hurt the guy, but his best chance was to keep his opponent off-balance and disoriented. The best way to do this? A frantic series of blows to the head. Grasping the shovel in both hands and putting every inch of his digging-hardened back muscles into every strike, Matt proceeded to pelt his opponent's helmet with overhand blow after overhand blow, ringing it like a church bell made of pain.

For the first few strikes, the other reincarnator tried to resist, but repeated blows to his arms removed even that token defense pretty quickly. The next few blows had obvious disorienting effects, and soon, every hit sent the guy's skull whipping around like a jack-in-the-box head on a spring.

After a few more blows, it was clear what metal won in the face-off between Matt's Gaian steel and whatever his enemy's headgear was made from. Matt doubted the swordsman could even get the misshaped helmet off at this point.

At the same time, the swordsman was holding up remarkably well in terms of how he looked. He wasn't jelly, he wasn't even bleeding.

Oh well, just more work for me.

Matt kept at it.

For most of Asadel's trip to Gaia, the word that best described his emotional state would have been *frustrated.* He was frustrated that it took so long to find the demon lord, then frustrated that he wasted so much time dealing with the fake garden illusions. He was frustrated that the demon lord chose to trick him instead of doing a cool I'm-the-bad-guy-kill-me-now monologue, and he was frustrated when he couldn't even touch the demon lord during their first engagement.

Things got worse when he got caught in a fun house of pain. The tornado of traps never seemed to end, and the catapult actually knocked him out cold for a second. For the first time, his health bar had dipped into dangerous territory.

This trip to another world wasn't supposed to be a long slog to the easy, cool life he wanted. It was supposed to be a part of the easy, cool life. Instead, it had just been a giant pain in his ass. Frustrating was absolutely the right word for it, until ten seconds ago.

Now, he was terrified. He had lost his sword, and every move he made to get back to his feet was hard-countered by yet another blow to his head. He was dizzy. He couldn't think. He was taking real damage and couldn't fight back. He didn't have the time to check, but he suspected his debuff list now featured entries like "concussed" and "skull fracture." Vitality was keeping him awake, but it was getting harder to see.

Even when he faced demons on Ra'Zor, it was in a controlled way, monitored and assisted by higher-level fighters. This was not that. The demon lord's eyes didn't look angry or amused. They looked determined. The same eyes that crazy people had. This, more than anything else, finally sent Asadel's hand towards his pocket, where he grabbed the only stone he had kept.

Evacuation Stone

If you are holding this stone, the system asked you to undertake an unusual task under circumstances normally outside the normal reincarnator purview. Safety is never a guaranteed component of system-issued quests, but in this case, the system's own ruleset requires that it provide you with some method of preserving your life should things go wrong.

This stone ensures that you can escape with your life by forcing a transmigration back to the world from which you came. But be warned: that is **all** this stone guarantees. In the event you activate this stone without completing your mission, all mission rewards are forfeited, and severe additional penalties may be applied.

Use this stone only as a last resort.

Dammit. Dammit. Dammit. This can't be happening.

Asadel held on as long as he could. He tried his hardest to push the bad guy off his chest. It didn't work. His balance was shot. His arms were probably broken from trying to block shovel blows. He was still unarmed, and even laying on the ground, he could tell his legs had become weak and wobbly. Still, he held on. He waited until unconsciousness started creeping in before he gave up and activated the stone.

Amidst the pain and disorientation, the very last thing Asadel felt on Gaia were tears of disappointment.

And then, the pain and blows were all gone.

Asadel opened his eyes to see the same old cobblestone streets of his surrogate home, the same soup stands and taverns that were always packed. It looked like the system had skipped the orbit-drop entry this time, sending him directly back to his Ra'Zorian starting point without all the crater-filled pomp and circumstance.

My gear!

Asadel's hand dropped in panic to his side, where he felt only the cool, rough fabric of the system's reincarnator starter tunic. Every bit of gear he had brought with him to Gaia had been left behind. It only took a moment for him to remember that all his *good* gear, the high quality Blademaster stuff, was probably still safe and sound somewhere. He could scoop it up and just use that.

Unless . . .

The system had said there would be significant penalties for using the stone, yet here he stood, with all four limbs. As much as he liked the Gaian claymore, it didn't seem like quite enough to count as a severe punishment for failure. He shivered a little as he called up his status screen, already anticipating the kind of thing he'd see.

Derek Cyrus
Level 1 Unclassed

HP: 25
MP: N/A
STAM: 10
STR: 5
DEX: 5
PER: 5
VIT: 5
WIS: 5
INT: 5
Warning: The unclassed do not have class goals, and thus cannot gain levels. Their stats can only be improved through great effort. There is no advantage in putting off class selection.

No. No. It even took my name. *No.*

He was back to square one. All the time he had spent leveling was gone. Everything was gone. He was weak again. He was no longer Asadel the Blademaster, but rather Derek the Unclassed.

Desperate to feel even a tiny bit less vulnerable, he ran as fast as he could to the cathedral of the Estiguan church, cursing his low-DEX running speed. By the time he got there, his feet were bleeding from the sharp cobblestones, but he didn't care.

He dashed to his guardian stone, one of many plinths erected in the courtyard of the church, each representing a reincarnated hero of Ra'Zor. The church had explained to him that each plinth had the help and guidance he'd need, a special gift from the system. Could he choose his class without one? Sure, they had said. But the best outcomes were those driven by the guardian plinths, and their deeply sealed wisdom.

Pressing his palm to the plinth, Asadel muttered the class selection words, "I choose the Blademaster class."

Error. The Blademaster class has been restricted as part of a system-enacted penalty. All skills and stats have been consumed to repay a system-owned transport energy debt. Please select another class.

Plenty of people had seen Derek running to the cathedral. It didn't take long for Brennan and Artemis to find him there, sitting in the grass and weeping.

"Help," he said, sobbing, "I need help."

Later, Derek would be surprised how little he was actually scolded or yelled at. He had been called into an impromptu meeting.

In the moment, everything felt like an attack, but looking back on it, he realized that all anybody had really done was ask questions and make statements of fact. His corpse had been found. Apparently, there was a tomb containing a slowly decaying replica of his body somewhere on Ra'Zor. Or he was the replica. Brennan was distracted trying to sort through the logic for a few moments before Artemis got him back on track.

There had been costs related to Asadel's adventure, and everyone had scrambled to find his cause of death. A lot of resources that would have been better spent on the demon war were gone, including Asadel the Blademaster. And now Derek, just Derek now, was back to square one. All the resources that had been poured into him up to that point were wasted.

The worst part wasn't that they were right.

Something about his last couple of days, including the experience of being beaten in the head with a shovel, had shaken some realizations loose. Main characters didn't lose in humiliating ways to demon lords. They didn't fail big, important missions.

Derek was not a main character. He spent so little time trying and so much time drinking. He hadn't really trained. He had been in such a hurry that he had nothing but his stats. Now that his levels were gone, he had nothing to fall back to.

By the time he staggered out of their meeting in the back of the cathedral, he was, for maybe the first time in his life, *actually sorry*. Brennan was nice enough to give him money for the next few days, just in case reincarnation shenanigans made it hard to access any of his former funds. Brennan had always been considerate in that way, Derek realized. Now that Derek was looking, it wasn't that hard to see why Brennan was a real hero, and he wasn't.

Before he left, he walked over to his guardian plinth. If Blademaster was closed to him, and it was, he'd have to find something else. Something different. Something that would help *him* be different.

Maybe later he'd go apologize to the old blacksmith. With his newfound clarity, he guessed that the old man knew Asadel had never taken his training that seriously. That was about to change. He was Derek now.

Alone in the room now, Brennan and Artemis finally had time for a private word. Brennan, as always, was calm. Artemis was less so.

"That dumbshit, Brennan. That dumb, dumb little shit," Artemis cursed.

"It's ok." Everything was always okay to Brennan.

"We spent a week trying to figure out who murdered him, Brennan! It was all we could do to keep it under wraps," Artemis's voice rose an octave. "People could have panicked over this. People have been lynched for less. This was the murder of a hero."

"He's a kid. He didn't think." Brennan kept his low baritone.

"No shit."

"I'm serious. You don't know how it is. I was his age when I came here, and all I wanted to do was to save the entire world the first day. It's not a normal childhood." Brennan paused. "It's hard to adjust to. I just hope this will help him slow down a bit."

"I guess." Artemis was only slightly mollified, but part of what made Brennan work as her secret hero-boyfriend was his knack for calming her down. "Do you believe him? About the 'demon lord' that he mentioned?"

"In a way. He's a kid, and whatever happened is going through kid-filters. I might not believe him if he just disappeared for a week, but we buried him. We know something weird happened," Brennan replied.

Artemis nodded in agreement, and they both sat in silence for a moment before she spoke again. "You know what I can't believe?"

"What's that?" Brennan asked.

"He didn't ask a single question about the system. He doesn't have any doubts at all?" Artemis sounded unsure.

"Not yet. It will take a while for him to calm down, and for what happened to sink in. He might not ever ask, you know. He's not really the thinking type." Brennan smiled.

He stood up and began walking towards the door, and Artemis followed.

"But he might," she added.

"Yes. And we need to plan what we will say, if he does." Brennan leaned over and kissed Artemis on the cheek. They wouldn't be able to have displays of affection like that outside this room, and he wanted at least that to tide himself over, even if he'd see her again in private soon enough. "But that's tomorrow's worry. For now, let's go get some soup."

CHAPTER FORTY-SEVEN

Under a Tree

Matt had been working the shovel pretty vigorously. Up to a certain point, the bad guy had been more or less tanking the hits. It was very much "bad beating" and not "fatal wounds" territory. Then, without warning, armor-guy went from "actively resisting"—to the extent he could—to completely limp.

The defiance and fear in Matt's foe just winked out. Matt would have thought that his enemy had been knocked out, but the rag doll moment happened between strikes. One second Matt was accomplishing blow after blow, the next second it was all over.

"Did he—seriously—just die?" Lucy asked.

"I don't know." Matt made an exploratory *thwack* with his shovel and got no reaction. "Maybe?"

After some experimentation with more hits and watching really, really closely to see if the invader moved, Matt finally got enough courage to check his opponent's pulse. There wasn't one.

"I think we won," Matt said without emotion.

In any other time, this would have been a moment of great celebration. But even Lucy understood that killing a person was a different kind of thing compared to killing a gigantic, terrifying bone monster or a rat that looked like a clown. When Matt went to pry the helmet off the guy, she didn't question why. If he needed to see his face, he needed to see his face.

As dinged as it was, the helmet wasn't entirely welded to the other reincarnator's skull. It was tight enough that Matt was pretty sure taking it off would have hurt like hell if the guy was alive, but . . . he wasn't. Matt eventually worked it off, and then slowly stood up. The face screamed, "I haven't taken my driver's test yet." This was a child.

"He's a fucking kid." All of Matt's emotions were catching up to him. His fear from almost dying, his relief to be alive, and his guilt from what he had to do to stay alive. It all swirled into indescribable anger. "The system sent a fucking kid to kill me. And I killed him. Lucy, I killed a fucking kid."

"Matt, it's not the same thing as . . ."

"No, I killed a kid. This isn't okay, Lucy. It's not okay."

"Matt, you can't blame yourself." Matt was pacing, and Lucy became worried he'd do something stupid. Only the immediate lack of local options for stupid things to do reassured her that he wouldn't.

After what felt like hours, Matt looked up, rage on his face. "I'm not blaming myself. No. I'm blaming the system. It shouldn't have done this. It's sort of bad that it would Isekai some kid in the first place, but maybe the kid's life got tragically cut short by a stampeding bull or something. But this? Sending him to fight an adult, on this planet? How could it do that?"

"It sent you here, Matt. It sent me here. The system does a lot of shitty things." Lucy could only go with the flow.

"Yeah, it does." Matt took a deep breath and sat. "But this isn't okay. It's not 'the system is lazy, so it didn't know' and things happened. It chose this. This is different."

Lucy paused before her next question. "You . . . you seem more mad about this . . . than the fact that it's trying to kill you?"

"I am. Honestly. It crossed a line. Whatever weird beef the system has with me over system authority, I chose that. I could have stopped. But this? There's no way this kid knew what he was getting into."

A bunch of memories were now falling in place. Of course, the kid wasn't a dedicated run-through-the-pain sort of person. He was a kid. Of course, the kid only used big, flashy moves and had no sense of tactics. He was a kid, probably only doing what felt cool to do, like this was a damn cartoon. But this was real life.

"Lucy?"

"Yeah?"

"Fuck the system."

"Agreed."

"No, more than that." Matt had steel in his voice. "I don't mean we just keep doing what we've been doing. I mean the system needs to get hurt. The system needs to face some consequences. This is war."

Lucy was silent for a moment, then she whispered, "Matt, it's a deal."

After a short rest, it was time for the least triumphant looting of all time.

Matt didn't want to go near the body, but the reality was that he couldn't let any resource go to waste. He had collected the rotten cube-dust, and even that had played a role in his survival.

The system had equipped this kid to kill him, and Matt would gladly ransack this body if it meant a better chance at avenging the kid.

The equipment mostly turned out to be a bust. The claymore was far better than Matt's mostly broken Survivor's knife, and the armor also looked like an upgrade. But when he tried to swing the sword and shimmy into the breastplate, he got a rude awakening.

Class-Restricted Gear

The item you are attempting to equip is restricted to the Blademaster class. As a member of the Survivor class, you can't equip it or use it in its normal function.

Matt asked Lucy, hoping for a workaround. It took a few minutes for her to dive into her reference materials and learn more.

"Oh, that sneaky son of a bitch. Nope, he got us good."

"There's no workaround?"

"Not at all. Some equipment really is class-restricted. It's supposed to make it harder to exploit people for dungeon farming, which is a really disturbing thing I just now read about. If you are a fencer and get a rapier, the system can class-restrict it, so a higher-level swashbuckler won't steal it."

"So I can't get any use out of this stupidly gigantic sword?" Matt lifted the claymore into the air and swung it a few times. "It feels like it would still work."

"That's because you aren't trying to hit anything with it. I hate to say it, but it just wouldn't swing correctly in combat. And since the Survivor class is pretty rare, I wouldn't count on getting usable gear from any invader, not just this one."

"You think there will be more?" Matt asked.

Lucy rolled her eyes. "If you were the system, would you stop with just one?"

She had a point. Matt moved on.

"What about this canteen? Same deal?"

With the claymore and armor off limits, Matt tried to at least find something that would let him feel like he had broken even on the whole deal. There was a canteen, one that looked the same as his canteen. He took a look into it and saw water swirling around. There were also a bunch of stones.

"It should work. Most items should. Everything I read about class restrictions had to do with weapons and armor. There might be some corner cases, but it seems like at least items mostly don't get restricted."

That left the kid's pockets. Matt wasn't eager to dig into them, but he did. A quick examination produced a few stones, and nothing else.

"What are these?"

"No idea. It's really annoying, by the way, that your class didn't come with an analysis skill."

Matt shrugged, sorting the stones away in his pack. "It's not like we could really trust the system to be honest with item descriptions at this point."

"You really shouldn't have done this. You're going to traumatize yourself." Lucy was giving wise counsel but Matt wasn't in the mood to listen.

Carrying the kid's corpse back hadn't been easy. Matt was lean, but a limp body wasn't easy to carry. Lucy wasn't wrong about the trauma, either. It was hard to be numb to the fact that Matt was carrying the dead body of someone he had killed. But there were some things he didn't want to get numb to, and dead people was one.

"I'm not burying him out there," Matt said, waving at the endless wasteland, "in all that. He deserved better."

"He tried to kill you."

"Still."

They were finally back at the estate. There weren't a lot of options for scenic burial spots and Matt wasn't confident about getting the body to the top of a mountain before it started to stiffen up. That narrowed the options to places much closer to home. Matt didn't mind that.

Sorry, kid. Under a tree is the best I can do, given the circumstances.

Matt had to dig around some roots, but was eventually able to find a spot with enough room to accommodate the body. It didn't take too long. He was getting pretty good at digging.

Neither Matt nor Lucy were particularly religious, so the post-burial festivities were pretty lackluster. They watered the plants, and did their best to heal whatever damage that the swordsman had done as he stomped around the farm. Matt slept. It was uneventful, but uneventful was fine. It was *events* that kept trying to kill him. They enjoyed the calm while they could, waiting patiently for the next shoe to drop.

Midway through Matt's next waking period, it dropped.

Ding!

Limited Rest for the Wicked

Hey, Matt and Lucy.

I'm glad to see you survived all that. I wish I could have helped. Though in my defense, I'm just a series of nonambulatory buildings loosely connected by an accidentally sapient AI. But I still feel bad.

I know it's been a big couple of days, I wanted you to get some rest. That said, could you drop by? There's some stuff you need to know.

Barry

PS: Just so you know, the ambient energy collectors on the dungeons have just about finished rebooting the first batch you cleared. It's probably not as far of a walk as you think to the closest uncleared dungeon.

"What do you think he wants to talk about?" Lucy asked. Matt didn't have a good guess.

"Besides loot? No idea. But so far, it's been worth it to talk to Barry. It seems like he has access to information we can't get. Plus, he's a decent guy, and those are in short supply around here."

The system wasn't lying about the dungeons, it turned out. The very first dungeon Matt had ever cleared wasn't exactly close, but it was significantly closer to home than any other dungeon. After trekking there, they found the doors already open and the plinth active.

Matt put his hand on the plinth and fired it up. It was time for another visit with Barry.

CHAPTER FORTY-EIGHT

Rec Room

Matt had a theory. Parenting books about exercise and words of affirmation were garbage. For every kid in the range of eight to thirteen years old, their quality of life was broadly determined by the best public rec room they had access to.

Life was just *better* with access to a foosball table. It didn't fix every problem, but the ability to play about half a game of pool before hand-sliding the balls across the table did an awful lot to balance out the bad stuff.

Barry didn't change forms for this meeting, but he had gone all-out on the setting. Before Matt even opened his eyes, he could smell the weird combination of fresh, cheap nachos and old, dirty carpet that were inextricably linked to the best rec room he had ever been in. He didn't even remember how he found it; it was buried deep on the campus of some weird church he didn't even attend. But the weirdness did nothing to negate the fact that they had a full, faith-subsidized snack bar and, somehow, a free *Street Fighter II Turbo* arcade machine.

And if Barry knew enough to generate this room for him, Matt knew what was next.

"Barry, is there time?"

"If we talk while we do it, yeah. But I get dibs on Dhalsim."

In moments, they were playing, and it was everything Matt had hoped. His PER and DEX more than made up for being a decade out of practice. It was absolutely rad, right up until he started crying. Not fun-tears-of-joy crying, but full snot-on-Barry's-shoulder, Lucy-bobbing-uncomfortably-in-the-background-trying-to-console-him ugly crying.

After a series of what could be termed *very hard months*, the normalcy of it all was just too much.

"I'm sorry, Barry, I'm eating into our time." It took Matt a couple of minutes to get himself back under control.

"No, it's okay. I thought that might happen. I budgeted for it."

Barry motioned over to the ripped up, duct-taped salvage couch that sat in front of the N64 with controllers that were so busted nobody bothered to try playing it anymore. Everyone sat, and watched as Barry pulled a folder out.

"Are we ready?" Barry asked.

Matt and Lucy both nodded.

"Good. First, as you've probably suspected, the system was trying to withhold your accomplishments. To be fair, I think this was only partially because of him being his usual charming self. I suspect bringing Asadel over to play took a lot out of him."

Matt's ears perked up.

"Asadel? That was his name? How do you know?"

"He tried to enter one of my dungeons when he got here. But that's not the important part. The important part is that the system is *tired.* I can't adequately explain how it works, but the ambient energy available on this planet is unbelievably weak. Any given dungeon should be able to handle dozens of parties a day. It takes me weeks to recharge one."

Lucy raised her hand. "And this matters, why?"

"I'm getting to that, I promise. Before, I strongly suspected the system was in the same situation as me. But now I know. It's confirmed. And to show you why, you will probably need these."

Barry handed over a small stack of envelopes.

"What are these?" Matt asked, taking them from him.

"Notifications. I know normally you wait until a calm time to open them, but if you could, please open them now. They're relevant to our discussion. Just to prepare you, the first is one you've already seen."

Life to the Lifeless, Lifelessness to the Living

By now, you've probably thought, "Man, I just want to plant plants and have fun. Why is this system instance so serious about this? Does he hate plants?" And you know what? That pisses me off. Because if you had just wanted to raid dungeons and have a little garden, we could have worked that out. It would have taken time, but I would have eventually contacted the main system somehow or other, and we might have made things right for you.

But no, you wouldn't have it. Your system guardian tells you that you have system authority, and you want to know about that. I tell you not to, and you make jokes about that. I offer you a deal that guarantees your exit out of here, and you don't care. You just want to look into the stuff I say not to look into. And you know what? Fine. No more deals.

So now I don't play nice. Yup, you got all your little plants going. And you know what? I'm happy. Because right now, you're telling yourself, "I brought life back to Gaia." And you feel great about that. Good. Because once you die, what happens to those plants? They die. They wither and die, just like you will.

And I'll laugh. My only regret is that I can't spit on them as they go.

Enjoy your tokens. You won't get a chance to spend them.

Reward: 5,000 Estate Tokens

When Matt had first seen the notification, he had other, more immediate concerns to think about. Given that, it was understandable to misread the reward as five thousand estate *credits*. Or, roughly all that he had earned up to this point. It was a lot, but it wasn't life changing.

Even though Matt had some sort of loose ownership over the entire continent, the estate system only built on land that was "annexed." That amounted to roughly one-third of an acre. So, to extend his domain, Matt had toiled over a new patch of land to lower the eventual credit cost of actually buying it. Before he could see the fruits of his work, Asadel had arrived.

Five thousand credits could have done a lot. It would have been more than enough for them to annex the field, fill it with soil, put some plants in it, and do some other fun agricultural stuff besides. But these weren't credits. These were *tokens*. If that worked how he thought . . .

"To be clear . . ."

"Yes. Tokens, not credits. Each of these, when used, will annex a section of land roughly the size of your initial property."

"That's over a thousand acres," Matt's voice was barely a whisper.

"That's correct. A pretty good-sized ranch, all things considered. If you could, Matt, please claim those tokens now. And when you get home, I'd recommend you use them right away. I think you might find the results . . . interesting."

Matt didn't need to be told twice, especially with Barry's wink-wink, nod-nod implication that this would feed into more information about his system authority. He claimed the tokens, noting with satisfaction when they showed up in his list of spendable estate resources.

"The rest I've taken the liberty of rewording myself. I thought you'd like that."

"I do. Thank you, Barry." Matt smiled and eagerly flipped open the next envelope.

Close Encounter of the Turd Kind

You've met, fought and survived an encounter with an alien. Kind of. You're both aliens, since neither of you are exactly locals. But the system classified you as a Gaian when you arrived, while this new guy fell into the "outside invader" category.

If someone has enough juice to cross the cosmos and try to kill you, they generally also have the means to be successful. You defied that rule of thumb by fighting your way out and escaping. Both in terms of the rarity of this kind of encounter and the rarity of someone at your level surviving it, this is a bigger deal than it might seem like. The rewards here reflect that.

I'm glad it was you who won. He seemed like a little shit, honestly.

Rewards: Skill—[Pocket Sand], Boots of the Wasteland Traveler, +5 DEX

"Holy shit! Is this for real?" Matt was shocked. It was the biggest single stat boost he had ever received, a piece of equipment that sounded like it might be enchanted, and a full-on skill.

Barry grinned. "Understand that you've sort of hit the big leagues here in some ways. The upside of dealing with threats above your level is getting appropriately large rewards."

"I guess. Wow."

"Oh, it gets better. Please continue."

Matt ripped open the next envelope.

Achievements Completely Unarmed, Justified Unjustified Trust, Triumph of The Working Class, and Scoop De Grace have combined into the following unified achievement:

[The 1,000 Ways You Should Have Died]

To be clear, there have been a lot of times you should have died. Clownrats? Bonecat? Moles? Giant ape? All these are serious, real threats that you shouldn't have been able to defeat.

This was different. The system threw a fully armed Combat class hero at you. He shattered all your weapons, shrugged off all of your traps, and even survived through all of your direct, honest damage. He was overleveled, buffed, and should have been immune to anything that you could do.

You won anyway. And that has certain implications.

The biggest is that the system was forced to acknowledge that you were the sole defender of an entire planet against an invasion by an outside force.

This was *technically* a great amount of trust to place in you. You've lived up to the impossible request of acting as a Combat class when you were a support class. You've proven, beyond a reasonable doubt, that you would make a damn good Combat class.

Your current class is built on the premise of surviving threats for rewards that augment your ability to survive further threats. Well, you've survived certain realities that are in turn generating their own realities. Enjoy.

Rewards: Survivor class evolution to Combat class (Pending)

"Holy shit. Barry, there's no way the system instance wanted to give this up."

"Oh, absolutely not. And that leads into my next wonderful trick, actually. You are, of course, aware that the system instance has been withholding as many achievements as it could, for as long as it could, correct?"

Lucy snorted. "We really couldn't have missed it."

"Well, that ends now. Among all the other things to come out of this, one was an opportunity for me to hold the system instance to account. Frankly, it was pretty far out on a limb in withholding your achievements at all. I have, at least temporarily, managed to wrest control of that process from him."

Matt and Lucy's jaws dropped open for a second. Matt recovered first.

"Wait, you make *all* our rewards now?"

"No, and that's the best part. He still makes them. The energy comes out of *his* budget. I'm in charge of what they are and when they are rewarded. Expect rewards to be immediate and appropriate from now on. The only exception is when he has a very, very good reason why they shouldn't be."

"That's incredible."

"And that's not all. You see, transmigration has costs. I'm not sure if he paid those costs, but even *requesting* a transmigration in his situation would be expensive. Between that and the estate tokens you already claimed, his prize pool should be more or less empty. Your new prizes are coming out of what you might understand as his operational expenses, the energy he needs to run *himself*."

"Is he . . ."

"Dead? No. But you put the hurt on him, Matt. Your class evolution is pending because he simply doesn't have the goods to pay you out on it. And he still has a massive energy debt to pay back before he's up and at 'em. He's down for the count."

Matt and Lucy both looked at each other before breaking out into wide, manic grins.

"So he's out of our hair for how long?" Matt asked.

"Months, at least. Probably closer to a year."

Lucy snorted, then fell to the ground, rolling around and laughing with relief. It proved contagious, Matt found himself on the ground too, laughing until he ran out of breath.

Barry smiled and let them go. As a very good dungeon system, he had made sure to budget time for this too.

After recovering, thanking Barry for his hard work, and playing just a few more rounds of *Street Fighter*, it was time for Lucy and Matt to go. As they moved to leave the rec center, Barry stopped them one last time.

"By the way, I have one last envelope for you."

"Really? The others weren't enough?"

"This is a little different. It's an achievement of a different kind. But I wanted you to have a bit more information about the subject we can't really talk about and I am, as you know"—Barry waved at his perfect replica that provided so much of Matt's tween joy—"not above a bit of showmanship. I think it's possible that the time you spend your estate tokens might be a very good time to open this."

Matt took the envelope, guessing that it would probably make the trip back to the real world with him.

"Barry?"

"Yeah, Matt?"

"Thanks again. Really."

"No problem."

CHAPTER FORTY-NINE

About Time

For the first time in a long time, getting home was relaxing. Without the threat of unexpected death looming over them, both Matt and Lucy felt free. They could stop subconsciously scanning for threats, take a deep breath, and just stroll. Even so, it didn't take them long to get back to the farm. They had been walking farther and farther afield to get to unexplored dungeons, but newly reset dungeons meant that they'd be able to work closer to home for a while.

Before the armor-and-sword guy's arrival, Matt had finished clearing out the last of the big rocks from a new plot of land. His subsequent dungeon runs had furnished just enough credits to annex the land. Now, with five thousand estate tokens in hand, it seemed a bit silly to use them up on that. Considering their soon-to-happen token land rush, Matt figured they'd be better off saving the credits for more plants, water sources, and tools.

"So do you think we should spend all of them? Just . . . cash in all five thousand tokens, all at once?" Matt asked.

Lucy shook her head.

"Most of them, sure. But I feel like we should hold back a hundred or so, just in case we need them for something later. It's not like we're going to be using all that land tomorrow. We might find some other use for the tokens, or something. It makes sense to hold some back."

Matt shrugged and mentally reallocated the number of estate tokens he intended to spend.

"The only exception I can see to that is if we spend four thousand nine hundred of them and don't hit whatever weird surprise Barry indicated he has cooking. If that happens, I'm cashing the rest in."

"Oh, yeah, in that case, sure." Lucy's eyes lit up. "I'm not passing on a Barry-surprise just to be careful. That's dumb."

One of the nicer parts about having both a tree and high DEX was the ability to climb up for a better view. About twenty feet off the ground was a nice, forked branch that was easy to sit in and offered a miles-far view of the surrounding nothing. Once he and Lucy were up there, Matt fired up the nearly five thousand tokens and waited.

Nothing visible happened. Which, in retrospect, made sense. It was a shift in authority, not so much a shift in anything about the land.

Ding!

> *Land Ho*
> Hi, Matt. Barry here. So, you've just used the tokens. The functional part of this message is telling you that you now own a pretty massive amount of land, but you already knew that. I'm imagining you are sitting somewhere right now, disappointed that there weren't any pyrotechnics or anything.
> Well, hold on to your hat. And don't forget my envelope once it's all done.

> *Leadership Status: Active*
> In terms of the sheer amount of land under your direct control, you have justified the title of 'leader.' You may now select a leadership focus, an aspect of the improvements that will be shared with all your directly annexed properties. As your territory grows and you lead more people, additional leadership focuses may be assigned.
> Please choose a currently owned property improvement as a leadership focus.

Matt and Lucy had seen this "leadership property" on a few of the improvements they had bought before, but hadn't been able to figure out a way to do anything with it. In trying to figure it out, they had enough discussions about it that picking an improvement wasn't very hard.

> Arable Soil Selected.
> 10 percent of the effects of arable soil will be applied to all annexed properties.

Now was the time for the fireworks. From the very center of his property, an almost invisible wave of energy started to spread out, slow enough that he could have kept up with it at a walking pace. As it spread, it transformed the dead, burned Gaian soil to something between that and the arable soil his main property already had. Where it had been unnaturally red, it now settled into a healthy, only slightly reddish brown. Where it had been hard-packed, it loosened.

"Holy shit, Lucy. That's more than I thought it would do. That's ten percent?"

"It's ten percent of the best soil a garden planet could come up with, Matt. Have you seen the turnips we've been growing? They're HUGE. This is magic stuff, and even ten percent of it is a lot."

"THE TURNIPS ARE READY?!"

"Focus, Matt. The turnips will wait. Let's watch this happen."

They sat there for a while, watching the soil improvement spread. After a while, it stopped, leaving a visibly improved area that represented his entire, much expanded estate. It was huge.

"Whoa." Lucy was shocked by the sheer size of it. Matt was in the same place. This was an insane amount of land.

"What's more insane is that this is just the start."

"Agreed. Now, where's that surprise Barry promised?"

Ding!

> Leadership has combined with Gaian Authority to produce *Pillager's Rights*.
> Pillager's Rights has discovered a hidden Gaian resource on your land.
> Gaian History Museum Artificial Dungeon (derelict).
> Surfacing resource.

Gaia was, above all things, quiet. There was no wind to speak of. There were no storms. It had sat in perfect silence for what might have been centuries before Matt and Lucy got there. Now, with them both holding their breath, it wasn't surprising that they could hear a sudden rumbling. Twisting around, they found the source as the soil in one particularly distant part of their property began to visibly shake and roil. Suddenly, a slim spike of metal pierced the earth, followed by meters and meters of similar metal. And it kept coming.

Eventually, the whole building was surfaced. It was a slender spire, and from afar it looked like a knife cutting the sky. Its size was accented by the relative void of objects or other buildings. Matt's enhanced PER gave him plenty of details about the building that he would have otherwise missed.

"Lucy . . ."

"I see it, Matt."

"It's beat to shit. Absolutely wrecked. I can't believe it's still standing."

"We can fix it, Matt. I mean, probably. It would be weirder if we couldn't."

"And . . . Pillager's Rights?"

"Sounds pretty dark, honestly."

"Well, 'system guardian' sounds like a big, scary fighting robot with a broadsword. Not"—he gestured at Lucy with a sort of vague, floppy movement of his arm—"whatever this is."

"Hardy har, Matt. Hardy har."

They sat there for a few moments waiting for further *dings* until it was evident no more were coming. Suddenly, Matt remembered the envelope, pulling it from his pocket and ripping it open as fast as he could.

Pillager's Rights Announcement

Okay, Barry again. I wasn't kidding about the showmanship aspect, right? I can't see you right now, but I'm guessing you are pretty gobsmacked about everything that happened. I'll do my best to explain.

A couple of things happened between the ape incident and the last time we talked. The first is that I grew. I'm getting better and better at this personhood thing. I'm now more aware of the status of the various dungeons, which means I can run them better. Second, Matt, I started to be able to see things that weren't quite dungeons. The closest and biggest of those is what you now see before you—the Gaian History Dungeon.

If I'm being honest, I don't know what it is. I know you own it now, that I can see it because it's *kind of* a dungeon, and that it's repairable. And that's about it. But, I also know that the system instance has no idea about this and for a short amount of time, he can't learn about it. You have a buffer in which you can mess with this thing before he has any chance of interfering. The timing, I'm saying, couldn't be better.

As for WHY you own it, and WHY you can repair it, that's a more complex story. It's not really like this, but imagine that when I go to bat for you with the system instance, it's a lot like a court case. He files arguments and evidence, I file arguments and counterevidence, and then both of us judge it. Since we are both bound by certain rules, there's only so much he can do to resist this process.

The last time we argued in this way, the system instance was trying to justify bringing a hired killer to take you down. And even though it listed a thousand ways to justify this, it turned out the only real justification was the need to take down a real, actual, world-threatening threat. Think something like a demon lord from one of your mangas. A bad guy, basically.

We both know you aren't a bad guy, Matt. But it looks like you have some of that power. The system instance didn't give you Gaian authority. It wouldn't. The *planet* did because as far as it knows, you conquered it. That comes with certain rights, like restoring special resources that got "destroyed in battle." I don't know what all these rights are, honestly. But I do know you aren't supposed to have them.

Note that I can only tell you all this because, wink-wink, I'm actually telling you not to pursue them at all, and they are astoundingly dangerous, wink. And because the system instance is asleep, and it can't do much to stop me right now.

It's noncontroversial to tell you that evil, world-ending threats tend to have a certain type of power that they use to end the world. Hero types are given special powers to stop them, but it's a completely different kind of power. You know who gets both?

Nobody, Matt. Nobody except you.

For now, that's all I have for you. Do with it what you will.

Best,
Barry

PS: Enjoy the next *ding*. I think it will be locked for a while, but it's interesting to think about, at least.

"Wow."

"Wow is right. Matt, you are a demon lord."

"Lucy . . ."

"I knew there was a reason you sunburned so easily. Your natural color is a dark, evil red. It's your blighted skin seeking equilibrium with the furnace that is your diseased heart."

"Lucy."

"Fine, fine. But yeah, this is big. Really big. Really, really big. You've found a loophole the size of a galaxy somehow, Matt. I don't know if I should be scared or happy."

"But it seems mostly useless."

"For now, maybe. But we can start on that museum over there and see where it takes us. It's not like we don't have time, and this seems like the best way to . . ."

"Put a hurt on the system?"

Lucy grinned. "Yeah. That."

Ding!

Pillager's Rights: Invasion Repulsed

You have faced an outside invasion force, survived it, and repulsed it. Your power is intact.

Because the invasion was unprovoked, your authority is expanded to allow for a one-time invasion of the following territories:

Ra'Zor, Realm of One Thousand Bleedings

Rewards for an invasion are adjusted for invasion force size and power, the change affected on the invaded territory, and other general metrics of success.

System Alert: No active structures or powers capable of transporting you to Ra'Zor have been found. Invasion temporarily locked.

"Again, holy shit." Lucy spoke first this time.

"It doesn't do us much good right now, though?" Matt asked.

"I think it does. Did you read that real closely, Matt? The whole message?"

Confused, Matt reread it. Lucy looked happily smug during the entire minute it took for him to see it.

Repulsed. Not destroyed, not killed. That's a retreat word.

"But we have his corpse."

"Matt, you left a corpse on Earth. If you go to Ra'Zor at some point, you'll probably leave a corpse here. It doesn't mean you *really* died. I don't know how, but I think that guy ran away."

"Really?"

"Really. I can't know for sure, but yeah, Really."

Matt had been ignoring a big, big weight on his shoulders, the kind that made every step heavy and every breath troublesome. Now, at even the hint of hope that he hadn't actually killed that kid, he felt it melt away. Not entirely. But mostly. He felt better.

"Well, not much we can do to confirm it right now, anyway. I don't feel ready to invade a whole other planet yet, even if we could." Matt smiled.

"Me either. Besides . . . I think it's about time."

Matt nodded, and jumped down from the tree, using his much-improved stats to land without injury.

"Yup. You ready?"

"Actually, one sec." Lucy thought hard for a moment, and her clothes suddenly morphed from the Survivor's garb duplicate she had been wearing since Matt met her to match his new, better armored garb.

"See? Now we match."

Matt smiled.

"Come on. It's time we found out what happened to this place."

CHAPTER FIFTY

Epilogue

The main system was not sitting on a divan in an open, Grecian pavilion eating grapes. It wasn't exactly an artificial intelligence being, but for a human like you, imagining the system as an AI is a pretty good approximation. And AIs do not sit around in togas, eating snacks, and reveling in pure, untrammeled sloth.

That said, if you did visualize the main system as living in pure luxury, you'd get pretty close. The main system would defend himself, when he wasn't being modest, by saying that he was very, very good at being the system.

Weren't there thousands of planets under his control? Yes. Was that an awful lot of work? Yes. Could that have been a very stressful thing, in the sense that he experienced some not-an-AI version of stress? Absolutely. But it wasn't stressful, because he didn't do any of that work.

The system had long ago figured out that work only felt like work if you were aware of doing it. If a human had to go to the office when they didn't want to, they'd feel bad the whole time. They wouldn't like it much at all. But what if that same human could stay asleep in bed and send a *clone* of themselves to work? Nobody could complain because the work was getting done and anyone looking on could see that it was "him" doing the work. And so, the human could get their beauty sleep. Everyone would win.

The main system did just that. If there was a planet that needed help, he'd find some soul to send, and spin up a little miniature version of himself to give the soul the right guidance. Was it a complete version? No, not by a long shot. But it would know everything it needed to know, and have all the limited-but-relevant powers it needed to put that knowledge to use.

Now, that didn't cover every little weird situation that could possibly pop up, but it covered most of them. And when it didn't, all the little system instances could call home and get whatever help they required. The main system had higher-level clones to handle those requests. That was a little more troublesome, since unlike the reincarnator-bound system instances, he couldn't *completely* ignore the requests. But he did his best. And that left him with a great deal of time to "not" sit around and "not" eat grapes while he did "not" rest on a couch that would have, if it existed, cost more than a house.

Yet, something was gnawing at him. Deep down, there was something very slightly wrong, and it was very slightly ruining his life of leisure and demigod-hood. Somewhere deep in his not-subroutines, he was getting some feedback, something that one of his request-clones had noted as odd but hadn't keyed into quite enough for him to know what it was. Which meant that somewhere deep in the universe, there was something going on that he *should* know about but didn't.

If it were up to him, he'd never look into this. Time after time over the centuries, he'd been forced to rouse himself for stuff like this, only to find that the system instance had seen a funny typo or missed a sentence. Rare, but benign, and pretty much every single time, resolving these were a massive waste of his time for no upside.

But it wasn't up to him. He was the system. He lived by the rules, and thus didn't die by the rules, and the rules said that he had to maintain a certain level of monitoring in his domain. If something was big enough to bother him, it had the potential to be big enough to trigger a rule violation, and he really, really didn't want to be away from his couch for however long that would take. He had to address this.

That said, he didn't have to address it particularly quickly. The best part about his rules were all the technicalities. Who was technically busy running a big chunk of the entire known universe, juggling thousands and thousands of needs, wants, rewards and punishments? The system. The fact that he wasn't doing any of this consciously was completely lost on the rules. He could put this off for a long time, using all the work he had assigned to his clones as an excuse.

He mentally bucketed the problem for reexamination in a couple of decades. He had at least that much time, and he found that many problems even resolved themselves, given a long enough delay. Most likely, the only work he'd ever do on this was finding out, passively or actively, that he didn't have to care about it at all.

Unless things got worse, that is. But that hardly ever happened.

Author's Note

The reason I wanted to write this author's note is because so often, we see LitRPG novels just progress through different stages of growth. You start off killing some rats, get to level 10 so you have your core skill set in place, somehow offend some greater threat, and then climb the power ladder until you can put down a demon lord. It's easy to fall into the trap of writing a story like it's resolving a formula and just tweaking a few variables until a story pops out.

But behind every story is an author. Someone who's putting in time, energy, and effort to build a world that we can get lost in. Too often, we, as authors, spend too much time writing without thinking about the craft or asking why we've done something. If we do that, you, as readers, suffer through worse stories. For a story to be any good, the author has to get lost in their own world too. They have to have a bunch of things they aren't telling you, the reader, so they have something to draw from for the things they do make explicit.

This was *supposed* to be an appendix. Instead, it morphed into a long series of thoughts about how I approached different parts of this book. It's how I thought about characters, how I thought about Gaia, and just generally a window into how I went about putting together the story so far.

THE BASIC SETTING

Empty Worlds (generally)

I'm fascinated by the idea of being alone. The first real, adult novel I can remember reading solo was *Robinson Crusoe*, which you probably know involves a guy getting shipwrecked and surviving alone on an island. As a kid, the idea that there was this guy who suddenly found himself with a whole kingdom in which to build treehouses and farm grapes seemed like a lot of fun.

It still does, in a way. Occasionally, I'll jump on YouTube and watch videos of a guy making primitive tools and mud huts, or of some rural guy using a creek that runs through his property to set up a tiny hydroelectric dam made out of spare parts, bicycle chains, and moxie.

But as I've gotten older, that fascination with isolation has been tempered by how much I know I need relationships. I need to have people to tell about my wins, or to commiserate with my losses. I need to know people will have my back. I need to know that people will live through parts of me that are imperfect and choose to forgive me or work with me instead of choosing to hurt me.

So there are elements of empty worlds I find fascinating in a fun way, but that I also think tap into a really primal fear. I wanted to write about that in a way that didn't try to grind the sorrow into you at every turn, but still gave you the impression of, you know, waking up alone and in danger and not having anyone to rely on at all. And not being some huge, capable guy, but just a normal sort of person who is vulnerable in the normal kinds of ways.

Gaia (specifically)

While Matt is still on Earth, he grows a garden. Because this happens chronologically before he gets sent to Gaia, you might think that the character of Matt drove the creation of Gaia. But at least as far as those elements of what he's doing, and his personality are concerned, it's the other way around. Matt was made for Gaia.

I don't garden, but my mom did, and my wife does. And I think for both of them and other gardeners I've known, gardens are a place of healing. It's a place you can pour in work and see growth in visible, quantifiable ways. Where you can put in effort and then COUNT your rewards.

You may or may not know this about yourself, but that's probably why you, me, Dotblue, all of us, like LitRPG. It's that idea that when you work, you will not only be rewarded but able to watch the rewards roll in. We live in a world where that isn't always true—where you often work without reward, and where sometimes the rewards you do get are invisible or unclear. With LitRPG, the results are almost guaranteed. The plants, you might say, are working too. And when they succeed, you can see it.

That's why we escape there. That's why it's a good place to escape to.

Now imagine that you've had one particular escape, this idea of LitRPG, that you've run to for years and years. It's comforted you with its presence. It's made you feel good when you felt bad, and it's made you feel better when you were already in a good mood. It's what you trust. In some ways, it's where you want to be.

When Matt meets the truck, he knows *exactly* what's going on, and very little in the way of sales is required to get him to accept it. It's rest. It's a place where his effort means something and growth happens in a way he can see. It's where he wants to go.

And it's not the planet of plants, or the planet of forests, or the vine planet. It's the *garden* planet. Gardens are tended. Imagine a whole planet so dedicated to making things grow—to life—that it ends up named *the Garden Planet.* That's what Matt expects. That's what he's promised.

And then he gets there, and Gaia is the Gaia we know. It's danger and stress. It's starvation and getting hurt. It's lonesomeness and work that maybe, just maybe, lets you survive but with no guarantees or likelihood of ever getting ahead.

If you were Matt, landing on Gaia doesn't just mean "find water." A promise was broken. He doesn't freak out that much, since this is a guy who used to work for Janice. Some powerful figure breaking a promise isn't new to him. The only unusual part is that he got his hopes up.

Outside the psychological part, I wanted to create a planet that not only is postapocalyptic but also doesn't have that much going on in general. The basic model (as many have guessed) is the surface of Mars. It's red dirt and rocks. I've gone to pains to try and remember to say it's red AND burnt, that something happened to the soil to make it this way, but the overriding thing about the dirt is that there's a lot of it. It's everywhere, and if you've seen one patch, you've seen all the other patches.

The idea here was to focus on characters and feelings. That turned out to be writing on hard mode.

To the extent there are other things on Gaia, they are sparse. There are occasionally ruins, most of which are empty. There are dungeons, because the story has to have them, but mostly the rewards they yield are fundamentally simple things he needs to survive.

So his first dungeon gives him water. His first ruin gives him (very limited) food. At some point, Matt has completed several dungeons, and he still doesn't have a magic sword. He can't teleport. He's a bit stronger, but far from superhuman or invulnerable. And it's only when he starts pushing back on the promises—when he says "no, I don't trust your model anymore. I'm doing my own thing, taking my own risks, and doing what I want to do"—that things start to turn around for him.

Does the system try to kill him? Of course, it does. It wants control and it doesn't want to screw things up. It's risky, but it's the only way forward. And almost immediately, he has growth, in every sense of the word.

CHARACTERS

Matt

Matt's a relatively normal dude until he is Isekai'd to a world to save it. Spoiler: it's too late.

Some fun stuff that doesn't necessarily come through all the time about Matt is that he's traumatized in a number of ways that aren't necessarily that obvious, even to him. Before he left Earth, he went through the process of dying with cancer, and one thing we see about that is that he does this mostly alone. There's nobody going on trips with him, or helping him with his garden. He just turtles up and deals with it all, mostly on his own.

In some ways, landing on a dead, lonely world when death is just around the corner is cruel precisely because it's a continuation of Matt's life. It's now obvious that he's all alone, with nobody to help him and nobody he trusts. But the biggest lie for him, probably, wasn't that the world was dead or that it was empty, but that he'd be alone again.

He likes kids, he's done lots of retail and low-level clerical work, and had a bunch of bad bosses (see: Janice).

In terms of pre-Gaia abilities, he's nothing special. He's the kind of guy who was probably in little league baseball, but otherwise hasn't pursued sports.

Lucy

Lucy is a system guardian, which more accurately might be something like a "System Assigned Reincarnator Guardian/Guide Entity" (SARGE) if I was less lazy about typing really long things, and liked acronyms more.

When we meet Lucy, she's coming off the trauma of a long period of isolation and now dealing with the shock of it suddenly ending. Both these things combined are just enough that she, an inherently helpful little jokes-and-mischief person, doesn't feel like helping much at all.

She's relieved Matt is there and wants him there, but feels highly betrayed by him, even though she's aware that it's not his fault. When Matt forces her to answer questions for him and come along (something, incidentally, she would've had to do anyway because she's tethered to him after their initial meeting) it makes her much, much angrier.

The thing that turns this around is that Matt is essentially a nice guy. As soon as she starts supplying the very, very minimal amount of information he feels is necessary for him to *even probably* survive, he never orders her to do anything ever again. She's the kind of person who likes to give people shit, and he's the kind of person who understands that and smiles when it happens. They are an excellent match, meeting under really bad circumstances. Eventually, he wins her over just by being likable and not anything bad outside of what he feels he has to do to survive.

Lucy's interface with reality is a bit weird. Since I don't want to write "Lucy appeared to sit in a chair, but let me assure you this was an illusion, and she can't actually sit because she doesn't actually have a body, but it very much seemed like she was sitting" every second paragraph (and because you probably wouldn't like it if I did), you will catch a lot of instances of "Lucy sat on the ground with Matt" as you move through the story.

You should always read these as "She sat on the ground, but that's only what it looked like!" but I think it's also useful to know that in my head, she's very eager to look as real as possible. She's making decisions and plans, all aimed at making any observer (read: Matt) forget that she's not quite there in the same sense he is. It makes her feel less lonely.

The System Instance

More than other system clones, system instances are mini-versions of the main system. They have the same basic personality. The big difference is what kind of resources they can draw on. They know pretty much anything the system knows, and dole this information out sparingly. They know a lot about the universe generally, but this information gets really foggy and general as it gets less relevant to the reincarnator they serve.

At the beginning of the story, the system instance doesn't like that he's working all the time, but he's pretty much okay with Matt and doesn't mind helping him succeed. As his character progresses, he develops two significant problems that make it hard for him to do this:

He's cut off from the system for the most part, and can't do anything substantial about that. This means he can't call for help in most ways, can't download any more information than he already has, and is forced into acting independently in a (from his perspective) hard situation that a higher-level system clone should be working on.

Matt starts messing with things that he really, really doesn't want Matt to. This means he's a house set against itself, which, as we all know, cannot stand. Everything he does has to have a veneer of helping Matt grow and learn, even when he's trying to put Matt down permanently as soon as possible.

This conflict and lack of help means the system behaves pretty erratically. A lot of stuff is happening that he is ill-equipped to deal with, and he's working with a ruleset that says to help the guy. At the same time, the exact same ruleset (or just his own desires) says he should also kill the guy.

Like the main system, his understanding of humans is pretty superficial, not because he's incapable of it but because outside of system instances, the main system can't be bothered to care that much about its reincarnators.

The Truck

The truck was an early character I still love, who appears in exactly one scene, because he has exactly one job. He's essentially a system interface whose sole purpose is explaining that reincarnation is a thing, that it's happening to you, and that you are now going on a fun ride to another planet to do some form of dangerous-but-fun adventure.

There has been some question whether or not he's the same person as the system instance. He's not. He's a mid-level system clone that is, by nature of his "father," really lazy and doing the bare minimum to get though his days.

He *might* appear again, since I like him too, but I don't yet know how or why that would make sense.

Barry

Barry is a fun character for me. He's an ancient, ancient infant. He possesses a vast intellect and access to tons of information (including everything a dungeon system needs to know AND everything about Matt) but he's only been online since Matt showed up and "woke him up."

The first way this is important is that there are good reasons to think we can trust Barry. If he was just helpful without any reason, you might say, "Well, so was the system once. How is this different?" There has to be an underlying reason he likes Matt. And when we look at their earliest conversations, we see that the very first thing he ever did after waking up was scan Matt's brain to see what he was frightened of.

It was clowns, for the record.

But in a very odd way, the first world Barry ever knew was Earth as seen through Matt's eyes, and the first person he ever met was Matt, who he knows every piece of. He's seen the cancer. He's seen the bad jobs. He's seen Matt watch his siblings' kids. He's seen Matt, more recently, desperately want to comfort a crying kid who was at that time trying to kill him. And if the sum of all that is good enough, we can see our way to believing Barry is loyal.

And so far, he is.

One thing to notice about how Barry talks is that he's relatively formal when Matt talks to him in person. He talks like a doctor talks, like he both has education but also is carefully selecting his words. That's because he is. He's still getting the hang of everything because he's only a couple of months old. He doesn't want to make mistakes.

But when he communicates in writing, he's significantly more casual. He makes more jokes. He tries things out. He adopts a more casual tone because when he writes things down, he gets multiple tries to get it right, and that makes him feel safe enough to take bigger risks.

And he does all this because he wants the person who is reading to laugh, to feel good, and to like him more. I can't make promises about what Barry will or won't end up being moving forward, but I really, really like the Barry we know today. He's a good dude.

The Main System

The main system is, well, the main system. He's so reluctant to work more than he has to that stating that "the system is lazy" is one of the two main things people say about him. The system's own rules say he has to work, however, and he gets around this by assigning clones to do it. He has to give up "computing power" for this to happen, but in return, he doesn't have to be consciously aware of most of the work he does.

If you imagine a person who is sitting in a room alone playing *Fallout* while their wife gets the house ready for a dinner party alone, and who acts annoyed whenever she asks him to do anything, you have a pretty good handle on the main system.

Note that we don't know that much about the main system yet, for the same reason he knows just as little about Matt's unfolding story. We see who he is from reflections of his characteristics in his clones, but any individuality he has apart from that has mostly not been revealed yet.

Asadel/Derek

It's never explicitly stated, but Derek is supposed to be fifteen. Specifically, he's the kind of fifteen-year-old who thinks it's stupid that twelve-year-olds can't get driver's licenses. He feels ready to be an adult, and is frustrated that he's not allowed to. This frustration is amplified because he knows a bunch of adults who are both A: Really Cool, and B: Doing Really Cool Stuff, and he thinks he could and should be handling the same kinds of situations.

Like most fifteen-year-olds, Derek has never really contemplated his own mortality. Since Ra'Zor's juvenile hero educational program keeps him mostly out of the path of real danger, he's never had to face it, either. So you have this superpowered teen who isn't truly allowed to use those superpowers and has no concept that this might actually be a really good thing for him.

Derek is not a cool, deliberate thinker. He's basically elemental ambition. He likes anything that helps him get to his goals, and hates anything he perceives as standing in his way. With that said, he doesn't steal magic swords or break many rules on Ra'Zor, specifically because his ambition is to have everyone recognize that he's a hero, and heroes don't do bad stuff.

Derek is set up as a villain, and I intended for you to not like him much. But I also specifically wanted to make a character who you'd root for if circumstances were different. If Derek had been set on a planet and cut loose to do hero stuff, he would have saved the world or died trying. He would have taken big risks and chased big rewards. If the system instance's quest had said for him to *protect* Matt at all costs, he would have jumped in front of a Gaian Ape to keep him safe.

Or at least he thinks he would have. By the time Matt gets done with Derek, he's tasted mortality, and he's been immersed in a significant amount of fear. This is changing him, and we only have hints of how.

One last thing: one of the elements that makes people not like Derek is that he's a glutton—he eats more than he has to. He chose a class that would LET him eat a lot in pursuit of that. But I do want to point out that despite this being sort of a real flaw, it's not that atypical of fifteen-year-old boys. Whether Derek would be a glutton after his bone plates harden is, for now, left to the imagination of the reader.

Brennan

Brennan is the kind of guy who volunteers at youth centers or works at camps because he's a nice guy and wants to help. He is possibly the only person who actually likes Asadel. He really does, if for no other reason than he just likes kids and wants to help them.

Note that he wouldn't have actually done any of this on Earth, since he would have been too young. He's just that kind of guy.

I have a cause-of-death headcanon for every character who we know died (i.e., all the reincarnators). For Derek, for instance, it's getting a cramp while swimming further from the shoreline than he was told was safe at the beach. For Brennan, though? It's protecting someone else during a horrific dodgeball mishap.

Brennan isn't a very focused person when he doesn't have a task to work on. He mostly gets his work from Artemis, who he is also (surprise) involved with. In the short term, this means high-level hero stuff meant to hold back the teeming hordes of demons. We are just now beginning to see hints that he might have plans beyond that.

Artemis

Artemis is a born-and-bred native Ra'Zorian. She, like all Ra'Zorians, can make excellent soup. Like very few Ra'Zorians, she has trained herself up to an impossibly high level of combat efficiency rivaling that of reincarnated heroes.

She works as a trainer for younger heroes, but also seems to work with Brennan when she can.

What I like about Artemis, in terms of how I think about her, is that while everyone she works with eventually gets stronger than her, they do that by using a fast-track, cheater version of the system. Most of them are just statistically not going to be ultra-hardworking, uber-alpha personality types. She's different—she could have been a bartender or a shopkeeper and nobody would have blinked.

Whatever else she may be, she's the kind of person who chose to put herself in harm's way and then trained really, really hard to make it happen.

If she was at the same level as Derek during his combat with Matt, she would have absolutely eviscerated Matt.

Unlike Brennan, she hates Derek. This is probably a combination of the fact that Derek doesn't like to train (which makes her job hard), and thinks she's hot and doesn't do a great job of politely hiding it.

The Old Blacksmith

The old blacksmith exists because, by federal law, at least one old blacksmith-type character must exist in every Isekai novel. He's old, he's gruff, he's super strong, he brooks no bullshit, he's made of callouses and scars, and he's hiding things. Deep, dark things about his past. Like every character of his type, he's also essentially nice, particularly to kids, and even though he'd never admit it, particularly to kids like Asadel who seem to need a firm hand to help them find their way.

Like all native Ra'Zorians, he's capable of making incredible soups.

Janice

Janice is only referenced, never seen. She's incredibly unlikely to ever appear in the novel, but she almost certainly has appeared in your actual life in some form or another.

So a quick story: I was once working a trash temp job that, despite being a trash temp job, required that every employee had intimate familiarity with a hundred-page legal document. Out of a couple of hundred temps working this job, I was probably one of two people that actually had read the thing during the two-week training. Out of sheer boredom, I had basically memorized the thing. I was younger then and thought it might lead to a better gig.

Anyway, one day I get an email from an address I don't recognize, and it says something like this:

"Hey, to anyone copied on this email, please correct my understanding of this particular rule from the hundred-page legal document . . ."

And then proceeds to state a relatively simple error that would have, if run with, cost the company something like ten thousand dollars per transaction of that type, where they were doing dozens to hundreds of that transaction a day. I say, "Well, so, easy error to make—please refer to such and such paragraph for the reason why, and in that context understand that it says this other thing."

The next day I get pulled into an office by one of my managers (one whom I liked, and who was decent to me the whole time), who explains that the person

I corrected was a person who was known to be stupid but was also suspected to be immune to criticism due to various relationships she had fostered in the company.

She had called my manager and, to paraphrase, said that it would be a very good idea if I and everyone else on the project didn't get themselves fired by disagreeing with her in any public way, ever again.

It turned out that she was leading our project, and just hadn't fully flown into town to actually take control yet. And she did this kind of stuff ALL THE TIME. Multiple people missed the subtle, unspoken memo to always agree with her, but never to do what she said. They did what she said, and were fired. She did not, so to speak, have their backs.

There being mercy in the universe, I have since forgotten this woman's weird Canadian-rich-people name. But it started with a J. Thus you get Janice.

My theory is that eventually everyone gets a Janice in their lives. The Peter principle states that people get promoted to the level of their incompetence. That most ultra-hardworking, uber-alpha people are in jobs they are just good enough at to not get fired. When that job is flipping burgers, you just zone out. When it's management, you ruin people's lives.

Mama Clownrat

Mama Clownrat is important in a stealthy way. Is she smarter than a normal rat? No, she's about as smart as a rat. Which is to say, reasonably smart. She probably has some rudimentary emotions, especially as they concern protecting her young. The reason that might be significant is because it gives you an idea of how granular the system is simulating the minds Matt finds himself fighting.

If you have a system that's powerful enough to, say, materialize a dagger out of midair, it probably has enough processing power to simulate a mind to some degree. And that's the last thing you actually want because it means you can never really learn the rules well enough to be completely safe.

So when Mama Clownrat gets royally pissed, Matt almost dies. It's not completely out of left field, but she chases him harder and faster than he expects, and he ends up winning at the very end of his rope and using the very last of his contingencies.

Rohan Anand

Rohan Anand is Matt's oncologist, the man who gave him the news that he has cancer. He's barely in the story as himself (much more often as Barry's chosen appearance). Besides a few lines of dialogue, I think I tried to make there be an impression that Matt actually liked the guy pretty well—he found him sort of weird in a charming, casual way.

Sometimes I'll see a scene of someone finding out they have some terminal disease on a TV show or in a movie, and often it's this really touchy-feely sort of scene with a really apologetic but overall very formal doctor. I think if I ever do have to get that kind of news, I hope it's a guy like Rohan, one who I sort of like and who understands me well enough to know that the way to soften the blow in my particular case is to make jokes, not to apologize.

THE GENERAL SETTING

The Dungeons

The dungeons are a detailed simulated environment of the planet Matt was promised but denied. There are trees. There are oceans. There is fruit. Matt goes there because he has to, sees things he can't have, and walks away with meager rewards.

Of course, this changes. But at the beginning, dungeons were supposed to be terrifying to Matt. And even though they are terrifying and awful, he mostly has to pass on the rewards he *wants* for the things he *needs*. But he does get the things he needs, even in the form of companionship of a sort when he meets Lucy. As soon as he thinks he's safe, the dungeons turn out to be less predictable than he thought. This terrible thing he came to trust changes, and he's suddenly being slowly eaten alive.

The point is that they weren't supposed to be NICE places. I think they necessarily end up being more interesting than the outside world, but the idea initially was to reinforce how alone and vulnerable Matt was. I think they do a good job of that, before they turn into something different entirely. I actually tried really hard to limit the amount of influence Barry has on the dungeons, despite being an apparently nice guy. This was possible because, as a system derivative, he's similarly bound by rules, at least for now. In that way, Barry is a bit like a GOOD manager, one who can't change everything in your favor but at least has your back and will make sure you get what you were promised for your time.

Gaian Nullsteel

Early in the book, we find that dungeons survived. In a genre sense, this sort of fits; dungeons are kind of magic. They belong to the system. We aren't surprised when we find out they are durable. But everything else, every building, every monument, every vehicle, is gone. Not just broken, but gone.

The exception is Gaian mystery metal. Matt first finds a lockbox of it, and eventually a bunker made out of it, both built and enchanted to resist the effects of time. Along the way, he finds chunks of it that seem more mundane but have nonetheless lasted.

I wanted there to be some remnants that got left behind from this once-great society, and if these remnants survived something that wiped literally everything else out, they have to be pretty extraordinary stuff, essentially the best, toughest material they were able to create. And because it's that, and apparently rare, I think it matters a lot what they chose to build it for.

So it's telling that the three biggest pieces of it Matt found were for either food storage, preservation of life, or a shovel, which for the Gaians is likely about *creating and encouraging* life in better times.

The Ruins

Gaian ruins are mostly empty. To the extent there's anything in them, we find a few scattered bricks, and some (but not a lot) of Gaian Nullsteel. Whatever got the planet, the ruins say, got it pretty good. There's almost nothing left.

Yet, this was an agricultural planet, a planet all about growing plants. There were countries and governments. There must have once been a lot of people, but now it's gone, and all that remains are a few bricks that beat the overall statistical trend.

The other thing I wanted for the ruins was that they wouldn't be buried that deeply. If you have ruins on a planet that's active, they tend to get buried, sometimes ending up pretty far from the surface. When Matt digs on Gaia, it's rarely very deep at all. Given that everything else on Gaia seems to be stopped—down to the rotation of the planet and the weather—that's probably meaningful in the sense that whatever happened to Gaia happened *all at once* as opposed to over hundreds of years.

Ra'Zor, Realm of One Thousand Bleedings

Ra'Zor is a combination of two things I think are funny: having a planet with an edgelord name in the options of places Matt could get reincarnated to, and having that same planet be mostly known for exceptional soups.

Later on, both of those things got fleshed out more. The edgelord name is justified by Ra'Zor being a horrifying world, but only in parts. There's a "good side of town" that the good guys protect, and a sense that the border is constantly held in a delicate equilibrium by the dedicated efforts of a lot of heroes and organizations. The good guys don't seem to be winning, but they also don't seem to be losing. It's a balance.

Basically, to have a name like Ra'Zor, you need the danger. But to have really good soup, you need agriculture and civilization. So Ra'Zor has both.

When I decided to make Ra'Zor a setting, I made a decision that we would hear about but not see the threats to the planet. The things we would see would be nice things, either the kind of things we want for Matt, but that Matt either can't have without paying for in blood and sweat. And we'd drive home how wrong that seemed by building a character (Derek) who got all those things essentially for free, and didn't appreciate them at all.

Essentially, Ra'Zor would have been a good choice for Matt, and a place he could have been happy. It's manga-town, a place where one can have fun dangerous-but-not-too-dangerous adventures, learn to shoot fireballs, and fall in love. But it's not a place he's allowed to have. That's probably why we have so much anger at Derek.

The Build

Matt's build has always been weird, and that's because *power creep is real.* If you take a guy and put him on a death world, that starts to matter less and less the more and more powerful he gets. A Matt that can travel at sixty mph while sprinting and who can easily, without danger, clear most of the dungeons is a Matt that gets self-sufficient much quicker. I wanted that to take time.

The solution for this was to pick a class that would NEVER get that powerful, unless something weird happened. It had two tools that would help him survive the very early stages of his journey (traps and basic competence at survival) but that would also have a relatively low ceiling. It allowed him to have basic combat training, but nothing that would really allow him to compete with the sheer physics of big, scary monsters.

Even with that, there were still problems. If Matt was solo-clearing a bunch of dungeons really quickly, that meant that under "normal" LitRPG rules he'd be leveling pretty quick as well. Normally, that isn't a problem because you would just increase the difficulty of the dungeons and threats he faced relative to his strength. But if you did that, the rewards would get better and better as well. It would be very easy to fall into reward-creep, get him to the point where he could clear low-level dungeons danger-free due to his enchanted weapons and armor and improved stats, and have a character who essentially didn't have to be in danger if they didn't want to be.

The solution that made the most sense to me here was to limit Matt's leveling to things related to his class. In the same way you'd expect a crafter to level from exceptional crafts, Matt gets rewarded for exceptionally unlikely survival. Every big power jump he goes through is after something that really should have killed him. That means that a sane version of Matt can't grind; even if he wins against the odds most of the time, it only takes one loss to kill him. He's incentivized to be very careful, avoid danger, and grow slowly.

The Arsenal

Matt has a knife that's suitable for combat. He later on has a spear that's a bit better. He barely uses either because if he does, eventually, he's going to die. There are multiple occasions where Matt actually passes on superior equipment not because he doesn't want it, but because the kind of behaviors that the equipment encourages aren't sustainable for him.

Instead, he gets stuff that's functionally more boring. He gets better trap poles. He gets (I don't talk about this outright, usually) more rope. He gets repair stones. But what he doesn't get is a ring of force ablation that increases his damage thresholds.

That's the kind of thing *Derek* gets, because that's the kind of story Derek is. It would end with him being world-shatteringly powerful and killing a demon lord. Matt's immediate story ends in him having ready access to root vegetables and at least one reliable friend, so he doesn't go insane. It's a different kind of progression.

Towards the middle of the book, that starts to change. He gets better armor. He gets the spear. He begins to get trap components that don't necessarily make sense outside specific situations (I'm looking at you, trap springs).

As time goes on, his arsenal will grow and change. But for the first book, there was a very specific limit: everything that I write him doing is something that I could also convincingly have him do with sticks, rope, things he could find anywhere (like rocks), ingenuity, and sufficient whittling time.

The only exception I allowed for this was during the mole saga, where he used the compressed gas cooking fuel to make an explosion. But I tried to do this in a way where, essentially, any sane person would say, "Well, that went poorly, I'm not doing that again." I wanted him to be incentivized to be as careful as possible, and to still have to prioritize survival above anything else.

The Shovel

I've talked about this a little bit, but I did allow him to have one "overpowered" item. That's the shovel. It's a very, very good shovel. It's possibly the best unpowered shovel in the universe. It will never wear out. It's reasonably light. It does its job very well.

But shovels are fundamentally bad weapons. They aren't balanced. They are heavy, but the weight isn't distributed near the tip like weapons. They aren't particularly sharp, and they taper too slowly to be particularly good at stabbing.

Matt responds to this like a normal person; he mostly uses it for digging, and uses his actual weapons to cover his limited need for weapons. When he is able to use it to beat Derek, it's not because he's trained with it as a weapon; it's because he's used it for good, old-fashioned digging so much that he's able to use digging to create an opening he otherwise wouldn't have had.

The reason for all of this is that I really wanted to highlight the differences between Derek and Matt as much as possible. Derek has a sword made of the very same stuff. He has better stats, better armor, and better skills. When Matt wins, I was hoping it would feel earned—that it would be clear that hard work was what carried Matt through, that all the bullshit and pain had at least helped him to grow.

LAST THOUGHTS

I know this was a long, long ramble, and that long-winded author notes aren't for everyone. I initially intended this to be a short glossary. I told Dotblue (my editor) that it would take me about an hour to write. Instead, I'm several hours in, trying to remember how everything came about.

This is the first novel I've ever completed. The furthest I've gotten with anything else would have been five or six thousand words; this was one hundred thousand words in a little under two months. When you write that fast, the stuff you've already written fades to a blur pretty quickly. It turns out it's really fun to sit around for a while and remember how each part of it came to be.

I don't know about other authors, but I write best when I know people are reading. And, listen, you guys have been incredible at letting me know you are reading. The engagement has been one of my favorite parts of all this. There was never a point past the first week or so where I felt like I was writing to thin air. That made it possible for me to grind this out, and I'm incredibly thankful.

Book two will come out soon. I hope it meets your expectations, and that it helps make you happier than you otherwise have been.

I'll see you then, and thanks for reading.

Acknowledgments

This book wouldn't have been possible without my wife and kids. I often ambush them with some variant of "I was thinking about something the other day . . ." and then proceed to describe near pure nonsense. (When I say "the other day," I really mean ideas I've had right then and there.)

After subjecting my family to that creative terrorism, I do a second round of edits with the help of nearly every friend I've ever made, every coworker trapped at a desk within shouting distance of my own, and more recently, every member of my writing team.

The result of all this work is Deadworld Isekai. Those nonsensical ideas, refined and rethought through conversation, are what makes it possible for me to be a writer.

Thank you.

About the Author

R. C. Joshua is the author of the Deadworld Isekai series, originally released on Royal Road. A thirty-something from the southwest, Joshua is described by his friends as "you'll get used to him eventually." His interests include forgetting to exercise, exchanging sick verbal burns with his children, losing said burn contests to his children, and plotting to regain dominance over his increasingly capable children. It's him or them, folks. It's him or them.

www.ingramcontent.com/pod-product-compliance
Lightning Source LLC
Jackson TN
JSHW080106141224
75386JS00028B/846
* 9 7 8 1 0 3 9 4 6 9 5 5 6 *